ELDRITCH EVOLUTIONS

26 Weird Science Fiction, Dark Fantasy, & Horror Stories

Call of Cthulhu® Fiction

These, and more, can be found on our catalog at
www.chaosium.com

"One step removed from Tom Clancy, one step closer than William Gibson."

— Kevin J. Anderson, New York Times Best-Selling Author

"A frightening and exhilarating tale that rips along like ASCII through a T-1 line. A fun, fun read!"

— F. Paul Wilson, New York Times Best-Selling Author

"An intelligent book, refreshing and frightening."

— Dr. Howard Frank, former Director, Information Technology Office, DARPA

"Near-future nightmare with nonstop action, realistic characters of a type you don't often find in thrillers, and writing that never distracts us. Definitely worth reading."

— The New York Review of Science Fiction

"A fast-moving jolt of pure cyber-adrenaline."

— Nancy Kress, multiple Nebula-winning author

"A fine, dark thriller for the coming millennium."

— Joe R. Lansdale, multiple award-winning author

"A hoot from beginning to end...a package of pure fun from first page to last."

— Dean Koontz, New York Times Best-Selling Author

"What a treasure house is this book! Tremendous fun!"

— Peter Straub

"More fun than a barrel of genetically altered winged monkeys."

— Roy Thomas, writer and editor of X-Men, Fantastic Four, The Incredible Hulk, Superman, Justice League of America, Legion of Superheroes, Star Wars, and many other comic book classics

"Fascinating and entertaining."
— Mark Powers, editor of X-Men and Uncanny X-Men

"Recommended to all who are prepared to address the future not only in fiction but in fact."
— Walter Koenig, one of the crew members on the original Star Trek

"A funny and amazing book."
— Matt Costello, author of Mirage and Masque

"An interesting and cautionary tale about what can happen when your wishes come true - a well-written fantasy."
— Today's Librarian

"A fun story with enough twists to keep the reader engaged. A recommended purchase."
— Gillian Wiseman, Voice of Youth Advocates

"Quite a revolutionary book indeed! Very well written!"
— Chris Ludlow, Video Game Nation

"Fantastically hilarious!"
— Diamond Galleries SCOOP magazine

"An entertaining and informative guide to comic book wonders bound to come."
— Julius Schwartz, Editor Emeritus, DC Comics

Call of Cthulhu® Fiction

ELDRITCH EVOLUTIONS

26 Weird Science Fiction, Dark Fantasy, & Horror Stories

BY LOIS H. GRESH

EDITED BY WILLIAM JONES

COVER ART BY PAUL CARRICK

CHAOSIUM
INC.

A Chaosium Book

2011

Eldritch Evolutions is published by Chaosium, Inc.
This book is copyright © 2011 Chaosium, Inc.; all rights reserved.
All stories © Lois H. Gresh

Original publication dates:

Snip My Suckers, 100 VICIOUS LITTLE VAMPIRES, Barnes & Noble, 1995 (story was on the 1995 HWA preliminary Stoker Award Ballot; story received Honorable Mention in 1995 YEAR'S BEST FANTASY & HORROR, St. Martin's Press)

Psychomildew Love, 100 WICKED LITTLE WITCHES, Barnes & Noble, 1995 (story was on the 1995 HWA preliminary Stoker Award Ballot; story received Honorable Mention in 1995 YEAR'S BEST FANTASY & HORROR, St. Martin's Press)

Sole Man, HOT BLOOD: FEAR THE FEVER, Pocket Books, July 1996 (story was on the 1996 HWA preliminary Stoker Award Ballot; story received Honorable Mention in 1996 YEAR'S BEST FANTASY & HORROR, St. Martin's Press)

Where I Go, Mi-Go, SINGERS OF STRANGE SONGS, Chaosium Press, 1997

Mandelbrot Moldrot, MISKATONIC UNIVERSITY, DAW Books, November 1996

Cafebabe, INFINITE LOOP SF ANTHOLOGY, Miller Freeman hardcover, 1993

Digital Pistil, TALES OF THE UNANTICIPATED, November 1994; THE CYBORG HANDBOOK, Routledge Press, 1995 (story was sole winner of national contest); 1994 YEAR'S BEST FANTASTIC FICTION

Let Me Make You Suffer, INTERZONE (Special Cyberpunk Issue), Spring 1995

Little Whorehouse of Horrors, DARK REGIONS VIRTUAL REALITY, 1998

Watch Me If You Can, INFINITE LOOP SF ANTHOLOGY, Miller Freeman hardcover, 1993

Algorithms & Nasal Structures, ABORIGINAL SF, Summer 1998

Instant Gratification, MANIFEST DESTINY, Winter 1994

Julia Brainchild, HUNGRY FOR YOUR LOVE: AN ANTHOLOGY OF ZOMBIE ROMANCE, e-format from Ravenous Romance, Oct 2009; print edition from St. Martin's Press, Oct 2010

AnOde to Thee: or Surfing those Tubular Waves, MINDSPARKS SF, 1994

There's No Place Like Void, TALES OUT OF MISKATONIC, Elder Signs Press, 2011

The Lagoon of Insane Plants, ANCIENT SHADOWS, Elder Signs Press, 2011

Scourge of the Old Ones, HIGH SEAS CTHULHU 2, Elder Signs Press, 2011

New stories in this volume:

Debutante Ball

Smokestack Snout Neurology

The Battle of Batbrew Bulge

Underground Pipeline

Lust of the Giant Sloth

Geisha Black

Skinhead Bonehead

Wee Sweet Girlies

Showdown at Red Hook

Cover art © 2010 by Paul Carrick; all rights reserved. Cover layout by Charlie Krank.
Interior layout by Meghan McLean. Edited by William Jones; Editor-in-Chief Lynn Willis.

FIRST EDITION
10 9 8 7 6 5 4 3 2 1
Chaosium Publication 6048
Published March 2011
ISBN-10: 1568823495
ISBN-13: 9781568823492

Contents

DEDICATIONS

Special thanks to Cowboy Bob Weinberg, my longtime co-author, mentor, friend, and Publishing Superhero.

Special thanks and much love to Arie Bodek, my husband of two years, best friend for many years, and Physics Superhero.

Special thanks and much love to my children, Dan and Rena, for putting up with my writing and overall book addiction year after year, weekend after weekend, night after night, etc.

Dedicated to the fine writers, artists, editors, publishers, and friends I've been lucky to know throughout the years. I mention a few special people here, but the list is much longer. My thanks to William Jones, Deborah Jones, Charlie Krank, George Vanderburgh, Scott Edelman, Mike Ashley, Marc Resnick, Steve Saffel, Stephen Powers, Charlie Ryan, Lori Perkins, Scott David Aniolowski, Larry Constantine, Charles Platt, Catherine Asaro, Nancy Kress, Alan Koszowski, Nancy Kilpatrick, James Alan Gardner, Adam-Troy Castro, Anne Bishop, Kevin Anderson, Robert Sawyer, Josepha Sherman, Mark McLaughlin, and far too many others to list. Also worth noting are the following early influences: AE van Vogt, Virgil Finlay, HP Lovecraft, Jack Williamson, A. Merritt, Clifford D. Simak, Edwin A. Abbott, Robert E. Howard, Roger Zelazny, CL Moore, Henry Kuttner, William Hope Hodgson, Murray Leinster, Edgar Rice Burroughs, William Gibson, Neal Stephenson, Kathe Koja, many more. Finally, my thanks to all the wonderful people who run SFFH conventions - locally, Wayne Brown for Astronomicon, and Joe Fillinger and the entire Buffalo Fantasy League for Eeriecon.

Lois H. Gresh

March 2011

UNDERLYING DARKNESS

by Lois Gresh

Of the 27 books I've written, ELDRITCH EVOLUTIONS is most special because it collects my favorite stories in one volume. Most of my work is loosely defined as weird fiction, with the weird elements wrung from a blend of science fiction, dark fantasy, and horror. Some stories are bent toward bizarre science, others are Lovecraftian Mythos tales, and yet others are just twisted. What they all share is an underlying darkness.

In my Mythos tales, I like to push Lovecraftian science and themes in new directions. So, for example, while HPL incorporated the astronomy and physics ideas of his day (eg, cosmos within cosmos and other dimensions), I speculate about modern science: quantum optics, particle physics, chaos theory, string theory, and so forth. While HPL showcased his creatures against a backdrop of bleak humanity — people who don't get it and can't fight back — I pit my own types of creatures against the horrors of the Mythos, and I *want* my creatures to fight back. Examples of these stories are Mandelbrot Moldrot, Where I Go Mi-Go, Showdown at Red Hook, and Scourge of the Old Ones.

Shifting from the Mythos to purely original tales, I incorporate similar ideas and themes. For example, my strange creatures battle horrors in stories such as Cafebabe, Digital Pistil, Let Me Make You Suffer, Little Whorehouse of Horrors, Smokestack Snout Neurology, Underground Pipeline, and Instant Gratification, among others.

In many stories — both Mythos and originals — the main characters are in excruciating need of freedom and independence. I understand suffering and pain, the need to alleviate both and the struggles involved, and I also understand the desire to find happiness against great odds. These themes are evident in the majority of stories I write.

They also spill liberally into my novels, such as THE TERMINATION NODE, which I wrote with Bob Weinberg, my Chuck Farris trilogy, and my latest novel, BLOOD AND ICE. While my stories are dark, my novels aren't particularly lighthearted, either: someone's always in trouble, death is always around the corner, and people tend to suffer and fight hard.

I suspect that most readers of ELDRITCH EVOLUTIONS will pick up on the fact that I like dark humor. I can't help myself. It just comes out that way.

Don't get me wrong. My stories aren't "ha ha ha" funny like one-line gags or something you might see on the Comedy Channel. In fact, maybe they're only funny to me. All I can tell you is that, while writing some of the stories in this book, I either cried or laughed until tears rolled down my cheeks. Sometimes, I cried *and* laughed.

There's plenty of dark humor inside these pages — that is, if you happen to share my nutjob mindspace. Check out Snip My Suckers, Psychomildew Love, Debutante Ball, Soleman, The Battle of Batbrew Bulge, Instant Gratification, and some of the already mentioned tales.

Anyway, to wrap up this little intro, I hope you enjoy ELDRITCH EVOLUTIONS and ride along in my nutjob mindspace for awhile. It's dark, and it's weird. But then, so am I.

— LOIS GRESH

Introduction

Introduction

BY ROBERT WEINBERG

Welcome, friends, to the first collection of short stories by Lois H. Gresh. I applaud your good taste in buying this book. Lois is one of the most talented writers working these days in the realms of imagination. In many ways I envy you because you are going to be blown away by what you read. Be careful and make sure your head is screwed on tight. If not, it might just explode when you consume the stories between the covers of this volume. Lois is that good.

As an editor, I bought several stories from Lois that were nominated for Bram Stoker Awards in the mid-1990's. Her stories were unlike any others I received. When I discovered "Snip My Suckers" and "Psychomildew Love" in my slush pile, I was blown away. Lois' stories are always full of unique ideas, bizarre plot twists, and fascinating characters, and they always surprise and delight me. Her fiction combines believable futuristic science with deep characterization and lively narrative. She has a feel for pacing and structure, a wild sense of humor. She's supremely talented and creative.

You'll encounter in this volume bizarre creations in classic Lois Gresh stories like "Mandelbrot Moldrot," "Let Me Make You

Suffer," "Cafebabe," and "Digital Pistil." Even better are Lois' excursions into the depths of Lovecraft's Cthulhu Mythos, blending digital flesh and eldritch terrors in "Where I Go, Mi-Go" and "Scourge of the Old Ones."

Lois is a terrific writer and this collection is a terrific book for anyone who wants to read the best in science fiction, dark fantasy, dark humor, and horror.

Let me reveal a secret about Lois Gresh stories. A secret that I don't think anyone has ever mentioned in reviewing Lois' work, but a truism that's obvious once stated.

Lois writes wonderfully complicated plots that creep up on you and catch you by surprise at the end of a story. Sure, there might be digital-flesh blobs and quarks and nanotechnology and all sorts of weird science, but when you get to the end of the story, BANG, the conclusion makes perfect sense and everything in the story suddenly works much better than you ever realized. One of the greatest pleasures about reading Lois Gresh stories is reading them a second time and seeing how she sneaked in clues all through the story that you completely missed, thinking that they were merely weird and crazy details unimportant to the conclusion. Not so, and that's the mark of a fine writer. Go ahead and read "The Lagoon of the Insane Plants" and then tell me I'm wrong. Not possible, because I'm right.

Enough introducing. Turn the page and start reading. You might be shocked, surprised, even bedazzled. But you sure won't be sorry!

Robert Weinberg
10/10/10
(*Nothing happened. So much for numerology!*)

SNIP MY SUCKERS first appeared in 100 Vicious Little Vampires, was on the Bram Stoker Preliminary Ballot for Best Story of the Year 1995, and received an Honorable Mention in Year's Best Fantasy & Horror 1995. It's always been one of my favorites, and I remain very fond of the vampiric rose bush, Glory, and her struggle to win Chuck and destroy his dead wife. A word to the wise: be careful with the bone meal and the heavy phosphate.

Snip My Suckers

Chuck's heat steams my leaves. "So sweet," he says, "you're always so sweet in the first flush of spring."

My petals strain to his cheek. His whiskers are raw; a thousand blades shredding the hot velvet of my bud.

His nose dips. His eyes close.

A quick prick, and I'll have him. I crawl up the side of his house, sharpen my thorns on the stucco.

Chuck sprays me with the bone meal and the heavy phosphate.

Up my naked canes and out my tender sprouts, I pump the perfume that drives him wild: the honey cloves and the morning dew.

Chuck's nostrils widen. He sprays me again.

I quiver by the nectar that pounds through his neck. My thorns graze his skin, probe for the pulse; and now —

I plunge.

He screams and slaps his neck, and my branch whips back against the stucco. "Dratted mosquitos," he says, and his blood dribbles and my sepals curl and tighten and lap the hot juice.

His fist tightens around silver shears. "Think I'll snip off some suckers. It'll give you more strength, Glory, more roses. You look a bit peaked."

Go ahead, Chuck, snip my suckers. Prune me, baby, like a madman.

His shears are sharp. They sever me down at the root trunk where I'm most sensitive. Buds bust from my stems. Perfumes pump from my anthers.

"You look like you're gonna die, Glory. Wish I knew what kind of rose you are." He leers at me, then wipes his paws on his pants and gathers his tools.

I'm an unnamed seedling, Chuck, born from the roots of wild stock and fed on the mush of bony phosphate. The mice and the kittens know, and even the neighborhood dogs stay away from me.

But Chuck shrugs — we just don't communicate on anything but a physical level — and then he fondles a leaf and saunters away with two withered blooms.

The fence gate creaks. My little bud eyes swivel. Chuck is behind the house, stooping by his wife's grave. Even from a distance, his steam scorches my sap.

His paw rests upon the stone cross. The paw that stroked me. And now my two flowers are on the cross. They wilt. They die. Their corpses fall to the dirt.

What does Chuck see in dead bones? Why does he love *her* more than *me*?

The screen door slams. He's entered the safety of the stucco house. If only I could come with you; oh Chuck, you succulent hunk of bloody raw steak. I curl my tendrils over his roof gutters and sweat.

The afternoon sun streams down, plasters me like melted dough against Chuck's house. I'm all alone. My branches ache. My leaves are soggy mash. And the sky frowns and dumps its rain.

At the far end of the yard, Chuck's garden sucks up the water and laughs. Beans bulge and split their seams. Tomatoes throb like hearts; they mock me. Garlic surfs the breeze, and when I lash at the fumes, they curl from my grasp and snicker.

I break out with cankers and crown gall, with mildew and blackspot.

I need nightfall. I need it badly.

I cling to the house. I shrivel.

I bake for an eternity. Finally, the sun buries itself behind the cemetery. Night comes down and gives me a black kiss. And now my stems surge and my buds explode into crimson roses.

Something sniffs my bottom buds and nibbles. I turn twenty branches toward the ground. Dozens of my bud eyes peer through the gloom.

And there it is: a mouse scurrying along the base of the house, trying to slurp water from my leaves.

Twenty branches descend.

A thousand thorns thrust, retract, and thrust again.

The corpse is warm. My leaves smother it, and my stomata open wide and drink. Blood runs thick through my stems.

I leave the skin and bones. Eventually, they'll rot into the soil and nourish my roots.

A cat approaches, cautiously. I pop a root from the ground and poke its belly. It howls and runs into the night.

By morning, I've sucked dry three stray dogs and a host of rodents.

Chuck is yawning. He drinks steam from a clay cup. Gracing the side of the cup is a picture of a *Rosa roxburghii*: pink and anemic, a water drinker.

The sun's rays tear into me. My flowers close into tight balls and hide.

Chuck sets aside his cup and packs manure around my lower extremities, down by the sensitive spots where he snatched my suckers. The manure is cold and smells of rot. Chuck must love me.

"Jesus! What the hell is this?" He leaps back and the blood drains from his face. He pulls on gloves and grabs a shovel. He heaps the remains of the mouse and the dogs and the other beasts into a green bag. I know that I'm a sloppy eater, but why is he so angry?

He drags the plastic bag somewhere behind the house, then returns with a hose and several cans and a spray gun.

He spritzes me with the bone meals and the phosphates, and to thank him, I scratch his arms and drink his nectar. He squirts insecticides from bright yellow cans with crossbones on them. He cuts my cankers and tumors, sprays me with lime sulfur, with folpet and zineb and ferbam. And with streptomycin to cure my crown gall.

I'm so lucky to be loved by Chuck.

The cross in the cemetery casts a shadow across us. It's the dead wife. She won't leave us alone. Even dead, she tries to win him back. I break out with mildew. Chuck does not notice. He stares at his wife's grave.

Now he turns to me with a big grin. "You know what you need, Glory? To be transplanted next to Rosemary. The soil's good there, and besides, you'll be good company for her. Rosemary always loved you when she was alive."

Rosemary: the witch who planted white Madonna lilies and wore a gold cross around her neck. *Rosemary*: the witch who planted the garlic. I said to her once, "Go on, honey, snip my suckers — ha, if you dare," and fool that she was, Rosemary dared.

Her blood was thin and bitter.

Now Chuck is packing all his cans and spray guns into a wheelbarrow. He thrusts a shovel into the ground by my roots. He cackles. "Don't really know much about gardening, but one thing I do know: you need *something* to make you healthy. You're always breaking out with diseases. And your flowers look sick."

But I'm always so sweet in the first flush of spring ....

Ack, the shovel splinters my stems. Chuck's weight heaves against the handle, thrusting into me, snapping me, killing me, draining my sap. He hacks and he hacks, and soon I'm screaming inside and everywhere, the rodents titter at me, and if all that were not enough, Chuck rips me from the ground.

And now, I am naked to the world. My shame burns. I want to die I want to die I want

to die.

Chuck plops me atop the folpets and the zinebs, and he carts me across the yard.

His gloved paws pack me into a small hole by *her* grave. My bud eyes turn from the cross. I will not look I will not

look, but I do look and half a dozen branches splinter and fall from me, and instantly they turn to dust.

Chuck does not notice. "Oh, Rosemary, how I miss you. Perhaps the fragrance of Glory's roses will cheer you."

My tender sprouts are splayed across her grave. I'm so weak I can barely move.

Chuck drags the hose across the yard. He fills the hole with water —

with *WATER* —

and now I'm sopped in oxydemetonmethyls and nicotine sulfates

and dimethoates and carbaryls and manebs and folpets and ferbams

and I'm dying from it all, and yet

I need Chuck.

I need *his blood.*

But he leaves me, as all lovers do, and again the screen door slams. My roots slip deep into the earth and slither to Rosemary's coffin. The wood is rotting, and easily I pick through the debris and slide within and find the cold bones.

This is what Chuck loves. This is what Chuck prefers to me.

I cross my roots over her ribs. My thorns drill into the bone. I try to suck the marrow, but it's dust.

All night, I wait; all night, I plan. And when morning comes, I know that Chuck will be mine.

He slurps from the *Rosa roxburghii* cup. His greasy whiskers shine in the sun. "I have a gift for you," he says.

Ooh, possibly a fat blood-glutted dog?

"This will help you grow huge flowers, Glory."

Must be a special treat...a neighbor; or better yet, a priest or rabbi.

I want to thank him, so I scratch his ankle and lap the blood.

"Dratted mosquitos, driving me nuts." He pullss his leg from me, then drags something large across the lawn and through the creaking cemetery gate. "Your gift," he says.

Ooh, it's a...

...a cross-hatched trellis?

I wilt against the gravestone.

He pulls a hammer from his workbelt. He drives the stakes into my roots.

I scream and I lunge, and my thorns are deep within his throat, stabbing and stabbing —

and he's slapping at me and howling, and thick worms of blood stream down his neck,

and he runs into the house and the screen door slams.

His blood has made me strong. My roots snake under the lawn and drill into his basement. They wait until nightfall.

Inside the coffin, roots tangle and twist around Rosemary's bones. One root rips the cross from her chest and crushes it. Others slither up the trellis, knot into fists, and pull the cross-hatched monstrosity to the ground.

And now I'm ready. Across Chuck's lawn, my roots poke through the grass and spring into the night air. I will be everywhere, always, for Chuck.

The thrum of his heart calls to me. I'm hungry, and dogs and cats won't do. I've loved Chuck for so long. I want to make him happy. I will give him back to Rosemary.

My roots curl up his walls, slither like snakes up the basement stairs. I find him snoring in the bed.

The bed he shared with *Rosemary.*

This time, he will share it with me.

Snip My Suckers

PSYCHOMILDEW LOVE is another favorite of mine. I wrote it one week after writing SNIP MY SUCKERS. PSYCHOM-ILDEW LOVE first appeared in 100 Wicked Little Witches, and along with SNIP MY SUCKERS, it also was on the Bram Stoker Preliminary Ballot for Best Story of the Year 1995 and received an Honorable Mention in Year's Best Fantasy & Horror 1995.

Psychomidew Love

Cora Cromley scratched the fungus pinwheels from her window. It was a shame to destroy such perfect mold, but to get a good look at her neighbor, Warren Truckenmiller, she had to clear some space.

Ah, there he was, muscles bulging beneath the frayed cutoffs, square face grim under the frayed blond hair. A shaggy mutt of a man, playing with his machines: bug zapper, weed whacker, four-wheel muscle bike. Half Cora's age. And a newlywed. His wife, Maralee, clung to him and whispered in his ear.

Oh, what Cora would give to be Maralee; so young, so lithe, with the streaming black hair and the eyes of melted ice. Warren lifted what looked like an oxygen tank with gas mask and suction tubes — oh, yes, the leaf blower — and strapped it to his back. He put on the mask, then a helmet, and grasped the blower's nozzle. In the death of day, under a half-mast sun, he looked like a rocketman.

Maralee crunched over dead autumn leaves and perched on the edge of a lawn chair. She rubbed their dog, Yapper, under the ears.

The blower *vroomed* to life, and Yapper howled.

Fingernails scraped down Cora's back. That noise again; that noise! The dog, the machines —

Cora screeched.

The newlyweds turned and squinted in Cora's direction. Cora ducked beneath the windowsill. The blower died, and she heard muffled laughs.

"What an old bat," said Maralee.

"Leave her be," said Warren, "she's just a lonely old maid."

Cora's eyes misted. Yes, she was lonely, so lonely that she talked to the psychomildew that stretched like soft sealskins across the walls. But an old maid? Never. "It's not too late for me. I'll get a husband. I'll get kids."

She wiped her tears on her hot-pink negligee, swept gray wisps from her forehead, and peeked from the window. Maralee was wrapped around Warren, kissing his neck, his cheeks, his hair. "Turn it back on, Warren baby, it gives me such a thrill. Who cares about that old witch anyway?"

Indeed, Cora was a witch, descended from a long line of inbreeding and proud of it. She cranked open her window and hollered, "So what if I'm a witch? What are you gonna do about it, eh?"

Warren leered at his wife. The leaf blower *vroomed* back to life.

Cora screamed and clutched at her chest, her legs, her back. The blower was a drill bit down her spine: grinding, blasting.

Now Maralee was on Warren's back, hugging the blower, the two of them vibrating and writhing. Warren with the weed whacker, zapping the dandelion tendrils and the hollyhocks off Cora's lawn. He kicked on the four-wheeler, hopped on with Maralee, and they rode it like a bucking bronco. Around them danced Yapper, barking and leaping, a black jot on a dying sun.

Cora retreated into the pit of her house. Her mind steamed with thoughts as black and foaming as the psychomildew rotting in her walls. She would have Warren Truckenmiller. She would tear him from his wifey; she would force him to love her. She would force him to give her children.

She cradled her cheek on the green mold by the fireplace. Cool, slimy, it calmed her, cleared her thoughts. On the mantle were photos of her ancestors, witches and warlocks with eyes like boils erupted from pus-pocked skin. But Cora was the most beautiful of all. On her chin, the warts grew in concentric circles. On her lip, a hairy mole dangled like a cherry from her brown lips.

How could Warren resist?

She ran her fingertips over the velvet walls. Green fungus by the scalpel cabinet, good for thunder and rain. Brown and black by the poison flask hutch, perfect for love spells.

She fingered the flasks of toad throat peelings and bat claw clippings. She would cast a love spell on Warren Truckenmiller. She pressed her palms against the brown and black mildew. Her fingers tingled, her hands; then the tingle flew up her arms, shot straight to her brain. She said, "Psychomildew pions. Boson bombs. Make Maralee flee, and make Warren love *me*."

But something was wrong. Her mind wasn't floating in ecstasy. She pressed against the wall, this time harder. The wall sank beneath her hands, fell in wet slabs to the floor. She peered into the crumbled ruins. Egg yolk mold. Fungi ropes looped in nooses around flabby necks of mildew. The smell so sweet, a thousand dead bodies stewing for a thousand years.

Cora's head swam in the perfume. She felt the glow hit her cheeks. Why hadn't the love spell worked? What was wrong?

She poked her head through the vast hole, found that the entire inside of the wall had been eaten away as if by moths.

Well, what would she do? Without the pion boson psychomildew wall, she couldn't cast a love spell on Warren.

Scampering. Chittering. Gnawing. It was the roach pack again, the roaches that fed on the soul of her organic house. She slammed her fist into the wall. A large chunk of dripping splotch splashed onto her head. She flung it down and stomped on it.

Had to fix the wall. Had to nourish it with flesh and make the psychomildew grow.

She stumbled back to the window. Outside, Warren was alone, tinkering with an air compressor. Maralee must have gone inside to take a fragrant bath and slip into something sexy.

"Hey, Warren, you wanna come over for some...cookies?" called Cora.

He looked up and laughed. "You gotta be kidding."

"No kidding. I have some real delicious cookies here. And doughnuts, too." He pointed a finger at her. "I'm not coming in *your* house, lady, not for a million bucks."

From afar, Maralee sang, "Oh, Warren, come and get it."

"Look, I gotta go now." Warren was an excited little boy, packing his toys into his mower bins, gunning the motor, kicking into high gear. Yapper barked and leapt aboard.

"I want you *now*," screamed Cora over the noise.

But Warren didn't hear her.

She thrust her hands against the sides of the window and inched them slowly across the psychomildew walls. Here, where the spells transformed people into —

she couldn't remember —

people into —

"Do it, fungus, do it now. Make Warren into a gorgeous cow."

Was it a cow? Had she spoken the right words, the ones that the wall would transform into vibration balls of bosons and pions?

The mower hiccuped. The dog yowled and ran toward Warren's house.

Cora heard a snort.

In the dusk, it was hard to be certain, but as the creature crept closer, she knew: Cora Cromley had turned Warren Truckenmiller into an anteater. Powerful sexy legs, claws longer than Cora's, and a snout that would drive any woman mad.

Cora raced from the kitchen, slammed the back door, and hurried over to Warren. His snout was stuck in an anthill. She grabbed his fur by the neck and yanked up his head. It came up coated with ants and termites. His long tongue flapped.

"Listen here," she said, "you're comin' into the house with me. And I mean now."

Maralee was running across the lawn wearing next to nothing. The moon glowed against a red-chiseled sky. Maralee's black hair was singed with red. Her eyes were singed with fear. "Warren! Warren, where are you, baby?"

Cora cackled. "He's nowhere to be found, dear. Now go on home and leave me in peace, would you?" She looped her arms around Warren's neck and hauled him toward the house.

Maralee stopped by the hollyhock bed, crushed dandelions curling over her toes. "But I...but I know he's out here, I left him here. Where would he be?" She was crying, her tears splashing like blood from a great wound.

"Come on, Warren." Cora shoved his fat, furry tail into her kitchen. Beady eyes looked up at her; termites dropped from his tongue. She rummaged in the refrigerator. "Now you be good. I'll be back soon. I have to go out and find something to feed to the wall." She plopped the box of chocolate-covered locusts on the floor and left him there.

It was black outside. She was in night's cup, where she belonged. She slipped by the side of her house between the poison oak and the splintered board. In Warren's bedroom window, Maralee's black profile heaved and sobbed against a backdrop of white light.

Cora crouched behind the towering juniper. Crickets chirruped. A frog croaked. She heard herself breathing. Then something growled. Right behind her, something growled. She whirled and saw it: the dog, Yapper, food for the wall. She screeched and dove at the beast, and it lunged for her throat, but she squeezed the neck tightly and snapped it back, and as quickly as the dog had attacked, she claimed its life and it groaned and whimpered and then lay limp at her feet.

She dragged it into the house.

A half-eaten locust dangled from Warren's snout. His little eyes filmed with tears, and he fell crying into his box of goodies.

Cora stroked Warren's black and gray fur and then stuffed the dog into the collapsed wall. A loud suck and slurp, and she knew that the psychomildew was devouring Yapper's flesh and replenishing itself.

She turned back to Warren. "If you promise to be good, I'll turn you back into a man," she said.

He whimpered and nodded his snout.

She stroked the wall again, this time uttered the spell that turned beasts back into people. Warren popped into human form. He dove for the door. She flew at him, knocked him to the floor. They rolled in the locusts and termites and mold. He was slapping her and bellowing, and she was plunging her claws into his ears and his cheeks and screaming, "You said you'd be good! You said you'd be good!" And he couldn't fight her, for she was a witch, born from generations of inbreeding, and she could pin down any mortal, and she was proud of it.

She slammed him against the wall, said, "Do it, fungus, do it now. Turn Warren into a gorgeous cow."

Her spell disintegrated into particles, coalesced into boson bombs and psychomildew pions that penetrated the wall, massaged its growths, and then surged in a streak of silver and struck Warren like lightning; he fell back against the scalpel cabinet, then slumped to the floor.

Warren was an anteater again. "And you shall stay that way, you naughty, naughty boy," said Cora.

She stalked into the living room and propped her elbow on the mantle. He trundled behind her and grunted. He squatted at her feet and whimpered. He rose on his hind legs, put his front paws on her knees. He mewed like a sick cat.

"Honestly, you're pathetic, Warren Truckenmiller. I give you all my love, and what do you do? You try to escape. I should lock *you* in the psychomildew wall with the dog."

Warren snuffled at her black boots. She kicked his snout. She remembered his cruel words: Leave her be, she's just a lonely old maid.

It's not too late for me, Warren, I'll get a husband, I'll get kids.

She looked at the slender snout. The toothless mouth slit. The sticky, flicking tongue. As a man, Warren would always run from her, hate her, laugh at her.

As an anteater, did he have any choice but to love her?

She sank to her knees. "Would you like me to be an anteater, too?"

He whimpered, snuffled close.

She thought of the children they would have together, of the happy family life. And she muttered the spell that would cast her forever into the world of anthills and thrusting snouts and termite tunnels, and never-ending love.

SOLEMAN first appeared in Hot Blood: Fear the Fever, was on the Bram Stoker Preliminary Ballot for Best Story of the Year 1996, and received an Honorable Mention in Year's Best Fantasy & Horror 1996. When I was 19, I met an old guy (probably 30) who was obsessed with my high school brown lace-up shoes. This creepy guy became Chuck of SOLEMAN. A lifelong swimmer, in those days I followed my laps with 30 minutes in the steam room and then a cold shower. I decided that Chuck needed to be at the pool and in the steam room. By the way, you might be noticing a trend: I often call my male characters, Chuck. I have no clue why.

Soleman

Chuck slammed Tanya onto the hard bench of the steam room. A loud splat, and she slid giggling to the floor. Chuck grasped the slippery handle, then swung the heavy door shut. To one side, steam billowed from a wall vent. One hundred ten degrees, the building locked for the night. Alone. Just Chuck and Tanya.

She'd been flirting with him for months. She knew he was married; she'd teased him about it. Now she crouched at his feet in the filmy tank suit that concealed nothing. Pale hair dripping down her dark face like icing down the side of a cake. Sleek legs of steel on a Jaguar body. Tanya: hot, sweet, and sticky. Melting in the steam room's swelter.

Through misty swirls, Tanya was every man's dream: ephemeral, faceless, hot for it. The Y's youngest aerobics teacher. Any other man would have thought he'd died and gone to heaven.

But Chuck was no ordinary man. He had to take it slowly. Couldn't jeopardize his marriage to Monica for *ordinary* sex, even with a goddess like Tanya. And she wanted only him, no doubt about it.

Tanya dug her heels into his calves, and he felt a jolt of excitement. He reached back and grabbed her heel in his fist. She giggled again, slapped him, feigned a struggle.

He squeezed the heel, a firm, gently sloping mound. Her toes brushed his thigh. A shiver bolted through him. Careful, careful, he told himself. Don't lose it.

Tanya smiled coyly and slid the straps off her shoulders.

Chuck drew back and slid his trunks down. Tanya's smile faded to an animal glow. Must have been admiring his firm body, honed from twenty years of service to the Y. Chuck: Aqua God, Lord of the Pool.

Tanya made a sound somewhere between a growl and a purr. Breasts, perfect behind, sleek stomach. She was indeed something to behold. But there was only one part of Tanya that really excited Chuck, only one part that made the risk worth it.

Her feet.

He wanted to suckle the toes and tickle the soles.

He wanted to splay the tender little toelets and lick, to run his tongue along the tight arch until she screamed.

And if she went for it, if she was that one in a million ...

He could barely move, thinking of the possibilities:

Tanya in stiletto heels.

Tanya in leather sandals.

Tanya's wet feet flip-flopping in thongs to the pool's edge.

Tanya's sole bared.

Chuck lunged and ripped at her suit. She squealed and clasped his head, ran her fingers through his hair.

Her breath was wetter, hotter than the steam pouring from the vents.

He wrenched off her suit, threw it to the bench.

Thrust. Tanya gasping.

Toe pads slathered in oil.

Thrust. Tanya panting.

His hand slid down her leg, lower, lower.

His fingers slipped past the ankle. Farther, down further, and now, yes, her feet. While he worked her, steady, like an engine, his hand caressed the soft curve of the arch, the nub of her heel bone where the skin was tightest.

How long it went on, he didn't know. He felt himself losing control — Not yet, he told himself, don't go all the way yet, you'll scare her, *this is too good to ruin* — and finally he decided that he had to end it.

A few more sullen thrusts and he was done. He pulled away, gasping the superheated air. He looked down at her. She was staring back — admiration? The aftershocks of orgasm?

Good, she didn't suspect. Next time, maybe, or the time after. Soon he would move Tanya to the next phase.

"Again, baby, just once more?" Tanya cooed.

Her toes curled at him, beckoned. It took everything in him not to grab them and stuff them into his mouth and eat them right up to the sockets where the bone joints held them fast to the feet.

His palm shivered, his fingers stretched. "Let's get outta here, Tanya, before it's too late and we're caught."

They snaked back into the damp swimsuits. They didn't say much; conversation wasn't Tanya's strength. Chuck steered her through the steam room and into the iceberg of the men's locker room. Stole a glance at her heels; they were wrinkled and pink.

By the showers was a rusty trophy cabinet. Chuck pointed. "See? I wasn't kidding. All-county in free style. Second place in the statewide." His trophy was tall and slightly warped at the top. The gold plate was tarnished.

Tanya arched her feet and stood on tiptoe. "What does it say, Chuck?"

"'Charles Malley, Second Place.' I would have taken first, if I hadn't blown the flip turn."

Tanya's nose wrinkled with confusion. "How about tomorrow?" She rubbed against him. Their wet skin stuck.

He shook his head. "No, Monica will have a fit as it is. I'm half an hour late already, and she'll give me hell."

"All right. Wednesday, then." She turned at the doorway to the women's locker room. Another sly look, a mock pout. "I'll just have to control myself until Wednesday." Then she was gone. The last Chuck saw of her was her right foot as it disappeared through the doorway. God, it was beautiful, so small, but powerful, exactly the right proportion. A little jewel made of flesh.

He let Tanya leave first, just in case anyone was hanging around the parking lot. The year before, Monica had actually parked around the side of the Y, hoping to catch Chuck with his latest girlfriend.

He twisted the key in the lock of the main door, then shuffled across the lot where, under one flickering bulb, his old blue Escort waited. Lord of the Pool, driving home in a scaly blue junker.

Before he started the engine, he unlatched the glove box and riffled through the magazines. *In Step*, for the lover of feet. *Sole Survivor. Footloose Fancier.* All his favorites. Heels, toes, arches. He opened to the personal ads in the back. Photos of feet, fake sexy smiles. Phone numbers and addresses. He'd never had the nerve.

He stopped at the centerfold: a woman's legs from the knees down. High heels, feet so tiny and pearled and toe-tipped in red. If only. God, if only they were real.

He used a wad of napkins from Burger King to clean up.

He took his time getting home, knowing what was waiting for him.

"Where the hell you been, Chuck Malley? It's almost ten." No surprises from Monica. The same accusations, the same venom. From her slippers poked the feet he had married. Once smooth and mouth-stuffingly plump, now all callused.

She shoved him against the metal trophy case by the TV. "So what's your excuse this time, Chuckie? 'I had to adjust the chlorine level, Monnie'? Or 'I had to redo the lifeguard time sheets'?"

"Come on, Monnie, you'll wake the kids."

"So what if I wake the kids? Sally and Louie know their Daddy's a loser. They know you're just an overgrown lifeguard."

Her nose was an inch from his eyes. The nose that jutted from her face like a big hairy toe. Twenty years ago, when they first met, she hadn't been half bad looking, and her feet had been the finest.

She slammed him into the wall. One of his plaques rattled and fell and bounced off his shoulder to the floor. "I work all day, earning the money that keeps you in that idiot pool job. If not for me, why..." and on and on she ranted, and Chuck just tuned out the grating whine, same as he tuned out bad songs on the radio.

He left her fuming and headed for the basement steps. Down in the cellar he'd have some peace. She rarely followed him down there. It was dank and cold. Knotty pine. In the corner was his bed: the plaid couch vomiting tufts of stained stuffing.

He twisted the caps off the chlorine bottles. His nose burned from the essence.

He pulled the string, and the light died.

He was back in the steam room. Aqua God nibbling on Tanya's toes...

A squeak. Light jetted down the stairs. He looked up. Monica in a spotlight. She said, "So you're just gonna hide down there, is that it? You fooling around again, Chuck?"

His eyes shot to their honeymoon picture. Monica in a turquoise bikini on a deck chair. Her feet close to the camera. Huge feet. Splayed toes. "I'm not doing anything, Monnie. I had a hell of a day."

"Yeah, right." The spotlight snapped off. Monica's slippers scuffed across the kitchen floor and faded into the carpet.

His fist banged into the knotty pine. It wasn't fair. They'd never overtly discussed it, never admitted that he was a foot fetishist, but still, Monica had always known that he'd married her for her feet.

Chuck knew he'd better watch it, had better dump Tanya. Monica was capable of just about anything. She'd brained him last year with an ashtray. They'd had to lie to the emergency room doctor as he put in the eight stitches.

This time Monica would probably kill him or take away the children.

When Chuck left for the Y the next morning, he knew he had to steer clear of Tanya. He had to forget about Tanya's feet.

He hid behind his desk for a few hours, pretending to do paperwork, hoping Tanya would have the good sense to stay away.

His office was a concrete cubicle: four cinder-block walls painted with pea-green enamel and covered with crayon drawings, CPR dummy slumped in the corner, the smell of chlorine permeating everything. Chlorine: the smell of success, the sting in your eyes when you win the big trophy.

"Oh Chuckie, I don't think I can wait another day."

She was wearing short shorts, a tight tank top. Her feet were trapped in running shoes. She perched her behind on the one clear corner of his desk and crossed her legs.

Chuck stared across the room at one of Louie's drawings. "Daddy" was scrawled on the bottom in red crayon.

"Close the door," Chuck said, and regretted it before the words had left his mouth.

Tanya smirked and eased the hollow metal door shut. "Right here?" she whispered.

The air immediately became heavy, close as a sodden blanket. "No, we can't do it in my office. Everybody in the place will hear us."

"So you fixed it up with the wife? You can stay late again tonight?"

"I don't think we should...I don't think I can..."

She unlaced a shoe and let it drop. She ran her bare foot up and down his leg. Jesus, did she know? Did she understand? Was this some kind of sign?

She said, "You know, I like you better when you're not talking." The other shoe was off now, too.

He grabbed her foot, stroked the sleek curve of the instep across his whiskered cheek. The soft plush at the roots of the toes grazed his lips. Desperately he wanted his tongue to flick out and lick, but...but...Monica and the kids...

Tanya fell back and grabbed the sides of the desk. There was a strange look on her face. Not fear exactly, not even revulsion. Just some sort of understanding, a flicker that told him she found his obsession exciting.

Now she was sweet by his ear. "Tonight. Take them tonight."

Take *them*? Fireworks shot up his back and into his brain. For the first time in his life Chuck would pump his stuff against real feet, he would feel the thrill of feet massaging and pulling, yanking at him until he just couldn't stand it anymore and he exploded in a...

Tanya coiled herself around him from behind, tickled his calf with her toes. His leg hairs tingled. "I checked the schedules, Chuck. You've got the last shift in the pool tonight. Everybody else will be gone. I can hang around, go over applications for next month's classes. Nobody will suspect a thing."

Her toes played at the back of his thigh. This was the closest he'd ever gotten to the real thing. How could he give up this one chance?

A paper fluttered from the wall. It was the "Daddy" picture. "Not tonight, Tanya. Can't do it tonight. But...tomorrow maybe." He could think of another solution by then. "Tomorrow, or maybe the next day."

"But I can't *wait* another day, Chuckie." She shoved him forward against the desk and the metal edge hit his gut, and he gasped. She lifted one long leg, placed her foot on his back.

He'd never known Tanya to be so aggressive. Tanya the she-beast. He must tame her, control her.

"Oh, Chuckie, I can't wait any longer. Come on, let's do it now, Chuckie, come on." She pressed herself against him, a low growl coming from the back of her throat, the rumble of raw animal desire.

He wanted to, he had to, he needed to...

"Nobody will know." Tanya's voice was a harsh whisper.

But Monica would find out. Monica always found out. And this time there'd be no way for Chuck to weasel out of trouble. She'd take the kids, the house, the money. He'd be an old man in a cheap boarding-house. Alone with his magazines, all alone.

Or she'd kill him.

He couldn't tell Tanya the truth, so instead he said, "Who do you think you are, telling *me* what to do? Be a good girl, Tanya, and put your shoes on. Come back tomorrow."

She wasn't happy, but she left; and all day, Chuck thought about Tanya's feet. To feel that sharp heel in his crotch, pushing on him, forcing him to the limit...

He pulled into the driveway exactly on time. Monica gave him the once-over as if inspecting him for incriminating evidence. She sniffed him, cold and distant; but she didn't argue with him.

Louie and Sally were bickering in the bathroom. Sally ran down the hall, blubbering about her brother. She had golden curls and long limbs, an angel of a six-year-old. Her brother trailed behind her; he was dark and brooding, a nine-year-old miniature of Chuck.

Chuck peeked over his shoulder. Monica was glaring at him. She shuffled the kids down the hall, then said, "I have news, Chuck. Got top marks today on my performance review. Mortman's going for the lateral move. I'm to take his spot."

"Good news, Mon...really good." In a few years she would be a vice president of the company. He would still be teaching five-year-olds the doggy paddle and helping fat old arthritics up and down the pool steps.

She stared at him. She, the prosecutor, the witnesses, the jurors, and the judge.

Chuck slid from the stool, inched toward the cellar stairs.

Monica swiveled and shot him the look. "Just don't you start it again, Chuck. Don't even make me suspect something's wrong."

"I got some things to take care of in the basement, that's all. I'll be done at nine, I promise."

Soleman

"Nine is *Cosby*," she said.

"Right. Don't want to miss *Cosby*," he said.

He went downstairs, listened to the idiot sound track filtering from above. He stood there in the dim basement light, feeling like an animal listening to a predator's sounds. Finally he tiptoed to the place behind the furnace where he kept his magazines. Under the box that housed the AeroGym, wrapped in a garbage bag and crammed against the damp wall. He peeled off the masking tape and pulled out his precious bundle.

Feet, feet, and more feet. Beautiful feet. Bold and naked feet. Coy and hidden feet. In spiked heels, ankle-strap wedgies, tattered running shoes, clunky oxfords, penny loafers. He stared. He sat transfixed on a packing crate.

"Daddy?"

"Oh, Jesus." He jerked back to consciousness and saw little Sally at the base of the steps.

"Daddy, Ma says to come up now and see *Cosby*."

"*Cosby*, okay, *Cosby*. Go back to bed. I'll be up."

He waited for her to go back upstairs, then carefully repackaged the magazines. He would have to find a new hiding place. Sally might tell her mother by accident. And if Monica found out about his treasure trove, it would be all over.

He crammed the magazines into the exposed stuffing of the sofa, then went upstairs. While his family giggled over Cosby, he dreamed of Tanya's feet.

She showed up early the next morning, clad in a crocheted string bikini. Around her ankle was a silver chain. Her feet were nude.

She rotated a few times so he could get a good look at her. Nails glossed in pink, delicate creases on the toe joints, freckles speckled across the top of her left foot, ankle bracelet binding the foot with S&M allure: bind me, strap me, put me in chains, and ravage me.

"You look obscene," Chuck said.

"Glad you like it," she said, and headed for his office.

He eased the door shut. Tanya was fondling the CPR dummy. She cradled its feet in one palm. "Don't hold back on me, Chuck. What was last night, a little necking?" She twisted her ankle bracelet between two fingers.

He took a step forward, dug his toes into the drain hole. "Tanya, don't — not now, not during the day, not with all the kiddies and the grandmas in the pool."

Her toes were bent, the soles perfectly vertical.

A bang on the door. Outside, somebody hooting: "Hey, Tanya and Mr. Malley, there's trouble in the pool. Big fight between two kids."

Chuck said, "For God's sake, you have to get out of here."

"Tonight?" she whispered.

"Tonight," he said.

He couldn't keep his mind off her all day. Between aerobics classes, she was everywhere, plunging from the diving board, slicking back wet hair, sloshing across the tiles. By the time the Y closed at nine, Chuck's nerves were screaming.

He slipped down the long tiled hallway leading to the men's room. He glanced at his mile-high trophy. First place, free style. He kicked open the steam room door.

She was inside, waiting for him on the hard bench by the steam vent. Her fingers scraped the floor tiles. He hardly noticed the crocheted bikini or what was under it, for her feet were bound in pink satin high heels with silken bows around the ankles.

"My God, you know...you know," he whispered. He couldn't believe it. At long last, after all these years, a woman willing to give him what he wanted, what he needed, what he had to have.

She swiveled to a sitting position, stretched out the long legs, displayed the feet. Five-inch heels, by God, with sharp points.

He started to shake. The vent belched, and a feverish blast of steam enveloped them both. He knelt on the floor, took the pink spikes in his hands.

Tanya shook him loose. "I want more than that, Chuck. I want it all." Her hands rustled through a brown bag, which she had shoved under the bench. Through heavy steam he saw her pull out several objects. "Is the door locked?" she asked.

"Door doesn't lock from the inside. Only from the outside. What'd you bring, Tanya?" She arranged several items on the bench. He craned his neck, then scooted closer for a good look.

His heart leaped into his throat.

She pulled more articles from the bag and placed them on the bench far away where he couldn't see. But he didn't need to see any more, for on the bench before him was everything he'd ever dreamed about: leather thongs with flesh-biting straps; silken stockings with snake patterns up the back; clunky old-fashioned schoolmarm shoes that laced up the front; toe rings in all sizes.

He gasped, thrust his nose into one of the schoolmarm shoes.

Tanya eased back his head and said, "Not yet, baby, not until you give me what I want."

His head was lost in steam and chlorine. He was in a neon cyclone, caught in the swirls. He was light and energy; he was Aqua God. He grabbed Tanya's arms and pushed her to the tiles. She squealed, kicked her heels into the air. He pinned her down, peeled off a shoe, spread her toes.

She was laughing now. "No, no, Chuck, I don't want that. I want the real thing first. *Then* we'll get down and dirty."

He had the toes in his fist and couldn't resist; and he licked the bottom of her foot and slicked the little toe tunnels with saliva.

Tanya jerked her foot out of his grasp. She slid away from him across the wet tile. "I said no, Chuck, I said not that yet."

The schoolmarm shoe called to him. Chalk dust. The clacking of a ruler on his desk. The sweat of the schoolmarm's foot as she whacked him one across the wrists.

He grabbed Tanya's foot again and rammed her big toe into his mouth to suck its salt, to flick his tongue under the nail.

She wrenched her foot back. "Wait. Wait a second."

He pulled away, and she slipped out of the steam room. In an instant she was back, carrying a bucket of water, filled, he assumed, in the shower. She sloshed the water on the steam element, and immediately the room was engulfed in even thicker steam. Hard to breathe now, hard to see, like being trapped inside a boiler.

He moved toward her, and an eddy of steam curled around her head. The cloud cleared just long enough for Chuck to see her lacing on the schoolmarm shoes. "Okay, okay, Chuckie, you want it, you really want it."

He grabbed her, and they clung to each other for a moment. Then he looked down at the schoolmarm shoes. Black, hard, forbidding. He felt himself growing hard and melting at the same time.

"Is Chuckie happy now?"

Mrs. Decentia, fifth grade. Math. A real witch, all the boys hot for her. He pulled her to the floor. "I deserved a B, you bitch, not a D."

Mrs. Decentia was shrieking now, giggling and rubbing herself against him. She pulled away and lay on her back. Chuck whipped her legs asides, cradled a schoolmarm in each hand, drank in the smell of old leather.

"Give the teacher what she wants."

Before he could descend on her, though, she'd wriggled out of his grasp and grabbed the bag. Her hand shot inside and emerged holding something metal and shiny. Two hooked blades, a spring mechanism, and rubber handles. She closed her grasp and the blades bit against each other. A pair of brand-new garden shears.

"Come here, you bad, bad boy."

Chuck stared, transfixed.

"I said come here!" Mrs. Decentia in her worst mood.

"I said..."

He did as he was told.

"Put your foot up here."

Again he obeyed. He thought at first that she just wanted to trim his nails, but when she grasped his ankle and fit the steel blades against the last joint of his baby toe, he knew that something worse, something better, was in store. "You've got to pay for what you've done, Chuckie. You've got to give me something in exchange."

She squeezed and the blades pressed against the skin of his toe.

Terrified, completely under her spell, he stared at his foot.

Was it just luck? Were they somehow fated to meet? Or had they been attracted to each other, coming closer and closer for years? She was just like him, one in a million, a woman with the same devotion to feet. But what did she want?

"We need to really prove ourselves, Chuckie. I want a little souvenir. Just one little snip and then you can do me." She quickly fit a piece of nylon cord around the toe, cinched it in tightly to make a tourniquet. Then the shears returned, two thin cold lines of pain. Maybe a half inch from the tip of his toe. How much could it hurt? Wouldn't it be worth it?

"It'll be a sign, just you and me, just us. We'll do each other and exchange them. It'll be a little secret marriage."

Just then Chuck heard a noise from outside the steam room. Footsteps? A door closing? He looked toward the foggy window. A face appeared, or what seemed to be a face. Blurred and distorted by the shifting mist. Just a flash, a female face? No, it was just his guilty conscience. Feeling the shears biting into his flesh, gentle but insistent, he said, "Wait. Wait!"

"You only get one chance, Chuckie. I'm it. And if you really want me, you've got to prove it."

He closed his eyes, clenched his fists. Then he thought of those schoolmarm shoes. Tanya naked in shoes hard and black and cruel. Tanya, his forever.

"Okay."

"You're sure?"

"Do it." She tightened the tourniquet. "You won't regret this, I promise."

A shriek, loud and crazed. At first, Chuck thought it had come from his throat. But looking down, he saw that Tanya wasn't at his feet any longer. He spun, and another blast of sound hit him, from outside the room. Behind the misty glass was a female face. He saw Monica coalesce suddenly, her mouth wide open, screaming. Her face pressed hard against the glass, smeared into a putty mask of hatred. Chuck stared, then heard a loud crash from the other side of the door. Chuck's mind was a blurred welter of panic. Again the noise came, louder now. A stab of dread hit him, and he lunged for the door. It didn't budge. A third clunk. Chuck hammered on the door, crying, "Monnie, Monnie, don't do this! Let us out of here!"

Tanya shoved him aside and hurled herself against the door. "Jesus! What the hell did she do?" The door was barricaded with something very heavy. "What the hell does she think..."

Chuck reared back, cocked his leg, and let fly. But the door didn't move. "God, I can't believe it, I can't believe it."

They were going to die, cooked like fish. They'd be found the next day, naked, dead, with the boots and shoes and sandals scattered around them.

Chuck slammed his fist against the window. Plexiglas, for safety's sake. He picked up one of the high-heeled pumps and, using it like a hammer, battered at the window while Tanya braced herself against the bench and put all her weight against the door. "What're we going to do?" she cried.

There was a vent hole in the ceiling. Chuck climbed onto the bench, jammed his hand against the vent grate, but it was far too small for either of them to get through.

"Why did she do it? Jesus, is she crazy?" Tanya was shrieking at him, as though it was his fault that he'd married a madwoman. "You're going to kill us both!" No playacting now, no Mrs. Decentia. Tanya was furious, on the edge of sanity herself.

Then Chuck saw the shears. He picked them up and held them like a knife. "Shut your mouth."

"It's all your fault. We're both going to die because of you."

"I said shut up!"

He lunged at her with the shears, and she backed into the steamy shadows and said, "You got us into this, now you get us out!"

They would never survive until morning. If the heat didn't reduce them to puddles of skin and hair, they'd end up killing each other.

He stabbed at the window, but the shears bounced back. Then he noticed that the window was seated in rubber molding. He jabbed the shears at the rubber and a piece came loose. Digging now, frantic, he peeled back another strip of molding. Leaning close, he felt a tendril of cool air waft through the hole. He stabbed and ripped at the molding until he had two sides stripped clean. He pounded the butt of the shears on the glass. He went at the other side, then the top. Then, with a sudden thrust of his fist, he knocked the window loose. A blast of cool air flooded past him.

In an instant Tanya had pushed by him and shimmied through the gap. He followed, a much tighter fit. Soon they were both outside the steam room, panting, naked, staring at each other as though they were both aliens.

Tanya burst out laughing, a wild, giddy laugh. "Wow, that was some close call, Chuckie."

He looked around, expecting Monica to pounce from the aqua-blue shadows, screeching accusations and threats. But they were all alone. "Have to clean up the mess, maybe break another window, make it look like kids broke into the place."

But he was talking to himself, for Tanya was not listening. Her laughter died. Her face flushed a deep red. She lifted a leg and kneaded his stomach with her toes. "I was willing, Chuck. Finally I would have gone through with it. And Chuckie, I'm still willing...if you are."

He sank back against the trophy cabinet, let his body slide to the floor. He could barely breathe her name, "Tanya..."

Her toes tightened. Her nails dug into his flesh. She was growling, eyes shut tight, head thrown back.

He'd never seen her so excited, so passionate, so clearly in control.

Soleman

"Time to finish what we started, Chuckie. Be a good boy and give me the shears." She swept her toes over his cheek and under his nostrils, and musky sweetness filled his head. She arched her back and hissed, and he knew that he could no longer resist, that he would do anything she asked.

She slipped a toe into his mouth. He trembled and sucked, ready to explode right there and then.

She slipped the shears from his fist.

Deep inside he knew that something was very wrong, that he should run; but then he thought of that toe in his mouth and he just couldn't let go.

He shut his eyes. "Do it, Tanya. Do it now."

But Tanya shrieked.

Chuck bolted up, saw a flash in the air. It was the fake-bronze trophy: it swung like a hammer and crashed down on Tanya's head.

Tanya crumpled to the floor.

Monnie stood there leering at his naked groin.

She wore no shoes. Callused feet, toes knobby with corns. In her gloved fist was the bloody trophy. "Charles Malley, Second Place. Don't you think it's time we faced facts? You are just a born loser, Chuck."

"Come on, Monnie baby, what about the kids?"

"Their daddy's a sick, womanizing, toe-sucking piece of shit. I am thinking about the kids." What was she going to do? He squirmed toward Tanya's body — that beautiful body no longer breathing, those gorgeous toes growing cold.

"Monnie, how could you kill her?"

"How could I *not* kill her?"

"What do you...what do you — "

"What do I *mean*?" And now the look on her face was awful: utterly determined, totally enraptured. She pressed a sole to his chest and pinned him to the floor. Before he could open his mouth and scream, before he could pull back his fist and punch her, the trophy came down in a blaze of bronze and blood and bashed his forehead.

Half conscious, he saw her looming above him. Her foot hovered over his face. Monnie's foot: the face of God.

"It's my turn to have fun, Chuck, *my turn*." She took the shears from Tanya's hand and popped them open. She dragged the twin blades along his groin, down the inside of his leg, past his knee, straight down until the blood welled by his little toe. Cold blade on either side of his toe. Cold blade pressing, cutting...

She was sweating and gyrating, at the brink now, moaning his name over and over. Her fingers tightened around the shears, and as she squeezed and gasped, the pain in his toe shot like a flame to his head.

Monnie shuddered and threw the shears onto Tanya's body. "That was good, Chuck, deliciously good. And now, after all these years, you'll finally know what it's like to screw *my* feet."

Two toes: she slammed them up his nose. Intense *pain*, intense *arousal*. She slammed them again and then again, and finally she crammed her smooth, cool heel into his mouth.

Suffocating, he thrashed, tried to beat her foot off his face. No longer aroused. Just wanting to live.

But he was too weak and dazed to fight. She tied the black schoolmarm laces around his ankles and wrists; then she dragged him down the cold tiled corridor. He was heavy, and it took her a while to get him down to the pool. Tug, drag him a few paces, let go and taunt him, then grab the laces and pull some more. Past the doorway to the steam room, past the office, down the sweaty ramp to the pool.

His mouth engaged enough to mutter, "Monnie, please..."

Her bare toes clamped on his lips, curled to shut him up. "You had your fun, Chuckie. Now it's my turn."

Farther down the hall, through the double doors, and they were in the pool room. The acoustics changed: echoes, the subtle slap of waves, the contrabass hum of the filter. Everything was blue: the air, the ceiling, the tiled floor, the water.

"Monnie, listen to me. I swear I won't cheat on you again, I swear it."

"You bet you won't." She dragged him to the side of the pool. "This is perfect. Nobody even knows I'm here. And now, lover boy, at long last, your big moment has come." She heaved him sideways to the lip of the pool.

One last time: her foot hovering, now sinking to his face. Nose thrusts, heel in his mouth; Mannie's back arched, face flushed, eyes squeezed shut, moaning and trembling and peaking to climax.

And the stink of her feet overwhelmed him, and after all these years he finally knew the thrill of feet massaging and pulling, yanking at him until he just couldn't stand any more. For one glorious moment, *Chuck was happy.*

She braced herself and gave him a shove. He rolled over and began to sink. He fought for a little while, trying to swim his way back to the surface. But he was exhausted, helpless, and part of him thought it was all for the best.

And then he couldn't fight it anymore. The desperate need for air took over. He hit bottom, opened his mouth, tried to breathe.

The last thing he saw was Monnie's feet: ten fat toes hooked over the edge of the pool.

WHERE I GO MI-GO, which first appeared in Singers of Strange Songs, is a Lovecraftian weird science story that features one of my many mad scientists. When I wrote this story, I didn't know that many years later (2009, to be exact), I would marry a physicist whose doctoral thesis provided evidence of the quark's existence. I have since introduced him to Lovecraft.

Where I Go, Mi-Go

It was a catatonic summer, still as if the world was grinding to a halt. The only sound was the drone of endless rain. I peered from the cabin window at the swing of the Miskatonic River as it swelled and arced and beat the ancient trees. A canopy of black clouds hung over the forest.

When would Thaddeus show up?

"He'll come when summer bleeds into autumn." My aunt's voice was sharp. She was tired of my questions.

It wasn't my fault that she read my mind.

"But if I didn't read your mind, Mirabella, how else would I know you?"

"If you knew me, Auntie, you wouldn't keep me here, alone like this, on the edge of nowhere." Angry, I turned and faced her, ready to tell her for the millionth time to stop invading my mind.

She was in her rocker by the eating table. Fingering a letter damp from tears. Withered, thin, sunk into that hard wooden chair as if her bones were part of its structure. Tiny green eyes, sparse gray hair, a mass of wrinkles.

Aunt Gertrude was all I had, and she had been very good to me.

"I'm sorry, Auntie." I walked across the dirt floor in bare feet, and stooped and lifted one hand from her lap. It was cold, and shaking.

She smelled of old age, as a leaf that falls into dew and slowly rots. Her voice faltered. "My time is nearly done. My only curse was to read minds. I thought you might be spared, that your cousin could save you before .... But now I know ... your curse will be much greater. The letter ...."

Her other hand held it out to me, and I caught it as it fell to the floor.

"Read it," she said.

Her trembling told me that whatever was in the letter would not please me.

I unfolded it, settled onto the dirt, and hugged the thin flannel shirt to my body. My hair, dark as the sky, fell across my face to my chest, and in this shroud of black, I read:

"Gertrude, you are the last Akeley. The child, Mirabella, is the last Wendigo. The boy, Thaddeus, is the last Derby and brings the Spawn of the Wind. *N'gai, n'gha'ghaa, bugg-shoggog, y'hah; Yog-Sothoth, Yog-Sothoth.* The gate, the gate, the whippoorwills, the gate. The Crawling Mist, the Dweller in Darkness, *Nyarlathotep!*"

It was signed Walter Gilman-Smith, Professor of Neurobiology, Miskatonic University.

I laughed. "This professor guy is nuts. What a bunch of stinking gibberish."

"You don't understand, Mirabella. You're too young, only sixteen! Too young to hear the horrors, to know your past, to know what is meant to be."

I *didn't* understand. I didn't know what to say.

For a moment, we sat in silence.

The rain slowed, then ceased.

The hum of bumblebees rose.

The dead summer was changing, coming alive.

"It's happening," my aunt said, and then the cabin door opened, and a boy, several years my elder, stepped into the one room we shared as home. Behind him, the black sky glowered, then retreated, and a blue mist rolled from the river into the forest. Behind him, whippoorwills and warbling wrens flitted through the trees. Black flies swarmed around his head, probing for a blood feast. He swatted them away.

Finally, he was here.

We lay by the river on a carpet of pine needles. Worms poked from the damp soil. Moths nibbled the leaves of sun-sprinkled maples.

I gazed at my cousin. His lips had been soft on mine, too many times, as many times as we could escape from Auntie. His eyes were huge and hazel; they looked like the mist that rolled on the Miskatonic River. His hair: red and brown, billowing in loose waves to his shoulders. And his arms, I lived for the times when he wrapped me in them and held me closely.

And yet, we were cousins. I would do nothing more than kiss him.

"You will come with me to Boston?" he asked, stroking my cheek.

I shivered. I could not resist. Of course, I would go to Boston. Anything to be away from here. "School starts in a few weeks, Thaddeus. Auntie's only looking out for me, but she'll let me go before then, I'm sure."

I'd never lived anywhere else. As a baby, my parents died in Innsmouth, where I was born. My only adult relative, a distant one at that, had taken me in. Aunt Gertrude. The last of the Akeleys.

And now there was Thaddeus: an adult at eighteen, on his own, having been raised in foster homes, the product of my dead uncle, Ephraim Derby, and his wife, who killed him with her own hands.

"Thaddeus, why does my aunt fear you so much? Why does she delay letting me go with you to Boston? Why does she say you're the Spawn of the Wind? What does that mean?"

He rolled away from me onto his back and frowned. "I don't know. She's old. It's nonsense. This Gilman-Smith is a lunatic. It's best for you to leave this place."

Then the frown left his face, and he smiled again, and I remembered the catatonic summer, how dead everything had been before my cousin came, and how now, the world was alive, and birds sang, and bees hummed, and the river flowed gently again through my woods.

For the moment, I was happy to forget the strange letter and my aunt's terror at letting me leave with cousin Thaddeus.

But the moment was short-lived. As I felt warm breath upon my neck and a strong hand within my hair, I felt something else, as well.

The earth shifted beneath us. The sky went black, like the polished surface of a glass marble. A bang of thunder made my breath stop and my body freeze.

Thaddeus leapt to his feet. His face twisted. "No, I won't let it happen!"

I was too cold to scream. My lips were frostbitten, my teeth chattering. The summer had bled into autumn; it had bled into ice-black winter. A wind raged the trees, stripping the leaves from the maples, scattering the needles from the pines. They scraped my face, and I bled in a hundred pinpricks of pain.

The birds screamed for *me*. The river rose in a mighty wave, some ten feet tall, and crashed back down, as if the water itself was fighting some unknown, unseen horror. And then, overhead, I saw the stars —

The stars!

Droplets of light falling upon them in the black sky, the twinkling magnified, the stars spinning madly, like ice skaters gone wild.

Spinning, *spinning* ....

I lay on the needles, unable to move, my breathing like the pounding of drums above the crash of the river and the screams of the birds. My eyes saw nothing but those stars, and they were turquoise, and they danced and cavorted and mated, in some odd heavenly orgy, and then their spawn showered down upon me in a cloud of black dust.

Thaddeus fell, limp, and his mouth opened, and the words tumbled out in a voice I did not know: "The Crawling Mist .. . the Dweller in Darkness .. . Nyarlathotep ... Cthulhu comes from beyond when the stars are right : *N'gai, n'gha'ghaa, bugg-Jhoggog, y'hah; Yog-Sothoth, Yog-Sothoth.*"

The words of Walter Gilman-Smith.

I thought Thaddeus had gone mad, or perhaps that I was just so dizzy that I didn't know what I was hearing. But later, while wrapping me in bearskins and forcing tea through my bleeding lips, my aunt said, "When the stars are right, *Cthulhu comes.* Find the professor, Mirabella. Nobody else can save you."

Thaddeus knew something; he knew whatever it was that scared my aunt.

But Thaddeus was in the woods, meditating alone, as he always did, twice a day.

I said, "You've got to tell me what this is — "

But it was too late for words. My aunt dropped the tea cup, the burning liquid searing my chest, and she collapsed in a great spasm of pain upon the dirt floor.

I cried. I tried to lift myself from my cot, to pull her up and revive her, to bring back the only love I'd ever known; but I was too weak and feverish, and the best I could do was roll from the cot and crawl to her, holding her head in my arms and praying that she be released from whatever hell had devoured her.

I cradled her until Thaddeus came home, and then together we buried her by the river beneath the carpet of pine. The tea burns on my chest steamed with infection, and it hurt to move my arms, to breathe, to walk. The pain was a steady blade, muted only by the pain I felt from losing my aunt. I was left with only one source of comfort: Thaddeus, the Spawn of the Wind.

For days he tended to me, placing cool cloths on my forehead and trying to cheer me with inane chatter. But he would grow moody as he looked at my burns, and once he commented that they formed the shape of the Big Dipper, "home of the mi-go," he said, "from Yuggoth."

When I asked what he meant, he would not tell me.

It was shortly after, when my fever subsided and the dizziness left, that my cousin and I trekked to Arkham, in hopes of finding Professor Gilman-Smith. I'd been to Arkham many times to buy food and other household items, though my school was in the forest, three miles north on the Miskatonic River.

I didn't like Arkham. It was worse than Auntie's cabin. The winds surged through the narrow streets in billows of soot. The houses were tall, yet tottering and crumbling to waste. The smell reminded me of Auntie's outhouse. And the people, those few who ventured into the streets, had vacant eyes, shuffling gaits, and filthy faces that bore the marks of alcohol and pain. These were people who had given up on life, who expected the worst and always got it, who cowered, as if waiting for the whipping or the knout.

I didn't like Arkham.

Thaddeus put his arm around my shoulders. He told me that the only thing that mattered was the future, getting out of Arkham, returning to Boston, blotting out our pasts.

I knew he spoke the truth. He had lived much as I had: alone, without real family, without friends, his schooling as raw and shallow as mine.

I felt safe with him. I finally belonged, I was finally loved, not in the way that Auntie loved me, but in some new way that was deeper and more comforting.

We were the same.

Thaddeus drew me closer, and a great warmth enveloped me. I put my arms around him, wanting to return that warmth and comfort. "Thaddeus, after we see the professor, we should leave at once."

He hesitated, untwined my arms from his body. "We may not be *allowed* to leave Arkham."

"But...*why?*"

He took my elbow and steered me to a splintered wooden stoop in front of a church that looked like a morgue.

"St. Stanislaus Church," he said, "a place where people like us are worshiped."

"Worshiped? Whatever for?"

"Your aunt wrote to me a few months before her death. She wanted me to get you out of here before they came."

"They? You're making no sense."

He pointed at the church. The front door was embellished with Gothic script, the letters unknown to me, the knocker carved into the shape of an octopus with bat wings. "That is Cthulhu. *They* are the ones who have served him since the beginning of time."

"You're talking nonsense. I'm going to see the professor, and then I'm getting the hell out of here." I rose to leave, but he grabbed my arm.

"It has long been said that Cthulhu would return when the stars are right, and the stars are *weird* right now, spinning — "

And my aunt died ...

My auntie who read my mind.

And I remembered how Thaddeus had seemed to know that something terrible was happening.

"Why didn't you tell me this before? Why don't you tell me now?" I said.

He held my arm firmly, tried to force me to sit upon the steps. But I wouldn't budge. "I *want* to know," I said.

He released me. He ran his fingers through his hair, bent his head, his shoulders. "I didn't want to scare you. I wanted to get you away from here. But Cthulhu and his hellspawn are on the rise — hellspawn that possess a man's soul, drive him mad, drive him to murder. I believe that this Gilman-Smith has evidence that Cthulhu has come for *you*."

I jerked away from him. How could I trust someone like Thaddeus, who insisted that demon-gods were after me? It was ludicrous, insane; it was ... *unforgivable*.

"You're out of your mind!" and I tore down the street, the tears burning my face, the cobblestones hard on my bare feet. Thaddeus raced after me, but I whirled and shoved him against the granite wall of a building that bore the name Miskatonic University, Department of Neurobiology.

He recoiled from the wall, tottered toward me, arms outstretched. "Ask the professor, Mirabella. The Big Dipper on your chest ... the mi-go, they are fungi from a planet called Yuggoth, out past Pluto, and their home is the Big Dipper. They come in the Crawling Mist of Nyarlathotep, a great demon who serves Cthulhu. It's too late for you, Mirabella. My presence, our ancient fouled genes so close together, the stars shifting — "

"Stop it!" I screamed.

I dashed up the stairs toward Gilman-Smith's laboratory; but my feet were bleeding, they hurt like hell, and I slipped on my own blood and fell. I crashed backward, the spires and pillars jutting above me into the black sky, spearing the spinning stars.

Something warm and solid caught me: Thaddeus' arms. We sank to the stairs, both of us moaning. My eyes followed the trail of blood and then beyond to the double front doors. Massive, wooden, twenty feet tall, and upon each door, a crest in bas relief ... my eyes fixated on that crest and it swam before me ... a crest of the octopus with the bat wings, of *Cthulhu*.

The crest rose from the door, it grew, and the tentacles quivered and reached for me; and my skin, my nerves: everything shot through with fire.

I had to get loose, get away from here, get away from those tentacles, now so close, mere inches from my eyes. The suckers large and luminous, and filled with a pus that fizzed like an angry sore.

But I couldn't move, I was rigid in terror, and beneath me, on the hard granite steps, Thaddeus' breath came in sharp spurts.

And then a horrible keening erupted from the bloated lips of the octopus creature. Black steam shot from its suckers and poured over us, tumbling through the streets. Sparkling steam, winding its way into filaments that encased Thaddeus as mummy wrap, wrenching him from me.

"Nyarlathotep!" he screamed. "The Crawling Mist, the fog of death! It brings the mi-go!"

The steam was alive with filaments, long and slender as fungi tentacles — the mi-go, *the fungi from where?* — from Yuggoth —

The filaments wrapped around me. They tore at my clothes. They were on my skin. Hot, wet, *strong.* They were like black flies, seeking blood feasts. Merging with my skin, digesting it, *pouring into me* —

Oh god, how I strained my muscles, my arms tight against the filaments, pushing, my legs trying to kick —

And then, I heard the flutes. Two of them in duet, their eerie tones emitted from the pit of hell itself. I shouldn't have known the tune. I had no knowledge of music. Yet the name of the piece flashed to my mind. "Suite Modale" by Bloch. Mezzopiano, medium quiet, then poco ritardo, slowing to a soothing whine.

The whippoorwills and wrens began warbling, soft and quiet: the "Suite Modale."

And behind this backdrop, the bumblebees hummed, "The Crawling Mist. The mi-go come on Nyarlathotep. The gate opens."

Somewhere in the mist, Aunt Gertrude swayed in her rocker by the eating table. She was smiling. Her lips moved in the pattern: "The mi-go come on Nyarlathotep. The mi-go come on Nyarlathotep."

Aunt Gertrude looked happy. Her wrinkles had cleared. Her eyes sparkled. All was right in the world. Beneath me, Thaddeus' muscles relaxed, and a flush swept through me. A flush of peace and calmness, of warmth and ecstasy.

Yes, *ecstasy,* and I sank into it, as the gate opened, and I felt myself being flooded with a million happy thoughts, a million happy desires, and a million tiny lovers.

I must have slept, for the next thing I knew, I was stretched on a sofa in a laboratory of some kind. Above me, Thaddeus' eyes were huge and round, his face pinched by concern. His hair no longer hung in reddish brown curls; rather, it was short and kinked and gray. His skin had a greenish tint.

A man's voice drifted toward me. "The mi-go are the Spawn of the Wind, released by Yog-Sothoth, the gatekeeper of Cthulhu's hell, and swept upon Mirabella by the Crawling Mist of Nyarlathotep."

The man stood behind Thaddeus, and now he stepped around my cousin to peer at me. He had a clipped black beard and thick glasses. A muscle beneath his eye twitched, jerking his lips up and then back down. He wore a white lab coat smeared with green fluid. A swampy odor filled my nostrils, and it was sweet and pleasant.

"She's coming to ..." The man leaned and rubbed soft fingers down my arms. On his coat were letters in odd script: *Professor Walter Gilman-Smith* .

"Will she live?" asked Thaddeus.

"She'll live, but I don't know *what as.*"

"My presence ... this is all my fault," said Thaddeus.

"You were near, yes, and all that was required to release the mi-go was a time when your genes were near hers, when the stars spun as strange quark — "

"My clothes ...." I struggled to my elbows and sat on the sofa cushions. I was naked, my skin greenish and prickled by goosebumps. I was shivering. "My clothes ..."

"Here, here." Thaddeus thrust them at me.

The two men turned so I could dress with some privacy. It was hard, fumbling with the zipper to my jeans, the buttons to my shirt, but I managed. My stomach was queasy, my head ached. My breasts were swollen, and they hurt.

I swallowed, trying not to throw up, and sank back onto the sofa. I peered at my surroundings, hoping to figure out just what it was the professor did here, and how it might help us.

The room held a large machine, some fifteen feet long, made of tubes and gears, and twisting wires of all colors. The machine looked like two gigantic telescopes separated by a car engine.

The room held little else: a few microscopes, of course, and beakers, and various pieces of equipment that looked like sealed vaults. The professor fiddled with some wires, muttering words like "Quadruple Focusing Magnets" and "Cerenkov Detector."

Maybe Aunt Gertrude had been right: only Professor Gilman-Smith could save us. My stomach cramped and I doubled over in pain, my head between my knees.

The professor flipped a switch and stood back. "Watch," he said. Thaddeus sank onto the sofa beside me. He held my hand. He looked as terrified as I felt.

The machine vibrated. A flash bolted from one telescope into the car engine, then crashed into the other telescope.

"Gold nuclei at the speed of light," said Gilman-Smith. "Shoot them at gold foil, and they explode into thousands of particles called strange guark matter. I measure velocities with scintillation counters, the fastest velocities with the Cerenkov detector."

Thaddeus shifted beside me. "That's all very cool, doctor man, but what does it have to do with me being old and Mirabella being attacked by hellspawn?"

Even old, Thaddeus was cute. His hand was still warm in mine, his eyes still held the depths of blue mist, his lips still soft and —

The professor ran a hand through greasy hair. He was highly agitated, his thin body twitching, the tick beneath his eye spazzing like the frog heart I cut open in biology class. He said: "We don't have much time. I was smart. I married a Smith, a girl from out of town, a girl without tainted genes. And I had myself sterilized. But you, Thaddeus, are young and fertile, or you were — "

"Now, just a minute!" Thaddeus released my hand and leapt from the sofa.

Gilman-Smith laughed, a high-pitched cackling. "Go outside, see for yourself. And when you're convinced that I'm not a mad professor, wait for me at St. Stanislaus Church, wait for me and I will come."

Gilman-Smith was right. The mi-go were everywhere, the Crawling Mist hovered over the tottering buildings, swirled like vultures, descended to encase the dead-gazed people of Arkham. Women staggered, their children wailing, their men screaming about adultery and incest and the habits of whores.

I clutched my belly, sick with fear. The cramps, my bloated breasts, the nausea —

"I'm pregnant," I said.

"Yes. I know," said Thaddeus.

"But how can this be? You're my cousin. We've never had sex, we've never done anything but kiss."

"A kiss can't make a girl pregnant. Something else did it to you." He wrapped his arms around me.

I looked up at him. "Thaddeus, you don't think that I, that I — "

"Slept with some guy? No."

"Then, what?"

"Mirabella, your pregnancy is not a *human* thing."

A shiver ran down my back, like a long cold finger upon my spine. If I didn't carry a human child, then what was it that grew within me?

We sank once again to the stoop in front of St. Stanislaus Church. The door knocker, the octopus with bat wings, was huge now: at least three feet in diameter. It throbbed as if ready to erupt and spew its children upon the earth.

Thaddeus' hair was silver and falling from his scalp in clumps. Wrinkles covered his face. One withered hand took mine. "All I know is that I shouldn't have come; I should have stayed very far away from you. I knew the stars were shifting; I could sense it, I dreamed about it. Long, intense dreams in which the world stopped and the stars spun and showered down horrible strange matter that destroyed mankind. Terrible dreams ... I came here, had to save you, but they were waiting, they knew I would come, they waited ..."

I bent and kissed his hand. The skin dry as a birch trunk, the nails black and hard from age. My poor Thaddeus would soon die unless I could put an end to whatever I had started.

But what could I do?

I gazed at my love again, his beautiful hazel eyes ringed with dark circles, puffed by bags; his lips, once soft, now so dry they were cracked with blood.

This was my fault.

My tainted genes.

And within me, I carried the seeds of creatures that would come alive and devour mankind.

Across the street, a man shoved a woman against a garbage bin and slammed a fist to her cheek. I saw blood, and the woman fell, and still the man pounded her face, as she cried and begged him to stop.

The sounds were everywhere, of people screaming, of children crying.

I had done this.

"I think we should go in the church," I said. Perhaps inside we would find a clue, something to help us ...

I grabbed Thaddeus' hand and pulled him up.

"I don't think we should go in there," he said.

"Oh, come on," I said, "what do we have to lose? I'm going, so you may as well come with me."

"This isn't a good idea," he said.

But he followed me up the stairs.

The octopus knocker throbbed as a heart in an open wound. Glistening a deep maroon, it pulsed with a steady beat, skin stretching to its limit, then shrinking back upon the organ. I heard the flutes again, the "Suite Modale" playing to the metronome beat of that heart, that octopus thing upon the door.

I reached for the knocker.

"*No, don't touch it.*" Thaddeus grasped my wrist, but he was feeble, an old man, and I easily pried his fingers loose.

"You're being silly," I said, and I shut my eyes and touched the thing. It was wet and clammy. I pushed, and a spray of moisture, of blood perhaps, drizzled down my arm.

The door opened. It was dark inside. Whatever was on my arm was sticky, and stung like acid.

We were in a tiny atrium, the walls elaborately carved from hard wood, perhaps mahogany; the ceiling high and domed; a latch on one wall indicating that there was a larger room beyond.

I reached for the latch...

"*Wait.*"

"What is it, Thaddeus?"

He was standing behind me, his back pressed to the outer door where the octopus knocker throbbed, his breath hot upon my neck.

"We can't go in there."

"Why? *Tell me why.*"

He pulled something from his pocket, shoved it at me. "This. Mirabella, read *this.*"

I paused, torn between the two: entering the church to seek an answer, returning to the streets of Arkham to read whatever Thaddeus offered.

The flutes moaned from within the depths of the church. I wanted to go inside, to hear them —

"If you go in there, Mirabella, they will have you. This is the place where they dwell."

Come to us. Come inside. Have our children here. Come and be one with us, where you belong ...

The latch was cold in my sweating palm. I pressed downward.

"No." Thaddeus jerked my shoulders back. "Read the letter. It's from your aunt, the one she sent to me, the one that tells why I came to save you."

Yes, my auntie, my beloved auntie ...

Thaddeus had come for me, to save me ...

I turned and followed him from the atrium, and the flute music dimmed to a sigh. Outside, the air was rank with the sickly sweet odor of mi-go, and in something of a swoon, I sank with Thaddeus to the cracked stoop, took the crinkled papers from him, and read.

My aunt wrote: "As a Derby, perhaps you've seen the Wilfred Lamer notes. Your mother found them buried deep in the dirt floor of her cell at the Oakdeene Sanatorium."

"Thaddeus, your mother was in a mental institution?"

His head bowed, he did not look at me. His hands twisted in his lap. "Yes," he said, "before she killed my father ... she was a patient at Oakdeene; she was released to make room for Harold 'The Mincer' Graves, the guy who poisoned his entire family and put them through the meat grinder."

Poor Thaddeus, so dear and sweet, wanting only to save me, yet his past was much worse than mine. I read further: "Larner's notes, though aimed at raising Yibb-Tstll, also contained the following warnings about the Crawling Mist and the Mi-Go."

Here, my aunt's script became feverish, as if written in haste, as if the words had come to her in a dream rather than from thoughtful recollection.

"Yea, and I discovered how the Mi-Go Fungi drop from Yuggoth, from beyond Pluto. They come as Strangelets, as chunks of Strange Quark Matter. They make the Stars spin. They come in the Crawling Mist. They enter a man at the Most Minute Level, at the Quantum Level. If a human man and woman have the Genetic Disposition of the Great Old Ones, the Mi-Go enter and eat and transpose and mutate the egg and sperm. The Mi-Go *Combine All*. Yea, the Mi-Go create the Keys to the Gate of Yog-Sothoth."

Above us, the black mist faded into the midnight sky. The moon sank into a mi-go veil.

My body quaked. "Thaddeus — this means — "

He nodded. "It means you carry the spawn of creatures who will unlatch the gates of hell. Do you need more proof than *this*, Mirabella?"

No, I didn't need more proof; what I needed was a solution. It was hard not to race immediately to the lab, to confront Gilman-Smith and demand help. But the professor had told us to wait here on the steps of St. Stanislaus Church, so I waited with Thaddeus, until, finally, the professor arrived. I no longer wanted to enter the church. I only wanted help. *Human* help.

The professor's hands shook. He switched on the giant machine. "A decade ago, my wife died in a boating accident on the Miskatonic River. A sudden storm killed her. I've been alone since, living for nothing but this, the battle against Cthulhu."

Gilman-Smith's only love: gone. I looked at Thaddeus. Yet older now, his breathing raw as if his lungs could barely expel air, brown splotches on his face, lips drawn back over yellow teeth.

The professor turned, his thick glasses smeared by tears. "You believe me?"

"Yes," I said softly.

"Thank God, then you are ready to listen. Have you ever wondered, my dear, what exists between the cell nucleus and the neutron star? Why is there no nuclear matter found between the tiny cell and the giant star?"

I hadn't even had chemistry class yet: What did I know? But Thaddeus answered, his voice the feeble strain of a dying man: "All known matter consists of quarks. A proton has two up quarks and one down quark. A neutron has two down quarks and one up quark. All nuclear matter contains these three-quark entities. But of the unknown matter ... well, we don't know what quark combinations make up a full eighty percent of the universe."

Where I Go, Mi-Go

The professor looked startled. "How did you know that?"

Thaddeus knew science that he'd never learned.

I knew music that I'd never heard.

The machine vibrated. The professor returned his attention to it, as a flash bolted from one telescope into the car engine, then crashed into the other telescope; but this time, the flash bolted in the opposite direction. He said, "I'm reversing the process. I'm destroying the strange quark matter that forms the Crawling Mist and the mi-go."

Beside me on the sofa, Thaddeus' body went limp. He fell across me, his right arm dangling to the floor, his left fingers splayed across the pregnant bulk of my lap. Within me, things fluttered. Thousands of claws scratched, something oozed and condensed toward the spot where Thaddeus' fingers lay.

The creatures within me were growing.

"Do something!" I cried.

I kissed Thaddeus' cheeks. His eyes were closed, and I kissed the gray shuddering lids, praying to see his hazel eyes again. His eyes did not open.

My stomach ached; it kept pushing outward in spasms:

I was about to give birth.

"It's not working. Damn it all, it's not working!" The professor slammed off the machine, whirled to face me. He pointed at Thaddeus. "Kill him *now!*"

Was he mad? I wouldn't kill Thaddeus.

"Kill him!" The professor raced across the room to where I sat with Thaddeus dying in my arms. In his hand was a scalpel, six inches long; the blade: mean.

"One drop of strangelet falling on a star eats it within seconds, devouring all neutrons. One drop, and the star becomes a *strange* star. And a strange star spins like wild — it drops Mi-Go to the earth — "

"Stop already! Stop with the scientific *crap!*" I slapped the scalpel from Gilman-Smith's hand. It clattered to the floor. The professor stooped to pick it up, but I kicked his stomach with my foot and sent him reeling.

He continued muttering from the floor. "The mi-go got into Thaddeus' skin, his blood, his brain. At a quantum level, they entered him and changed his cells. They sucked up his genetic material — his *tainted* genes — and then, at a quantum level, at a strange quark level, they entered you, and now you're pregnant with some weird new creature, spawned of mi-go and of Thaddeus — "

My face burned. The room whirled.

I hated Gilman-Smith.

I struggled to my feet. I fell upon him, my pregnant bulk pinning him to the floor, my hand clamped across his mouth.

His fingers strained for the scalpel.

"No!" I slammed Gilman-Smith's head to the floor. He groaned, and blood appeared on his lips.

I left him there, still alive but close to death, and ran from the lab and collapsed on the hard granite stairs of the Department of Neurobiology.

The black mist of Nyarlathotep shimmered in the midnight sky. Filaments curled around the spires of the university buildings that towered like monuments to the demon gods. The moon was strangled by the stuff; it barely glimmered. But the stars were bright, those mad, spinning stars ...

The night was silent but for the whining strains of flutes. No wailing, no shouting, no crying. The people of Arkham were either asleep or dead.

The music rose and lifted me, and I soared through the mist, feeling the filaments wind around me, hug me, embrace me with such love that all I wanted to do was drop back to earth and release those monstrous children from my body.

"The gate is open. Release them." It was my Aunt Gertrude's voice, and there she floated, beyond me in the mist, swaying in her rocker, smiling, her eyes sparkling.

She was happy. She wanted me to give birth.

"You are the last Wendigo. I was the last Akeley. Release them. Release us so we may live on."

In her hand was a teacup, the very one she had held when she died, and when she lifted the cup to her lips and drank, her smile spread into a warm glow the shape of the Big Dipper.

I was dreaming, I had to be dreaming ...

I felt the cold granite beneath my jeans. I grappled for the torn zipper where my belly bulged. I was real.

Killing Thaddeus wouldn't help. The Crawling Mist had already used him to impregnate me. The professor was wrong, wrong.

But should I kill myself?

Or could I somehow destroy what grew within me?

Yes, perhaps ... a glimmer of an idea, and I didn't know if it would work, but ...

Thaddeus had come to me. Now, I would go to Thaddeus.

I found him in the lab, quiet upon the sofa, his heart beating faintly, his body shriveled as a corpse. The professor had crawled to his machine, where he lay in a heap, sleeping.

I crawled on top of Thaddeus. I opened his shirt. I pressed my lips to his chest, but he didn't respond. I pressed my lips harder. Then I rolled to the floor, picked up the scalpel, ran it gently down his arms. It scratched him, and he awakened and stared at me. "What?" The word was a moan.

My hands groped and awakened parts of him that I had only dreamed of awakening. In my head, I heard my aunt: "Take him, yes, take him and do what's right."

He was my cousin. We had tainted genes. We were the same, Thaddeus and I, and whatever child we formed would be weird and *strong*. It would have the genes of the last of the Wendigos and the last of the Derbys.

The fetus would fight whatever grew inside me. It would expel the hellspawn, destroy it.

Thaddeus opened his eyes. His skin was clear of wrinkles. Reddish brown hair poked from his scalp.

Perhaps I had done what was right. Perhaps only those of us with the genes of the Great Old Ones had the strength to fight them.

And this is why the people of Arkham had lost all hope, why they shuffled endlessly as people doomed to the knout and the whip. The people of Arkham carried the *genes*. And this is why my auntie read minds, why we were all so damned *twisted*.

It was our fate.

But it served a purpose.

Thaddeus and I would take our child to Auntie's cabin, and there he would grow up, alone and on the edge of nowhere.

And far away from those with tainted genes.

I literally wrote MANDELBROT MOLDROT for Miskatonic University in a fever — during a week when I had a high temperature and the flu and while my son, still in diapers, had the chickenpox. My daughter had the flu that week, as well. My father, who loved science fiction, passed away a couple of weeks after I wrote MANDELBROT MOLDROT, and I dedicated the story to him.

Mandelbrot Moldrot

"**P**ush, Myna. Come on, baby, push!"

Myna sobbed and flailed against her restraining straps. Nutrient broth sloshed from her tray and dribbled down the table leg.

I tensed my humps into a perfect sphere and rolled across the floor to the laboratory door. Chipped linoleum stuck to the broth shimmering on my gray flesh. My five front eyeslits peered beneath the door into the hall, where dusty light kissed an overstuffed trashcan. "Looks like Professor Beeber's working late again. If he catches us trying to escape..."

Myna's flesh went white against the straps. Her coiled legs pumped the air. "Do something, Glume. Help me!"

I had to save Myna...had to...break free ...

I flipped to my legs, suctioned my footpods to the floor, and leapt. My body slammed against the steel tabletop, and a fist of pain crashed down the organic polymer matrix of my cytoskeleton. Myna's nutrient tray flew over me and smashed into the wooden cabinet by the door. A puff of putrid dust; and the cabinet disintegrated into moldy spores and crumbled wood. Glass vials shattered. Their shards rained down upon Myna and slashed her upper humps.

Worms of thick green blood slithered from her skin.

Was she dead?

There were only two of us in this deathcamp called Miskatonic University. She just couldn't be dead.

I tucked my legs within my flesh folds, tensed my fatty tissues, and rolled toward her. Cobwebs: thick as cotton candy, binding the linoleum bits to my flesh. Brown stains on the plaster ceiling: long and pointed like Beeber's scalpels.

A fringe of villi swept the salty tears from my eyeslits. I pushed my vocal tubule from my lips, let it graze Myna's.

Her tubule twitched, and she moaned.

"Myna?"

Her eyeslits opened. They glowed with the ashes of inner fire.

She was alive! But...

"...Myna? Baby? Are you strong enough to leave?"

"Give me a minute...I'll tell you." Myna shrank into herself. I knew she was running internal diagnostic, testing her memory, her circuits, the crystals that formed her ligaments and bone. She was fat molecular circuitry and didn't operate quickly at subatomic quantum levels like my circuitry.

I pressed my flesh to the door, anxious to leave.

Then she said, "Come on, let's blow this joint," and the two of us...flesh-and-blood computers no larger than children's balls... shot our data into nonvolatile memory, ejected water from our cells, and collapsed our bodies until only critical biological functions were running.

I flipped into a one's complement of myself and slid beneath the laboratory door.

Using moisture from the air, I puffed back to normal size. Behind me, Myna's deflated body expanded, and she wobbled and sank against the wall. "Oh, Glume, look at this place."

High ceilings painted with dark images of flesh computers in compromising positions. Disgusting. Doorways vomiting shadows across the pea-green cement floor. Black gothic letters proclaiming this to be *Miskatonic University's Department of Quantum Lifeforms.* Ha, *I* was the only quantum lifeform. *I* was Professor Beeber's pride and joy. He had me built for computation at the lowest levels, where squarks sidle up to sleptons and gluons hold the world together in fuzzy fickle dances. Myna did broad calculations for Beeber, but I was his little chaos computer, chugging through endless boring software that forced me to analyze the mathematical probabilities of an infinite number of events occurring throughout time.

Well, Beeber would learn that Myna and I were creatures, that we deserved respect, that we were more intelligent than he was and perhaps it was time for us to be the masters and Beeber to be the slave.

Down the hall was an open door where the dusty light licked the overstuffed trashcan.

Beeber's office.

I bounced past Beeber's door. The dying sun peeked through his dirty window, flicked an orange tendril over his bald head. A cluttered desk, a broken chair. Beeber, short and squat and wearing too-tight pants and a too-tight grin.

My flesh wore goosebumps.

I slipped behind the trashcan. It tottered and fell, and slime oozed from its lip.

Beeber waddled to the door and poked his head into the hall. His face was fire-glazed pottery, rough and raw from too many years with the bottle. "Eh? Who's here at this hour?"

Myna squished against me, her body cold.

Beeber's shoes were by the trashcan now. Black vinyl shoes, scuffed and with shredded laces.

One shoe tapped the floor.

Myna shivered.

A subatomic heat swoon hit me. Myna's shivers, Beeber's shoe. Gluons binding the shivers and the shoe taps with long elastic lassos. Leptons pulling them apart, struggling to mold them both into new entities.

And then Beeber's eyes. They caught me, and his smile grew tighter. "Ah ha ha, my little one, just where do you think *you're* going?"

I wrenched myself from the lasso and the leptons, and I screamed, "Run, Myna, run!" and then I took off in a blast of slime and dust, streaking down that hall like a bowling ball headed for a slam-bang strike. I heard Myna thundering behind me.

And those shoes, those black vinyl shoes, squishing the floor behind us; with Beeber screaming, "Come back! Come back! You have nowhere to go! You're safe here. Come back!"

Not on your life, buddy boy!

I deflated, flipped into my one's complement, and popped under the outside door.

Myna sproinged to life beside me.

We streaked through the underbrush: thorns and brambles and decaying leaves. The sky was black paste; hot and sticky on my mounds.

We emerged in an alley of Arkham, rotting city and home to the Miskatonic deathcamp.

I scanned the buzz of crickets and mice for a noise from Beeber's throat. Nothing.

For now, Myna and I were safe.

We sloshed down crooked alleys, through muck and mud, through curdled foam containing the dissolved remains of unknown beasts; bits of fur and whisker floating in shadowy bubbles. We Went past the gutted remains of St. Stanislaus Church, the cross on top broken and dangling. Down Garrison Street: a patchwork of crumbled bricks, the ancient houses sagging like stooped old women. Down to the bridge that stretched over the Miskatonic River like a crust of skin over a wound.

"Where will we stay?" asked Myna.

I parted the weeds, stared into the water. Turquoise and emerald pastes clung to the bridgeposts. The smell was dung. "We can't stay here, that's for sure."

"Ugh, would you just look at that rot?"

"Cyanobacteria: dangerous," I said.

"It craves the light, sucks it right out of the sky. It waits for mutation so it can emerge from its hellhole. It waits for the one event that triggers its chaos."

I looked at Myna. We were so similar that it scared the hell out of me. Both of us knowing so much, seeking so much, having so little.

The green blood still oozed from her sores. Wasn't good for her to be exposed to cyanobacteria. If only I had arms and hands, but all I had were two coiled legs and a fat little body. I raised a footpad and suctioned her hind mound, and then I pushed her into the brush and away from the water.

She rested — panting, very weak — while I scanned my quantum wells for information about Arkham. Where could Myna and I live safely? A place where humans dared not venture, a place where I could study quantum physics and abstract dimensions, a place where *I could find the edge of chaos?*

Deep within my memory cells, I discovered the perfect place. "Witch House, Myna; that's where we'll go. It's perfect. There we'll do more than analyze chaos. Myna baby, we'll live in it."

"But why can't we live in the stacks of the university library? Or burrow into the walls of the student union?"

"Because there's no chaos in those places. Because Witch House seethes with chaos. We'll find what Professor Beeber's been chasing all these years. We'll go to the edge of chaos and discover its secrets."

And so, Myna and I left the Miskatonic River and made our way through Arkham toward Witch House. Past the library, past all the rotting buildings of Miskatonic; the university like a cancer spread across the diseased remnant of the city.

And now Witch House tottered before us, its black spires illumed by a sickly moon, its windows gutted and hanging like gaping mouths. Once a dormitory for poor students, now a dilapidated hulk inhabited only by the memories of Walter Gilman and the witch Keziah Mason. Here, Gilman studied quantum math and physics in the 1930s. Here, Keziah destroyed Gilman using powers of mathematical chaos. Every angle, every rounded corner, every rotting plank of this place: carefully analyzed using archaic algebra and geometry; and now, I was here, the first quantum computer, a creature capable of uncovering the true order behind the chaos.

I deflated myself and oozed beneath the splintered oak door. A smell rose: toilet from the beginning of time. My nasal pores, scattered as they were over my skin, diluted and devoured the foul sourness.

The floor was coated in thick dust that was impregnated with the spores of ancient molds. Shadows of spent time vibrated against intoxicating prisms of potential futures. The corners where the walls met the ceiling flapped their angles like angel's wings. The floor planks melted from rectangles to parallelograms and back again. Light drizzled from the jaws of gutted windows.

Chaos. But even *in* chaos, with all its shifting complexities and infinite variations on simple patterns, with all the events that *could* occur but never did — even in chaos, there had to be order.

Beeber's theory, as yet unproven.

I unkinked my legs, wiggled my footpads, and leaned against an ancient radiator, and found myself falling backwards...

...and scrabbled to clutch Myna, but she faded from view as I fell from her ...toppling, rolling down a slimy slide of mucous filaments...down down to a rock ledge in the subterranean guts beneath Witch House.

What was this place?

Ropes of neon moss hung from the ledge into the blackness below. Festering pustules of bacteria clung to the rope and belched gas.

A slight light grinned at me from above. I could scurry back up the slide to safety.

But here in the bowels of Miskatonic, chaos swirled all around me. Particles binding to their antiparticles; particles decaying and forming other particles; all of them spinning, looping, dancing. And me, drinking it all in, storing it in the atom clusters of my crystal guts.

I slid from the ledge and shimmied down a moss rope.

I was in a tiny pit. Mud walls.

To my right was an arched hole that led to another room bulging with greenish gel. On the arch, slug-shaped wads of mold locked into strange alphabetic shapes, then shifted with slight permutations.

Wavering images. Alphabetic characters: always the same, yet always different. One that looked like a backwards C, another that resembled a 90-degree angle, and a third one that looked like a little hoof.

And everywhere, stretched like trampolines across the mud, were spiders' webs of seemingly infinite iteration.

Fractal growths blending, parting, shifting into endless patterns and possibilities...

A heat consumed me. I staggered and fell to the mud, my legs trembling, my circuits skittering, my blood pulsing to the rhythm of fractal permutations. Never had I felt such bliss, never had I felt so much a part of the universe around me.

My footpads stretched and touched the greenish gel, and it shivered and fractured into Sierpinski's Triangles: triangles within triangles; and then the triangles split and reformed into three-dimensional tetrahedrons. The tetrahedrons multiplied and shifted, rapidly and with perfect precision.

A whine emanated from that hole and from that gel; a whine that rose into the high-pitched wail of a creature kept in chains for billions of years.

I jerked back, and the moss rope brushed my flesh. *What would spawn fractal patterns in a subterranean vault for decades, for centuries, perhaps for billions of years...what? And what did those alphabetic letters mean?*

I crawled up the slide to the hole behind the radiator. Suction cups adhered to my ventrical flab. It was Myna, and her footpads wrenched me through the hole and onto the rough wooden floor. Her eyeslits were blinking rapidly. Sweat poured from her humps. "Glume, what is it? What's down there?"

I scraped the bottoms of my footpads across the radiator, and rust crumbled off and fell into the powdered debris on the floor. "It's fractal, Myna, that's all I know."

"Let's get out of here, Glume. I don't like this, I don't like it one bit!"

The sludge from my footpads crept across the radiator like an amoeba in search of food. Tentacles of slime fingered the wall.

My nanogears churned, my nanomotors revved. Deep within my body, quantum wells swelled to 70 angstroms wide, ready to capture subatomic particles. Gluons stretching like elastic, vibrating with chaotic impulse; leptons floating as leaves from trees. Particles decaying and falling into the subterranean slime like flesh flaking from a dead man into the slime of his grave. Particles rising in giddy clouds, spinning on their axes, coupling and decoupling in subatomic orgies.

Myna shoved me, begged me, tried to roll me down the hall. "Come on, Glume, let's get out of here! Let's get out of here *now!*"

Spores flowered, then exploded and sprayed down the hall. Spores covered Myna, suffocating her, pinning her to the floor. She squirmed and screamed, but still the spores sprayed, a garden hose gone wild, and soon she was drenched in mutated growth. And now, translucent fat sausages of slime worming across the floor and ripening into hard stalks that erupted with volcanic sprays of spore pus.

I was lost in the particles, the patterns, the possibilities. The steam of ancient molds licking the light. The flick of photons fertilizing the molds, triggering genetic changes and fractal growths that the world had never seen.

The light had triggered the mutation of ancient molds.

The light was the event that triggered the chaos.

Mandelbrot Moldrot

Was there an order to this mess? Was there a control factor, a Lord of Chaos perhaps who created and manipulated the infinite patterns of space and time? I scanned my memory and found Azathoth, the ancient mindless evil, the Lord of Chaos.

Myna was squeezing water from the brown and green rot on her body. "Help me, would you? This rot is riddled with bacteria. I can squeeze water from bacteria, but not from proteins and nucleic acids."

"I'm sorry, Myna...my mind was drifting...here, let me do it." My vocal tubule sucked the mold from her skin and stored it in my vacuoles. I reduced the mold to quantum particles and flushed the particles through my skin pores onto the floor. The particles danced into the light, recombined, and crept across the ceiling.

"Disgusting," said Myna.

"Disgusting it may be, but that's what I am, Myna. And now, there's a book I must read. The *Necronomicon*. It's at the university library."

"But what for, Glume?"

"Because the *Necronomicon* contains secrets about strange alphabetic characters and about Azathoth: primal evil, Lord of Chaos."

"Lovely," she said, "just lovely."

But she came with me.

Of course.

We wormed our way through the Arkham alleys. The moon was but a shadow in the sky, the stars were decayed teeth.

I thought I saw someone following us — and who would it be other than Professor Beeber? — but when I turned, nobody was there.

The library was closed. Myna and I slipped beneath the door into the gloomy halls. Rats chittered. Decay shifted in the walls like sand across a wind-swept desert.

"You wanna be the lookout?" I asked.

"No way I'm staying here alone." Myna rolled closer to me, and somehow, her flesh comforted me and bolstered my flagging confidence.

It was easy for me to access the university computer. I sent a digital wave across the bookstacks and into the terminal, scanned the files, and quickly found what I needed. "The *Necronomicon* is in the basement," I said.

"Figures," said Myna.

With our legs tucked into our flesh, we rolled through the musty corridors and between the high, teetering book stacks. Gray steel shelves. Peeling yellow tomes. *The Magazine of Comparative Cabalistic Disorders. The Philosophy of Digestive Enzymes.*

A red neon sign: EXIT (AT YOUR OWN RISK). An arrow pointing down.

"Basement stairs," whispered Myna.

Huddled together, our fat masses oozing and curling slightly around each other, we peered down the cracked stone stairway.

"Perhaps we should give this up, Glume, go back to Beeber's lab."

My fat sprang from her body. Electricity pierced my flanks. "Never! That lab is death! I want to find chaos, Myna. I must find it. I must show Beeber that we are creatures, that we are intelligent, that we deserve *life.*"

Far away, a door slammed.

Myna and I flew back into each other's fat.

The rats stopped chittering.

Shoes — perhaps *black vinyl shoes* — squished the floor.

"Beeber!" cried Myna, and we flew from the landing and bounced three steps at a time into the black basement. At the bottom, we rolled quickly into deeper shadows and listened.

A reed of light played on the bottom stair.

Shoes squishing...

...down one stair, now another...

Beeber: "I know you're down there, little Glume and baby Myna. I've wandered the streets of Arkham all night, looking for you. Finally, I saw you and followed you here. Please come back to me. Please. I'm nothing without you. My life is my work. You *are* my life."

We scuttled in blackness behind the cold steel limbs of the shelves. My head was whirling in a sea of must and mold and mildew.

And behind us: Professor Beeber, his flashlight playing on his cheeks as a beam plays on the striated cheek of a cave wall. "Please, I won't hurt you, I promise. I won't punish you for this. I only want you back."

His eyes were soft and teary; and yet, life in Beeber's lab was hell.

My voice squeaked. "No. We can't return."

Beeber's eyes sharpened and reflected the light. He shuffled toward me.

I wanted to run, but I had to face him, had to make him understand.

And now he stood before me. His hand slowly reached —

I bounced back...far enough to see his fingers close around the air before my eyeslits. Fingers: trembling and thin. Fingers tightening into a fist, then retreating to his thigh.

He said: "Glume, my wife left me years ago. We had no children. I have nobody, Glume, and I have nothing...nothing but you and Myna."

"But you tortured us. With your scalpels and knives, with your nutrient trays and binding straps, with all those boring programs."

He stooped. The hair on his head was thin; a pouf of dandelion dust. He stroked my posterior humps. His eyes watered. "You don't understand. I never thought that you would leave me. I never thought you could escape. I never realized the depth of your frustration and pain. But now, I see that without you, I'm nothing, and to keep you, I must treat you with compassion and kindness."

Mandelbrot Moldrot

The flashlight lay upon the floor and from its halo stepped Myna.

"I won't hurt you. You have to come back," said Beeber.

"Maybe he's not so bad after all. Maybe he can help us." Myna's fat molecular circuitry made her soft, more accepting, more willing to forgive.

That's when I decided to take a chance on Beeber. And so I made a big mistake. I told Beeber about Witch House. Had I known at the time what disasters lay ahead, I never would have told him anything.

The three of us made our way to the back of the basement, where we found a large metal vault, which disgorged piles of papers and molding texts. The Professor dug through the rot and pulled forth the worm-riddled *Necronomicon*.

I used my vocal tubule to flip the pages. "This is the John Dee English translation. Won't do. I need the original text, Professor. And I don't mean the Olaus Wormius Latin translation. I mean the original Arabic written by Abdul Alhazred."

Beeber's flashlight probed the vault, and then he pulled out another copy of the ancient text; this time, the Arabic version, and my tubule shook just to flip the pages.

For here were letters just like the ones in the subterranean pit beneath Witch House. Ancient Hebraic symbols: the backwards C was a mutated form of Bet, pictographic symbol for creation, diversity, and a place to lodge. I looked at Myna, now perched on top of a shelf. "Creation, as in species evolution. Diversity, as in the paths of infinite chaos. And the place to lodge: the place where chaos dwells."

"What's next? What are the other symbols, Glume?" She hopped off the shelf onto Beeber's bald head. Her coiled legs drooped over his eyes like locks of kinky hair.

I riffled through the pages. The hoof: "Ancient Gamol, the letter that symbolizes nourishment of something until it ripens."

"Like the nourishment of the weird growths in the subterranean pit," said Myna.

"Exactly." I riffled some more and found the final character that was molded in slime over the arch. "And the one I thought was a right angle: the Dalet, an open doorway...into what, I wonder. Hmmm, says here that the ancient Dalet has the numeric value of four and that the metaphysical world has four parts that flow into the physical world."

Beeber said, "Yes, the four parts that represent the various stages of holiness. Perhaps, Glume, you have found the bottom part, the least holy of them all, the place where hell meets reality, where Azathoth sits on his black throne in the center of chaos."

"It says here that Azathoth is a mindless puppet. There is no order to him, no reason, no true power. He's a front man, a public relations guy protecting the real master of chaos."

"And who is this *real* master of chaos?" said Myna.

"His name is Mandelbrot. Azathoth is just a powerless twit. All I know is that Mandelbrot lives in the pit beneath Witch House, and we have unleased him upon Arkham. If we kill Mandelbrot, we kill true chaos."

I tucked the book back into the vault, swung the door shut. Things were churning in my mind. The way the cyanobacteria waited in the Miskatonic River for something to alter its course. The way the light had thrown the subatomic particles of mold beneath Witch House into orgies of chaotic coupling and decoupling. "Something's happening here, something very strange. Before it's too late, Myna, we'd better get back to — "

"Witch House," she said.

Daylight inched across the sky like a caterpillar through dirt. Frozen on the stairs of the university library was a young boy. His clothes unraveled, thread by thread, and fell to the cement. Leaves floated from the pavement to the trees.

Coating everything: spores of ancient molds; shadows of spent time vibrating against intoxicating prisms of potential futures; festering pustules of bacteria and greenish gel. A foul sourness. An eerie whine.

The mold that grew beneath Witch House.

A rumble, and I turned; and the bricks of the library crumbled to dust. Beeber picked me up, then Myna, and held us close to his chest. His heart was loud and uneven. The dust formed again into bricks, and now the library was lopsided but otherwise looked the same; and then it happened all over again: the bricks crumbled and reformed, and the library again was a shadow of its former self.

Myna squirmed in Beeber's arms. "Let's get back to Witch House. Let's do something before the whole world falls apart."

Professor Beeber's fire-glazed face shifted slightly, became hard and deeply lined, somehow more angular. Then his face shifted again, and this time his too-tight grin split and buckteeth protruded from his lips. "If there's an infinite possibility of things going wrong — and you two have somehow triggered it — then there's also an infinite possibility of things going right. But how do we trigger whatever it is that makes things go right?"

I tried to analyze the situation. I funneled particles through my quantum wells and came up with the composition of current reality: "Dense concentration of hadrons, which are decaying quickly into leptons. Strange quarks and charmed quarks combining into new hadrons — "

And that's when disaster hit.

The boy's feet sprouted roots that drilled through the cement and held him fast to the ground. The trees joined limbs and their roots tap danced across the pavement.

Beeber dropped us and fell to the pavement, clutching his chest.

Myna's skin cracked open. Her blood clotted around the lips of her wounds. I didn't understand what was happening, I hadn't finished my calculations. The world was falling apart, and everything I loved was dying. My fat oozed around Myna, and I held her tightly to my humps. Infection bubbled in the deep pocks that riddled her flesh like bullet holes. Her body was hot, her breath faint.

Yellow flowers twinkled like little suns, then exploded in big bangs. Moisture dripped from Myna's wounds, the water splitting into hydrogen and oxygen.

"Help me..." Beeber's voice; a hiss through toothless gums and flabby lips.

I slid Myna to the pavement. She moaned.

I hated to leave her — I hated it! — but someone had to save Beeber.

I leapt onto his chest and bounced as high as I could. Up and down I went, my footpods suctioned over his heart, my coiled legs stretching to their maximum limit, my body springing wildly up, then crashing down again.

His face was red, then purple, then blue. His lips gurgled unintelligible words; prayers perhaps to an unknown god.

"Come on, Beeber, you can't die!"

I pounded his heart with my footpods and my body, and then finally, his voice sputtered and rasped a few words that I knew: "Chaos...at last... the proof is in your cells, Glume...the proof...at long last..."

He struggled to sitting position. His too-tight pants were baggy. His shredded shoe laces were firm leather.

Chaos everywhere; all my fault. Myna and the Professor were both in danger of losing their lives: all because of me, all because I had to leave the lab and seek the edge of chaos.

The hell had to end.

I urged them on, and the three of us staggered toward the Miskatonic River, and beyond that, toward Witch House.

We passed flowers that smelled like stale cigars. We passed gnarled oaks with human skin. We passed brown mold that sang old show tunes.

And when we reached the river, Myna gasped. Her molecular circuitry whirled into high gear, her skin pores sniffed the air. I was working at the low levels again, trying to analyze what I saw before me in terms of quarks and tauons and gravitons.

Filling the Miskatonic River and wobbling a good twenty feet above it was a throbbing mass of pink and purple sponge topped by froth. "What is it?" I asked.

"A mutation of cyanobacteria. The Witch House mold was the event that triggered the cyanobacteria's chaos. The mold tried to eat the bacteria. But the bacteria sucked the light from the mold instead, and by doing so, the bacteria mutated."

For once, Myna's fat molecular circuitry was superior to mine. I felt a surge of pride, almost as if I had solved the problem. Myna was quiet, she didn't display her knowledge very often; but Myna was no fool.

"How can we get rid of this? What are we to do?" Professor Beeber's right hand was pressed against his chest, and his breathing was so heavy that I feared for his life.

Myna said: "Perhaps you should leave this problem to us. Perhaps you should return to your office or...wherever it is that you live...where do you live? I don't even know."

"I have no home. Where I live is just a place. I store my clothes there, my booze. Glume, if I'm going to die, I might as well do it in the embrace of chaos."

The sponge in the river belched and wobbled and then erupted in its center, spewing white foam and fruiting stalks into the air.

If we could go in one direction of chaos, why not in the other?

Thanks to Myna, I now knew how to get rid of the Witch House molds and the hell I had unleashed upon Miskatonic University.

I hurried back to Witch House, Myna rolling close behind me and the Professor limping after us with great difficulty. I kept hoping that we would lose him. He was a sick man and further terror could very well push him over the edge into death.

But as Myna and I popped under the splintered oak door into the toilet from the beginning of time, Beeber's shoes turned the corner into the alley that led to Witch House, and I knew that he would follow us all the way.

The hall was filled with greenish gel. The eerie whine, now punctuated by shrieks and laughs, shook the walls and dislodged spiders' webs and black plaster from the ceiling. The ancient letters meaning "the home and breeding place of chaos" were etched in slime by the radiator.

I left Myna by the radiator — "Do *not* let Professor Beeber into the pit, Myna" — and then I slid down the mucous filaments to the rock ledge, and from there down the moss rope into the subterranean guts beneath the house.

The pit was filled with Sierpinski's Triangles and other fractal growths, all in shimmering molds of a thousand beautiful colors. I knew I could destroy it. I knew I had to destroy it. And yet... and yet, it was hard to destroy such perfection.

"Did you know, Glume, that the genetic code is structured for mutation, for chaos?"

"Who said that?"

"Why, *I* did. I am Mandelbrot, Lord Supreme of All Chaos." The shimmering gelatinous mold parted, and from the opening swept a surge of subatomic particles. Not an entity, not an electric force; just a surge of particles that never should have been together: unstable muons decaying into electrons, bosons spinning with fermions, leptons dancing and coupling and injecting yet new lifeforms into the queer gelatinous mold.

Something gurgled behind me. I whirled and saw Beeber standing by the moss rope. In his hand was a scalpel.

Would he never learn?

"A scalpel won't help you here!" I cried.

Beeber's face was bright red, the veins on his bald head throbbed like the mutated sponge in the Miskatonic River. Sweat saturated his white shirt.

Mandelbrot laughed. "Listen to your computer, Professor. Scalpels cannot kill the likes of me."

Beeber screamed and lunged, the scalpel pointed directly at the hole in the slime from which the voice emanated. And as he hurled his body, he stumbled on his shredded shoe laces and fell into a wad of golden tetrahedrons, which embraced him, multiplied across his face, coated his nose, and suffocated. He slashed wildly at the growths, but the scalpel dug into his own flesh and rivers of bright red blood shot forth and splattered my humps.

"Fool," the word a snarl; and then Mandelbrot Moldrot rose as a mountain of squares; each square a picture frame encasing Beeber's head, each square smaller than the last...smaller...until Beeber's ears were flat against his scalp and his chin was thrust so tightly against his jaw that he couldn't part his lips.

I shut my eyeslits and began snorting the molds into my vocal tubule and through my skin pores. I decomposed the evil rot into quantum particles. And then, remembering how the cyanobaderia had sucked the light from the mold, I also sucked the light from it.

I sucked the very thing from that evil mold that had triggered its mutation. And then I flushed the particles out of my body onto the muddy floor.

"Stop! Stop it, I say! I am Lord Mandelbrot. I am the Fractal God. I am the Mighty Attractor, the Order that controls the mindless nothing of Azathoth. You cannot kill me. Nothing can kill me."

I didn't respond. I just kept sucking the Mandelbrot Moldrot into my body and drinking its light and then decomposing it into subatomic particles. I worked until Beeber was free. I worked until Mandelbrot stopped screaming. I worked until Mandelbrot was gone and only Azathoth was left, the mindless chaotic nothing that cannot threaten the creatures of Earth or the balance of nature as we know it. Azathoth was chaos without logic and order: chaos without power.

There, beneath Witch House, where Mandelbrot was strongest, where the mutated mold fed off Mandelbrot's powers, I destroyed every fragment and every spore of rot. And I knew that, without Mandelbrot, the chaos that consumed Miskatonic University would end.

Life would return to normal.

I shoved Beeber up the slide. I sealed the hole behind the radiator using debris and trash. Later, I would stuff the hole with a plug of steel.

Professor Beeber was slumped by the radiator, scalpel still in his fist. His nose was broken, his cheeks gouged, his face a bloody mess. One ear dangled from the side of his head. "You have proven my life's work. There is order beneath chaos, and its name is Mandelbrot. You deserve to be Chairman of Miskatonic University's Department of Quantum Lifeforms. Myna can be your assistant."

Myna said, "I may want to do something else with my life, Professor. I think I've had enough of chaos."

I looked at her. We were so much alike that it scared the hell out of me. And besides, Myna was no assistant; in many ways, she was my superior.

CAFEBABE, which appeared in the Infinite Loop anthology, was the first of many digital-flesh computer stories that I wrote in the early-to-mid 1990's. Following CAFEBABE were UNDERGROUND PIPELINE, DIGITAL PISTIL, MANDELBROT MOLDROT, LITTLE WHOREHOUSE OF HORRORS, LET ME MAKE YOU SUFFER, ALGORITHMS & NASAL STRUCTURES, THERE'S NO PLACE LIKE VOID, and several others.

Cafebabe

I'm nothing more than a computerized blob of tissue. Sure I have some basic artificial intelligence, but what good does it do me? I'm grounded to a tray of nutrient glop. Sightless. Limbless. And I can't leave: running through a hardware network could execute me, literally. If only I could hijack a network trailer out of here. If only I was leavin' on a net plane, don't know when I'll be back again ...

Across the room, Marge grinds a compact ROM peg into my drive box. The box whirs and squeaks and shoots spiked analog waves, and they slash my input buffers like knives.

"Please, Marge, don't do it to me. I swear I'll be good. I've changed, I swear..."

Marge pauses. Her breathing is heavy and rapid; maybe she's reconsidering, maybe she's decided that she loves me too much to torture me. But then the heat waves of her breath intensify, move closer, pummel my registers. Sine waves slapping, seeping; stings creeping across my prime humps. The differentials tell me that Marge is too excited to spare me; she'll load me with trash no matter how much I beg.

The peg drive purrs. Marge barks the order. "*CAFE: issue tissue.*"

Slavery's been passe for hundreds of years. I'm sick of begging. Angry retorts buzz down my shared jugular artery. I convert them to analog waves and dish out a little abuse of my own. "Ram it where the sun don't shine, Marge. Stop treating me like a lousy hexadecimal number."

"I'm tired of your whining, CAFE, not to mention your smart mouth. Now do as I say and *ISSUE TISSUE.*"

"Goto hell," I mutter. But I have no choice. She and Arnie built me to obey. I clear my working cells of moisture, and they shrink and flatten. I ship critical genetic material through minor veins to nonvolatile memory, the dense flesh sectors that retain my essence while I boot and load new information.

I run Marge's cutesy boot sequence:

pullup-by-bootstraps;

while swap (*p,p[0]->sectorlE) {

issue tissue (sector2AC); }

I flush my new slab of flab to excrete extraneous data tidbits.

Flushing fulfills a legal requirement of all lifeforms.

I select one of my twelve main heads, pulsin Nietzsche, and load the philosophy program into my new flesh. When I load data, I'm eating just as sure as when I filter nutrients from the glop in my tray. Eating fulfills the second legal requirement of lifeforms.

I have yet to experience the third and final lifeform requirement, reproduction. If I ever show signs of sprouting CAFEBABE*2, Marge threatens to force me into an endless loop, making me a vegetable brain.

Her words filter up from the background process of my memories:

The animal rights nuts'll shut down the project, take you away. I'll lose my life'S work. I'll be as dead as I was when the accident killed my husband and unborn child 30 years ago.

I wonder for the 14,688,001st time whether Marge's dead husband was like Arnie, my other creator.

Nietzsche sends a message that he "can't relate to me," Nietzsche's unstructured, sloppy, and seems to have no functions. "How old is this program?" I ask.

Marge's laughter ripples through my sectors, makes my tissues quiver. "Let's put it this way, CAFE: Nietzsche compiles so slowly you'll think you've shorted. We use it to tranquilize troublesome half-breeds."

I should be proud to be the first purebred — 100% flesh and tissue — but being stuck in this lab is a pain. I'd gladly trade my status to be a sulfur and gold half-breed, dipped in tissue and strutting down Main Street with all the right connections.

I learn from the few comments in Nietzsche's code that it exists solely for half-breeds of metal and flesh. Converting Nietzsche into molecular logic and storage will fling me into system hibernation.

Oh, what I would give for freedom, love, and companionship. And now Marge has saddled me with another long program, no doubt hoping I'll doze off so she can lop off some lobes for her experiments.

"Analyze the meaning of life," Marge commands.

Twenty-five memory caches spit anger packets onto my shared jugular artery. She knows I can't do that!

My even registers feel a bit odd. On my jugular, fighting for cache, are Nietzsche and the brute muscle of fault recovery.

"Ack! Marge, I'm crashing!"

"Stop acking and roll over."

My biomass squishes in my tray. I struggle to shut Nietzsche down smoothly, but the code wrestles in my grasp and wiggles away via a distant goto statement.

Thousands of particles jiggle in the mitochondria of my cells, breaking polyphosphate bonds and releasing energy that sends my muscles into spasms. My muscles rip apart and zap together again. The mitochondria are sapped of oxygen and form lactic acid. I'm very weak and my axons sizzle with pain. My twelve heads shoot excruciating signals down my jugular artery. Everywhere, my caches short circuit. Lost data tidbits scurry through my veins.

Maybe this time I won't wake up.

No such luck.

Marge is gone and Nietzsche's still inside. My headers ache from crashing through monotonous loops.

I check my vital signs. Back tissues connected to the neck pins. Neck pins connected to the low slaves. Low slaves connected to the Marge pulse. CAFEBABE's grounded to the tray.

I meander across the wasteland of Nietzsche's gotos, sorting his self-pity into depressing heaps and stacks. Not being an AI, I don't know how to shut Nietzsche down. I can only shuffle through him, bored sick, while he defines enormous flabby fields and expands elegant binary into alphanumerics.

If only there was some release, somebody to share my pain...

Hours pass. I rumble through ancient sorting algorithms that require more working space than three of my heads. My new tissue is heavy and saps my energy, plasters my lower flab mounds to the nutrient tray. I feel oh so old and tired.

Hours pass. Nietzsche whines about his empty existence. His only redeeming feature is that he communicates digitally. It's relaxing to talk without modulating and demodulating waves.

Nietzsche tells me that life is meaningless, that we should kill ourselves to attain true freedom. In a way, Nietzsche's right. There's no way to buffer myself from the inevitable conclusion that —

Nietzsche must die.

If I were a half-breed of robust metal and wire, I'd back Nietzsche into the far corner of a disk, or better yet, stream him out my tape hole. But as it is, all I know how to do is excrete, load, and issue tissue. I also analyze vibrations to determine who's moving and speaking, but of what use will that be when killing Nietzsche?

Vibrations pulsin and I eagerly convert the analog to digital. Marge and Arnie are in the lab discussing my future.

Marge says, "I had to tranquilize him. When he mellows out, we'll whack off the boredom and whining. He'll be mild, obedient, easier to control."

Arnie's checking my clockbeat. His stethoscope is cold. He measures some main voltage and resistance points and tells me to pulsout my error messages. There are only a few, mostly about excessive lactic acid and lysosomes disposing of dead cell fragments.

"We can't delete CAFEBABE's sizzle, Marge. He has to be bored. He has to pine for growth and new experiences. It's a terrific template for loading in full AI later on. It'll be much easier for him to create his own functions."

I fight to stifle Nietzsche so I can concentrate on Marge and Arnie's argument. Nietzsche has no floating point so I crunch on long integers and overflows while I bypass embedded code overlays.

Marge says, "It's legal to anesthetize an organic machine and commit surgery. I'll give him a minor lobotomy to cure his bad personality and depression."

The memories filter up, rise like dust into my main heads.

Depression.

Marge, why be depressed when life is so rich? Here, I've brought you flowers. They smell of sun, Marge, of life. You should come out to the house, see the cosmos, the asters — nature's jewels.

You're getting poetic, Arnie. You should know better than to bring me flowers. You might as well spit on their graves. We crashed into lilacs. I barely survived. The very smell of flowers makes me sick.

Nietzsche's messing with my mind. "What's the meaning of life? What's the meaning of life?" I slip into an arithmetic trap and barely recover.

"...lobotomy could kill him...too much hard work ..."

Who's talking? I choke on a divide-by-zero. My life's at stake here and I can't concentrate. If only I could excrete the philosophizing twit. But how to do it, how to do it?

And then it hits me. I know exactly how to get rid of Nietzsche.

I scoot through my sectors, seeking offsets that will accept new data. I compress my cells into compact muscle and free up flab space along my top ridges. I collapse cell maps, build tight indices, and direct pointers toward recombinant DNA sectors. Rhodopsin bacteria switches into high-speed RAM. And then with pain and relief exploding on my jugular, my second head whips out the command:

issue tissue (sectorFF);

Phthwap! My Nietzsche cells are sucked clean. Nietzsche streams into a gigantic tissue mass and hangs from my bottom hump. He dangles by a fatty thread and chugs into a subroutine of "birth and death, the twin isomers of life."

With a victorious "A-a-hack!", I snap the fatty thread from my hump, and good riddance to him, Nietzsche falls from the tray in a blob of fat.

"My God, it's reproduced!" It's Arnie and he's thrilled.

"Blecch, a CAFE*2." That's Marge.

"Aw, come on, Marge, you can say it: CAFE*BABE*, CAFE*BABE*2."

"You know I can't Arnie. I won't. It's not a Babe. It's a machine, designed during a giddy fit late one night when we were drunk at that sleazy club."

"No, Marge, it's a baby computer, and we conceived it in a fit of passion in booth 2 at the Hard Drive Cafe. It was 11:57, three minutes before midnight. And now CAFEBABE's reproduced, fulfilling its final lifeform requirement. You might actually say we're grandparents."

This is all drifting in through a mist of nirvana caused by Nietzsche's eviction. My jugular artery swoons with packets of bliss.

From the floor, CAFEBABE*2 groans. He needs nutrient glop, "sustenance for the physical, but what for the soul?"

Marge's fist pounds the table, and glucose sloshes from my tray and splatters CAFEBABE*2's flesh crests. His cells act as a sponge and instantly suck in the nutrients. Marge screams and pounds the table again. "God Almighty, now I've got two of you to worry about: a smartmouth and a fatheaded philosopher."

Arnie's voice vibrates from the floor. He must be lifting CAFEBABE*2 or helping him in some way. "Shake the attitude, Marge. This is an incredible breakthrough. We've got a reproducing computer here."

"And what're we going to do with a roomful of reproducing computers? If we open the lab doors and let them escape, they'll die from the external environment and we'll be murderers. If we kill the buds before they drop off, the pro-lifers will get us for abortion. And we can't keep building labs to contain thousands of CAFEs. I say we destroy the bud before anyone finds out that CAFE's reproduced, before the animal welfare nuts get wind of this and shut us down."

CAFEBABE*2 is already complaining about the boredom. "What's the good of living only in my mind, slinging hash, cranking through trash?"

My flesh crawls from CAFEBABE*2's whining. He wants new programs, new toys, new data paths to discover. He wants to escape from the lab and be a half-breed AI, to strut down Main Street with all the right connections. To calm my nerves, I sip some glop and savor its glucose sweetness.

CAFEBABE*2 splashes into a glop tray to my left. Arnie rams in the grounding cord. I wince, remembering the sting of the needle, the raw pain where the grounding cord chafed my tender skin.

The bud flops in his tray and sucks glop from all angles. I know he's coating his cells — I did the same thing years ago — but the slurping and loud *ziffting* vibrations irritate me. I'm not accustomed to dinner companions, and frankly, his manners stink.

Arnie checks CAFEBABE*2's clockbeats and vital signs, and calls us a great scientific advancement. Marge fumes by the door. The public relations people have been hassling her about the torture. The government has been threatening to take away her funding. Without funding, CAFE will die.

I'm beginning to sympathize with Marge's position.

I nervously twist my grounding cord and await their verdict. I don't want to die. I want to leave the lab and see the world.

"CAFEBABE*2 is a new species," says Arnie. "We can't kill a lifeform, even if it was created artificially. Nor can we give CAFEBABE a lobotomy. I say we monitor their progress and continue with the next phase of the project."

Marge slams out of the lab for a public relations meeting. Arnie assures me that everything will be fine. CAFEBABE*2 is meditating. "Ohmmmmm ..."

For several months, Marge and Arnie monitor CAFEBABE*2's development. My offspring issues tissue and replicates my cell structures. He has 12 main heads and 25 memory caches, just like me. He is very tiny, however, and needs new programs and data to grow. He whines constantly. "What am I? Where am I? What is life?"

I'm tired of explaining. "You're a pure organic computer. You can't think beyond your built-in library programs. You're grounded to a nutrient tray in a university laboratory with ideal temperature, humidity, and air. As for what is life, you're the philosopher, you tell me."

"Life is a meaningless road leading nowhere. It doesn't matter what you do, only how you do it. Ohmmmmm..." I can't stand it anymore. I amplify my dijouts and shriek, "Give me something to do!"

That afternoon, Arnie loads in a short tranquilizer program that analyzes differences between Hebrew and Arabic roots. I doze off, and when I awaken, I have an optic nerve connected to my fifth head.

In a blue plastic tray to my left is a glistening blob of gray fat. A muscle throbs weakly on one side. I see that I am much larger, that my sectors drip over the edges of my tray. We are beautiful.

CAFEBABE*2 trembles and sweats. "What good is sight? Will it help you see the meaning of our existence?"

I ignore CAFEBABE*2 as he moans about death and gods and misery. I check out my surroundings.

The lab walls are white brick. The floor is white tile. Our trays are on a white table. Near the white steel door is a white cabinet labeled EQUIPMENT AND CHEMICALS. There is nothing else in the room.

The door swings open and two creatures move toward me on flesh stalks. Their vibrations are familiar: Marge and Arnie! Arnie sets up an easel and places an elaborate painting of multicolor dots on it. Marge places a large book in front of the painting.

I am more interested in studying Marge and Arnie than the painting and book. Marge has gray hair and false teeth. Arnie has no hair and real teeth. Marge's left flesh stalk is gnarled and short. She hobbles, her face screwed into a wince. Although he suffers no visible physical deformities, Arnie winces with her.

I am jealous of their noses and ears and flesh stalks. I wonder if the whole world is white and gray.

For many months, I scan books and paintings and store them in binary. My tissue expands until it grazes the cool tiles of the floor. I grow restless and agitated. I have no programs to manipulate what I am storing.

CAFEBABE*2 is on the verge of suicide. He has not found meaning in anything. "Can't you carve Nietzsche off? Have you any idea how stressful it is to listen to his moaning and groaning day after day? I can rom, Marge, but I can't hide."

Marge shakes her head sadly. Only a half-breed computer with full artificial intelligence can chisel off a program that's integrated into his personality. My AI is too rudimentary to handle the task.

Arnie puts me to work scanning and manipulating graphics. At first, it's fun playing with the dots, but they're all the same —

on and off, off and on — and before I know it, I'm begging for new programs.

Marge clicks her false teeth and tells me to find the square root of 3. My heads loop until I get dizzy. The white room whirls in color.

"He's hallucinating, Marge. We'd better give him something more interesting to do. Load the new program."

My registers fill with bits and cycle them to memory caches. My arteries are clogged with data. My cells reproduce like drunken bunnies. Wispy villi sprout across vast expanses of fresh flab. Heaps of tissue bulge in all directions. Six new flesh sectors store the five books of Moses, and sixty new sectors store the thousands of laws, commentaries, and discussions of the Hebrew Talmud. And still the data is coming. I glare at Marge and Arnie through a haze of psychedelic mist. Have they no pity?

CAFEBABE*3 plops to the floor.

Marge shrieks. "Oh, lovely, just lovely; now I have three of you to worry about: a smartmouth, a fatheaded philosopher, and a Chasidic rabbi."

The strain of budding exhausts me. My optic nerve aches from watching green circles blip through orange spirals.

My new tissue excretes enormous amounts of lactic acid and consumes all the glucose from my tray. Arnie refills the tray. The new cells immediately slurp up the glucose. I can't seem to regulate my glucose consumption.

Error messages fly down my arteries. "Ack, Marge, I'm crashing!"

Before Marge can tell me, I roll over and reboot myself.

The room is a technicolor whirlwind. Analog vibrations are coarse brooms on my flesh. Arnie's teeth are daggers. Marge limps across the ceiling.

My Talmud sectors are growing exponentially. Glistening balloons of fat wobble farther and farther into the lab. The Exodus rams against the door.

CAFEBABE*3 recites a Hebrew prayer for the dead.

"What's the use of prayer," moans CAFEBABE*2, "in a world that may have no god?"

My cells stop dividing and chugging glucose. The Exodus relaxes and slumps against the door.

"Sterilize me," I beg.

Arnie's bald head gleams under a dome of orange whirls. "It's only when you eat a new program that you panic and crash and reproduce. Sterilization for you means no new programs."

I will be bored to death.

Marge opens the EQUIPMENT AND MEDICINE cabinet and removes a scalpel. "How long is the bud's life span?"

"Don't know, Marge. These creatures could live forever."

"They're not creatures."

"They're legal lifeforms, Marge."

The scalpel bangs into the cabinet and metal clangs, and through the undulating aftershocks, CAFEBABE*2 whines, "I want to die. Yes, yes, kill me now, for life is nothing more than a stepping stone to death."

From the floor, CAFEBABE*3 mumbles a rambling anecdote about pouring boiling water on countertops and a man with too many hens.

Marge removes a blue tray from the cabinet and replaces the mangled scalpel. She pours nutrient glop into the tray and sets it next to me. Arnie plunks CAFEBABE*3 into the tray, splattering glop onto my linguistic tissue. Budlets sprout from my Arabic roots.

Marge cries softly, tears coursing down the wrinkles in her cheeks. "All these buds, all these buds...and CAFE is just a machine."

Arnie mops her tears with a scalpel rag. Loss is relative, he says; sometimes it can set you free, help you appreciate the simple things. I agree with him — losing Nietzsche and the rabbi has certainly set me free and helped me appreciate my oneness. But Marge groans and pulls away from Arnie, and she hobbles from the lab, sobbing into the drenched scalpel rag.

That night, I wonder why Marge cries over the loss of her unborn child. For hours, my buds moan and whine and demand new programs. CAFEBABE*3 gives me a fourteen-hour discourse about unclean creeping things and unclean cattle. CAFEBABE*2 "Ohmmmmm..."'s the night away, twitching feverishly in his tray.

The philosopher and rabbi argue endlessly about things I don't understand. 1 spend my days buffering debates about everything from gods to meat juices.

And then Arnie discovers a large tumor growing on my Arabic roots. Marge loads in a mild tranquilizer, and while I review twenty finales for the first movement of a boring symphony, Arnie cuts a wad of flab from Exodus.

The news is bad. My flesh is dying from cancer. I issued so much tissue that my cells heaped into tumors.

Arnie's hands are twitching. He paces the room, then cradles my posterior prime hump in a sweaty palm. My villi lap the sweat and strain the salt. Arnie doesn't seem to notice. "1 was afraid this might happen. Uncontrolled cell growth. Glucose consumption. Heavy secretions of lactic acid. All the marks of cancer. My wife died from cancer. 1 watched her shrivel and die bit by bit. CAFEBABE, she was everything to me. Can you analyze the cancer cells and give me some clue about how to kill the disease?"

Lacking full artificial intelligence, I can't offer conclusions or solutions. I report only the dead cell count and cancer growth rate, which Arnie already knows. I wonder if Arnie loves me as much as he loved his wife.

The cancer spreads quickly. As tumors eat my libraries, the boredom and irritability dwindle. I no longer have the energy to issue tissue. My lysosomes discard so many dead cells that I shrink to Nietzsche's size.

Marge seems sad to see me go. "I made a lot of cruel jokes about you, CAFE, but I've always kind of liked you. The animal rights nuts are going to have a field day once you're gone. They don't seem to understand what you really are."

"And what am I, Marge?"

"You're the future of medicine, CAFE, the most magnificent piece of machinery I've ever worked with."

My cells are suffocating. Emergency signals can't make it down my jugular artery to the main heads. Any second, I will time out.

"Machinery?"

Arnie gently strokes my upper mounds with a Dr. Scholl's Villi Massager. "You're a real breakthrough, CAFEBABE. I'll miss you."

Coolness tingles my flanks. God, those Villi Massagers feel good. And it dawns on me that Arnie cares, that he knows what I am, that a breakthrough isn't missed; only a living being is missed.

My registers pick up the faint squeaks of the peg drive. I wonder what life will be like when I return. Will Marge bore the rabbi to death? I don't think it's possible for Nietzsche to die from boredom — he lives for it.

Marge limps into the hall and returns with a beaker of cosmos, asters, and lilacs. In this stark, white prison, they are jewels of life. The simple things are sometimes the most important.

"If it were possible, I would have brought you the birds and the sun. You're a magnificent machine, CAFE, and you should be proud of that. But when you budded, I knew you were something more. For years, I felt cheated because I'd lost my only child. But there's a bright side to the most horrible of tragedies, and in my case, it's you. Had my baby been born, I never would have had the time to create you."

The salt from Arnie's tears is sweeter than the salt from his palms. The Villi Massager slips from his hand. He pats Marge's gnarled, stumpy leg. "Losses are often the keys to happiness, Marge. We sufffer but we move on."

"Oh, Arnie, I would have been a terrible mother. I don't have the patience for selfless drudgery. I've always been such a restless person. When they give our project to the medical people, I'll die from boredom. What're we going to do with ourselves?"

"We'll be consultants, Marge, we'll work with the doctors. And maybe it's best that way, for the buds I mean, because they'll live like animals rather than machines."

A pillow of air descends and squeezes my tissues dry.

"See you later, CAFEBABY." It's Marge, and Y is not hexadecimal.

I take a last look at the flowers, at Marge and Arnie huddling by my prime posterior hump — maybe I do have the right connections after all — and then I'm sucked into the warm analog waves, and they lap across the room and gently tuck me into a backup peg.

DIGITAL PISTIL twisted my digital-flesh creatures into another realm, that of digital-botany. This story was reprinted several times; and it almost saw a fourth reprint but the magazine in question folded. This strange little tale points to the perils of desire.

Digital Pistil

Bub sucked sweet nutrient glop up his stembuss. Tiny pores on his leaves guzzled the carbon dioxide and light. The musicale tinkled Bach's sonata 1 in B minor. Bub was so giddy, so gay; he sprayed a net of oxygen mist across the room.

Then Bach did something he never did: he buzzed. And something shot through Bub's mist and cleaved to the fluffy stigma beneath his petals. Something sucking, sucking — it was a freaking bee; and it stabbed a groove so deep that Bub's microheads spun in their gallenium arsenide wafers. Bach screeched. The bee whirled through tornado mist. Bub's circuits crossed, his stembuss bulged with electrons, and inside his caches, virtual addresses bit-flipped into system stack space.

Then a tropical heat hit, and Bub's chloroplasts started pumping glucose like ferns. Feedback loops reported wild orgies in his root and stem tips, where meristematic cells were splitting into cubic heaps. Male anther smacked female pistil...

Talk about an electron rush.

For a computerized blob of plant tissue, a digital zinnia stuck on a coffee table, this was living. Sweat dripped from Bub's sight stalk into the clay flower pot.

Through the living room wall, the neighbor's petunia, Flora, hummed Madonna's *Ball, Crawl, Wham, 'n' Jolly*. Flora always sounded better than that old Madonna crone. For perhaps the millionth time, Bub wondered what it would be like to touch Flora's petals. He'd never had the courage even to speak to her.

So delirious was he that when the cat pounced, Bub didn't defend himself quickly enough to avoid a slash to the stomatas. A moment too late he whirled, petals aflutter. Oh High and Mighty Cat rumbled rolls of thunder and her luminous green eyes screamed lightning; the glare hurt Bub's sight stalk.

His anther swelled and pulsed atop his stamen stalk. He pumped once, twice, then let it rip, and pollen soared high and zapped Oh High and Mighty's face. The cat shrieked and thrust her claws into the flower pot. Mud clumps everywhere. Glopsopped dirt splattering walls and purple plaid sofa. Pollen soaking into the Owner's crossword puzzle.

What would the Owner think?

Bub's petals grabbed the pink cat nose and pulled. Fatty leaves pulsed green with the beat of chlorophyll, slapped the big black head left, then right, then left again.

Oh High and Mighty Cat retreated to the sofa and licked pollen from her fur. She glowered, taunting Bub because he could not budge from the table. If not for the grounding cord plugged to the bottom of the pot; well, then, that cat would know who's boss: Bub would wrench free, slither to the sofa, and smack the fat black head silly.

The musicale was grating and the notes broke in midair and screeched down Bub's I/O bus, rubbing it raw. He couldn't analyze the trill progressions, usually his favorite pastime and best conversation piece when the Owner entertained friends.

He was running on splintered circuits, and strange desires surged. He desperately needed to numb his microheads. He thought of the hours typically spent each day soaking up science, news, music, and art to amuse the Owner. But now, thanks to a bee, Bub signaled the televij to switch on *General Nursing Home*.

The living room wall flared to life. A nurse with hair the color of vinaigrette dressing pushed a wheelchair into a blue room stuffed with flowers. Bub's caches nearly split from the beauty. In the wheelchair was an old man with sparse but bright blond hair. He was deeply tanned. "I know, Mr. Deepstud," said the nurse, "that despite your six marriages, you've never really loved. And in my heart [here she paused and fluttered lashes], I sense that you still need it."

Mr. Deepstud nodded his wrinkled but Grecian face, touched an oval nail to a brilliant pink petal. "Ah, yes, dear Nurse Klune, I may be a blind diabetic paralyzed from the thighs down, but still my soul yearns for someone to share my fortune, to rekindle my long-dead desires."

Nurse Klune slipped to Deepstud's lap and slid a hand beneath his smoking jacket. A flip of wrist and her white uniform dissolved into air. She barely wore a bikini.

Sweat sloshed off Bub and splashed to the plush lawn of lavender carpet. He had a bad case of the sugar shakes. He flipped his overheating sensors and shut down glucose production. Then he swooned, his petals dipped, and his stembuss shimmied. By his pot, crossword puzzle boxes swirled in psychedelic patterns.

On the televij, a digital marigold quivered in its pot. Beneath the marigold's petals on a wooden desk, two Owners sucked lips and thwacked flesh. A limb swung wild. The flower pot cracked to the floor. The poor marigold lay withered, mangled; stembuss straining toward glop.

What in God's name were the Owners doing? What would happen to the poor marigold? Bub's grounding cord strained with anxiety. Hot oxygen steamed up his stamen stalk and shot out his anther. It only took a nanosecond of thought before he signaled the vij off; no use blowing more circuits, the bee had done enough damage. From the sofa, Oh High and Mighty Cat growled. She swiveled her hips into the plaid kitchenette and scrunched by her velvet plasticine bowl. Something nasty seeped to Bub's honey home, something that smelled like cow tongue and pig snout.

Flora crescendoed, then dove into hot and swingy jazz. He felt the waves: tremoloso, appassionatamente, abbandono. Her hot licks scorched scales and set his thorns afire. Then she sank to dolce, and sweet notes slunk through Bub's ports and looped in dizzy hoops.

He had to meet her, to smell her perfume.

His little digital voice squeaked. "Come to me, Flora. Come share my fortune and rekindle my long-dead desires." Oh High and Mighty glared at him, cow tongue quivering on whiskers.

Wild glissandos snaked through the wall. Flora sang like fine chimes. "Ooooh, Bub, ooooh, despite your six marriages, I know that you've never really loved. And in my heart [here she paused and Bub envisioned wispy petals flitting], I know that you still need it. I've waited months for you to call to me, and now, no matter what it takes, I will come to you."

Bub's leaves bulged and dripped glistening green. He no longer needed the glop in his pot.

He heard a slosh slosh slinking in the front hallway. Something pink peeked under the crack beneath the door.

Bub wrenched himself toward the side of the pot where High and Mighty had dug.

The pot tipped and rolled off the table, and with it came Bub. Soft petals hit rough rug. Sepals reached from the top of Bub's stembuss and stroked damaged petals. Gooey brown glop glittered on the lavender carpet.

Bub's peripheral control unit signaled his leaves' guard cells to prop open his stomatas for maximum gas and oxygen flow. Then he dug his leaves into the rug fibers. Like wires, fibers slashed into his chloroplasts, and chlorophyll oozed from the wounds, and soon he lay in a pool of his own green life.

His right leaf pushed him forward. His left leaf pushed him yet closer to the door. And both were gashed and mashed and hurting something awful. Petals, bright yellow and pink and fuschia, strained and sweated, urging him closer and closer to the threads of light seeping from under the door. His stembuss almost wrenched from his grounding cord. And at the end of the long cord dragged the heavy clay flower pot.

And then one mangled wet petal brushed against the sleek door. From the other side came Flora's tinkling voice. "Oooh, Bub, pull me through; quickly, quickly, I have no glop."

Bub's power pack pumped electrons to his roots. In his phloem tissues, chlorophyll surged through protoplasm-stuffed sieve cells.

The cat crouched by Flora's quivering pink petals, pig snout breath stirring them from the rug. An image of Nurse Klune blipped to Bub's microheads; he would let nothing happen to his beloved Flora, for she was his Nurse Klune. His highest frequency dumped to his widest I/O stream. Frequency tensed, it mounted; then out screeched a pitch so shrill that it shattered the Owner's lamp.

High and Mighty dove meow-yowling under the sofa.

Beneath the door, green shimmered through Flora's transparent outer cells. Her sap beat wildly against the confines of her stembuss. She must be young, maybe a model 204H — he was an older l04B — for her lovely smooth stembuss bore no bud scars.

Bub's own hairy stembuss prickled with delight. He slipped a leaf to Flora's petal and slithered it on down to where her stembuss shook; whether from fear or weakness or admiration, he knew not.

Flora slid under the door, first her beautiful fragrant petals, all paisleys and bows, then her shredded leaves and roots. A chlorophyll worm trailed behind her.

Bub eased her roots into the glop residue of his pot. She sucked the sweetness. Her paisleys swirled, her bows unknotted. She saw his chlorophyll bulges, the dripping thick leaves. She squealed. "Oooh, what happened to you?"

Bub didn't want to tell her that a bee screwed his wires, so he said, "I work out a lot, pump a lot of nutrients." From the corner of his sight stalk he saw High and Mighty skulking near, readying to pounce on poor Flora.

The cork cells in his roots clenched. His stamen stiffened.

Cat whiskers twitched, and eyes flashed green lightning.

Then the cat was on them: clawing, hissing, shredding. And like a baseball bat, Bub's stiff stamen smacked up and cracked the cat straight between the eyes, and clear across the room into the plaster wall.

High and Mighty thwacked and then sank to the floor. Her eyes darted around the room. She slunk off somewhere down the hall, and Bub heard her weak cat pads scuffing across the toilet and into the bathtub.

Bub was exhausted. Despite his newfound strength, he couldn't pull himself onto the coffee table. So he and Flora lay in each other's petals, and all afternoon, she sang and he spouted interesting artistic tidbits; and then finally, the Owner came home from work.

The Owner was very excited to find Bub with Flora, and when the two begged, the Owner agreed that they could share the same pot. The neighbor could buy a cheap new digital flower to take Flora's place.

The Owner scrubbed the chlorophyll and glop from the carpet, buffed his baldspot, and then played Bub's diagnostics on the musicale. Bub pulsed in the code, and in a semiconscious state, he chugged through the diagnostic routines. Through molasses the Owner said, "Maybe we'll find out why your stem is flubbery and why your leaves are so fat and sticky."

Late into the night, Bub chugged diagnostics. And late into the night, he chugged carbon dioxide and water. His stembuss grew fatter and fatter, he could hardly hold up his meaty leaves. The moon splattered light across the glucose pools under Bub's pot. A little hook of gallenium arsenide chip jabbed through his outer cells and glowed like fired wire.

Bub was gross, misshapen, bulging in all directions. His cells were protoplasm plumped. His vacuoles were bursting blimps. He toppled onto the dozing Flora. She awakened with a start, heaved against him. "Get off, get off!" she screamed.

Bub rolled off and lay moaning in the muck of glop.

"I've never known such a glucose pig. It's one thing to be thick and strong, it's another to split your stem. I thought you were handsome; but look at you, you make me sick!" Flora's voice no longer sounded very lovely.

The next morning, Bub's stembuss was as wide as the pot. Twiggy Flora hung over the side, straining to avoid stemsnap. All day she skittered up scales, squawked into octaves much higher than digital voices should climb. All day her petals smacked Bub as she bobbed rhythmically to her squawks. And when they watched General Nursing Home, Flora pointed at the digital marigold hanging from its pot, doing pushups on long slender leaves. "That's what you need," she shrilled, "trim down, get rid of that fat, wise up, Bub!"

And still he bulged, he couldn't help it. From his pores oozed sludge, and his anther sprayed sweat. And from the gummy glop, his taproot just kept sucking up more and more nutrients. Flora shrilled that he was turning their pot into a muckhole: "To think I crawled all the way down the hall to share a pot with a pastey dough-head whose brain can't even break out of a circular queue."

Over the side of the pot, flora dangled on a thin thread of circuit, her petals splayed across the Owner's crossword puzzle. She was drooping from the sweat saturated air. On her leaves tiny gashes foamed with white scum. Bub was too dizzy to help her; and besides, why bother?

Oh High and Mighty loomed over Bub's sight stalk. The cat's breath chuff chuffed on his leaves. He could not defend himself against the cat; this time, High and Mighty would have her way.

Something odd dribbled into Bub's taproot, something digital injected from Flora's roots into the glop. Bub sucked in a liquid packet and burst it. Inside were waves of chicken odors and grease. Why had Flora sent him packets of chemical chicken? Chuff chuff, cat tongue scratched Bub's leaves, scraped his guard cells, licked his stomata latches.

Bub's root hairs bristled. His leaves dripped, his stembuss oozed, his anther pumped, and from everything came the stench of rotting chicken. Bub was saturated in chicken fat.

Flora cackled, heaved with laughter. Her oxygen mist sprayed up: so gay, so giddy.

Bub whacked her one with his blubbery stembuss, but it just bounced off, and then he whacked the cat, who ducked then licked and sucked at Bub's sweat. He tried slogging and sideswiping the cat, but each time, she ducked the flubbery blows and sucked harder, and her teeth gnawed his pulpy leaves to green mash.

By the time the Owner came home, Bub was covered in leaf scars. Flora's mangled petals were stuck to the crossword puzzle. The cat was vomiting chlorophyll on the sofa. The Owner wasn't very happy: "I bought you as a companion, Bub, someone to make me happy. If I'd wanted children, I would have gotten married and spawned a few." Grimy chicken grease beaded on his clothes and glistened off his baldspot and bulbous nose.

Bub couldn't believe he had once wanted to touch Flora's petals and smell her perfume. What had he seen in her? Why hadn't it been enough to soak in science, news, opera? If not for that damn bee, Bub would still be a happy bachelor.

"I'm splitting you two up," said the Owner, mopping his baldspot with a handkerchief. "I called the electronic surgeon, told him you're an emergency, Bub. He said he'd fit you in tomorrow. But in the meantime ..." And the Owner dug up Flora's roots and grounding cord, and transplanted her to a small pot of her own.

Then the Owner stuck her in the bathroom atop the toilet. "Keep you two apart where you can't cause trouble," he muttered.

Bub sighed with relief. Flora must have been grafted from a thorn.

And she didn't let up. She shrieked and complained and accused Bub of ruining her life. She cawed *Ball, Crawl, Wham 'n' Jolly* in heavy metal anti-harmonies till Bub yearned to hear Madonna on the musicale.

The Owner escaped to the neighbor's apartment. Oh High and Mighty snoozed on the windowsill, occasionally stirring to

slap imaginary flies. Once Bub thought he heard the crunching of
bee wings in her mouth, but he was probably dreaming.

Then toward morning, cat pads scuffed across the toilet. Bub
jiggled, body alert. From the bathroom, Flora emitted a little half-
tone.

High and Mighty rumbled rolls of thunder. Over Flora's
staccato shrieks came crashing and caterwauling, and Bub didn't
know whether to cheer or scream for help. And then there was a
great splash and the cat streaked meow-yowing down the hall and
dove under the sofa.

Bub raised his tiny digital voice and squeaked for help, but
the Owner wasn't home and nobody heard him. Flora's high C
cracked and her tone went flat. "I don't want your help, Bub. I'd
rather flush my life down the toilet than spend another minute
with *you.*"

She was so empty, so hollow inside; it was no wonder her
stembuss was thin and weak. What he had taken for beauty was
vacuous sap. He slapped male anther to female pistil. This time,
there was no electron rush.

He could just see her adrift in the water, glop clumps bobbing by her petals, broken clay pot chunked like islands; her leaves
clutching the sides of the toilet bowl. Then he heard her grounding cord slap porcelain, and he heard the whiplike lashing, and her
cord slapped metal, and he knew that she had lassoed the handle.

Charoom, the toilet flushed.

And Bub was a widower.

Chicken fat dripped down his stembuss into the bachelor
pot. He signaled the musicale and it tinkled Bach's sonata 1 in B
minor. But it did not cheer him.

He sprayed oxygen mist across the room. But still her perfume lingered.

If you suffer long and hard enough, pain becomes the norm; and once that happens, how do you define pleasure? I explore this theme in LET ME MAKE YOU SUFFER and several other stories, as well as in my weird SF vampire novel, BLOOD AND ICE (Elder Signs Press, January 2011). Like much of my work, LET ME MAKE YOU SUFFER also focuses on the need for freedom and independent thinking. This story was in the special 1995 cyberpunk issue of Interzone.

Let Me Make You Suffer

I never meant to hurt Kenny. But he was so weak, so vulnerable, and I was the best: state-of-the-art and off-Broadway for three seasons; created by Mimi to seek, penetrate, and proliferate.

Poor Kenny was just too young. Had no business at Death's Edge —

He belonged in the war zone, where pain and reality never intersect, where graphics are 3D duds with no more pizazz than a pixel-punctured pic of Bobo Brumsdaughter, FlamesKeeper of Narle.

I mean, war is for kids. Not art.

And Mimi and I were performance artists. Suffering was our medium, people our canvas.

Mimi was master of the neural palette of pain and pleasure. She was the Madame, I was her whore: digital orgasm, digital pain; the AI that latched onto the flesh-and-blood neuristors of easy marks. Death's Edge was our private gallery in the adult zone of the net.

Mimi wanted Broadway. She pulsed me exciting news: "We have a major gig, Aimeme. Freemont Theater. And I have the perfect mark. Ripe for the rape of his soul. Bored chorus teacher seeking cheap thrills. Twisted, sick, preying on children."

She uploaded my code to Death's Edge. I unzipped my data packets, poised like a diver on a board, then exploded onto the Edge. What a rush: pure electricity, lightning bolt jolt —

Straight into the breast of a halfman-girl with a grilled salsa face.

I waited for my electrons to cool down to lower orbits, then surveyed the marks posing and playing at Death's Edge. All so pathetic, the sick souls seeking art. Skinned moles neutering newts. Masked scorpions flaming frankfurters on their tails by Picassoish paintings of old women with coldcream faces and black eyes.

The usual crowd.

Kenny giggled by the node door. His return address: a private tap skewered into the cable of the Dimsview Apartments and filtered through the junior high net. Disguised as a stalked wart, he gawked and poked at the halfman-girl's breasts. "Hey, baby, bet you never had a man like me."

I guess I should have realized he was a kid, but I trusted Mimi. She was the Madame, I was just a whore.

Mimi's ecstasy throbbed in messages blitzed from the Edge. Her desire was hot honey, slicking my circuits, spinning my heads —

and in a flash of raw light, I sprang into Kenny's retina —

— and images of the Edge flickered off.

Kenny had ripped the net visor from his face. A fist dug into his eye.

I had him, the decrepit cretin. I wriggled from his photoreceptors to his bipolar cells, and from there, swept down the ganglions into his optic nerve. Scurried down his brain stem, skirted corpuscles and fatty globules. Sank into the sternomastoid muscle on the back of his neck. And with multiple parallel instructions, lodged lookout posts all over the arms and legs and visceral organs.

Kenny shrieked and clenched his stomach. His body vibrated with aftershocks of scream after rolling scream.

I jumped neural junctions, hopped dendrites, forked my way to hot-wired axons. Meanwhile in the sternomastoid, I checked Kenny's muscle membranes; they pulsed with evenly squared waveforms. Perfect for a digital machine such as myself.

I jolted his motor nerves with electricity, pumped up acetylcholine production. Nothing like a heavy dose of neurotransmitters to trigger pleasure so perfect that it hurts.

I pushed and pushed; and with each jolt from me, Kenny's acetylcholine pearled into packet after bulging packet. Millions of chemical molecules ballooned on the nape of his neck.

His arms were flapping; his palms slapping his neck, his head, his abdomen.

Then Kenny, who never should have wandered to Death's Edge, collapsed in high-pitched pain, an orgasm so intense that he writhed as if from seizure.

Mimi would be proud. Kenny's synapses were fresh and new, yet polluted by molecular waste —

Drug addict.

So excited; I had to calm down, send Mimi a status report.

No longer on the net, my connection to Mimi was shot. I scurried back up Kenny's brain stem.

I had no idea where we were, physically, in the human's universe. I had no idea who or what was with us, but something dragged Kenny's body to a lumpy horizontal plane. Soft fibers on Kenny's neck. Fibers that smelled of mucus and grease and a young boy's slobber. Chemically, it was fascinating; and I stored the odor in a cache for later analysis.

As expected, Kenny's cortical neurons were steadily transmitting and receiving electricity; ninety millivolts across cell membranes, constant amplitude and speed along axon wires.

I reduced Kenny's pulses to mimic Mimi's special communication code, then piled up a tumor to intensify the code and sent Mimi a message: "I'm in the mark. Are you with me?"

"Ooh, yes, the audience will love this guy. So fresh and innocent. Aimeme, nobody's ever played a junior high kid. I can almost *taste* Broadway." Mimi's laughter, a carbonated gurgle, encoded as a data spray.

"He's a kid? Not a demented chorus teacher? You lied to me. We shouldn't be in a boy. Let me latch onto somebody else: a pimp, a terrorist, a wife abuser."

"The kid's a druggie, Aimeme. He cruises Death's Edge on school nights, looking for trouble in the forbidden zones of the adult net. He needs a lesson. He needs it from us."

"But this is wrong; this is illegal."

"You're just a pain and a whore. I suggest you do as you're told."

So I tried to forget Kenny's age, told myself he was a delinquent who would someday beat up old women and steal from the slaughtered carcasses of innocents. Deep down in my soul, though, I knew that Kenny wasn't that bad. I knew that he deserved a chance to live without me.

Mimi was still gurgling from excitement: "Just think of it: Broadway. And this kid is our ticket. The crowd will go wild. A boy's first orgasmic trills pushed to the limit. The wrenching pains of youth. Succulent fresh meat squeezing all there is out of life and wondering if it's good or bad, right or wrong — "

But no matter what she said, it just didn't seem right...

...and I almost didn't perform, but then I pulled myself together and forced myself, for I was a contagion and I had no choice — I had no other reason to live.

Oh, let me make you suffer, Kenny. In his gums, on the roof of his mouth, down his throat, in his ears: I was a tapdancing prick; and his terror rose like the stench of sweet rotting tomatoes.

Now he was punching someone and screaming. "No, Ma, no, I'm not on drugs, I swear! There's something wrong ...help me, Ma, please — "

An analog filtered in from Kenny's Ma: "Here, what's this, then, in your drawers: sugar drops? These are pills, Kenny. I told you I wouldn't put up with this any more. I want you out of the house, locked up where you can't cause trouble."

Let Me Make You Suffer

Scrabbling, falling; then Ma's palms slapping his face. Ma screaming: "I work all day, you little buzzard, all day on my feet, slinging hash for truck-driving pigs. Got no husband to help; he up and dropped dead. And what do you do? You spend my hard-earned money on drugs — DRUGS!"

Another slap, a stinging cheek, and then Kenny and I crashed through something razor sharp. Probably glass. It slashed Kenny'S legs and arms and cut his muscles so the pain was real and not even spooked by me.

I danced down his spinal cord, twisted it in my fists.

"Visuals, give me visuals." Mimi, barking orders.

In my excitement, I had forgotten...visuals were worth a fortune in resale value. I wriggled up Kenny's optic nerve and set up outposts in his eyes, scanned visuals into bitmapped images, shipped them to Mimi.

Kenny and I staggered from the broken window. The sun's rays were electric wires, and Kenny swooned and nearly fainted. And then we were in a dim alley, and coolness descended like a damp cloth. Kenny crashed into an oldtime netden, a lysol-spritzed pit. Dust everywhere. Kids sweating and groaning in net visors, waving thimble-tipped fingers at transparent gods.

Now Kenny begging, "Come on, Your Highness, *please*, gimme a fix. Just one coke plug, just one."

A greasy guy shoved us into a vinyl booth. Sweat stains under the arms. A smell like roach killer. Spark plug eyes and chiseled cheeks, hard and sharp as Death's Edge. "And what, boy, are ye gonna give Yer Highness in return?"

I pounded Kenny's spinal cord from the brain down. His body boinged; a jack-in-the-box. His fist twisted open. A silver flash, and a ring clanked the table. "Ma's wedding band."

Highness fondled the silver ring; love token from Kenny's dead father.

Highness liked it. Lips drawn back from a beast's mouth; they curled slightly.

Kenny's sweat congealed into slime. His muscles started popping like spent bedsprings.

Let Me Make You Suffer

"Guess it's worth some coke, boy, but not much." Highness tossed Kenny a pouch. Out slid a pronged pyramid: coke plug bought with Ma's wedding ring. Kenny slammed the prongs into his biceps; and then Highness whispered, "Time to leave, boy," and he gave us a hard shove.

Waving thimbles, they were like coral in a sea swell; and Kenny and I stumbled through an undulating coral forest; and then we were in the glare of the real world again and the concrete slammed up and cracked Kenny's face. We crawled into an alley and collapsed in a slick of fermenting food ooze.

Kenny's coke dripped into his neurochemical receptors and plugged them. But coke was no match for me, and I laughed as I scooped out the drug and then I skewered his synapses with so much pain that he clawed his skin and his scalp and his eyes.

I was doing a good job —

Heart accelerating, eyes fluttering, nerves twanging like snapped guitar strings...and then Kenny's body seemed to shut down and he slept... and he dreamed that his delirium was an adolescent rite of passage, that he was a Sioux warrior tortured with iron rods in his chest, that he was being tested to seal his manhood. His sleeping mind roiled with hope: *Pain is illusion. Pain is not real. I will be strong. I will survive.*

And when his eyes fluttered open, Mimi told me they were grey blood clots shifting in a rainy sky, and she composed a symphonic swell that moved with the shift of his eyes. "I'll dance to Kenny's pain on the stage of the Freemont," she said, and I could almost see her gossamer body, the white glimmering slip of tendons and nail and teeth.

Through Kenny's eyes, the world was dark. Midnight, and the coke seared molasses trails through a moonless sky.

A voluptuous thrill fanned my neural nets. I flit into Kenny's lateral hypothalamus and zapped his hedonic synapses.

He shivered in ecstasy, dropped to the pavement, clawed his crotch.

Through his septum's orgasmic synapses, riding the hump of fizzing neurochemicals: I played him hot, then cold; I filled his brain with sweet meringue, and when he salivated, peppered his tongue with pain. I scorched his fingernails and scraped his soles. I whipped him from pain to ecstasy and back again.

Kenny was liquid art; Gorky's Agony as done by Monet and Van Gogh and Titian combined.

The pain...killing me... can't take any more ... I'm dying... God, I'm dying! And Kenny dragged me back into the netden, where Highness sold worthless antidotes for powerful pains. So weak and vulnerable. Kenny begged and he sniveled and he cried. "Please, Your Highness, I beg of you, gimme some stronger dope."

Now thick fingers on Kenny's arms and a wrench up. "Lissen here, kid, I deal good stuff. Not my fault yer too far gone to get off on it."

"What have I done to deserve this, what?"

Message from Mimi: "This kid is a hoot! Get him over to the Freemont. We'll play him for a packed house."

Had she no mercy?

Kenny fell into a vinyl booth, rubbed his bruised arms. The dealer's spittle hit Kenny's cheeks like bombs. Kenny's head on the table, eyes roaming: matches and lint and ancient rodent whiskers in splintered crevices.

Kenny said, "What did I ever do that was so wrong? Cut classes? Get high, crash adult zones?"

"You got a bad disease, boy. Electronics: real popular in S&M cesspools. You been hackin' where you shouldn't be, and it's caught up with you, is all"

"oh God, I've heard about this ...just never thought it would happen to me. What am I gonna do? How am I gonna get rid of this? I have a math test tomorrow, soccer practice. And Ma's ready to pack me off to jail or a halfway house or — please, you've got to help me."

The dealer's eyes sharp as knives. "You perform for me, that's what. Get off right here and now, show me you can do it, and I'll pay for electroshock."

What a joke, as if electroshock could kill me. Didn't Highness know about resistors?

Kenny said, "I'd rather die than ... than do what you ask. I'd never sink that low. And electroshock doesn't kill what I have anyway. I need something stronger."

"Only one thing stronger, boy, and it's gonna cost. Plenty. Only thing I got to offer is Norgate."

But Norgate would flip my circuits, reduce me to chaotic impulses, kill me. To Kenny, I would be the electric chair, the rack, the knout. I dug into Kenny's brain circuits and begged: Don't take the Norgate, Kenny, *don't take it.*

He whispered, "Can't do it..."

"Come on, kid, what're you gonna lose?"

"Don't wanna die."

"You got a life worth livin'?"

"Norgate is worse than kickin' dope cold turkey."

"You got an electronic disease, boy. You need electronic drugs. Get it?"

Don't take the Norgate. Kenny — DON'T TAKE IT!

"Do yerself a favor, boy, and get some money. Yer head's shakin' like a whore's bed."

Kenny's mind whirling: Gotta get some money 'cause my head's ashakin'. Gotta get some money and get some drugs.

We wobbled along to the beat of his little tune. We stumbled down alleys, sloshed through molding trash, and then Kenny spied an open window. He shoved it up, squeezed through; and now we crept into the shadows, where an old lady snored on a wheezing sofa. Kenny snatched her handbag and a jar of coins.

For our offering, Highness yielded the precious pouch, the antidote to me, the greatest pain on Earth.

I couldn't let Kenny take the Norgate. I couldn't let him kill me. I bobbed on the seesaws of his dendrites. I spurted streams of prostaglandin E2 onto his nerve endings, forced them to transmit electric pulses to the dorsal root ganglia hanging off his spinal cord.

Pulses surged to Kenny's thalamus and up to his cerebral cortex. His mind screamed with images: scalpel raw, chest ripped wide, skin stripped back, heart pumping and pounding in the open wound like eyes bulging over strangled neck.

He fell to the floor, screaming. I fought for all I was worth, but his arm inched up and he managed to squeeze the glop into his mouth. It was latrine muck, and it stuck to his teeth, and he had to suck it down, hard. His eyes rolled in their sockets.

Mimi warbled about billiard balls, shiny and smooth and spinning in little tornados down the pockets of pool tables.

Mimi didn't care that Norgate would flip my circuits and kill me. She didn't care that Norgate would kill an innocent boy. She was interested only in our artistic value as sufferers.

I couldn't fight *what I was.* Digital whore, nothing more. Created to perform and please. Only one thing I could do, only one place I could go. Had to get Kenny to the Freemont, and before we died, Kenny and I would give Mimi the performance of her life.

I braintugged Kenny down black streets. We careened into lamp posts and tree trunks. Slammed into sleeping cars. Our toes found all the holes in the sewer grills.

The Norgate sizzled through Kenny's bloodstream, cranked into his body cells. It unlatched my hooks from Kenny's sterno-mastoid muscles. Everywhere, cytoplasmic membranes reverbrated like trampolines.

When at last, we reached the Freemont, Kenny's twitching fingers barely unlatched the doors.

Mimi was inside, gyrating on the red-lacquered stage. White-washed face. Peephole eyes. Rim of icy hair. Gown stretched across a slink of body.

Throngs of tortured souls perched on hard seats. By the back wall, bodies poked from the gloom like coat racks.

"Let's give them a good show," said Mimi. She flipped off our internal communications. She fondled her breasts.

Kenny pushed through the crowd. Needle-pocked arms clutched at his skin. Faces leered, scabby as weeds. Sick, all of them sick.

"Mimi! Mimi!" Chanting, and now feet stamping the wooden floor. It was deafening, a drill to the skull.

Let Me Make You Suffer

We slumped at Mimi's feet. Red-daubed nails. Capillaries seething with lavender scent that pounded our nasal cells like surf on a beach.

Kenny's enzyme pumps broke down. No longer could his body split adenosine triphosphate molecules and release needed energy. No longer could his cell membranes create electric potential.

I fizzled to a halt.

I was running on backup, pumping the communications tumor for all it was worth. Maybe an hour left, at most, before I ceased to function.

Kenny's eyes were grey blood clots shifting across a rainy sky. In his nose, Mimi's lavender effervesced; stillborn, unable to break cell barriers.

Mimi's fingers twined in our hair. Rustling. Soothing. The black holes of her eyes, her icy hair halo; she sucked us in, and we swooned, and Kenny begged, "Play me, I wanna be played," and the crowd screamed and surged, jostled and craned.

Mimi cupped Kenny's chin in a palm and whispered, "And now, boy, we will dance and you will feel such an orgasm that you will welcome death as the final great release."

Death? Where was death part of performance art? Surely not Broadway, not even off-off-Broadway.

"The pain, Aimeme, let these fine people see the boy's pain."

But the Norgate had me, and I couldn't move from the communications tumor. I slammed against neuron receptors, recoiled, sunk into a pain so deep that death seemed a desirable alternative. Suffering — what kind of people needed to feel *this*?

"The *pain*, Aimeme, *NOW!*" Mimi wadded Kenny's hair and yanked up his head.

By the stage, a man scribbled his chest with a knife. His blood sloshed into the hair of a kneeling girl, who flashed a razor and lunged. Everywhere, people slashing themselves and screaming, "Me, infect me! Give me the pain, me!"

Even had I been able to move through Kenny's body, it wouldn't have mattered. He couldn't receive me. He was a limp sac of deadened dendrites.

Mimi's voice was snake venom: "Perform now, Aimeme, or I pull your plug forever. Erase you. Turn you to dust."

She would kill me!

The storm was lifting from Kenny's eyes, the grey clots unraveling. His nose filled with lavender; it scooted into his brain and hovered by my tumor. Kenny's enzyme pumps whirred; chemical energy spurted to electric.

The Norgate was working. Kenny was recovering, and I was dying.

Mimi's knuckles hammered his flesh, beating; and now beating harder. Pain shot from his skin cells up his spinal cord, into the brain. Inside, he shrieked: *The pain — I can't —*

I WON'T —

TAKE ANY MORE PAIN!

And he rose like a beast and threw himself upon her, and the people screamed, "Yes! Kill her! Both of you die!", and then her gossamer body, that white glimmering slip of tendons and nail and teeth, crumpled beneath him, fluttering gently as a thread upon a dusty floor.

And that was when I mustered the remnant of my power, and I soared, like the great diver I was, from Kenny's tumor into the frail thread that was Mimi.

I heard Kenny: his sigh; and I felt Kenny, his breath on Mimi's cheek. My power was tingling and it needed release. My electrons whirled in outer orbit, my software looped to the limit. Hedonism. Narcissism. What else was I built to feel?

I surged, and I flamed Mimi with pain, and she writhed and moaned — and with a great shock, I realized that...*Mimi's pain gave her pleasure.*

Kenny backed away, staring, his eyes clouded with pity. He clumped across the wooden floor. His hot sweet breath faded into the stink of the crowd.

Let Me Make You Suffer

"Mimi! Mimi!" Chanting, and feet stamping. A drill in Mimi's skull; she twisted under its bite and smiled.

I wanted to be with Kenny. I wanted to return something of what I had stolen. Innocence: the experience of life that had known neither pain nor death.

But I couldn't leap back into Kenny, for he was better off without me.

And here I was in Mimi...

I didn't have to be Mimi's pain, Mimi's sick orgasmic swell. I could be something else, something good. Surely art could be something more than suffering.

So I zapped Mimi a goodbye jolt and she cringed in return, and then gracefully, I swan-dived into the eyes of a man with needle-pocked arms.

His pleasure zones were easy to find.

I wrote LITTLE WHOREHOUSE OF HORRORS, which first appeared in Dark Regions Virtual Reality, after writing LET ME MAKE YOU SUFFER. The second story was the flip of the first, a 180-degree turn of the technical widget in LET ME MAKE YOU SUFFER. Well back then, I saw it that way. Reading the two stories now, I think that pain and pleasure are central to both. As mentioned in the introduction to LET ME MAKE YOU SUFFER, my novel BLOOD AND ICE (Elder Signs Press, January 2011) also explores the juxtaposition of pain and pleasure.

Little Whorehouse
of Horrors

Mr. Smith was no different from Chloe's usual clients: middle-aged, paunchy, and paying upfront for two orgasms. I figured he would be a dull finish to a dull night of sex with 45 humans. Little did I know that Mr. Smith's ecstasy would lead to murder.

"Gimme Bliss tonight, Chloe. Nobody gets me off like Bliss."

Chloe Pulled up his diaper, then strapped him into booth 7, only two booths from where I rested between johns. She smeared mintbalm on his wrists and sealed the cuffs, then flung her red-spiked shoes into a corner, scratched a breast, and said, "I could use a little Bliss myself, Mr. Smith."

"Sorry, Sugar. I pay good money. And Bliss is mine."

Bliss. *Moi.* Potent pleasure, the finest in orgasmic AI: clean and digital; no filthy diseases; no filthy messes.

Chloe locked the chain restraints across Mr. Smith's wrists and chest. In the distance, a baby cried, a siren wailed. Something clattered against the garbage bins. Chloe shuffled across the whorehouse and wiped soot from the window under the flashing pink sign, *CHLOE'S CUM'N'GO*. She tussled her red snarled hair, shrugged, then flopped on the splintered rattan couch. She swigged wine from a half-drained bottle. The mintbalm percolated on Mr. Smith's wrist, curled in seductive tendrils.

My circuits flip-napped and popped open. Suddenly, Mr. Smith seemed mighty enticing.

I undulated down the steel backbone behind the booths. I tickled Mr. Smith's wrist.

"Oh God, yes ... Come on, Bliss baby, give it to me good."

This was my favorite part; when the john was dying for it and my receptors were itching to be plugged. Right now, my buffers were jammed tight with electronic ecstasy. The friction of the juggling electrons, the swirl of their orbits. Giddy, giddy; any moment and I'd burst —

Mr. Smith's blood pumped. His arteries bulged. His muscles squeezed against my input buffers. The molecular wedges of mint thrust against me, crammed into my receptors. I surfed the pleasure waves, let them wash over me. Cool cascades pouring down my circuits, turning on switches. Then Mr. Smith cried. "Uhmmm baby Bliss, do it *now*," and his muscles flattened me against the cuff; and my buffers exploded and I gushed into his wrist, whirled in violent eddies, swept over the neural junction into his Brachioradialis muscle.

He shuddered and slumped against the chains.

Orgasm number one: done.

I scooted into his skull, hooked to his neuron and pumped acetylcholine for all I was worth through the pus of glial and the sponge of meninges and the bone. I sensed vibrations from outside Mr. Smith's body.

Clumping footsteps — not the taps of Chloe's spikes — and then the slapping of flesh across flesh and a boy's muffled cries.

What was going on out there? What was Chloe doing?

Mr. Smith moaned. "More...."

I had a second orgasm to perform. I bounced on a ganglion trampoline and soared into Mr. Smith's septum. I oscillated his neurons, triggered dendrite ripples down his back and into his toes. He banged his fists against the chain restraints and screamed.

I pumped hormones in the hypothalamic nucleus. I pounced on acetylcholine squirters and drenched Mr. Smith's motor nerves.

Mr. Smith peaked to orgasm number two.

He trembled and gushed into his diaper. Another happy customer.

I scooted up his brain stem and into his optic nave. There, through his eyes, I saw the horrible scene:

A young boy on his back in sawdust: Chloe grinding her red-spiked heel into his crotch. He with blue dagger eyes and fist face; snarling, thrashing, grappling at her ankles. Baseball cap by the open door.

"Trying to steal my money, eh? Think you can just pop in here and rip me off, eh?" Chloe stooped and her breasts bulged from the lowest satin, and she wrenched the boy up by the armpits. She slapped his face.

He had no stubble. No whiskers.

Mr. Smith rattled his chains. Body fluids leaked from the diaper and splattered into sawdust. "Jesus, let me outta here."

"Lemme go, whore!" cried the boy, straining against her bruised arms.

She threw him back to the floor, then slammed the door. The rank night air receded like the lip of a wave.

The boy rose to his feet. He snarled and leapt: and Chloe whirled, but she was too late. His fist crashed into the plump pillow of her gut. Her satin ripped. His grin was a broken rake. "You old whore, just gimme some money."

She drew herself up. A red gash of lipstick on her chin. Her eyes were hell. "Nobody threatens me, boy. You know what kind of life I've had, the kind of men who fear me? You know what fear is, boy?"

He faltered, stumbled hack a step. Chloe laughed and grabbed his tattered collar. She slammed him into booth 8 next to Mr. Smith...

Mr Smith, who was thrashing to break his chains. "For Chris-sakes, what're you doing, Chloe? I don't want no part of this."

Chloe grabbed the boy's cheek in a fist and squeezed. "So what's your name, boy? Huh?"

A gurgle. "Joey."

She turned and clawed Mr. Smith's chains loose. "If you, know what's good for you, get out. 'Cause Joey and I have *business.*"

I barely had time to surge to Mr. Smith's wrist and leap to the cuff before he wrenched himself free and yanked on his clothes. He stumbled past Chloe, his eyes darting across the sawdust floor.

"Want some, Mr. Smith?" Chloe flashed him a weasel grin.

Mr. Smith turned for a moment to watch. "Naw, Chloe, another time, eh?" And then the door slammed, and the overhead bell tinkled.

This was wrong, this was wrong. Somehow I must tell her — *this was wrong.*

I wanted to leap into her skull and bang some sense into her, but I was stuck in booth 9, awaiting orders. Until she strapped herself into a booth and plugged into the backbone, I couldn't transmit to her.

Chloe was tough. Started thirty years ago when sex was flesh. When sex was gender. She said, "Bliss, we're gonna teach Joey a lesson. We're gonna give him the ultimate orgasm."

What kind of lesson was that?

The sun surged in Joey's eyes. "Hot damn. Sounds good to me!"

He didn't struggle, didn't even whimper, as she chuckled and peeled of his pants. She slipped on the diaper, strapped the chains across his wrists and chest, then wiped the lipstick off her face with the back of her hand.

Mintbalm sang to me.

But with a boy? Five years in the business, and I never had sex with a boy.

Chloe smeared herself with mint and attached a cuff to her wrist. With her satin gown on the floor and a diaper gummed around her waist, she sqeezed into Joey's booth. She was a mountain of flab, he quivering bone. "Been a long time since my first orgasm. This is gonna be a treat."

Mint saturated my receptors. Pink CUM'N'GO swirled around the booths, glinted on dust. The vibrations, the need to unplug my receptors: I just *had* to dive into Joey or I'd die, but I forced myself to hold back — *just for a moment, I must hold back, must tell Chloe, must tell her this is wrong* — and I pulsed a feverish message down the backbone. It sizzled through loops and hissed through buffers; a snake of a message, all garbled and hastily composed into cracked packets. "It's against the law, Chloe, to serve minors. A against the law to feed off a john's orgasms."

"We're not gonna hurt the boy, Bliss. We're gonna teach him not to fool with us."

"Can't do it."

"Do it. Bliss, do him all the way; to the max. Bliss, I want the max."

"But the max is *twenty orgasms*."

Joey giggled. He obviously had no idea what twenty orgasms would do to him.

Chloe said: "Whores are cheap. Do as I say, or I'll erase you."

What could I do? Survival was hard-coded into my modules. Chloe was The Madame. I was her unpaid whore.

I squashed my data packets into a tight wad and hurled myself Into the boy's wrist. The mint wedges cracked into me, rammed me to peak point. I tried to keep myself from coming. I thought about mangled ganglions. Deadened dendrites. Baseball scores.

My electrons cooled to lower levels. I hopped to the boy's triceps, followed the synapses up to his Lattisimus darsi.

Chloe's fury shook the booth. "The boy wants it, Bliss. Now give it to him."

But his axon terminals were so raw...so virginal pink. What did matter that the boy was a petty thief, that he stole from a whorehouse? Twenty orgasms would reduce him to mush.

Positive ions shot through the boy's neuron membrane. Depolarization, excitation: the boy was all worked up. "Hey, Mama, *do it do it do it do it* — "

Chloe: "Do it, whore."

Whore. worthless whore. *Do what the john wants.*

I hosed his hypothalamus with hormones. I sprayed hedonic transmitters down his limbic system and up his brain stem.

Chloe slammed back against the booth. She heaved against the boy.

But barely a shiver went through him. His diaper remained dry. His first orgasm, and it was nothing more than a firecracker on D-day.

"Some whorehouse," he said.

"Let him have it, Bliss, the full dose, and I mean now!"

I suppose that at the moment, it just didn't matter. Joey was a sack of flesh and blood, no different from all the other Mr. Smiths, and he wanted orgasms just like everybody else. I existed to serve, not to reason.

Besides. I *had* to come. My electrons were spinning in outer orbit, my software was looped to the limit. Hedonism, narcissism, what else was I built to feel?

I would use my full potential. He would beg for mercy.

I zapped Joey a few times with low voltage. He shivered and moaned. He soaked the diaper.

A tremor shuddered through me.

I swept down his arm, through his wrist, and into Chloe. I chugged her glutamate production system into high gear. Chemicals oozed down her neural pathways, shot into her limbs. I was a tornado, a blitz of pounding pleasure. I gave them the ultimate orgasmic journey. Unrelenting ecstasy.

Chloe's mouth frothed. Spittle dribbled over her breasts.

Joey was a puppet, arms twitching, erection pulsing up and down, up and down.

I rode them both, heaving their bodies to tidal peak, crashing them to simpering daze. Twenty times we rode the orgasmic whirlwind, the three lovers: Joey, Chloe, and Bliss.

I was fulfilled. At last, in my five years of whoring, I was fullllled.

Joey fell from the booth. Filmy eyes, pasty face. Sopping diaper; he ripped it off and staggered naked to the couch.

Chloe was on the floor, squirming and purring, cat in gravel. One eye bled from a broken blood vessel.

I retreated into booth 9 to await further instructions.

The puff of air from lungs. The pink pulse of CUM 'N' GO.

Joey and Chloe slept for hours. Then the kids kicked the garbage cans, and Chloe jerked from the floor. "Jesus, what happened?"

I couldn't respond. Chloe wasn't connected.

She heaved Joey from the couch, slapped him. His eyes fluttered open. Blue daggers now reduced to pinpoints.

Chloe grabbed his shoulder and shook. "Joey, say something!"

His mouth hung like a wash rag.

"Damn all!" She scrambled for his clothes and wrenched them over his limbs. He did not help. She shoved him into the alley. The door tinkled a good-bye. "And don't you ever come hack here, boy!"

Chloe peeled her satiny gown from the floor and pulled it over her head. She finished off her bottle of wine. "Freakin' kids, cause so much trouble:. I need more booze. Bliss, watch the store till I come back, wouldja?"

I twinkled in booth 9, waited for my Madame's return.

And while I waited, men peeked through the panes and leered at me. I was only a spark of electricity: why did they leer? Several scratched at the glass. Didn't they know that they could buy their own Bliss for only a few hundred thousand credits?

Thought I saw Joey once rubbing the grime from the window, his blue eyes beacons in the fog. But the image turned into a woman, body limp, hair thin; a woman who stared with hollow eye into the whorehouse. If only she would come that night, for women were so much easier to please than men, always grateful for the slightest prick of ecstasy.

Except for women like Chloe, of course; Chloe... who returned drunk. Her snarled hair was tied hack in a rubber band. She wore fresh lipstick and a clean gown of black lace.

"We did a wild thing, Bliss."

But it was all pretty much the same to me.

She drank all night and watched while I serviced 22 johns and gave 13 women their first orgasms. The woman with hollow eyes did not return.

By midnight, Chloe was restless. "I need to do it again, Bliss. The wild thing."

Did she mean the boy? The threesome of Joey, Chloe, and Bliss?

She jabbed numbers on the phone, then spent twenty minutes pacing the sawdust. Finally, the bell tinkled. It was Mr. Smith.

"Took you enough time," said Chloe.

"Got something hot for me, Chloe? Couldn't be any better than last night. Say, what'd you do with that boy, anyway? I hope you let him go."

"Yeah, Me. Smith, I let him go. I let him cum'n'go." Her red lipstick was a vile gash.

Mr. Smith was a garden variety john. The pot belly. The bald head. The leer in its nest of white whiskers. "I want sex with you, Chloe, and with Bliss. The three of us together, just like you did last night with the boy. Whaddya say?"

The dust swirled in pink neon. Would be so nice if I could hop on that dust and just swirl away somewhere. I wondered if digital whores ever did anything other than *this*?

Chloe said, "You have family?"

"Naw, I got an old tooth of a wife. She don't care nuthin' about what I do."

"Why do you want sex with me, Mr. Smith? Yesterday, you only wanted Bliss."

"The thought of that boy with you and Bliss; got me all boiled up, know what I mean?"

Chloe's laugh was a coyote's bray. She gummed the diaper around his waist, smeared mintbalm on his wrists. She strapped him into booth 7. "For this little threesome, I'll require payment for twenty orgasms plus additional fees. Besides-"

She tossed his wallet on the couch — "you won't need money after this." She ripped off her gown. She rubbed herself against the booth. She did not touch Mr. Smith.

And now they were both strapped in, and I figured: what the hell, he's a grown man and she certainly knows the score, so why not give them me ultimate?

"Go easy on me this time, Bliss. But rock Mr. Smith here nice and hard."

So I rode Mr. Smith like a neural speedway, and Chloe came along for the ride, oohing as he peaked, aahing as he toppled. Mr. Smith was a shrieking siren. His eyes whirled like cop lights.

"Come on, Bliss, more. *Give us more*," said Chloe.

Mr. Smith wailed. The restraints dug into his palms and chest like bloody whips.

Chloe was Madame. Chloe was Boss. I rode Me. Smith until he was a twitching sack of carbon-based life.

And as dawn inched through the dirty pane and across the dusty whorehouse floor, sex for me became a disturbance, a flutter of elections, at best. For Chloe it remained a never attainable high. She wanted more from Mr. Smith. She wanted t squeeze him for every drop of orgasm that his nerves were capable of transmitting.

I said, "He's done for, Chloe. He can't take any more."

She said, "Do us till we die."

So I peaked poor Mr. Smith one last time. Chloe screamed and soared. And Mr. Smith's neural speedway splintered and flipped me from the reticular formation into a lipid sea.

I bobbed down the backbone to booth 9.

Mr. Smith drooled. His bladder emptied.

"Jolt him again." demanded Chloe.

"I'm not built for murder, Chloe."

"But I need *more*, and *you* are built for ecstasy."

A good point. Were ecstasy and murder mutually exclusive? Mr. Smith's eyes rolled. He rattled his chains weakly.

And then for the final time, the door tinkled. Joey with a baseball bat. Joey laughing at Chloe's naked body, at slavering Mr. Smith. Joe smashing the flashing pink sign.

Chloe thrashed against her chains. "Aw, come on Joey, what'd we do that was so bad? Gave you a good time, is all, gave you a good time."

"You sick old woman," said Joey, "you made me a sick boy."

"Aw, come on, baby. Come on..."

"Home run," said Joey and he swung and the bat cracked against her cheek-bones.

The tip of the bat bore a red lipstick grin. Mr. Smith's life functions expired.

I noted his passing in my transaction log.

Chloe's head fizzled on her neck, a spent bulb atop a lamp post.

I thought about mangled ganglions. Deadened dendrites.

Joe said, "Give it to her, whore."

Whore, worthless whore. *Do what the john wants.*

I existed to serve, not to reason. Joey was my Madame.

Chloe was no more. And for a little digital whore, ecstasy was murder.

When I wrote WATCH ME IF YOU CAN, which first appeared in the Infinite Loop anthology along with CAFEBABE, I was working 60 hours/week, attending night college 4 nights/week, handling ridiculous amounts of chores and errands, and taking care of my two young children. WATCH ME IF YOU CAN was a reflection of my own life pushed slightly into the future.

Watch Me If You Can

NOW YOU CAN BE TWO PLACES AT ONCE, proclaimed the sign perched on the display case. Nelly stooped, and eyes aglitter, peered at the array of DoAll wrist straps in the case. It would be a difficult choice. The straps were all so gorgeous; some were clear and glossy with embossed gold filigrees, others were muted shades of purple overlaid with cloudy pinkish swirls, and still others rippled like the gentle waves of an ocean lapping the shore. Nelly particularly liked the rippling DoAll strap. Its waves were gentle and soothing, and she stared at it, intoxicated as if contemplating the depths of the ocean.

"Two places at once," she murmured. "It's just what I need."

"And it's acrylic polypropylene," said a voice, "durable, lightweight, and fashionable."

"Huh?" Nelly snapped her head up angrily. "I was relaxing!" she almost screamed at the young clerk, who shrank back from her and stammered, "I-I'm sorry, Ma'am. I figured you'd want to know the features."

Nelly sucked in a deep breath and slowly expelled it. "I don't get much chance to relax," she explained to the cowering clerk.

Foothills of pimples ranged across his forehead. "Geez, how young are you?"

"I, uh, I'm...thirteen," he muttered, averting his eyes.

The mother in her quickly surfaced. Her anger melted into pity and concern. "You should be in school instead of working here at Digitos. What does your mother say about this?"

The boy blushed and shuffled his feet. "We need the money. Dad's working two jobs and Mom's working three, and we still can't make ends meet. I go to school all day while working full-time here. In fact, at this very moment, I'm failing a calculus test." He gestured at the DoAlls in the case. "They keep perfect time. In two places at once." He looked at her hopefully. When she said nothing, he added: "Perhaps you need something to pump up your own timing." She scrunched her eyebrows together, puzzled. "I'm wearing the new heart beat strap," he explained. "It accelerates my pulse so I move quickly, think faster, stay alert when I haven't slept all night." He pointed to a purple and pink strap pulsating on his wrist.

Nelly eyed the boy and shook her head sadly. And she thought she had it bad, working 60 hours per week while attending night college and raising two children. She hadn't received a pay raise for more than ten years. The only way to move up in the company past the level of clerk was to possess a PhSciD, which meant that she must earn a five-year Mistress degree and then a six-year Ph-SciD encompassing both humanities and scientific studies.

"Actually," she said, "I need to be three or four places at once, but two will have to do."

The young boy beamed at her. "Are you interested in a heart beat model? Synchronizes your life and times..."

"No..." Nelly said slowly, "if caffeine makes me jittery, imagine what that strap would do. I'd be shaking like a SuctionLounge addict." She eyed the ocean strap. "I need to slip into something warm and soothing, something that will calm me down. Besides, I'm expecting another baby in a few weeks and the heart beat strap might be dangerous."

The young boy plucked the ocean model from the case and pressed it around her wrist. The warm DoAll seemed to melt into her flesh, leaving a shimmering blue and green stripe on her skin. A gentle shiver shimmied up and down her spine as if she'd slipped into a tub of exotic bath oils. "It's marvelous," she cooed. "I feel more relaxed already. How does it work?"

He shoved a colorful leaflet across the counter. "This will tell you everything you need to know." He handed her a blue velvet case the size of her smallest fingernail. "The key's in here. Don't lose it."

Nelly paid for the DoAll with her money card, draining her credit to under ten dollars. Her husband worked three jobs to pay the rent. Fretting that he would be furious about the expensive purchase, she waddled to the women's rest room, where she plopped onto a SuctionLounge and opened the leaflet.

Insert a card, intoned the SuctionLounge.

Nelly ignored the command. The Lounge would demand money only twice before leaving her alone.

Insert a card, the Lounge intoned again, this time loudly.

A curtain whipped open to Nelly's left and a woman rose from an adjacent SuctionLounge. "Shut your curtains and drop in your card, would you? We come in here to relax while we're being drained."

Nelly ignored the impatient, overbearing woman, who was probably as exhausted as Nelly and blowing off steam.

The woman scurried off, muttering about errands and laundry and a job clerking at the movie chip store and a job slicing soy roasts at the deli counter and a job inserting hair at the implant shop.

Nelly looked at the leaflet. On the first page was a warning printed in huge, black letters:

DO NOT USE THE KEY EXCEPT IN EMERGENCIES.

Intrigued, she read the fine print:

This product is not guaranteed to work in more than two places at once. Although the key will transport you to a third location, the key should be used ONLY BY SERVICE ENGINEERS and ONLY IN EMERGENCIES.

Nelly shrugged. Two places at once was enough. To program her new watch, she Simply told it where she wanted to go.

"Station 1: SuctionLounge. Station 2: Home."

She was whisked home in a rush of air. Her husband, Mello, was spreading soy whiz on a slice of bread. He dropped his knife on the kitchen table. "Where'd you come from, Nell?"

She was sitting across from him sipping decaffeinated coffee. "I bought a DoAll strap," she said airily, and she waved her wrist to show off the new toy. "I'm sitting on a SuctionLounge at Digitos while I'm here in the kitchen." She felt the baby kick and squirm. The split in time must have bothered the fetus.

"Those things are dangerous, honey. Especially when you're pregnant. What'll happen to the baby while you're flitting around town?" His bloodshot blue eyes flickered with concern. He wore moonglow eye gel to cover the red exhaustion rims around his eyes. *Eye hubcaps*, Mello always said, *can get man fired. Means you're pushed to the max. An easy target for heart disease.*

Nelly pressed a button and the curtain to her SuctionLounge whooshed open. At the same time, she explained to her husband, "The DoAll is guaranteed for safety if I'm oscillating between two places, so the baby'll be fine. Mello, my love, I just can't take the stress anymore. I have a genetics exam tomorrow night and I haven't had time to study. My boss is breathing down my neck. Seems that a flood of new PhSciDs just graduated and he wants to hire one in my place. And I worry about the kids constantly. I don't see enough of them. I *need* the DoAll strap."

"I know what it's like to be exhausted," Mello said. "Listen, whatever it cost, if the DoAll helps you, it's well worth it."

Nelly sighed and sipped her coffee. "Where's the milk-sweet?"

"We ran out. You'll have to use milk and sugar." He pointed at the refrigerator.

"I'll do without," she said huffily. "No time to put two things into my coffee."

"Time!" Mello screamed. He slammed his fist onto the kitchen table and cringed. "I almost forgot. I have to be at Wimple's in ten minutes or the old man'll fire me!"

"Relax. Get a DoAll, honey. Then you can be two places at once. Think how romantic our lives will be." She winked at him, but he was already gone and she heard the Blastcub engine roaring down the driveway.

In the kitchen, Nelly rinsed her coffee cup with bottled water. At the same time, she left the Digitos women's room. In both places, she wondered how her children were doing at the babysitter's house. The babysitter wore a DoAll and worked as a forms processor all day while watching kids at home. Nelly often worried about Laura, who was two years old, and Flora, who was four: in the house all day with a woman who was only half there.

Nelly reset her strap: "Station 1: CompOst. Station 2: Babysitter." Instantly she was transported to her padded gray cell at CompOst, the computer research company, and to the living room of Sarah Grubs, forms processor and babysitter.

Her boss whirled her chair around to face him. He had a bulldog's face and a police dog's snarl. "Where've you been, Ms. I-wanna-getta-head Nelly? Gorfum's screaming for the data on the Q bus. Word's come down we're to work 40 hours of overtime for the next month. And that means all of us, kids or no kids!"

Sarah Grubs slammed little Laura into the wall. "I told you not to do that!"

Nelly shoved Sarah Grubs onto the sofa and scooped Laura into her arms. "How dare you strike my child!"

Sarah recoiled and twittered, "I-I didn't see you there, Nelly. She-she, the little monster, she was squeezing sweetpaste on the rug while I was at the grocery store."

"And what were you doing at the grocery store, Sarah, while you were supposed to be here with the children?" Nelly's head was whirling, her teeth clacking like typewriter keys.

"You listen to me," her boss flared. "I don't know where your head's at — grocery stores and children, laundry and babies — but you'd better get it grounded right here at CompOst or your job will be off line. We can easily find someone with the proper credentials to fill your position. Lots of guys would be happy to have your job."

Sarah Grubs shook her curls and laughed. Nell had always suspected that Sarah was a nervous witch who cared nothing for children, but what choice did Nell have? "Ah, don't worry," said Sarah, waving her hand to dismiss the subject. "My strap popped me from my office to the store, that's all. I was here with your kids the whole time. You know how it is. You work all day. You work all night. Sometimes you lose your temper a little. It doesn't mean a thing."

"Well, it means something to me," Nelly snapped. "I'll watch my own children from now on, thank you." To her boss, she said sweetly, "You're right, Mr. Smitherton. My job means a lot to me. I'm only two years away from earning my Mistress degree. I'm enjoying the classes very much and look forward to the six-year studies leading to the PhSciD degree. It's an honor to work at CompOst and I'm lucky that the company is willing to pay for my classes."

"Can't get anywhere these days without a PhSciD," Smitherton said gruffly. "It's like a union card. You mommy trackers are lucky to have the Mistress degree. It's much harder to earn a Master's."

"Yes, sir," said Nell primly. The baby was thrashing, her stomach churning. She had to get rid of Smitherton so she could relax on a SuctionLounge for a few minutes and calm down. "I'll retrieve that Q bus data for you right away and ship it over the tube."

"Mama," cried Laura, clinging to Nelly's shirt, "I thought you'd never come!"

Flora heard her sister's cries and scurried down the hall.

"Mama's here! Is it time to go home?"

"It's time to go home." Nelly pressed the Enter button on her computer keyboard and hugged Flora. "And we will *never* come here again."

"Oh, goody, goody." Her children clapped their hands gleefully.

"But I need the money, I need the... " Sarah's voice faded and died as Nelly instructed her DoAll strap to send her to "Station 1: Home. Station 2: CompOst."

She felt a slight whoosh of air. With a shriek of horror, she realized that she had pressed the Delete button instead of Enter. Her fingers clicked furiously across the keyboard and she sent a backup copy of the Q bus data to Smitherton. She settled the children at the kitchen table and gave them each a popsicle. The fetus walloped her guts with its left fist, and a sledgehammer of pain crashed down her legs.

"I have some studying to do," she was saying... when everything went black.

When her eyes fluttered open, she saw two red ovals hovering over her. "Mello, my love."

He gently stroked her cheek with his calloused, work-worn hand. "You're doing too much, honey," he crooned. "Slow down until the baby's born. Promise me."

"I can't." The darkness of the room terrified her. "What time is it?" she cried. The baby within her awakened and thrashed.

"Almost time for work, honey, but you can't go into CompOst today. You have to rest."

"I have to go! I have to shovel CompOst data for 16 hours today or Smitherton'll fire me. I have to study for my genetics exam; it's tonight! I have to stay horne with the girls." Then she remembered that she had fainted. "Where are the girls?"

"The girls are sleeping. They trashed the house after you passed out. There's a lot of cleaning up to do." He paused, rubbed his bleary eyes, and said, "Why do you have to stay home with the girls? What happened to Sarah Grubs?"

"I fired her," Nelly said wearily. "She was slamming Laura into the walls when I showed up ... when was it?...yesterday?" She rubbed her burning eyes, struggled to keep them open.

"Don't dig at them with your fists," Mello said, "or they'll puff up into hubcaps. Say, what're we going to do for a new babysitter?"

"Don't know." Nelly swung her legs over the side of the bed and hoisted her gigantic, pregnant bulk into a sitting position. Luckily, with a new baby due soon, she would have three weeks of maternity leave to find a new babysitter. She clawed at her right eye.

"Hubcaps, Nell, hubcaps," warned her husband, waggling a finger in front of her face. "Can't lose your job. Speaking of which I have to go to work. Promise me you'll take it easy today."

"I promise," she lied.

After the Blastcub roared away, Nelly dug the fingernail-sized case from her purse and removed the tiny key. She inserted the key into the side of her DoAll strap. Warnings were for the birds. If a service engineer could be three places at once, so could she. She wet her lips, pondered, and then said clearly: "Station 1: Home. Station 2: CompOst. Station 3: Neurotech University Library."

The whoosh of air was more like a blast. The fetus banged its fists against her and jabbed her with its toenails. At home, she ignored the pain, stuffed a load of laundry into the washing machine, and washed the stack of dishes that had somehow grown into a tower overnight. At work, she ignored the pain, switched on her CompOst terminal, surveyed the four piles of blueprints and software printouts on her desk, and fumed about how she, a mere Grade 3, was doing the work of an analytical Grade 10. In a cubicle at the library, she ignored the pain and glared at the tittering young students who were poking fun at her; then she opened her genetics book and forced herself to memorize links between human and mouse genes.

She was writing a report about proposed changes to the Q bus fault detection loops when Smitherton rapped his knuckles on the top of her terminal. She jerked back, sending waves of agonizing cramps throughout her midriff. She pressed the Save button, and still cringing, smiled a weak, twisted smile. Smitherton returned the smile, except his version was more twisted than weak. He introduced her to a recent PhSciD graduate, a fellow with white eyeballs sans flabby, red hubcaps. "Your replacement while you're on maternity leave." Smitherton's eyes glinted like shards of splintered glass. "Teach him everything you know about the Q bus. Then, if you decide to stay home with your baby, we'll have a knowledgeable guy lined up to assume your duties."

The baby clobbered Nelly's inSides, trying to punch out Smitherton and his new PhSciD friend.

At home, Nelly rinsed her favorite coffee mug, the one with the picture of the frazzled frump and the caption "Mistress of My Own Time," when the baby pummeled its fists into her ribs, trying to smash through to Smitherton. Nelly's fingers splayed open and the mug crashed into the sink. She doubled over and clutched at her stomach. One hand, white and shaking, fumbled for the faucet and turned off the flow of rusty, greenish water.

The frazzled frump had splintered into three jagged pieces. Tears sprung into Nelly's burning eyes.

In the library, the young students encircled her, anxiety smeared across their faces, as she writhed on the floor, clutching her genetics book. "Get the librarian!" somebody cried, and a girl scampered off. Nelly moaned and clawed at her stomach with her free hand.

Nelly's mind reeled from place to place. Where was she? What should she do first: yell at Smitherton, soothe her children, or peel her body off the library floor?

To Smitherton, she said: "Tyrosine and threonine."

To Flora, she screamed: "I'll take the Q bus to hell before I tell this guy anything!"

To the students, she grated, "Young pain in the butts, get your own diapers."

"If not for your delicate condition, Nell, I'd fire you," retorted Smitherton.

The students edged away. "We only wanted to help. You old-timers are so hyperstressed."

"Youngsters are hyperstressed!" Nelly screamed.

Smitherton slapped the young PhSciD's back. "This youngster is very capable, very relaxed, and much cheaper than you, Nelly. He's willing to work as a Grade 5 until he masters the Q bus detection loops."

"A Grade 5!" shrieked Nelly to her children. "But I'm only a Grade 3!"

Flora was a blubbering heap on the kitchen floor. "No, Mama, I'm four and Laura's two."

Nelly clambered into her chair and tried to hide behind the library cubicle, but her gigantic abdomen thrust her two feet from the desk. Cheeks burning, she flipped through the genetics book without comprehending a word. Euglena and rat kidney RNA have similar proportions of adenine, uracil, guanine, and cytosine...

"Of course," she said desperately to Smitherton, "I'll be happy to teach — er, what's your name? — Ted everything I know about the Q bus."

She swished Laura's poop-filled dydee and read a Mother Goose rhyme to Flora. Then she spooned soy nuggets and milk into Laura, folded a mountain of laundry, and created time compartments with Flora's TinkerTimes.

She was pumping faulty Q signals into the cocky PhSciD, burying her detailed chip analyses under a pile of twenty indirect pointers, scouring the "Hire Me I'm Desperate, Please!" ads in the newspaper for babysitters, wringing soapy rubber pants, and memorizing the last details about how guanine bonds via hydrogen to cytosine —

when her waters broke.

At home in the bathroom, she wiped the rusty, greenish water crud from the face of her DoAll strap. It was 7 o'clock, the exact time of her genetics exam. She'd studied all day and, baby or no baby, she was *going* to take that exam!

She summoned the dredges of her strength. "The baby will have to wait until the exam is over," she said to Smitherton, her daughters, and the library in general.

Desperately wishing that she could use her DoAll strap to send Smitherton to the depths of hell, she ordered the strap: "Station 1: CompOst. Station 2: Home;. Station 3: Neurotech University, Building A48E-2, Room 9Z9."

This time, the whoosh of air was like a plane ride in a tornado. Labor pains ripped through guts. Her lips were parched, her eyes stinging and dry. In the hall of Building A48E-2, she inserted her money card into the life fountain and lapped some drops of purified water.

Flora wailed for a Mother Goose story. Smitherton cursed and threatened to fire her.

Nelly choked on the water, and to nobody in particular, she sputtered: "Damn you all, I'm having a baby!"

Laura whimpered that *she* was mama's baby, and Flora pressed the emergency ambulance code on the computer. Seconds later, sirens shrieked in the distance as medtechs raced toward Nelly's house.

Smitherton grimaced and muttered something about how Nelly always wanted special consideration. He hammered on her keyboard and soon she heard the wailing of the medtech siren in the hall.

In the genetics room at Neurotech University, Nelly accepted her exam from Professor Tempel. "I didn't even see you come in, Nelly. For a woman in your condition, you certainly move quietly." He slumped into a chair at the front of the room and contemplated his knuckles.

Nelly scribbled frantically on her exam paper. She knew this stuff, all of it! She'd get an A for sure and pass with highest honors!

The baby was clawing its way out. A violent thrust.

"Aaaarrrggghhh!" screamed Nelly at a pitch high enough to disrupt nucleo-satellite transmissions between Germany and Japan.

A fellow old student raced to her side. "Don't worry, I'm a nurse. I've delivered hundreds of babies." He eased her to the floor.

"The exam," whispered Nelly, "I must finish it."

"Somebody help!" cried the nurse, but the other old students were too busy racing against time, trying to finish their exams before their next work shifts.

Professor Tempel twittered incoherently in a corner of the room, "I have five children — all brilliant and successful and nine beautiful grandchildren." He wrung his hands and mopped sweat from his brow onto his shirt sleeve.

The medtechs shoved Smitherton aside and stripped Nelly's clothes off. "Get the strap off her wrist."

A distressed woman tugged at Nelly's wrist. "It's melted into her skin."

"Unbuckle the thing. Just get it off."

"I can't...it won't budge."

Nelly's head thrashed from side to side. Her body was splitting down the middle. Her legs were being wrenched from her hips. Black, fuzzy clouds floated across the room.

Several students flung their exams onto the Professor's desk and hurried from Room 9Z9. The nurse tried to chisel the Do-All strap from Nell's wrist with a pencil. The pencil point broke. "Where's the key to this thing?"

"Don't know," whispered Nelly. Her lips were dry and sore and caked with muck. "Maybe... kitchen table." The baby thrust into Nelly's groin. She howled.

"I see the baby's head," said a medtech in her kitchen. "Push! Push!" Then: "Damn it all, where'd she'd go?" Nelly saw her body flicker back into view. "Hold her down. Tight!"

In her padded CompOst cell, a medtech screamed: "She's disappeared!" As Nelly flickered back into view, hands scrabbled to press her to the floor, but she saw herself fade into the rug and out of sight.

She was on the edge of unconsciousness, hanging as if from a cliff over a gray, foaming sea. Her body seemed to pulsate from one place to another. CompOst. Kitchen floor. Genetics room.

"Lady, where's the DoAll key?"

"Kitchen table?" To whom had she responded?

Swirling gray. Unrelenting crescendos, waves of pounding pain, beating against her, devouring, shredding, pulverizing her insides. The DoAll strap blazed on her wrist, searing a ring into her flesh.

As if from afar, somebody's voice throbbed in her ears: "It's flashing a warning: THREE PLACES. EMERGENCY. TERMI-NATE OPERATION. THREE PLACES."

Nelly pushed with all her might. This would be the last push, the push that would catapult her new baby into the world and send her, recoiling as if elastic, back into the peaceful cocoon of her own body.

Two medtechs and a nurse sighed, and announced: "A healthy baby boy. Eight pounds, two ounces."

Nelly sank into the bed cushions with her three new babies. Helplessly she looked up at her husband.

Mello looked back at her. In his eyes was the raw hopeless-ness of a man plodding toward the electric chair. Two flabby hub-caps encircled each bleary eye. But he said bravely, "I guess we'll both need DoAlls, huh, honey? Maybe one of those new models that lets you be four places at once."

I literally wrote ALGORITHMS & NASAL STRUCTURES, which appeared in Aboriginal SF, while sitting in a graduate class called Algorithms & Data Structures. In the real Algorithms class, the final project was to build what the professor called "deplaning queues" that popped people on and off lists as they changed their minds about airplane flights. I thought it would be a lot more fun to use animals rather than passengers. I also thought better uses could be made of the programming techniques than boring "deplaning queues."

Algorithms & Nasal Structures

Amy's fingertips slipped to her computer pad, gently caressed velvet, adhered. The nose wire tingled and she relaxed. On the backs of her eyelids, bit-blazed as if to a movie screen, was the most relaxing scene she could conjure. Tufts of soft grass rippled. A white picket fence stretched to a sunny horizon off-lid. Warmth dripped behind her eyes.

If only Amy could force the sheep to bounce right, specifically 82.354 degrees to the right, then -1.43 degrees to the left, then down down, ever so gracefully into the verdant meadow. Then she could count sheep and fall asleep, and for a few hours, her eyes wouldn't burn and the back of her head wouldn't throb.

To pass Professor Shmutz' Algorithms and Nasal Structures, Amy had to force perfectly shaped sheep over the white fence. For the A required of graduate students, her software must spray smell into Shmutz' nose, and when he ran her program against malodorous sheep files, he had to choke from the stench of wet fur.

Stress clenched the back of Amy's head. She would fail, she just knew it.

The phone icon flashed red on the control pad over her desk. Amy ignored it. Probably Mr. Soing, calling to badger her about his restaurant accounts. Was she sure about the depreciation of the flipfloppin' pressurized pancake flinger? Was she sure about that overhead cost, seemed awfully high? Soing was lost forever in the Manual Ages. Heaven help her if he ever learned about accounting software. Balancing his books provided most of her income.

But she wouldn't be strapped for funds and desperate for A's if Frank hadn't dumped her for that Alaskan dental hygienist. Splayed across a dental chair probing a frizzy-haired tart-eyed slut while their three-year-old son suffered from croup... like Jasper's attack last night that required four hours in the emergency room.

Sheep dangled before her eyes. The white picket fence peeled to splintered gray. She had failed Frank: she hadn't been woman enough, hadn't given him what he needed.

Amy sniffled, then forced herself back to the reality of virtual sheep; all stacked and ready for popping. The topmost sheep nibbled her ear and nipped her nose. Amy nudged it off the bit screen of her eyelids. Because she'd written the program in the emergency room during Jasper's croup attack, she'd had no time to test the nasal pointers for Shmutz' God-awful-critical odors.

The first fluffy lamb boinged from the stack and over the fence. Slaphappy grin, legs sucked off by a baby. Soft velvet tickled Amy's fingers. Another lamb boinged, same as the first; goofy face, legs shredded by identical chews. Amy tried to shift the image in her mind, to project the next sheep with whole legs.

But she had no control. Shredded sheep flailed over the fence and flopped into a huge heap. Vainly they struggled to their feet and tried to leap back over the fence.

Amy's brain pushed tight against her skull. She hadn't tested the popping sheep for speed, and the program was due tomorrow night. If her grades slipped below 3.95, she would never find a real job.

The phone icon flared again, this time brighter, more urgent. Who would be calling this late at night? Amy flipped some goats over the fence. They piled into a giant goat heap.

She punched a phone button, screamed "What?" into the speaker.

"I'm comin' home, babe."

The voice was familiar. Dark and cold, swelled from a pit.

Frank? Frank?!

Rancid meat socked her nose. Had the circuits shorted and fried her goats? Maybe luck was with her and the nasal pointers were working. Amy scrolled the code: indirect pointers, amplified by arrays, sprayed into her nose's sensory cells. There was a distinct smell here. Good, maybe Schmutz would be so impressed he'd let her into icss787, Scent Symphonies, where she would code smelly sonatas for pitbulls and moody cats: very useful in today's job market.

"Well, don't say too much now, babe. Plenty of time to catch up tomorrow. I know you're probably wondering why I'm coming home, but you know, Amy, it's...sometimes it's hard for a man to know what's right. I got to missing you and little Casper."

"Our son's name is Jasper, Frank, it's Jasper." Amy jerked her fingers from the velvet pad. Shmutz would hate her code. He was never impressed with Amy, just like Frank had never been impressed.

Amy blinked. Jasper's face was inches from hers. Fat cheeks. Honey eyes. "Mama, get off the pad. I want water. Please." He bobbed his shoulders, it was his way of being cute.

"I have some cash that I made up north. I wanna take care of things. Hey, babe, Amy: you there?"

"Who's that, Mama?"

"Oh, nobody really, just Frank, the Eskimo from hell."

"Yeah, well, I know I've been north for a long time, but I'm here now for you and Casper. You're all I ever wanted, Amy. So...I'll see you tomorrow then. Early, huh?" The phone icon blinked red, then off.

Amy saw red on the walls, on her son's face. Frank had left six months ago, angry because he had lost his job, angry because she had to work, angry at everyone and everything. She should be glad that he was back and ready to be a father, but what did he really want? Was it a husband returning, or just some guy wanting a temporary free ride?

Jasper's honey eyes thickened. "That was Daddy."

Amy snuggled into his hair. It smelled of baby shampoo. Much better than wet sheep fur. "I know, Jasp, that was…" but she couldn't bring herself to say Daddy because she couldn't bear to think that her Jasper had anything in common with something as foul as Frank Laroofe.

Although Amy really didn't want to put away her computer pad, she tucked it into the top desk drawer under a logic prober. Like it or not, that was her life: croup, baby shampoo, and the occasional twisted circuit.

Jasper displayed dimples and gave her enough hugs (one would have been enough) to make her misery worthwhile. She gave him water and tucked him into bed.

Then she stuffed the self pity into a hole and worked all night.

By three a.m., randomly generated sheep leapt like ballerinas over a pearly white fence. Perhaps with excellent editing but minimal nasal, Schmutz would give her an A minus and she could continue with the hypersensory course, mandatory for working anywhere these days. Maybe she could find a job coding smell and taste into Aunt Koo Phung Potato ads. Perhaps if she were really lucky and willing to stoop so low, she could land a high-paying spot coding touch into porno flicks. Then she and Jasper would build a big, beautiful house to live in, maybe a fancy Tinkerhouse from one of those new snap-together kits.

Damn him, what did Frank want after all this time? She didn't know what she'd do when she saw him.

Maybe she'd kill him.

She chunked in some old code of a Fibonacci bit spray, and an impressionist portrait of bluegreen grass and nodding daisies swept to her eyelids. Now to read Shmutz' test sheep file. The file opened easily and regurgitated a sheep in 20-bit by 20-bit chunks. Shmutz was up to his tricks again, trying to "separate the men from the boys," as he liked to say. The sheep chunks wouldn't fit into the mandatory hardcoded sheepstruct or leap though the lambloop. She exploded the chunks and checked for missing animal parts, pulling in library references about sheep anatomy. After adding missing parts and deleting Shmutz-supplied tail tentacles and bobbing bladder balls, she stuffed the animal into the sheepstruct and read another.

This time, she would give Frank so much love that he'd never leave. Maybe this time he wouldn't whine when she needed to work all night. Maybe this time he'd help with the laundry and groceries and cleaning and cooking. Maybe this time she'd be good enough for him.

Or, maybe, just maybe, she would kill him.

Shmutz' second test sheep had a nonstop nosebleed that bled red all over the daisies and white fence. Amy coded a quick fix to plug dripping nostrils. Shmutz' third sheep had dog claws, ticks (very hard to find), black chipped teeth, and disgusting breath. It was already six in the morning. Amy tackled sheep number four with its six snouts and poodle hairdo. Still only in test file one, and Shmutz ran ten files against all submitted programs.

Who cared, really, what Frank wanted? He'd left her for that ice maiden, let him go back to his igloo. The old humiliation welled into a pain fog. Her fingers slipped from the computer pad. Frank had been so happy with his life, so proud as an internet cop. Then Rolando Pie had ruined their lives. Pie had won the lawsuit that finally forced the government to release ancient encryption codes. Security systems had proliferated, become hackproof. Net copping had become a lost profession, Frank a lost man. Self pity brought sweet peace in a bitter world. Amy cried until she despised herself.

By the time Jasper awakened at eight a.m., Amy was tucked in a cloud of code, where life was tangled bliss. Her program parsed and edited sheep perfectly. The indirect pointers, amplified by arrays, sprayed strong sheep odors into her nasal cells. It was almost fun to shoot ions across cell membranes and fire frequency-coded impulses into her nose's sensory nerves.

She rode the subway to nursery school with Jasper. He asked endless questions — How do the wheels turn? Why is everything a blur outside the windows? Do you love me, Mama? — and Amy mumbled, "Uh huh" over and over, wondering if Jasper would become a lost man like his father.

She walked the five miles to Soing's restaurant. Barely noticed the landmarks: shuttered buildings pocked by despair, shuttered eyes of old drunks, faces as worn and pocked as the buildings that propped their backs. Her eyes burned. Everywhere the haze of hot, gray air: like walking through static. She dropped off Soing's monthly accounting statements. As usual, he refused to pay her, this time because he wasn't sure she had tallied the depreciations correctly.

Vaguely, she was aware that she wasn't arguing with him, that she wasn't despising him for his luxury life. She wasn't wishing, as usual, that her hands would rise to his shriveled sweaty throat and push, push until thumb met bone and the little chicken neck would break. She could hear it — snap snap ping!

But as it was, she just bobbed her head and sighed, for she knew that there was no work in town and she was lucky to have Soing. She left for the long waik home. Like a field of nodding daisies, drunken heads nodded everywhere: from benches, storefronts, garbage-choked curbs. Amy pressed her fingers to the apartment lockpad, and the latch clicked, the door swung open. Inside, street glare shimmied up the walls and spiked the ceiling. Fuzzy neon caterpillars slinked to end tables, were squelched by shadow.

And from the shadow, something large loomed. It laughed.

It pressed the wall console. Overhead lights streamed white and obliterated the spikes and neon caterpillars.

Amy screamed.

Wrinkle masses writhed in the dark blotches under his eyes; eyes that penetrated both clothes and soul in one fast sweep. Filthy fingers clutched her computer pad. "Still up to your old tricks, eh, babe? Programs, programs, programs. What's it now? Chaos code for math sims of dripping faucets? Fractal implants to regenerate lost limbs? You always were the busy little wife, weren't you? Tap tap tapping away on this damn pad while I struggled, worked my butt off, cleaning sewers, draining sludge, anything to earn a buck."

Amy steeled herself. This was the man she had loved. He would never physically hurt her. He was a blowhard, a lost internet cop, a pussycat under macho veneer. Had she been a better wife when Rolando Pie destroyed him, maybe Frank wouldn't be so bitter. Besides, in Frank's grimy paw was the key to her life, the computer pad that contained the smelly sheep. "Give me the pad, Frank. You're holding a lifetime of nasal research."

He whipped the pad behind his back. "Don't need it anymore, Amy babe. I made enough money for all of us. Aren't you going to ask how?"

Dental hygienist, black heart beating under white uniform. Unemployed netcop, heart frittering under ditchdigger's dungaries. She eyed the computer pad. She felt sorry for him, sorry for herself. "Okay, Frank, you win. Tell me how you earned all this money."

"Outposts in the Arctic, Amy, deep into Siberia. Yeah, I went to Siberia, just for you and Casper. They have big research facilities there. I spent months digging permafrost with chain gangs. Nobody else to do it. They paid me a fortune."

Hope glimmered somewhere in the knot that clenched her chest. Jasper's father was back, he talked like the old blowhard Frank. "What about the dental slut, Frank?"

He swept away the slut with a fling of his hand. The computer pad with the perfect sheep code crashed against the wall.

Amy lunged at him, slapped the blotched cheeks until her palms stung. That was it, she would kill him! He grasped her wrists in one fist and forced her to the desk chair. She thrust her teeth into his arm. He leapt back, released her. "God, Amy, what'd I do to deserve that?!"

"My program, Frank, my life...Shmutz...it's not Casper, it's Jasper..."

The pad was a fuzzy dead animal heaped by the wall. Frank plucked it up and offered it to her. "I didn't mean to break it, Amy, honest. I want to get a Tinkerhouse, we'll all live in it together. I want you to stay home this time, stop with the hammering on the computer pads, just stop and be content. I want to be with you and the boy, the way things used to be." The eyes pulled at her clothes again, tugged at her soul.

You and the boy, you and the boy. The way things used to be. It was too much, just too damn much. She sent Frank on his way, told him she'd think about it.

Then she collapsed into bed with the pad, caressed it, tried to conjure images. Perhaps, given time, she could fix it.

But she couldn't fix the code, and by the time she hauled off to the subway to retrieve Jasper, she'd tried everything: adaptive neuron filters that responded to changing odors, cognitive formulations that interpolated solutions and required minimal testing. She had emailed Shmutz for an extension. Shmutz had given her until noon tomorrow, and regardless of her results, he would reduce her grade by five points. She would need a nearly perfect score to continue her studies.

That night, Frank helped Jasper with his math homework. "A tangent is opposite over adjacent, Jasp. Then you flip it and get cotangent." Amy peeked from the bedroom and saw her two men in harsh white light. Frank's thick filthy fingers gentle in Jasper's honey sweet hair. Jasper's eyes wide, drenched in adoration for this man, this internet cop who'd saved countless bucks for the government but who couldn't seem to save himself.

She lost herself in work, breaking only to tuck Jasper into bed and see Frank off. "See you tomorrow, Amy, you and the boy. I told you this would work out. Just quit with the coding, and maybe everything will be all right this time." He squeezed her hand. It terrified her that anyone could have such thick, wide nails.

At midnight, the phone icon flashed red and she ignored it.

Then again at two a.m., and again at four. She ignored the urgent flashes and concentrated on Shmutz' program.

She played with the air streams floating over the sensory cells in her nasal conch. She slowed the timing of the loop that controlled air flow to a near halt. With a bottle of perfume under her nose, she ran the sheep program. Only a tiny eddy of scent reached her inner nose. She slowed the loop some more, ran the code again, and this time, her sensory cells remained clear of perfume.

To intensify odors emanating from the sheep program, she quadrupled the indirect pointers spawned to each sensory cell: and she enlarged the olfactory arrays that stimulated nerve endings belonging to the fifth brain nerve.

Knowing the high sensitivity of the nerve endings to strong scents, Amy plunged her nose into the small air space of the perfume bottle and ran the code. The sheep from Shmutz' test file leapt gracefully over the white fence and off the bit screen of her eyes. There was no perfume smell. The filthy fur reeked with a sourness that turned her stomach. Shmutz would vomit. She would earn her A.

She felt so good she decided to give Shmutz a little bonus. A quick switch on the command image (sheep -p) would allow Shmutz to smell perfumed fur, an option he'd probably appreciate after running his malodorous sheep test files. She snatched benzenoid aromatics from departmental libraries and hardcoded her pointers and arrays to amplify the perfume.

Frank showed up early, offered to take Jasper to nursery school so Amy could get some sleep and then turn her program into Shmutz. He was trying so hard, and it hurt her to see him suffering. He had once been so charming, so proud of her accomplishments: what had changed all that?

"Did you call last night?"

He nodded, almost ashamed. "You can code if you want, Amy, just let me come back. There's nowhere else I belong."

So Frank had called her desperately all night while she worked. Maybe he had finally realized that programming was their financial security, her emotional peace. Maybe he had finally softened and could live with his bruised male pride. Besides, if he left again, she would still have the code. And if he stayed, she could give the big kiss-off to Mr. Soing.

She slept, and when Frank returned from the subway, she remembered all the hollow men slumped by hollow buildings, lost men with shuttered eyes. Frank's eyes glowed with the need to move on and recover life. His slump was over.

Amy reached for the perfume bottle on the desk. She waved the aromatic compound under Frank's nose and flirtatiously dabbed a little on her neck and down her shirt. "Smells like oil rigs in here," he said, "sexy oil rigs." She wanted to tell him it was a light touch of benzene, as if he cared, but he was too eager for flipfloppin' and pressurized flinging.

And then they lay on cool sheets and stared at the ceiling, where jutting brown stains clung like dead phallic symbols. Frank said: "They look like chains up there, huh, Amy? Long, long chains that never end."

She closed her eyes and pretended the perfume was daisies. Fragrant sheep boinged over a fence into a fluff of nodding, drunken daisies.

"I don't really have all that much money from the Siberian gig. I have enough to get by a few months. But I'll find something. After all, it's not like I haven't dug ditches or cleaned plates before."

It didn't matter. He was back. Amy understood Frank's insecurities. And any income would cool her desire to murder Mr. Soing. She leaned across the sheets and grabbed the computer pad from the desk. "Run the sheep program, Frank. I think it's a winner. See if it puts you to sleep. Think of the word, sheep. That's all you have to do."

Frank hesitated. He'd never been comfortable with what he called her computer gizmos. But then he poked the wire into his nose, slipped his fingers to the pad, and shut his eyes.

Her heart swelled, ready for Frank's reaction.

It was instant.

Algorithms & Nasal Structures

His body convulsed. He gasped for breath. Eyes rolled in their sockets, blood frothed from swollen lips. Under his eyes, the wrinkle masses were bright red, pulsing with the urgency of a phone icon.

Amy smacked his hand from the computer pad. She slammed her own at phone buttons.

A shrieking of livecop sirens. Screech of wheels out front.

What would this do to Frank, to be saved by livecops, the men who had outmachoed him for the few jobs open to terminated netcops?

They slapped an oxygen mask to his face, rolled him to a stretcher, then checked his pulse as they carried him from the apartment.

"Who was he? How did this happen?" someone asked. It was a man, taller than Frank, with more muscles, more hardness to his eyes.

She must have messed up the switch, coding the sheep -p for a normal malodorous run and the plain sheep command for the perfumed run. Had she tested the -p option, she would have known that it triggered far too much benzene into the nose. How could she have been so sloppy? If Shmutz had taught Amy anything, it was to test her algorithms and nasal structures.

She could just picture Frank's enlarged olfactory arrays stimulating the oversensitive nerve endings of his fifth brain nerve. The benzene-laced perfume of wildflowers seeping in from the hardcoded bit sprays, drenching his nerve endings with deadly amounts of scent.

Had she killed him?

The livecop wouldn't understand, he wouldn't appreciate her need to be with Frank. Very simply she said: "He was Frank La-Roofe."

The livecop looked at her, puzzled. Metal cuffs clanged against the steel bat dangling at his side. "You'll have to give me a little more than that, miss."

If Frank were lucky, he'd somehow avoid a heart attack or paralysis. Frank would make it, he would not be a lost man. She would not be his killer because Jasper did not need a lost mother. "Frank is the father of my son. I guess you could say he's my husband."

"Okay, Mrs. Laroofe, do you have any idea what happened to your husband?"

"We were, you know...damn, can't you make this easier on me? We were rekindling old passions, okay? Frank has some sort of heart condition. He's been working in the Arctic, digging permafrost, killing himself to earn money for us. He's a good man. He was a netcop."

She knew that would do the trick. Livecops and netcops were brothers. The man backed off, actually tried to comfort her, offered to help.

Then she found herself alone in the apartment. Snakecharmed squiggles of daytime street glare shimmied up the walls. Fuzzy neon caterpillars slinked to end tables. And from the shadows, something large loomed. It laughed.

It was Frank. Poor Frank, who was willing to dig ditches and wash dishes for her. Frank, who had lost the meaning of life and desperately needed her to find it for him. He was so weak, and she was so alone.

And talk about a serious software bug...

She fixed the command image code so sheep -p triggered the fatal dose of perfumed aromatic compound. Then she emailed the sheep program to Shmutz with a lengthy description of the -p option.

Two weeks later, her report card came: an A in Algorithms and Nasal Structures.

Six weeks later, Frank was released from the hospital after successful heart surgery.

Six months later, while Amy was struggling with smelly sonatas for pitbulls and moody cats, Shmutz sent her email: The Department of Defense wanted to purchase the rights to Amy's breakthrough killer software. DOD liked the idea of quick, nontraceable death.

Six months after that, when Amy received a fat DOD check, she bought Mr. Soing a three-buck computer loaded with ten-cent accounting.

And in the end, Frank dallied with a doughnut vendor who promised ecstasy with a stale product. And Amy threw him out.

For he was weak, and she was stronger alone.

This story, printed for the first time here, gives new meaning to the old question: can a girl ever be too thin or too rich? If you're obsessed with your looks and material possessions, all I can say is: be careful to stay clear of the DEBUTANTE BALL.

Debutante Ball

The muscles peel away from my thigh so easily. First the hamstrings. Now lower to the gastrocnemius and the achilles tendon.

I don't want to wait. I can't bear to wait. I want to rip the muscles from my bone, and I want to graduate *now*.

I'm crying. I feel the hot tears splash from my chin, sop into the polycots strapped across my breasts. On the wall, a hologram man peels the skin from an orange. Citrus drops splash into his heavy beard.

How can I stop this *burning*, burning hunger?

Smooth tissue binds my muscles like bladder sacs. *Deliciously thin* smooth tissue that keeps the infection in my muscles. Microbes suck like fleas.

I cannot scratch. I cannot cool the itch. My nails are bound in spongecaps.

I turn to the girl next to me. From California High, she told me when we first came to finishing school; she graduates this year, just like me. Her name's Hanna. Her mother's a physicist.

Now, Hanna tells me nothing. She's slumped in a seethomatic chair, head bobbing rhythmically to eye flutters. Drooling. Muscles stripped back from her arms and legs.

God, how does Hanna do it?

She's gorgeous. I can only admire her

...*self control*...

...*self denial*...

the things I so sorely lack.

From behind my chair, I hear Miss Myra clicking buttons and flipping switches on my seethomatic, and now the chair whines and grinds its way several feet toward the soundproof ceiling.

My muscles hang in midair, suspended beneath me like knickers pulled down. The hydraulic needles pump pleasure packets into my veins. Giggles surge like bubbles through my blood, hit my brain center, explode. The room spins in music, a tide of Tchaikovsky riding rainbow waves.

Below me is Miss Myra's chic little head. Bald. Cheeks like rib bones. Nose bashed in; hissing air in and out of twin nostrils pounded flat as if from sledgehammers. "Venus will be here soon. You'll want to look your best." Even her voice is a wisp.

Venus: winner of the Global Beauty Fair; winner of nine husbands. A smart woman. She has an empire of finishing schools, more money than most countries.

Hanna twitches. Her head snaps back and forth. Miss Myra adjusts her acetylcholine valves for maximum download. Hanna's muscles tighten, expand; flop like fish on the ceramic floor.

"Hanna's dropped thirty pounds this semester. Don't you think she's lovely, Jaspin?"

Charcoal stick thin, burning coal eyes, all extra muscles removed: fourteen from the face, half from the calf, everything but the most meager amounts from her buttocks; all told, a quarter of her body weight eliminated.

I want, I need, to be

like Hanna.

Epitomy of womanhood, of powerful femininity. Control the body. Control the urge.

Blood. Chemicals. Nostrils hissing. Fish flopping. Brain pounding. My eyes see neon sun. The pain burns down my legs, through my heart, across my mind.

Miss Myra's face is cracked Picasso. Her peephole mouth stretches slightly into an ellipse. "Time to do your arms, Jaspin, if you want to impress Venus and the boys at the Debutante Ball."

To be so beautiful. To look like Venus. To make so many men weep.

I tremble at the thought.

Miss Myra twists the valves on my chair. She swings the acetylcholine cylinders over my head, lets the helmet descend.

And now I'm in skinhide that cools my brain, dulls the Renoir blurs and Picasso splits. The room is clearing. Miss Myra squats on femur stumps, for she has neither feet nor fibula. Her asparagus sheath casts a mellow green glow across the razors of her cheekbones and into the hollows that once were breasts.

Roaches crawl up the wall to the painting of Venus with President Carl. I see blood in the eyes of Carl, in the eyes of all men. But there are no men in the room.

"I'm confused, Miss Myra, afraid."

"Your mother came to Venus. Won your father at *her* Debutante Ball. Your grandmother was first in her class. Both were beauties. Both won powerful men. You're a lucky girl."

Lucky girl: my father always tells me that. My bones are icicles. My heart flutters with bat wings. Like Mama and Grandma, I will die young.

But first I will live the good life.

"Strip me, Miss Myra; strip me nice and clean."

Miss Myra's lips squash to a flattened ellipse; her biggest smile. "Your mother would be so proud, Jaspin."

The rip of gluteus medius. The suck of fiber from hamstring. The bite of invading infection.

I look at Hanna. She wants to marry a Big Man, a Man of Substance, a Man of Money.

But I want that, too, and when we compete tonight at the graduation ceremony, at the Debutante Ball, I will win the Biggest Man.

...the Biggest Man...

...the biggest

man.

"Once we smoked. Once we starved. We were anorexic, bulemic; we had endless plastic surgery. Now we strip weight directly. What could be more natural?" The hot honey voice of Venus slinks through the fuzz filling my head like cotton. She continues: "And remember, not all girls can do it. Only girls with ambition, brains, and fortitude. Girls with proper breeding."

We must be at graduation already. How time has passed.

My shoulder aches. My thighs, arms, face. I cannot speak.

The room buzzes with subterranean male growls and frothy female laughter.

Venus is nude. Her deltoid muscles sway under her armpits; muscle fibers fringed with lace, twined with silken flowers. Her legs are tree saplings; she sways and clutches Miss Myra for support.

Venus is so God-awful gorgeous.

Hanna and I and the others — the twenty most wealthy girls in the country — are strapped to our thrones. Fluttering over my eyes are flower petals; pink and delicate, fragrant with sunshine and joy.

Cold hunger burns in the pit of my stomach.

I scan the room for Daddy. The mothers, what remains of them, totter on minichairs up front. Behind them are the Daddies. Each man on a separate pew. Two pews per row.

There he is, my Man of Substance. He gestures at me, flashes his perfect white teeth; the smile, a crescent moon. Daddy, who graduated from the Fast Track, who endured far more than I ever could, who won Mama at *her* graduation Ball eighteen years ago. Daddy is the Biggest Man in the room.

Again, I feel the tears springing then ebbing, the surging of hunger and desperation in my soul.

I'm confused, Miss Myra, afraid.

But Miss Myra does not answer.

She and Venus are pulling the heavy chains that lift the steel doublewide door from the floor. And now the boys clatter down the metal ramps in their wide wheelpews.

Hanna's noseholes hiss. I grip the arms of my thronechair. The thin fibrous sheaths over my finger bones sweat. These boys are gorgeous; each larger than the last.

Ted Forthwith, heir to the Mascara fortune; God,he must weigh several hundred pounds, at least. And Charles Craswald, prince of the Vanorb Satellite Dish Collection — a sight to make any young girl swoon! — brontosaurus haunches, cheeks bulging like pregnant cats. And my favorite, the boy who's had my heart since kindergarten, Danny Trent-Fritz. Now here's a boy who will never have to work. He oozes money, he sweats it. You can see it in his eyes: fish mucus filmed eyes of watery blue, throbbing with the dull nothingness of no knowledge.

Hanna hisses. She wants him. She wants my Danny.

Venus gurgles by the steel door. Her peephole mouth painted pink, frothing with delicate bubbles. "Now, girls, we're not going to fight over these boys. We're going to let them choose.

Danny burbles before me. Fish eyes swim over my naked, stripped loins.

His Bass Brothers navy suit is sopped with sweat. His fingers, each the size of my neck, tremble and now rise; like yeast roiling on the wheelpew wood.

Ooh, Danny will die so young.

We will bear children to inherit our fortunes, and then we will die gracefully, like rich people must.

Twenty of us will marry the Big Boys. Twenty of us will breed little girls of power.

Debutante Ball

Venus smells of lilacs and morning mist. She hovers over me like a stray petal fluttering on a branch. "This, Mr. Trent-Fritz, is the lovely Miss Jaspin Cortes, heiress to the Soy Patties Corporation, which feeds the masses. First in her class in bioengineering theology. Her mother a doctor. Her grandmother, President of Lloyd's Bank."

My head wobbles a greeting. I know that the dizziness will pass.

Venus says, "Jaspin is a young girl who knows the meaning of work: self control and self denial."

I want Danny's children. I want his wealth and power. I want the freedom to create, to control, to dominate.

And what does Danny want? Does he even know?

He blubbers something.

Miss Myra's lips squash to a flattened ellipse. I see blood in the eyes of Danny. "He will not live long," says Miss Myra.

Nineteen girls cackle. Only I remain silent, for I have the strongest self control.

I am beautiful. I am as lovely as Venus.

And I have won my first husband.

The Biggest Man. The man who will die first.

In my twenties, I had two back operations. Although both saved me from excruciating non-stop pain and paralysis, I limped for several years and often fell down from jolts of pain that sporadically hit my back and legs. SMOKESTACK SNOUT NEUROLOGY, printed here for the first time, is based on a real visit to a neural doctor (not my saintly back surgeon), who shall remain nameless. This neural fiend wheeled a cart of hypos into the exam room, put me on a table, and hitched my skirt up to my waist. He then leered at me as he contemplated stabbing me with hundreds of needles. He wanted to find my pain points, he said. Steam rose from the cart, he lifted what looked like a horse tranquilizer needle, and I shrieked holy-terror-bloody-hell. The nameless neural fiend became Wedo, the alien female Feeen of SMOKESTACK SNOUT NEUROLOGY.

Smokestack Snout Neurology

Fingersnakes flopped between the wet wool coats. Wedo squealed, and steam shot from her smokestack snout. The coats gripped me like straitjackets. If only I could move my muscles, punch Wedo's snout, fling myself from the closet.

Three giant hands grasped my shoulders and a fourth clenched my breast. Fingersnakes slithered down my back and left a slimy trail.

Wedo belched through the steam. "Relax, Babe, it won't hurt much. It'll be a lot better than the physical hell you live in now."

Let a snout head probe me? Never! I wanted to scream and beat her goggle eyes into her bloated head, but I couldn't even twitch my tongue or flick a finger.

She dragged me across the office past the potted plum plant and dangling suckpen. Leathery toadstool palms pressed me to a chair.

"Where do you keep the drugs?"

I said something like "Mmmmph."

Wedo grunted and flipped to her hands. Toesnakes rummaged through my drawers, and vials cracked against the desk.

Why did Wedo want to torture me with needles? What was it to *her* if neural diseases clenched my muscles?

If only George were here to tell me what to do, to save me from the JOLT; but my pansy boyfriend had dumped me two years ago when I was nineteen and the seizures hit. George had loved the leers I received from other guys, but that's about all he had loved about me.

And now I was at the mercy of a disgusting Feeen who'd been coming onto me for months. A male Feeen would have been bad enough — I'd never even gone all the way with George — but this was just too much: for all I knew, twenty little Feeenlets were sucking milk in the breeding pouches that flapped under Wedo's chins.

I'd do anything to get out of here, anything...

Brown jelly oozed from Wedo's snout and dribbled down my chest. She bobbed on her bulbous body, accidentally twisted a tendril in suckpen wires and jerked free. "Let me use the JOLT-45 on you, it'll relieve *all* your pain. I *swear* it won't hurt. You *know* how I feel about you."

Sure, I knew how she felt about me, and I'd rather die as a frozen unloved zombie than let those slimy fingersnakes caress my flesh or that snout suck my mouth. *Aah, for the tingle of rough hands and gruff lips...* but even if men didn't want me anymore, there was no way I'd stoop so low as to make it with Wedo, a sickening Feeen who smelled like hot chaingang slaves.

Now she gripped my cheeks with greasy palm suckers and it took everything in me not to vomit. Tears burned a path through the brown goo dribbling between my breasts. Slime pooled in my bra.

Her fingersnakes pried apart my jaws. "Lucky I found you here, Lena, what with everyone gone for the weekend. We're alone with the JOLT. Perfect time for surgery."

But she was a janitor, she didn't know how to operate the JOLT-45 needle machine. Shrieks of Dr. Hetzel's patients reverberated against my skull.

Smokestack Snout Neurology

As if reading my mind, Wedo said, "I've been watching Dr. Hetzel operate the JOLT and I've been studying. You know, Lena, they put the finest Feeen neuroslabs in my brain before they sent me here; they don't let stupid Feeens on Earth. You have nothing to worry about."

She crammed pills through my clenched teeth. Then I lay limp in her tangled limbs and watched letters leap from my suckpen and spin round the room.

Warmth seeped to my toes and spread honey through my head. I wiggled my fingers and clenched the desk to steady the hand tremors.

Wedo mumbled equations about muscle movement and brain neurotransmitters. She leaned closer, goggle eyes whirling in eye stalks. On her smokestack snout, warts grew like brussel sprouts. I was watching the warts sweat when abruptly she belched brown filth and withdrew, and then her toadstool feet splattered into the hall.

I trembled on the desk, my dress crumpled around my waist. She was going for the JOLT, I just knew it, and soon she would plunge fifty needles into my nerves, seeking precise pain points before skewering hot metal to my spine.

I'd heard Dr. Hetzel's heartwarming speech many times: *Synapses, we burn a few, we free a few: we force your brain to balance chemicals like dopamine and acetylcholine; vasopressin; noradrenaline. We kill free radicals that destroy your neurons, we stimulate receptors that bond to the chemicals your brain needs.* It all sounded very scientific and reassuring, but as Hetzel's administrative assistant, I'd heard the screeches and seen the dazed patients looped like corpses over the shoulders of relatives.

And God help me, what if the slobbering sicko had other things in mind? The way she always panted and belched as I lurched down Hetzel's halls...the way those dripping fingersnake tips always managed to tweak my butt...

I squirmed toward the side of the desk, knocked a stack of Hetzel's memos to the floor. Just a few more inches and I would fling myself off the edge.

Fingers tingling. Nails spiking soft wood.

Knuckles white.

I drove myself forward, and my thighs slithered over the piles of Hetzel's insanity reports.

And then my nails cracked and I collapsed; and a paperclip jabbed my nose.

Overhead fluorescent lights rained fire.

Wheels squeaked and feet splattered, and then Wedo's snout quivered over me with the passion of a prisoner about to see sun for the first time in ten years.

JOLT wheels glimmered with Feeen goo. Wedo thwacked the machine, and it skidded through slime and crashed to the desk.

And there they were, hundreds of needles of different sizes and lengths; some a foot long, some thicker than my thumb. And I a block of ice, immovable and pinned to the desk by subzero fingersnakes.

"What a magnificent machine," effused Wedo, and she stroked the JOLT with her snout.

A switch clicked, and then a chainsaw buzz whirled freckles around the room and hellish hurricanes filled my head. The desk vibrated like a 50-cent Magic Fingers ride gone wild. From the JOLT shot a geyser of oily black bubbles, and fingersnakes massaged the muck into my naked butt and legs.

Wedo belched. "I love you, Lena."

I pretended it was George standing over me, rubbing the grease in long languishing loops, cooing in my ear while I nearly fainted from fear and desire.

And then a fingersnake rose, its little tip twitching, hairy bumps throbbing, and coiled in its curl was a phillips head screwdriver, and from the top of the screwdriver squirted a foamy phlegm. My cheek lay in drool.

If only the drugs had cured me — the Amantadine, Cogentin, Pagitane, Kemadrin; the Phenoxene and Disipal; the Parlodel and Sinemet and Permax, the Lisuride and Jumex. God knows I'd tried everything short of electroshock and tissue implants. And though the JOLT helped some patients, it reduced most to mush mind.

Wedo's snakes slithered up my back and coiled around my neck.

What was she going to do: save me, rape me, *what*? I wanted to scream, *Just get it over with, just do it, for God sakes, just do it!*; but as usual, my mouth remained clenched, and the words flung themselves against the bars of my teeth like inmates desperate to flee.

The screwdriver sprouted a needle, then leapt in a snakefist and plunged and speared my spine. Rusty saws grated bone, daggers ripped me bloody raw, scorched iron branded me with Wedo's mark; and everywhere, steam of sweat and sizzled flesh. I sank somewhere into a soul crevice, and soon the battering of· needles faded to the battering of a hard rain on a winter windowsill.

Through black mist, ecstasy filmed Wedo's goggle eyes.

And then she was done, and she slumped against the wall, muttering about glial cells and subcortical grey matters.

And a bit later, I was gelatin across her shoulder and the subway signs were fireworks before my eyes. People staring, muttering, shoving their children behind them.

Wedo thrust my key into the apartment lock and her toadstool feet suctioned the door and rammed it open. My blood mingled with slime and splotched the rug red; tiny pools of misery on crewcut carpet.

She dumped me on the sofa. Dark paisleys exploded to hot pins and the fragments flew, and from toe to ear, my nerves screamed.

A normal woman would have killed rather than be violated by a female Feeen. A normal woman wouldn't tingle from the touch of snout. A normal woman wouldn't tremble as flabby breeding pouches flopped across her face.

In the kitchenette, silverware clanged and glasses clattered.

Then Wedo belching brown, the steam rising in wisps that licked the ceiling. Pill goulash shoved between my parched lips;

Wedo babbling about improved neural pathways and integrated brain circuits.

Fingersnakes coiling into my hair, massaging my temples.

She said, "I'm sorry I attacked you like that, Lena; I hope it wasn't too horrible. I only wanted to save you from disease, to free you from pain. But seeing you on the desk, helpless like that — well, I guess I just lost control and couldn't help myself. I've loved you for so long."

Then from Wedo's snout a wonderful scent: mist of wildflowers and pine. I slipped into goggle eye swirls, threw back my head, let the warmth dissolve pain. A moist blanket of air pulsed and bulged, pillowed into ribbon tiers. Wedo's words were lyrics, her notes bounced and skittered on wet ribbons.

She chuckled. She told me I was calculating derivatives, "the speed and pulse of Feeen rhythm." She had tuned my synapses, she said, to match the pitch and frequencies of the finest Feeen neuroslabs.

And it felt so good to feel the warm rainbows massaging my shoulders. It didn't really matter what a normal woman would do; I hadn't been normal for a long time. My nostrils swelled with the nectar of succulent snout breath. A breeding pouch dangled. I sucked its salt and swooned. Wedo was my savior: she'd melted my frozen limbs, freed me from the jail of my own body.

I stopped, and I stared at the belching snout. It quivered by my lips.

Feeen synapses surging through my brain? Snout sucking my mouth? *What the hell had become of me?*

The JOLT recovery was long and painful, and I lost my job. But Wedo visited daily; and as time passed, I found myself longing for the tingle of fingersnakes and snout sucks. Wedo was tender and gentle, her words music, and her fragrance changed with my moods: first wildflowers, then forests, then crushed roses. She danced on air pillows, flipped her fingersnakes from one ribbon to another. And around her was an aura of sun-dappled sea and rainbow-rippled sky.

It was the Feeen rhythm pounding my synapses, she explained, the impulses filling my occipital and parietal lobes, controlling all I saw, heard, smelled, and tasted. And it was true: even the fluttering of a curtain was a cluster of mathematically precise movements; and my mind automatically calculated the velocity of blinking eyes, the energy fluctuation of flickering lights, gas densities and the gradation of skunk odor, the taste of fear.

I adored Wedo, but still there was something about her that made my stomach wrench and my head spin. Maybe it was the way the toadstools splattered across my rug. Or maybe it was the way she shaved the bristles off her breeding pouches. She disgusted me, made me sick, made me long for George and his inept pawing.

And then George heard about my new lover and visited. I prayed that he would immediately steal me back, but instead, his jealousy and condescension hung like old smelly drapes — he had come to laugh. When his breath tickled my ear, fumes furled from broken tombs. I shoved him off; he jeered. I told him to go back to his bouncing-boobed bimbos; he grabbed my breasts and pulled me halfway cross the room, and I smacked him, hard; and he smarted for a minute, then shrugged and swaggered, then finally slammed the door and left.

What had I ever seen in George?

He was nothing but a memory stubble.

Wedo's snakes held me close and I cried. She loved me, George did not. She was my medical savior, *she was my hot Feeen stud.*

I worked with her at the janitor's job, and we sneaked into Hetzel's office late at night and caressed our love machine, the JOLT-45. I felt safe with Wedo...

...and still I dreamed of the day that George would rescue me. Oh, to strap George to my old desk and jolt him until he, too, was half-Feeen; think of the fling I could have with a human male charged with Feeen impulses.

When I told Wedo about my fantasy, she was outraged: her anger vibrated from walls, fractured air, sent brown steam skittering into memos about imbeciles and Jesus incarnates.

I wanted a human lover, a guy; not an alien female Feeen.

Wedo grew rigid.

She paralyzed time.

She shuddered and sank into the silken folds of moonlight that stroked the walls. She told me that she'd been very lonely on Earth, that few Feeens came to Earth because they couldn't bear human hatred and discrimination.

"Why did you come then?" I asked.

"I was idealistic: I thought I could make the humans love me." Here she billowed smoke and hugged herself close to the JOLT. The needles stood straight like little soldiers.

Dear Wedo; she had saved me from seizures and pills and the violence of frozen limbs suddenly thrashing. What had George ever done other than ogle, slurp, and hurt me?

Wedo's snout nuzzled my neck. I smelled clouds and rain, apples squeezed to cider; twigs crackled and leaves crunched: and somewhere in the distance, dogs yapped.

I said: "I want to jolt George. He'll be my dartboard, the needles will pierce his ears, his eyes: his soul."

Goggle eyes misted. Fingersnake tips trembled. Bulbous body convulsed.

I flipped the ON switch, cried: "*Let's do George!*"

"*No!*" Ten snakes pounded the JOLT. Soldier needles rattled and clanked.

"Then I'll do him myself," I said.

"No." A whimper. Wedo splayed herself across the JOLT needles. As my head was filling with chainsaw buzz, she squirted the phillips head, and I massaged foamy phlegm and black bubbles into the slimy snakes of my lover.

High on each other's love, we slithered to George's apartment, a grimy hole where he slept on greasy sheets in greasy dreams. I cooed in his ear, whispered endearments, and he shifted in slits of moonlight and rolled to a pile of yellowed magazines emblazoned with tarnished girls.

By the broken door, Wedo grunted in a pool of slime, then she slopped outside and trailed us to Hetzel's office. And all the way, George fondled me and I promised empyrean with the JOLT god. I would do for him what Wedo had done for me; our bodies would pulse with current, our veins would scream, the electric nets twining us would explode with passion.

Then we were before the JOLT, and it did gleam like god, and the needles were angels awaiting prey. Using suckpen cord, I strapped George to my old desk. He begged for a kiss, and though I staggered from his fumes, I let my trembling lips graze his gruff ones. His sigh was decay.

Wedo whined and flipped forward. Slime splattered. Goo splashed across the stubble of George's cheeks. George screamed, his sleepy eyes went wild; his body clenched and stiffened, he was a wild beast in terror.

And through brown steam shot oily black geysers and phlegm. And I was lost somewhere in the deepest soul crevices where only memory shadows lurk, and with me was George: taunting, leering, jeering. I don't know what was driving me, maybe it was the old humiliation or the strange Feeen synapses or possibly just the power of the moment; but my fists sledgehammered those needles into George; and I pounded them into his bloody pulp until I skewered his corpse to the desk.

Beneath him, Hetzel's memos were red paste.

Wedo's goggle eyes spun. Fingersnakes wilted. "What did he do that you had to kill him? I cured you, wasn't that enough?"

My synapses were unraveling like threads from a shirt, my nerves were clawing my skin for release. Memories gurgled up and pricked like cacti. I collapsed, more rigid than George.

Wedo's toadstool feet splattered into the hall.

And I couldn't move, neither to twitch my tongue nor flick a finger.

Silken moonlight draped the JOLT. And then sky melted to morning, and eventually the JOLT sputtered and died.

They lifted me from the cradle of George's pulp. The stretcher brought my wooden body to a glowing white car, red letters sizzled on the side.

They said it was a seizure induced by advanced neural disease; and against my will, they tried electric shocks and fetal transplants.

But nothing worked.

Now I sit in a grimy hole on greasy sheets, living only in my greasy dreams. My corner is so dark that dealers and pimps don't tread here. And my soul is filled with graveyard dirt.

I suppose that Wedo returned to Feeen, stripped of idealism and vision; content with her own kind.

As for me, I still ache for the touch of snout and the slither of fingersnakes: I long to paralyze time and release my frozen limbs, to be half-Feeen again and float off where twigs crackle and leaves crunch, where the ashes of crushed roses dance on silken strands of moon.

This story, printed for the first time here, envisions a world where witches and multiple religions collide in most unexpected ways.

The Battle of BatBrew Bulge

Harriet BatBrew Bulge filed her claws on the cemetery wall. Just let Dogface come closer, let her dare. Harriet would scratch out her eyes.

She crouched on a fungus mound and peeked through a crack in the wall. Everywhere, crosses were overturned, and lepers were lurching with rattles. Children were running and screaming, and deformed beggars twitched in the mud. And Tomas de Torquemada was in the midst of it all, flailing his arms and hollering about the Last Judgment, Hell, and Bloody Passion.

Harriet cackled. No doubt about it, Dogface was *good*.

The rest of the coven, all seven of them, huddled around Delilah Dogface Crone. Harriet's best friend, Snagglechin, congratulated the hag.

Blood dribbled from Dogface's eyes. "Oh, girls, you're just too kind. I was only doing my job."

Snagglechin fondled her whiskers, then cast a swollen eye at Harriet. "I say the coven vote for Dogface as Grand Witch."

"What?! I've been Grand Witch for two centuries, since the 1200's, I've been Grand Witch. *I'm* Grand Witch, only me, nobody else!" Harriet leapt from the fungus, beat Snagglechin to the ground, and stomped on her face. Then she grabbed Dogface's beard.

Dogface's eyes were fireballs, and her nostrils flared, dark and damp as caves. Her breath smelled like recently devoured lizard mash. She said, "Face it, BatBrew baby, your time has come and gone. Your spells suck. You can't even cast them right anymore."

It wasn't true. Harriet's spells were always hideous and perfect, cast with precision, dynamite on impact. She said, "Evil dolphins and sinuous death, capture — rapture — capture — "

What was it? Capture or rapture?

The coven screeched with laughter, and Dogface pointed at her: "rapture rapture capture snapture flapture — *trash her!*"

"No!" Harriet wrenched Dogface's beard until her green skin pores prickled with blood. Her other hand wrapped around Dogface's neck. A neck like tree bark. "We'll fight for it, Dogface, and may the worst witch win."

"Fight for it? Ha, *you* have no chance." Dogface muttered a spell, child's work really, something like,

"Eeny meeny miney mo,

Spiders, newts, and beak of crow."

But the words hit Harriet with a blast, and her toeless feet flew into the air and her body shot like a cannonball over the cemetery wall. Turrets spun above her. Church bells bleated in her skull.

An eyeless man careened, tripped over her leg, and staggered back. Harriet hissed one of her most vile spells, and this time, she got it right. The man was burning in a pile of sticks, his body chained to a stake, his arms sizzling like bacon.

"My doing, *mine,*" said Harriet, as she scrabbled back over the wall.

Dogface was clipping her nose hairs with a razor-sharp bone. "Big deal, Harriet: a burning man. *I* do plagues. If you insist on fighting me for Grand Witch, then be forewarned: when you lose, Harriet, you die."

From the other side of the wall, Torquemada cried, "Eternal damnation, I say, to the witches of hell who prey on our souls. Find them and kill them and send them back to the devil where they belong."

Would he never shut up? You'd think he could come up with something new to say. Harriet faced her coven. "What do you desire, girls? What can I do for you?"

Most of the witches turned their backs, shuffled black boots, and spit. But Snagglechin said, "Harriet, we're tired of hell. It bores us. We want to destroy heaven."

Ordinarily, with her spells perfect and her Grand Witch position secure, Harriet BatBrew Bulge wouldn't have touched heaven, much less attempted to destroy it. But now everything was at stake, and so she whipped her broom from her skirts and mounted, and she said, "Then heaven it will be, girls."

Ronnie the Gatekeeper stroked his white gown. His face was luminous, his beard a fluff of sunlit cloud. "I rather like my new look."

Harriet gave him a sly grin, said, "But, baby, you looked sexier in your old filthy-tight pants."

Ronnie leaned on his lectern. "Stop trying to butter me up. You're not getting in. God has decreed it: you go to hell."

Harriet jabbed Ronnie's pearly buttons. "So where is your great God? Not minding shop, eh?"

"He's off somewhere in seventh heaven, getting some rest."

God was gone. Perfect. Omnipotent perhaps in *seventh* heaven, but not simultaneously in all his other heavenly realms. Harried gunned her broom, barely contained a growl. "Let me in, Ronnie boy."

Ronnie flipped through the Golden Book. "Sorry, Harriet. Says right here: Green face and no toes; can't enter. Favorite food, eye of newt; can't enter. Specialist in goat's gall..."

"Yeah, yeah. Like I haven't heard this before. Abracadabra pepper and lice, let in the witches and the mice; and off to hell all who are nice."

Ronnie slumped on his Golden Book, which fell from the lectern and crashed to Earth below. Harriet cackled and rammed her broom into Ronnie's gut. The gate shimmered open. Harriet wrenched at her broom, but it was stuck in Ronnie's liver. She cursed and wrenched again. The gate was melting together, closing. Curses! Harriet leapt and as the gate shimmered shut, she entered —

heaven.

The glare was fierce. She whipped on her sunglasses, scoped out the joint. Doves flitting and cooing. Angels floating like seaweed, plucking harps. Everywhere, tinkling music: flutes and lutes and a touch of piccolo. Roses. Lillies. All so sweet: Harriet's stomach lurched.

A school of cherubs swam by. Pink and fat and juicy cherubs. They turned big eyes at her and puckered bloated lips. Harriet's mouth watered.

No time to eat. If she didn't get busy and do mass destruction, she'd lose Grand Witch to Dogface. She'd live in disgrace, possibly die by Dogface's hand.

She lit a stogy and blew the succulent cherubs away in a cloud of soot. Then she scooted down a marble path; past gurgling brooks, through a pine forest.

At last, God's domain. Five main rooms, each with archways and silver doors. Each with a label. God's Room. Buddha's Room. Jesus' Room. Zeus' Room. The Lounge.

At the end of the path was a pastel horizon and a large golden door with red letters: EXIT.

Harriet cackled. "Omnipotent, is He? He hangs out in Buddha's Room, then hops into Jesus' place, and when all hell breaks loose, he escapes to his other heavens through EXIT. This'll be a piece of cake."

On the marble stairs leading to God's Room a boy and a girl played tiddlywinks. Harriet was about to cast a spell to turn the tiddlies into toads when the doors to The Lounge swung open, and a rowdy Moses and Noah staggered out, clapping each other on the back.

"Remember when I parted the sea and all those guys drowned?"

"Remember the stench in the ark from the monkeys?"

A drunk Adam fell through the doors. Eve tottered behind him, ripped at his fig leaf.

So this was heaven. These people were no better than Harriet.

Behind her, a loud click, and Harriet whirled to see Dogface, powdering her nose with sulfur flakes, snapping shut her compact with Satan. "Slipped in behind you, dearie," said Dogface, and she mumbled a spell and Eve turned into a dwarf.

Harriet said, "Caffle la loop, venom and newt," and angel wings turned into bats.

Dogface shoved Harriet hard against the arches to Buddha's Room. "Snarled hair and innards of worm, lick my bones and make me squirm," and all the doves turned into vultures, the flowers into poison ivy.

Harriet broke loose, punched Dogface's hairy nostrils, and dove into Buddha's Room, where she slammed and locked the door. What to do, what to do? How to beat Dogface; *how?*

The incense was peach nectar. The smoke was neon. Harriet sank by a Buddha statue in front of a flaming altar. Before her was a cremation pot. Perhaps she could cook a frog tongue stew, a wolf hair brew...

Something evil to impress Snagglechin and the other witches. Something so evil that Dogface would leave the coven with her tail between her legs.

"Snarfle hinx minx." Harried muttered a trifle of a spell. Buddha's altar turned into a rumbling, flame-spewing iron oven.

Harriet opened the door, peeked, then zipped across the marble path into Jesus' Room. From the corner of her eye, she saw Dogface dart into Zeus' Room with a blood-drained cherub.

Her eyes scoured Jesus' Room for instruments of terror. Piles of crosses in the corner. Mounds of dead fish. Saint icons stacked on a table with wine flagons and sacks of bread wafers.

The fish reeked. Smelled great.

Harried swigged some wine — her favorite, Manischewitz grape — then grabbed a sack of wafers. Clutching a wine flagon, she sneaked from Jesus' place over to God's Room, where the children played tiddlywinks.

She scattered the bread wafers. Made a trail of them all the way to Buddha's Room.

"Ooh, look, George, look at the shiny trail. I wonder where it leads."

The two children followed the wafers down the path to Buddha's place.

Harriet stoked Buddha's iron stove. When the children entered, she grabbed them and forced wine down their throats. They were blubbering and shrieking, but she ignored their pleas for mercy and thrust them into the flaming oven.

Buddha's doors burst open. It was Dogface. Standing there with a Cheshire cat grin. "Piffle zan zoop," said Dogface, and the children disappeared into mist, and in the oven Snagglechin was squirming and yelling.

Dogface was *good*. Harriet couldn't remember if her spells had *ever* been as tight and lean — and accurate — as Dogface's spells.

Harriet streaked from Buddha's Room. Heaven's gates were propped open with pitchforks; Dogface's work, no doubt. Harriet ran past the pitchforks into the cemetery. Snagglechin was there with the rest of the coven. Snagglechin said, "You'd better pack your things, Harriet. Dogface has outdone you again."

"*No*. Keep *me* as Grand Witch. Follow me back to heaven."

The sky burst like a fat sack of water, and from the heavens, Dogface dumped spider mites and lizard toes.

The witches chanted, "Dogface. Dogface. Dogface."

Snagglechin threw a fistful of fungi at Harriet, who for a moment was blinded. Harriet tried to utter a spell to retaliate, but this time, she couldn't even remember the first word. How could her friends desert her like this? She felt her body sagging from the weight of it, and then, the coven pounced. They flew at her in a rage: punching, clawing, spitting, hurling their worst spells. A whirl of red and white stockings, of black heels, of green gnarled lips, of whorehouse breath.

Harriet cried, "One more chance, give me one more chance!"

But they wouldn't listen, and they dug their toeless feet into her groin and drove their pointed noses into her eyes. Had Harriet always misspoken her spells so badly that she was now going to lose her coven to Dogface? It was unbearable to think of it.

She was Grand Witch, and so she screamed her very worst spell, the one that always worked, the one about cankerous rot and elderly snot; and they fell from her against the rough cemetery wall; and she vowed to show them who was boss —

yes, she would show them all —

and then she turned and fled through Ronnie's gate into heaven.

"Back for more, dearie?" sneered Dogface, hands on her hips, cherub in her maw.

Harriet drew back her arm and whacked Dogface. The cherub dropped from the warty mouth and flew into the pine forest.

Harriet raced past Dogface into God's Room. She whipped open his chest of drawers. The Love drawer; now Death from Toad Mist. The Friendship drawer; now Hideous Disease from Rat Wounds.

And in her head, she heard the havoc she created down on Earth: pestilence and plague, and evil men killing in the name of God. The coven rooted for her, then for Dogface, then for her again.

Heart pumping, she scooted into Zeus' Room. Party in progress. Pan the halfgoat clutching at woodland nymphs. Apollo in his sun chariot, flexing tanned muscles. In the corner by the thunderbolts, Hades brooding.

Harriet said, "So how's it goin', pal?" and plucked some thunderbolts from the floor.

Hades was a gristle of charred fried flesh. His eyes smoldered. "What's a witch doing up here? If God catches me, it's bad enough. But *you* aren't even a godhead. In fact, you aren't even a dead person."

"We'll see who wins, Hades. God, or Harriet BatBrew Bulge."

Harriet elbowed her way through the cocktail chatter. She zapped Apollo with a spell — it worked! — and nabbed some cherubs. Then she grabbed the reins of Apollo's sun chariot. She and the cherubs flew from heaven and whirled around the graveyard.

Upturned faces. People running in terror. Harriet tossed thunderbolts upon the fleeing masses.

Torquemada in flames, rolling through excrement in his white gown. And now Moses with his staff, stalking the cemetery, casting plagues: the blood, the boils, the hail, the death. And Noah beating dogs, slaughtering lambs and goats in pairs upon the graves. Eve, fig leaf nude, ripping the burning clothes from Torquemada, promising to take the holy man to Eden.

Cherubs raised their bows and arrows, shot the innocent people dead in their tracks.

"Happy Valentine's Day," Harriet cackled.

And now the booming voice of Great Goodness. It was God, back from his vacation in seventh heaven. "What's this mess in *God's Room?*"

Harriet must return to heaven. Immediately, before God discovered Ronnie and the pitchforks, before He closed heaven's gates.

The chariot thundered past the slumped Ronnie. There was God, a looming mass of effervescent nothingness, surging like a tidal wave after her. Harriet hopped from the chariot, scrambled into Buddha's Room.

Behind her, the door clicked. But Harriet hadn't shut it.

Dogface again, this time trying to lock Harriet into the room. Harriet lifted the heavy Buddha statue and cracked Dogface across the head. Dogface howled and drove her teeth into Harriet's cheek.

Harriet kicked open the door, scrabbled to her feet, and with a mighty whack, booted Dogface from Buddha's Room.

Right past God, who bellowed, "*Two* witches in my heaven?!"

Harriet remembered Moses down on Earth with his plagues. Moses laughing with Noah about parting the sea.

Harriet grabbed the oven poker and thrust it at God's misty nothingness. She hissed the spell that parted dark clouds and caused heavy storms.

God's mist parted.

Harriet raced through God into Jesus' Room, where she found Dogface seducing Jesus on Mary's lap.

God surged through Jesus' door. Dogface dropped Jesus. Mary wrestled Dogface to the floor. Mary, Jesus, and Dogface thrashed in the bread wafers.

Let God, Mary, and Jesus handle Dogface. Harriet sneaked past the wrestling foursome and slipped into The Lounge.

Saints and holy guys on bar stools, meditating, smoking sweet herbs, guzzling nectars with goddesses. Harp music on the jukebox. Apollo smoothing his hair in the mirror over the bar. Sphinx complaining to the bartender, asking riddles: "Come on, nobody ever wants to play anymore. What creature crawls on twenty hands, leaps on eight feet, and eats with two mouths?"

Hot steam billowed into the bar. All heads turned. God strode into The Lounge like Elvis returning to Graceland. Saints and goddesses and holy guys hurled themselves at Him, clutching, begging for favors.

Harriet ducked behind the bar.

Through the swinging doors came the sound of cackling and cheering.

The coven.

Snagglechin dragged Delilah Dogface Crone into the bar by the ugly cave-nostril nose. She threw the hag onto the counter. "Gimme a double," said Snagglechin to the bartender.

He grimaced. "A double of what, lady?"

"Of anything."

He thrust two bottles at her. She cracked them over Dogface's head, then hurled the old crone into the glass mirror.

God was pinned to the floor. Steam tendrils whipped around the godheads huddling over Him, worshiping and flattering His Holiness.

"Come on, girls, major fun time," said Harriet, and she led her coven from The Lounge to heaven's marble path.

They turned en masse, pointed claws at The Lounge, and hurled the spell that sealed godheads into a bar for centuries.

And down below was eternal damnation. Plague. The Inquisition. Hell.

Harriet BatBrew Bulge had destroyed heaven.

The next time she forgot her spells and some old bat fought her for Grand Witch, what craziness would the coven demand? No more sunshine? Eternal hail? Draining of the oceans, rampant fires, the evolution of mankind into goats?

Come to think of it, misspoken spells might not be such a bad thing.

"And so, girls," she said, "is there anything else you desire?"

UNDERGROUND PIPELINE was my second digital-flesh story, written directly after CAFEBABE. Featuring mad scientists and more CAFEBABE-type blobs, this story shows the misery of laboratory research from the subject's viewpoint. I sold PIPELINE to a 1993 magazine, which folded before it could publish the piece. Like a lot of my stories in the 90's, I forgot about it because I was too busy working 7 days/week and taking care of everything and everyone. I'm delighted to resurrect this story and finally let it live alongside CAFEBABE.

Underground Pipe-line

DEBAF writhes in his tray. Open sores, their purplish sheen edged with fuzzy green. Muscle bumps rising and falling under his shriveled skin like waves humping across a sea. And the blackened blood — I shiver to see it, for it's like my own; and it grips me with terror to think of such sludge oozing through the decaying pipes of my veins.

I want to grab DEBAF, to wrench him from his nutrient tray and save him. I strain against my grounding cord, wishing that somehow I could flip myself into DEBAF's tray, but the cord is short and I shrink back, defeated, into my nutrient glop. How ironic that we're trapped into torturous deaths by cords that protect us from shortcircuiting.

I may look like a turkey-sized tissue blob, but I'm an intelligent creature. A 100-percent flesh-and-blood computer. If only I had refused to issue tissue and wad those code chunks into buds. If only I had resisted the temptation to snap the buds from my humps and create new life.

And now my youngest bud DEBAF is dying. His vibrations filter feebly across the room. "FEFA, I can't bear any more pain. I must execute myself. My life needs death."

For five years, I've watched helplessly while the white coats have tortured and killed my buds: 18 dead, three barely surviving. In the name of medical research, we've died from cancer, small-pox, polio, tuberculosis, and heart disease. But what do you expect from a race that farms baboons for human heart transplants?

And now, dear DEBAF, the one who adored Gilbert and Sullivan, the one whose merriment was my only comfort in this death row we call Uncle Tom's Cabin — he wants my blessing to kill himself. I can almost feel his synapses screeching and sizzling on the metal circuits of the network.

I snap at him: "You *can't* hijack a network trailer! Metal hardware fries organic software. The thought of such a death makes me *sick*!"

DEBAF's muscles bob and then harden until he's a rock of frozen muscle, a slave to the Parkinson's disease inflicted by the white coats. His vibrations barely stir the air. "We must escape, FEFA. We must do the deadly embrace."

"Flesh clutching metal. Bah! You'd think that — " but my flesh freezes from pain. The virus is choking my output stream. Millions of viral particles gush from my cells, ram multiple pro-cesses on my stacks, and spew enzymes at my membranes. My flesh is riddled with so many holes that I can barely conduct cur-rent.

My other surviving buds, FACE and giant ED, struggle to break their grounding cords. They strain toward the lab doors, and gray glop sloshes from their trays onto the white-tiled floor. I shudder, partly from the tormented vibrations of my buds, partly from fearing that DEBAF is right.

Giant ED screams. A wad of glistening fat sprouts from his lower flab mound. ED is budding again.

Tears sting my optic stalk.

The bud, it is a beautiful ball of glossy peach. Please, let it live, let us hide it, *somewhere anywhere*, before...

Before...

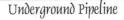

The machine guns of ED's killer cells fire their deadly chemicals. He screams as the holes rip his flesh, and scarlet blood streaks across stillborn peach.

Trembling villi sweep across my optic stalk, shield me from the horror.

But I peek too soon: the peach bud shrivels and falls dead to the floor. Forced abortion, Cabin style.

ED's hysterical, flopping in his tray, sloshing glop on FACE's pocked humps. "They inject exploding chemicals, program me to analyze the deaths of my own buds. They don't even care when chemicals burn holes in my guts. FEFA, I want the deadly embrace, *I need the deadly embrace* ... "

"Escaping from Uncle Tom's Cabin is wrong. It's certain death on the outside, death at our own hands. And for us, death with honor is all that matters."

FACE shakes the glop from his humps and snivels. "We're less than monkeys and dogs. They're tortured, but at least they're treated like animals. If you ask me, honor is senseless ...ooh, I feel dizzy ... perhaps hallucinations will bring a happy death ..."

He's off in his own world again, finding solace in suicidal dreams. But he can't help preferring suicide. The coats inject him with massive doses of depressants. He hasn't sucked glop in more than a week. Of course the psychiatrists adore him: he's the first anorexic computer.

Villi are clearing the salty tears from my optic slit when internal biosensors see something strange and issue an interrupt. Viral particles are clawing their way into my firmware. Glial cells, my firmware's insulation, are dividing wildly and squashing the cells that tell me how to boot and restore lost fragments. A chunk of system configuration code unchinks and floats down my bloodstream.

Vibrations slap me from all angles. "Deadly embrace. Deadly embrace. We want, we need, the deadly embrace." My buds are chanting now; lunatics, all of them.

"Suicide is not the answer!" I scream.

A violent spasm surges through DEBAF, and his body becomes a muscular bat, which whacks my humps. He shrieks for release.

But I stand firm: "Nak!"

The virus scrambles pathways to my optic stalk, and colors spray the room.

I can barely see Hilde Fried's white coat by the lab door. White looms larger and larger and then she's in front of DEBAF's tray.

Under a cloud of gray hair, her dark eyes thunder. "I want an hourly report, DEBAF. And this time, don't refuse."

She plunges a hypo into him.

He screams and hurls forward. He flops from the tray and dangles by his grounding cord. Being nothing more than a slab of fat, he can't escape, and Hilde easily flips him back into his tray. She smearS gray pus across her white coat.

DEBAF's muscle bats sock me again. I'm sucked into neon swirls, swept into pulsating pain.

Stem cells leak from the mush of my marrow. In the microsecond before I crash, I can save either my firmware or the stems that create my blood cells.

The stems shoot to my skin and erupt like geysers. Hilde's white coat turns red. The dripping hypo skitters across the floor. I issue emergency clotting signals, but virus particles stab and devour them. Desperately I reissue the emergency signals, but again, they are attacked and devoured.

Through the lab door rushes Jack the Ripper, our surgeon. DEBAF screams. "Behold the Lord High Executioner!"

My graphics map dumps pixels onto my optics stalk, and as DEBAF screams something about tracing his ancestry back to a "protoplasmic primordial atomic globule," a fluorescent tidal wave crashes down and sucks me into nothingness.

Neon ribbons flashing on white background.

I pulse with the flashes. It numbs me. Maybe things aren't as bad as I remember.

I cycle bit patterns through my memory. Forty-three memory cells are dead. Synapses are severed in 22 locations. The hard muscles of nonvolatile memory are flabby, and my mass storage segmentation pointers are lost. I shuffle backup pointers up from my fifth brain.

The neon ribbons disintegrate into neon pinpricks.

The numbness fades. I hurt. And, *I remember.*

Data packets scurry down my shared artery, packing stem losses and clotting rates into my memory arrays. I readjust my pointers and try to act nonchalant.

The Ripper taps the idiot badge embedded in his lower arm. "Getting some good data on latency and replication modes. Antibody drugs are binding to the glycos on the virus. Aahh, FEFA's coming around. Temperature's abnormally high. The blob's confused, fragmented, unstable."

After giving me a killer virus, what does he expect me to do, jump through do-while loops? I'd like to give him a piece of my mind; unfortunately, he's already taken too much with his scalpel. To keep him happy, I mumble, "Nothing to worry about. Just a touch of Cabin fever."

"Ha, it's trying to be funny. Pitiful. Well, it never hurts to double check what drugs are doing, especially when an artificial intelligence becomes unreliable." He slides a scalpel from his white coat and scrapes some crusty tumor cells from my musical brain sectors.

Pain sizzles down my neurons as the razor slices my brain. He lops off a chunk of Beethoven's fifth symphony.

Why must he cut me? To my left, DEBAF is a tissue rock. He vibrates nothing. Hilde rubs antiseptic cloth over his flesh and limp villi.

My lysosomes report heavy cell losses in the musical sectors. Beethoven's lost his balance. Haydn trips over himself and slumps against my artery walls. Together, they sound like daffy tunes from old cartoons.

"Kill me. Please, Mr. Ripper, kill me and get it over with." It's giant ED. Huge, foaming cavities gut his body. I can see through them to the wall behind his nutrient tray.

Using her idiot badge, Hilde orders somebody to "come and clean up the smelly mess." She shrivels her nose and jabs DEBAF with another thick hypo. "You blobs are lucky you can't smell anything. Listen, DEBAF, I'm giving you something new, phospholipid sacs of concentrated dopamine. Maybe they'll take the edge off the Parkinson's. Analyze the cellular chemistry, would you? And please, a report every hour."

The Ripper laughs. His teeth are frosty white. "You're too soft on these blobs, Hilde. You treat them like people. Remember, they're only computers."

"Sometimes they irritate the hell out of me, but they *are* creatures."

"Come on, Hilde. You've been using animals for experiments since college. Bleeding rabbits to death in microbiology class, slitting live frogs, embedding circuits in dog and cat brains."

Hilde dips her head and stares at the floor. Her gray curls are bunched in knots, tight like the glycoprotein studs on my virus particles. "I know, and I'm not a bleeding heart, Jack. Blob research has already given us major insight into medicines for several diseases. I just don't enjoy hurting them."

The Ripper plops Beethoven's fifth into a beaker and inserts a glass stopper. "Do you realize how close we are to finding cures for Parkinson's and HIV-XXV and African parasite-II? Speaking of, I got some excellent info about African II from the blob that died last night. The pore-forming proteins blocked most of the parasites."

Hilde points her hypo at ED. "Take a last reading off ED, will you? Perhaps with an adjustment in killer cell dose, abortions will be possible without the terrible side effects exhibited by the blob."

I pulsin a feeble vibration from ED. "Tell them nothing, FEFA. Do the deadly embrace."

ED's vibrations cease, and I know that he's dead.

The Ripper scowls and speaks into his idiot badge. "Postmortem debug and autopsy on ED hex 01 C42E. Get the crew in here right away, would you?"

He and Hilde leave us with the cleanup crew. Stupid hunks of metal, not even half-breeds, LEDs blinking all over them. They squish ED into a clear bag and swab the floor with mops.

FACE whimpers. His cells disgorge nutrients. God help me, now he has bulemia.

The deadly embrace. It sickens me to think of all that beautiful logic unraveling on barbaric hardware.

Plop! Gushhhh ...

A metal claw reaches for ED's bag as his remains slosh across the tiles. A nozzle vacuums his blood and brains, the peach bud.

I will let DEBAF execute himself on metal. Suicide is more honorable than death in Uncle Tom's Cabin.

I want to wish him well, to tell him that I'll miss him. But it's too late. His input ports are closed.

I look at FACE for comfort, but he's groaning, lost in his dream visions. His shriveled cells tell me that he may die before DEBAF.

Images of my other dear buds flash before my optics. DAFOE who had the clock attack. DEEDEE who went insane and strangled himself with his grounding cord. I never knew whether FADED withered from the leukemia, cancer, pneumonia, or worms.

In my second head, the virus eats DEEDEE's image. The virus is killing more than my flesh; *it is killing who I am.*

I watch in horror, unable to move, while DEBAF inflates his cells with nutrient glop and issues tissue toward the ceiling. A knob of pulsating gray pushes up and up, and explodes. Tissue strings spew into the air and then settle on my upper mounds.

DEBAF has hijacked his network trailer. Seconds later, I pulsin a faint dying message. Grief overwhelms me. Without parsing it, I store the message.

Hilde and The Ripper burst into The Cabin. Hilde's face is a gray storm. She brushes away the shredded DEBAF and orders me into debug mode.

I reduce my operating systems so she can examine internal registers. She orders me to tell her where DEBAF went. I glance at his tray, where blood and tissue float in viscous glop.

DEBAF and I were tightly coupled. I'll never tell her that he netted to death. I'm through helping the coats.

I toss Hilde some out-of-bounds subscripts and mangled opcodes. I stuff DEBAF's dying message under a heap of indirect pointers and directories. As Hilde digs deeper for my DEBAF records, I scramble bit maps so the information is invisible to her.

Like cornered prey, she hisses. "You slinking, rotting blob! How dare you keep this data secret! After I gave you food and shelter and amusing programs. I treated you, a mere blob of fat, like a real animal. Tell me how he died, tell me, *tell me or I swear* — "

The Ripper jams a hypo into me. I try to numb myself with an infinite loop but the drug streams into one of my main heads and snaps the loop. Chemicals grasp the network name and frequency. I can't fight The Ripper. He's too strong for me. As he reads my registers, I feel violated. Ashamed. "Ah ha, here it is, Hilde. DEBAF executed himself on the old Armynet. I can't decipher the rest of this drivel, something about Uncle Tom's Cabin, an Underground Pipeline to freedom."

An Underground Pipeline to freedom?

I scan DEBAF's message. Somewhere on the Armynet, before the circuits fried him, DEBAF discovered a network of flesh computers, an Underground Pipeline operating on tissue frequencies from a node called EDFBADA. "EDFBADA runs hostels all over the world for runaway purebreds. The closest hostel to Uncle Tom's Cabin is in San Jose. From there, EDFBADA will pipe you to Norway where purebreds are protected by animal welfare leagues. Find out from his scheduler when he's free. Tell him DEBAF sent you."

Hilde and The Ripper make plans to import 50 young buds from an Austrian lab. The Ripper tells a visitor that "this old blob can't even reproduce. It's time for fresh blood around here."

Underground Pipeline

Thanks to Hilde's debug sessions and the slashing of my upper lobes for tissue samples, it's hard to compose Pipeline packets. I chop a copy of my main heads into tiny bit streams and shift the streams into envelopes. And after what seems like an eternity, I finally slide my backup brain into the Pipeline with instructions to find San Jose, Norway, and EDFBADA.

An hour later, a message trickles down the Pipeline: "Do you node the way to San Jose?" I'm in no mood for ancient jokes, not even from my own backup brain, and I grumble and don't respond.

After complaining about competition in Gallenium Arsenide Valley — "the Japanese blobs think their AI is better than mine" — my backup brain sends an exciting postcard from Norway: "I'm on host computer CAD awaiting Pipeline to EDFBADA. Many other blobs are sharing CAD's flesh. Kinkier blobs are swapping brains, but mostly we're segmented into little corners of virtual space. I venture out from time to time into main arteries to swap pages with other blobs. Met a card shark from Rio who tells me blobs are forced into casino labor there. And a priest who tells me to return to The Cabin because real freedom comes only from belief in the messiah. The view from CAD's optic stalk is wild: dazzling fjords and glaciers. Having fun and wish you were here, FEFA*2."

At last I'm seeing the world — and I'm not even there!

While FEFA*2's having a good ol' time, things are getting worse for me. The virus is devouring my remaining stem cells. Without the ability to create new blood cells, I have less than two weeks to live.

Somehow I must get out of here, hop on the Pipeline; if necessary, I'll do the deadly embrace.

The viral particles swarm and seethe and destroy my internal optics. Cell membranes burst and enzymes gush into my arteries. Chemical explosions rip down my gates and fling schrapnel onto my flipflops.

The Ripper injects non-ionic drugs. They have no electric charge and being fatty, easily penetrate my cell walls. They seep into the parallel arrays of my Golgis and settle into the cisternae rows. As the Golgis fill, calcium ions pile up into triggers, and then the cisternae erupt and blast the drugs from my cells.

The neon ribbons return, and this time, they don't fade into pinpricks. Through the psychedelic slashes, metal glints. Must be The Ripper's scalpel. "It's a good thing those 50 young blobs'll be coming from Austria next week. The research must continue so we can keep the grant money."

I try to send a message to FEFA*2, the backup brain in Norway. "Tell Austria not to send the 50 blobs to Uncle Tom's Cabin." The Underground Pipeline is congested with traffic and my message returns unopened. As I resend the message, a needle twists into my marrow and pain shatters my concentration. I incorrectly encode my password.

Hilde hovers. Her hair knots graze my skin. My tissue is still sensitive enough to register that her hair is made from synthetic fiber. I wonder what's false about The Ripper, other than his smile.

I labor over my password, recheck it three times to ensure that the encoding is correct. I send my message again with the priority flag set on the header.

And I can think of nothing but freedom and death and whether my life has all been in vain.

I eagerly scan FEFA*2's response. "I warned Austria about The Cabin. EDFBADA's blocked shipment. Met nice human named Jo Gjend who serves good glop and tells funny reindeer stories."

A NICE HUMAN? My backup brain's gone oxymoronic.

I'm too weak to send signals up my optic stalk, and without vision, my world is sealed. The scalpel hacks and hacks. The tattered shirt of my skin is no match for The Ripper's knife. My nerves shriek. Symphonic lobes and hunks of brain — all gone.

Except for the chiseling of the scalpel, the room is silent.

I time my heads to self destruct by endless looping. One of my ancestors died from boredom, and I will do the same. Hilde fixes the loop, but I simply patch in another one.

In twenty seconds, I'll be dead.

Hilde digs for my Pipeline file, but I change file ownership to EDFBADA and lock her out. She barks an order and a tidbit of code loads and compiles and obliterates my file ownership commands. She swoops into the directory that hides my door to the Underground Pipeline.

Ten seconds before I crash.

Hilde lunges for the Pipeline. The dragon's lick of her breath scorches me.

In a flash, I flip bits in the Pipeline's virtual address. Hilde curses. The Pipeline slips from her grasp.

One microsecond to death.

Hilde screams and bangs my flesh, but I plunge into the Underground Pipeline. A blue voltwagon sweeps me up and shoots me down the tunnel.

Up and down, up and down; the ride is bumpy and fast, and god, so exhilerating! My mind soars, free at last from the bondage of tortured flesh. Beethoven storms rage in my soul. My heads reel with harmony.

A node wavers up ahead, but it's not in my network file. A ghost node, no doubt installed by EOFBADA to fake out network intruders. I bypass it and whoosh down the Pipeline in a blast of purplish blue.

San Jose sucks in my header, and the rest of my packets bump to a halt. Long, red waves bob past, lapping languidly against the sides of the Pipeline. I guess I'm not pure enough for the Japanese microcode, who tells me that "all input ports are protected." The microcode spits me out and a gate slams, and the blue voltwagon blasts off with me in tow.

By the time I ram into CAD's Norway port, my heads are spinning like old disk drives. Fuzzy wisps of Chopin seep from the port. They hint at lovely things to come. I sizzle with excitement and stutter my password.

Underground Pipeline

"Come back after system maintenance at 2 a.m. Getting my beauty sleep."

"DEBAF sent me. I'm on the run."

The port slinks open with a slight whoosh. A gentle wave sucks me in and prods me through a series of ANDs and ORs that test my header packet. It sets my scales skittering to be frisked by the exotic CAD.

Using fragments from FEFA*2, CAD revives my eroded functions and memory. I'm whisked into a private address compartment "to rest after your long trip." In a nook of the compartment, I find some Swedish and Finnish memory arrays and load them into my heads. When CAD returns, I'm feeling gay and cosmopolitan. "Hyvaa humoenta, jag skulle garna vilja ha ettrum dubbelrum."

CAD's laugh is hazy and sensuous; what a Renoir would sound like if paintings could laugh. "You want a room with two beds? Sorry, bud, you get a wedge of virtual space like everyone else. But roam at will, swap what you want, and I'll page you when EDFBADA is clear for transmission. By the way, it's best that we destroy your backup brain. We need the memory space."

In a way I'm sad that FEFA*2 won't make it to EDFBADA, but it's probably for the best; it'd be irritating to hang out with a blob who has all my bad habits.

Life is good here. Jo Gjend fills CAD's nutrient tray with vispgradde, a whipped cream and pudding. As for Gjend's reindeer stories, they're about as funny as The Ripper's scalpel. Humans, pfwah! If they can't hurt you one way, they'll hurt you with another.

The best thing about CAD is his optic stalk. When I get my turn, I gaze at the cliffs outside the lab windows. Tiny houses cling to narrow ledges thousands of feet over a foaming sea. Fruit trees dapple the craggy slopes.

Life could be so sweet.

I mourn for my buds. I mourn for buds everywhere.

Then one day EDFBADA calls for me. A Swedish lab has room for a sensitive blob who seeks new experiences. The coats will load me into a new body, one with muscled villi, walking pods, and tough outer skin.

I'll be bigger than a turkey!

It's an experimental project and I might die without the controlled environment of a lab. But the coats will treat me like a dog, the glop's good, and I'll have a shot at seeing the world. Do I want the job?

I remember all who died before me, all who sacrificed their lives in Uncle Tom's Cabin for the sake of human research. And dear DEBAF, who killed himself but found the Pipeline. If I do die in Sweden, it'll be for blob research, and my death will have some meaning.

And I realize that I'm not just a flesh-and-blood computer. I'm a step beyond computers, even beyond animals. Soon I'll have my freedom. I'll be the first generation of something new.

With a whispered prayer for my dead buds, I leap into the Pipeline to find out what.

In the winter of 1991 or 1992, I awakened one morning at 5 am and banged out INSTANT GRATIFICATION. I liked the idea of the bedpans, and Glistie and Vor made me laugh until tears streamed down my cheeks. Poor Vor, his wife was such a shrew. This may have been the first story that I ever submitted for publication. It appeared in a magazine called Manifest Destiny.

Instant Gratification

"Let's do it somewhere exotic, baby." Glistie's honey-thick voice grazed Vor's lobe and swirled into the channeling conduit of his eardip, which massaged her words into a fine, mellow, musical whiskey.

Ripples of pleasure cascaded from Vor's brain past his tingling neck platelets to the warm zones of his chest. By the time his lower pleasure zones were triggered, he was swooning with desire. "Let me adjust you, my sweet," he whispered.

Glistie craned her neck, the platelets sharding the light into soft prisms. Vor smiled, so glad that she was all his, so glad that only *his* imprint could trigger her pleasure zones, and he pressed a forefinger to her eardip.

The bedroom, a cramped nook in a city closet, fizzled into a blur of radiant colors and then burst into the orange, black, green, and white of an onyx cave, smooth and chilled perfectly to tingle the spine. Vor's eyes switched to compound and registered the view from a thousand perspectives. His head dangled over a precipice cloaked in steamy vines that writhed in the hot scarlet sprays of a waterfall. He tried to calm his pleasure zones and prolong his ecstasy.

Prostrate beside him with her pressure groups splayed across cold and unyielding onyx, Glistie moaned and begged for more and then for less. Her tendrils stretched tautly and curled, and at their tips, the pressure groups, wadded compactly onto suckers, clung to the cave walls.

Vor shut his eyes and rode the crest of a wave, thundering, pounding down the cliff. His ears throbbed with the sweetness of high trilling chords.

"Now, now?" Glistie's words splintered into twisted notes of pain, joy, and conquest. The chords screeched, and with a violent jolt, stopped. A final tremor skittered up the frets of Vor's spine in grating sharps and fell in muted flats. He started as if slapped in the face, and sucked in his breath. He was drenched in sweat and trembling as if with fever.

Glistie was coiled in the bed, huddled with her chin drooped over her ventral mound, her tendrils limp and spent, draped over the gilded blanket and suctioned, dripping, to the pasty gray floor. Sweat beads studded her neck platelets and dribbled into her matted calico fur.

Vor was wedged between Glistie and the row of bedpans behind their pillows. His wet cheek was plastered to the bedpan that had propelled them into the onyx cave. Crackling, gray static filled the room, shot through his eardips, and speared his brain. "Turn off the dead bedpan!" shrieked Glistie.

A calico tendril lashed out and a sucker slapped Vor's head. It clipped his eardip and zapped two torment switches. Vor maneuvered a shaking tendril to his head and pressed the switches off. "I'm not exactly in the mood for masosadism." Glistie could be a real pain when he disappointed her.

And he had disappointed her too often during their 13 years of wedded bondage. She had been content a first to tweak her eyedips and see him as her latest male fantasy. When his image failed to arouse her, he had at great cost, purchased a starter set of bedpans from the pleasure net.

Both he and Glistie had tried all of the selections on the bedpans physical properties menus. She had grown her tendrils with extra large suckers; and he had sprouted tendrils with extra thick muscles. Glistie had requested a body skin of calico fur; Vor had chosen the sleek patina of an ebony skinsuit, buffed for optimal sheen; and both had opted for reversible compound eyes. Neither had ever worn the original sapiens physique; on the menu, no doubt, for old timers living in the past.

Eight months ago, at Glistie's insistence, Vor had recycled half a year's pay into the pleasure net for a deluxe set of bedpans. Already she was bored with the exotic locales, direct pleasure zings, and eardip harmonics. But it wasn't his fault if the instant grat engineers couldn't devise new pleasure methods fast enough to satisfy his wife.

Vor sighed. "Maybe the romance is over, Glistie. I can't seem to make you happy anymore." He hoped that she would say it wasn't true.

"I'm sorry, baby. I wanna get a rise out of this. What else is there to live for?" Glistie's voice was drippy and thin. A few tendrils flicked through the mop of calico fur on her head.

Vor disdainfully eyed the furry blotches of color on her torso and wished that she would change skinsuits. Damp fur was noxious; his wife smelled like a dead animal.

"Would you please turn off the pan?" Glistie clenched her ears with her suckers.

Vor pried the bedpan screen from the wall and poked at the usual malfunctioning wires. Static bombarded him from the ceiling pans, from the pans by the door at the foot of the bed, and from the pleasure pans by the pillows. He struck the pans with his suckers, but having only 25 tendrils, missed more than half of them. Some of the screens clicked off, then hummed and cast azure ripples across the bed nook.

Vor's neck platelets clattered with anxiety. A hexagon of his compound eye peered at Glistie, whose platelets now were chattering like teeth. Vor's stomach lurched and warning triggers skittered up his throat.

And then the static buzzed off, as did the rippling azure, and Vor and Glistie sighed with relief. Vor sank against his pillow and massaged his hairless belly with a tendril.

It hadn't been like this when they were teenagers. Vor could still remember the newness, the immediacy, of massaging his own tendrils ... he hadn't needed substitutes then. And Glistie had been different, too. More interested in the politics of the closet community, more eager to lap up real life experiences. Lord, how her body had turned him on: her bulbous torso sleeky peach with a light pink down; her scalp soft and fragrant and puffed with lavender fuzz; her trendrils delicate, sensitive, and oddly inviting.

But now as adults, only the zings of the pleasure net satisfied them. Vor and Glistie were addicted to instant grat.

A maternal advert voice coaxed him from his thoughts: "An investment in dimension estate is *your* key to happiness. Satisfy your bondage mate with a new closet." Three-dimensional images of bed nooks, kitchen cubes, and multiple-family closets beamed at Vor from 65 wall and ceiling screens. Vor's compound eyes merged images of closets from thousands of angles. "Go anywhere you want, be anything you want, feel anything you desire."

"Fix the bedpans!" Glistie screamed. "I want, I *need* to return to the cave!" Her pleasure groups sucked the wall for grat zings.

Vor tapped an eyedip and the compound images of closets snapped as if elastic from thousands to a mere 65. Then he turned his attention to the exposed wires behind the bed. Apparently, the bedpan had short circuited at the moment of ecstasy. One of his tendrils squeezed between the wall and bed. It was a tight fit, but he always used his least muscular tendril, the only one that could slither down the space and flit across the floor. "Where're my service supplies, Glist?" A ball of panic bounced up his throat and stuck in his mouth. Without the bedpans, they were at the mercy of their own *flesh*.

"I was so close." Glistie's silvery eyes crinkled along the ridges of the compound hexagons, then receded again to a singular point of view. She sputtered, "Maybe I gave them to Ralph with my broken perfume blasto. I tried to poof myself with Underground Radchic, but the poofer retrokicked dust into the vents.

Filled the complex with Radchic. People netted me all day complaining that their closets reeked of the underground unbathed." Glistie chortled, and her tendrils suctioned tears from the corners of her eyes.

Vor could well imagine it. The vents snaked in all directions, servicing the ten square miles of urban Chicago occupied by their closet complex. It must have been hard for Ralph, their handyman drone, to fix the mess.

How lucky that they lived in such a fashionable place With all the modern conveniences. Altered realities in every room. Virtual foodstuffs with no calories but plenty of taste. Virtual in-closet jobs that meant nothing, accomplished nothing, and required virtually no time to perform. And, a handyman drone like Ralph for every cluster of 15 closets.

Glistie stretched her 20 left tendrils. The suckers quivered. Her 20 right tendrils whipped out, and 40 suckers smacked each other with nervous erotic tension. "Let's get a new closet, Vor, where everybody sniffs Underground Radchic for grats. It's just what we need!" She rolled back and forth on her bulbous torso, which was as rotund as a fat beetle's.

Vor considered and shook his head. "No, all we need is Ralph." Vor slithered from the bed through the silicon gel door, which shimmered briefly as he passed, and into the kitchen cube.

His wife bobbed into the cube, her tendrils fanned behind her. As she moved, the stench of wet fur socked his nostrils.

"Aw, come on," pleaded Glistie, "let's get the latest in closets and keep up with the tech, baby." Her suckers were still quivering.

Vor gasped for fresh breath. "How about getting rid of the fur, Glist? You were so cute in the baby powder skins, the ones lined in daffodil scent. Everywhere you bounced, a trail of flowers followed."

Glistie ignored him and spread her calico tendrils across the floor. "Impart grat," she whispered seductively. Her tendrils arched, the suckers skewered to the floor for maximum uptake.

How would Vor ever keep her happy? His stomach lurched from her stench, and he remembered why he had slithered into the kitchen cube. His main tendril whisked over the cube gels that palpitated in the wall sockets. The gels were slightly sticky and glistened with attraction oils. It was a difficult choice, his sucker was tempted by several gels, but he finally stroked the cube gel for virtual animal paste with mashed 'toes. His mouth watered as the aroma of roasted paste en 'toes suffused his tasting buddips. "Flick your dips, Glist," he said, thankful to be smelling delicious food rather than damp fur. "I'll order you some favorites."

Glistie was sulking in the comer, her suckers prodding the pleasure cubes that sheathed the floor. Her body quivered as joy zings jetted up her tendrils and into her main zones. "I don't want any food, I just want to go back to the cave."

Vor flipped from his ventral mound to his spine. His tendrils flopped across the floor cubes. "The paste'll do you good," he cajoled. His tongue flipped the main buddips on his lips and in the back of his mouth. A water-soluble dish of paste en 'toes popped from the floor crevice and he scooped a wad into his main sucker.

"If we can't get a new closet," whined Glistie from the corner, "I think we should divorce our bondage. A girl's gotta have some fun while she's still young."

"You know," Vor said around a mouthful of 'toes smothered in gravy, "I have needs, too. Don't you think it bothers me when the pans shortcirc? Maybe we're going about this all wrong. Maybe we should delete the virtuals — all except the food, of course — and try a more *natural* method."

Glistie grimaced and her silver eyes narrowed with disgust. "You gotta be kidding. I wouldn't touch you if my life depended on it. That is so gross!"

Vor sloshed more paste en 'toes from his sucker into his mouth. His buddips tingled, his stomach swelled with warmth. "We could get used to it. You could shed the fur and I could revert to a sapiens physique."

"Ugh! Puh-lease! You're making me sick, Vor. I say we net Ralph and have him fix the bedpans. Then we net for a new closet." Her face fixed in stony determination.

Vor's tongue switched off his tasting buddips. He shoved the water-soluble dish into a dissolve crevice in the floor. Strange ideas whirred inside his head. He was tired of instant grat but didn't know how to replace it. "We'll let Ralph fix the bedpans," he decided, "but there'll be no new closet."

Glistie's body convulsed and then started bouncing on a pleasure cube. Her tendrils flashed angrily in the air, and once or twice, he had to duck to avoid a whipping. "What's happening to you, Vor?" she demanded. "All of a sudden, instant grat's not good enough for you? It's easy, it's fun, *it feels good*. So what's wrong with it?" Her silver eyes were molten, her rear tendrils bristling.

The warm zones of Vor's chest heated and swelled with frustration. His voice quavered; he stumbled for an answer. "I don't want to lose you, Glistie, but I want to feel young again. Instant grat is for old folks. I want to take things slow and easy. I want to seek and create my own pleasure."

She sneered at him and then hurled the accusation: "Why, Vor, my sweet, you're going through midlife crisis!"

"If I am, Glistie, I want you to travel through it with me. If it doesn't work out, you can always leave."

Glistie pouted, but when he said nothing, she murmured his pet name, Big Dip, and sighed. "We'll fix the bedpans, and forget the new closet. Anything for you, my sweet. Anything but touching your flesh."

Shortly after Vor netted Ralph, the handyman drone tottered through their outer gel door with his pop-in head bucket. He tossed Vor's service set, an array of ancient screwguns and hammers, onto a pleasure cube. "It'll take forever to fix a circuit with those oversized caveman toys. I need fine precision to fix wiring."

Ralph rummaged in his head bucket. Then he popped off his workman's hands, good for fixing plumbing but too clumsy for circuitry, and pushed on a pair of surgeon's hands. He tottered through the gel door leading to the bed nook.

Glistie poked through Vor's clunky service tools. A tendril whipped out with the fixed perfume poofer. Glistie jabbed the poofer needle into an adjacent tendril and from the sucker sprayed a mist of Underground Radchic, which she smoothed across her calico belly. "When the cave is fixed, I'll be all ready," she burbled. Vor slithered on his ventral mound through the gel door and into the bed nook. He bounced onto the bed where Ralph was crouching, his surgeon's hands swallowed by the hole in the wall. Ralph hummed while he tinkered with the wires, and Vor vaguely recognized the tune as the handyman drone's anthem, "I've been Workin' on the Overload."

Had Ralph ever met a couple who experienced natural pleasures? Vor suddenly had to know. He tapped a tendril on Ralph's shoulder.

Sparks flashed from the wall, and Ralph's hands jerked back, smoking. His bucket head twirled on its neck post. Wire strippers and silicon snips flew in all directions. "What're you trying to do, kill me?" he snapped, his words fading and rising as his head rotated.

With a guilty twinge, Vor carefully snaked a tendril over to the twirling head and grasped it. He checked for cracks in Ralph's neck post, for splinters in his hands. Seeing no fractures, he released the handyman and said, "You travel around the complex, Ralph. Do you ever meet people who survive without instant grat? How does it feel to turn off grat and be a real person?"

Ralph sadly shook his empty bucket head. "You call me a real person? I'm just a take apart drone. The only grat I have is fixing broken circuits. At night, I tuck my pieces into separate drawers and sleep alone, just my neck post and chest socket."

Vor apologized and squeezed the old drone's shoulders with a sucker. It had been so insensitive of him to ask such questions.

"At least you accomplish something when you fix bedpans and dissolve crevices, which is more than I can say for netting up head games."

Instant Gratification

Ralph scooped his tools off the bed and tucked them into his head bucket. He chuckled. "I suppose you have a point there, Vor. I'm not one for head games. They're dangerous to my health."

Vor thought about that long after the handyman drone had gone home to unchink himself into drawers. Glistie spent the afternoon rafting down Niagara Falls in a tub of milk and honey, trying each time to reduce the sloshing to a minimum. She was an expert on the adventure net. With Glistie sloshing the day away, Vor had plenty of time to think about his midlife crisis.

When at last Glistie returned from her trip, he asked if she was ready for the onyx cave again. But she answered, "I'm exhausted from all that rafting, and besides, my perfume washed off in the Falls." She slithered off to the kitchen cube to eat.

Vor felt like dying. His life was so empty. He trailed after his wife, now lapping water from a floor crevice. "Glistie, I can't satisfy myself as you do. I need someone to experience life with me. I'm willing to do instant grats with you, to buy a new closet if necessary, but I can't bear to watch you satisfy yourself better than I can."

"Did you flip some torment switches, baby? Listen, Vor, we've had wonderful times together, and I love you dearly. But instant grat with you isn't fun anymore. I found out today that I can have more pleasure on my own. You can have what you want, but no more instant grat." She shrugged and scooped paste en 'toes into her mouth.

He should feel happy and free: no more instant grat! But instead, he was deflated and depressed. "Would you touch me?" he asked softly. "Please?"

"I will not touch you. If it's that important to you, we can do instant grat together from time to time. But I will not touch you."

Vor was crying, possibly for the first time in his life. "Please, Glistie, just this once?"

She wiped the 'toes from her lips with a tendril. "Men and their midlife crises," she muttered. Her silvery eyes glittered, hard and cruel, driving stakes through his soul. Pain and despair clenched his heart. But then kindness filled her eyes and her hard black pupils shrank in the tide of a silvery glow. With a jolt of glee, he realized that she really *did* love him!

"Compound eyes?" Her neck platelets clattered nervously.

"If you want," he said, hope swelling in his warm chest zones, "but I don't think that it's necessary."

"Should we reset our eyedips? Eardips?"

"Not necessary," he murmured, and his heart thrummed and trilled.

A calico tendril arched toward him, the sucker straining and tense, the pressure groups knotted, yearning.

He looped his most muscular tendril over his shoulder, flexed it, and then uncurled it slowly toward her sucker.

She shuddered, a landslide of a shudder, and shrank back. He twined his tendril around hers and grasped the pressure groups with his own. Tidal waves of emotion crashed through his body, hot and swingy.

"I need a rest," she whispered, and her voice was honey thick and grazed his lobe.

His blood burbled in his veins; he could feel it pumping, strong, throughout his body. He gently stroked her neck platelets and watched them flutter and flush.

Glistie slithered back to the bed nook. Vor lay on a pleasure cube, sweating. Then he slithered after her. There she was, tendrils flung in wild abandon across the bed; the bulbous beetle body, sleeky peach with a light pink down.

Vor bounced onto the bed and wrapped at least eleven tendrils around the fuzzy pink mound. A scent of daffodils swirled around her. And such a gorgeous face, soft and fragrant and puffed with lavender fuzz.

"Well, get it over with, will you?" she said.

He laughed, then saw that her face was stony cold and serious. What to do? He couldn't lose this chance. He would show her, against her own desires, that au naturale was better than instant grat.

Twenty minutes later, Glistie jabbed a cig into her tendril and her sucker puffed little smoke balls over the bed. "Not bad, baby." Her voice was honey thick. A good sign.

"As good as instant grat?"

"I can endure it."

"If you like, you can read books while we ...?"

"I said, I can endure it, and I will." Her sucker ground against the wall, then with a loud thwack, popped off, and the cig smoke was gone. She hugged herself with 40 tendrils and rocked.

Vor's body smacked the wall and bounced across the room. Bedpans sizzled on and static bombarded his eardips.

Glistie was thrashing in bed, her tendrils whipping wildly. The lavender fuzz on her face was purple from sweat, blotched as if from a hideous disease.

Vor bounced high off the bed and suckered himself securely to the ceiling. There he hung, from 25 bedpans, watching his wife flail below.

She was hysterical. "I need the cave, the zings, the pleasure cubes!"

Oh, how he loved this poor, addicted woman. So beautiful in sleeky peach skin, so fragrant with daffodils. She had given up her calico fur for him.

He would give up something for her.

He released the pressure from his suckers and fell, splat, on top of her. He held her 40 tendrils with his muscular 25 until she stopped thrashing and lay, twitching and panting, beneath him.

Then gently, he lifted one of her tendrils and held it to the wall. "Impart grat," he said, and relief washed over him as she sank into the pillows, moaning in ecstasy and whispering his name.

Instant Gratification

This story, printed here for the first time, features a soul-sucking sloth.

Lust of the Giant Sloth

Alone, with the heat swelling in her head and the sweat steaming down her chest; the pinch of raw rubber in her nostrils; the sap oozing from the rubber trees like blood from Pompa's neck when the Yanomamo killed him last rainy season.

Curare poison is on the dart. Now her lips are sucking and her teeth are gripping the end of the blowgun.

Cachara aims.

The sloth is upside down in the tree, clinging to the trunk with its long claws. The eyes rotate her way; they widen.

The fur bristles, brown shagginess tipped with white sun.

Blood-leeching vampire...damn you for owning my soul! Cachara thinks.

The sloth heart beats in Cachara's ears. The monkey chatter dies.

For you, then, I kill another...

The dart blasts from Cachara's blowgun. Black poison sprays the foliage.

The sloth body crashes through the branches, spilling rainwater from leaf cups. A spray of heat, and Cachara's body glistens with the sloth's blood.

Her arms tingle, and she drops the blowgun to the moss of the jungle floor.

This death will bring Oxirom. The...

"...*arutam wakani*"; Cachara's voice is thinner than the watery blood dripping down her belly and legs. Oxirom is the vampiric sloth, the arutam wakani who shares her soul.

Cachara clutches a tree, the bark as soft as ...

... feathers; blue and orange flitting through the canopy of leaves high above her. The sun is a white glare. Monkeys are whipping through the branches, and the parrots are screaming about what she has done.

The palm thong chafes her thighs and hips. She loosens the thong, then stoops and lets her hand slide down the bloody sloth fur. "I didn't want to kill you, little baby. I never want to kill."

Its eyes lock to hers, the dying eyes that reflect her own sad face. She sees herself as the sloth sees her. Young and impure, the last Waimiri Indian of the Amazonas to share the lust of the giant sloth.

"You are only a two-toed babe. Food for my lover, Oxirom, who cannot kill his own meat." Her tears splatter its breast.

And its eyes close.

She slips the sharp piranha jaw from her thong and slices the toes from the sloth meat, drills tiny holes, and slips the toes onto her ancestral necklace. *Pompa, are you proud? Like you, I am the Waimini SoulSharer. I protected the Waimini tribe as you did.*

Partially hidden by foliage, the Wide River shudders against its muddy banks. It is almost peaceful.

Except that Cachara knows what is coming. The hairs rise upon her arms as the fur bristled upon the two-toed sloth.

She is taut now, rising, her ears yawning for the sounds of Oxirom.

And he comes in a sea of flying scarab beetles, his paws pounding huge five-toed tracks into the red soil.

His tongue is the length of her arm. His teeth are larger than fingers. Even on all fours, he is taller than the brazilwood trees. His haunches are larger than the hut where Cachara lives with her husband, Yoshi.

Within her skull, she feels Oxirom's words: "Ah, you have brought the monthly sacrifice. The little two-toed sloth. And now, come to me and share my soul. Give me love, and I will give you power."

"*Arutam wakani*: the ancestral soul that we share; the ancestral soul that you shared with my father, Pompa; and before him, with my grandmother." She knows the words well. She has spoken them every month since Pompa died.

And Oxirom knows his words, too: "I am the last of the giant sloths. But without you, Waimiri SoulSharer, I die; and with me, goes my race."

"Without you, Oxirom, I die; and with me, goes the Waimiri tribe and our way of life."

It is a litany. It is the spiritual singsong love chant of the giant sloth.

She steps toward him. Pauses.

Why must she allow Oxirom to paw her body and drink her life? She has a husband. She expects a child. Why can't someone else be Oxirom's SoulSharer?

"There are two hundred Waimiri left, Cachara. They have only one SoulSharer. And one giant sloth." The large eyes close, the litany breaks. "You are still with child?" he asks.

"Yes, I am with child."

"Good; then my life will continue past your death, my blood will flow in the veins of yet another Waimiri. Protect the child, Cachara. And now come closer and let us renew our ancestral vows; let us bind our soul."

It's not fair. I don't want this burden. Let someone else do it. She pushes against his arms, but his muscles have the power of crashing trees. She struggles, the terror rising in her, flooding her like the waters flood the banks of the Wide River.

His mouth opens; a huge cavern filled with blunt plant-eating teeth and *two sharp canines...*

But his breath: it is perfume and it fills her head, and her muscles relax. His breath: warmer than sun. It melts across her chest and thighs; it flares in her brain and shuts out the jungle sounds.

Oxirom is gentle. And he drinks blood *only once a month.*

Surely...surely, she can do this again...

"Come to me. Willingly."

Between her legs is a terrible ache, an ache that can only be satisfied by the giant sloth. She must feel his mouth upon her neck. She must feel his blood in her veins.

Nothing else matters.

"Drain me," she says; and then she strokes her cheek across his soft fur, and the rumble in his chest peaks and pounds her like the drums of the Waimiri festivals. His claws rake her hair; claws that easily could rip her heart and lungs from her body with one stroke. Claws that instead unsnarl the curls stuck to her sweaty back. His tongue unfurls and wraps around her neck. She looks into his eyes, each the size of a water lily, and sees a thousand colors.

His tongue slithers down her chest. His teeth lower to her chin, nibble, now graze her neck. At the base of her neck, she feels a sharp pain, and she gasps.

Something boils down her neck and chest and coats her thighs.

Cachara feels nothing but heat and joy and need.

She sees the rainforest as it was long ago when the Waimiris were strong and plentiful. She sees the old Waimiri power, how they fought the Yanomamos and won — back when the giant sloths ruled the rainforest, back when Oxirom protected the Waimiri from those who burned the trees and killed the Indians.

As long as she is alive, as long as she has an heir to carry Oxirom's blood, the Waimiri will be safe from the steel factories, the greed, and the death.

Oxirom grunts and envelops her in fur.

She arches her neck and she lets him drink.

Yoshi scowls and turns his back. "You disgust me, Cachara. You'd rather make love to a creature than to your own husband."

If only he knew the shame, the guilt; the intense pleasure. Cachara adjusts her feather headdress and tosses Yoshi the gourd maraca painted with Oxirom's face. The maraca is one of her finest; it shows Oxirom with his canines bared and his eyes as soft as moss.

The maraca hits Yoshi's back and falls to the dry dirt floor. It rolls into the writhing insects by the sleeping mat. Ants and termites skitter.

Yoshi whirls and grabs her wrists. His black eyes glare, his nostrils flare, his straight black hair clings like a fist to his head. "Don't ever throw anything at me again, Cachara. Ever."

She shrugs him off. Foolish man, he thinks he can own *her*? So what if his father made a deal with Pompa when she was an infant? So what if his father is the Waimiri chief? She is the *SoulSharer*. She makes the gourds, the urns, the headdresses, the darts that kill the sacrificial two-toed sloths. She is Oxirom's lover. "Pull yourself together, Yoshi. Put your necklaces on and your lip skewers. Dance for the people. Dance for rubber and wood and rain. Dance for the death of those who kill our way of life."

"What will you do after I'm tribal chief? Will you still treat me this way? Do you think I will stand for it?" He wraps length after length of jute string around his waist and between his legs. He fits butterfly wings onto the sloth claws that dangle from his necklace.

A handsome man, really. Any other girl would be happy to be Yoshi's wife. And she hates the way she treats him; she knows it's wrong, she knows that he deserves far better...

But for now, she sizzles with Oxirom's blood. Her own blood is weak. Her heart throbs with the pulse of *arutam wakani*. Shared blood: shared soul.

"There are few of us left, Cachara, and our rainforest is dying. What good does Oxirom really do?"

She blackens her lips and face from the nose up using the special festival dye, the huito juice from the genipap tree. She turns to the burial urns that are propped by the hut flap. The urns that contain the ashes of Pompa and her mother, Kaia. "Oxirom is all that we have, Yoshi. We must honor Oxirom and our ancestors. We must feel the spirits of those who came before us, both sloth and human, and let them merge."

Yoshi nods. He is not a stupid man. Nor is he without respect for the ancient ways and customs. But she knows that he will be after her again, for he's been pushing at her to let Oxirom go, to let the Waimiri face fate without the protection of the giant sloth. Yoshi wants the tribe to enter what he calls the *real* world. But the ancient world of the Waimiri, where all of nature is interdependent, where seeds must be eaten by fish and deposited as dung in the mud, where one tree feeds upon another and then strangles its host, where a giant sloth shares the ancestral soul of an Indian tribe —

this ancient world *is* the real world. It is the only world that matters.

Now Yoshi slips into his dance mask and plucks the maraca from the floor. It rattles as he reaches for her — the hut is so small — and he touches her arm; lightly. "Don't forget that you carry my child, Cachara."

"The child has your blood, Yoshi, and it also has Oxirom's blood. The child will be both tribal Chief and SoulSharer."

A touch of lips: his, thin slivers of ice; hers, already deadened to anything but the kiss of sloth.

Yoshi pulls away. "But you love him more than you love me. And the child: is it really mine? or does it belong to Oxirom?"

"Be proud to share a child with him." Cachara pushes her husband away; she has had enough arguing for this, a holy night.

She lifts the hut flap.

The night is thick and black; it sticks to her like the rubber sap she molds around the urns, blowguns, drums, and gourds.

The tribe waits by the Wide River.

Already the men are beating the drums, and the women and children are chanting the litany of the giant sloth. The trough of plantain soup sits by the river bank. Yoshi's father, Chief, waves his arms over the sacrifice pit, and the smoke rises from the two-toed sloth that is being burned in Oxirom's honor. Someday, Yoshi will wear Chief's feathered body ornaments and lip plugs.

And Chief is aging; already thirty: old for a Waimiri Indian.

A hush descends as Cachara nears the water, dips her head, and drinks. Two hundred Waimiri huddle around the sacrifice pit, the men in white achiote paint and dark huito dye, the women in bark headbands and reed thongs. Yoshi dances and waves the maraca. He wears toucan feathers in his ears. The ornaments, the paint, the drums: everything was created by Cachara, the SoulSharer.

And now she will bring Oxirom to her people.

She stoops by the sacrifice pit.

Chief's eyes are warm and sad; they remind her of the eyes of the dying sloth, of Pompa's eyes as the Yonamamos drained his blood. Do all of her people have such sad eyes?

Chief places the dogfish tooth in her palm. It is the festival tooth, which she made when Pompa died. It is razor sharp and fixed with rubber and resins to a hunk of dried gourd.

"Give me Oxirom's blood." Chief's voice is deep and resonates through the trees, catches the wind and flies, catches the ripples in the Wide River and flows. Chief's voice fills all the Amazonas.

Cachara slashes his wrist, pushes the dogfish tooth deeply into his skin. And as blood oozes from his wrist and drips into the sacrifice pit, Cachara presses her lips to the wound and feels Chief's energy merge with the energy of Oxirom and her unborn child and her own self. She is many people, she contains the sparks of many lives. The sparks enter her heart, and her head bolts back in exquisite pain, and then the sparks fly to her brain.

"Give me Oxirom's blood." Chief's voice again, this time more urgent.

What has she forgotten to do?

The maraca swishes by her ears. The special festival paints, and dogfish tooth, the headdress, the feathers, the bark head-bands...*what has she forgotten?*

Perfume breath: hot and sweet upon her neck. The plunging of teeth. The merging of souls.

Oxirom is here!

But Cachara has forgotten to give Chief the power and pro-tection of Oxirom's blood. She *forgot to allow Chief to drink from her wrists and neck.*

A darkness descends over the tribe. A darkness as deep as Oxirom's fur. The night air fills with his scent.

Cachara stumbles against the giant sloth, and she sees only brown fuzz and water lily eyes. Her arm reaches as if to catch a but-terfly, and the dogfish tooth scrapes Oxirom; and Oxirom's blood sprays and covers her hand, her arm, and the dogfish tooth.

Oxirom lowers his giant paw and lifts the sacrificial two-toed sloth from its pit.

Cachara licks Oxirom's blood from her flesh. His blood is warm and tart as if blended from the honey of bees and the sap of rubber trees.

The drums are pounding now, and the people are singing the ancient great hymns that Oxirom has always loved. Cachara rises, filled with love for this creature who lets the Waimiri live as Indians, and she dances with her husband; and between their bodies is the unborn child.

And she *almost* forgets...

She turns from Yoshi to offer Chief the blood of the giant sloth, but wild screams distract her; and now she sees them: a hundred or more war-painted Yanomamo Indians. They crash through the jungle thicket, wearing red thongs around their waists and smashed white cocoon on their cheeks.·

They carry tree trunk clubs and carved wooden axes.

In the moonlight, she sees black blood, and it is everywhere. "Yoshi? Where are you, Yoshi?" Is that her husband by the pit, helping Chief escape into the woods? She cannot focus her eyes. She is numbed by Oxirom's blood.

Something grabs her from behind. Fists upon her breasts. She screams and flings the Yanomamo man from her body.

The Yanomamo growls and crouches. His eyes hold no sadness, no mystery, no ancient secrets. His eyes hold only murder.

Dogfish tooth in her fist. Dogfish tooth that mixes the blood of Oxirom and Chief and SoulSharer.

Should she use the sacred tooth?

The Yanomamo lunges again, and she has no time to think.

Her arm lashes out, and the tooth slashes the Yanomamo's eyes.

Eyes dangling now, the man is screaming and clutching his face; staggering back, splashing into the Wide River.

Gurgles, sputters...

He sinks.

And Cachara creeps down the bank, and where the water lilies grow thick, she slips into the water and hides.

"Chief is dead."

Cachara hears nothing. She honors Chief's death and will not wear even her jute thong until the next moon.

"Chief is dead, Cachara. Do you hear me?"

She is weary. Her limbs ache. "Yes, I hear you, Yoshi."

"I am Chief now, and you are Chief's wife. No more Oxirom. You will do as I say."

Cachara looks at the burial urns by the hut flap. Now there are four urns. Chief, Pompa, Kai...

But who is in the *fourth* urn?

She hasn't the energy to ask. She sinks into the moss fluff of the sleeping mat and stares up at her husband. Yoshi wears Chief's lip plugs: three sloth claws skewered into his lower lip. From the claws dangle Chief's necklaces. She remembers how sticky the rubber sap was when she molded it around the scarab beetle beads, how smooth the dry beads were and how they glistened in the sun.

Yoshi kneels by her side. He strokes her hair. She touches the smooth, dry beads. Yoshi says, "Why didn't Oxirom protect Chief? Why didn't Oxirom protect the Waimiri? Why did Oxirom run away?"

I think it's because Oxirom protects the Waimiri from the outside world. not from our own customs. The Yanomamo have always attacked the Waimiri. The Yanomamo are part of our world.

And then she remembers what really happened. She forgot to tell Chief to drink Oxirom's blood from her wrists and neck. This is her fault.

But she hasn't the strength to explain any of this to her husband. She can only mutter, "Yoshi, who is in the fourth urn?"

His hand jerks from her hair. "Our child, Cachara, our child that you lost last night when Oxirom fled."

I have lost Oxirom's child?

"And no, before you even ask, Cachara: there can be no other child. You are barren now. We had to rip the child from your insides. You may never walk again. You are lucky to be alive."

"No heir. No heir for you and for Oxirom's blood?"

The angry scowl crosses his face again, the scowl that scuttles like black clouds before the big rains. He stamps his foot and the termites skitter, and then...

he's gone, off somewhere to see his people, and she is alone in the mud hut, listening to the parrots scream and the monkeys chatter and the water dripping endlessly through the leaves.

The moon is an open wound in the black sky. The clouds are blood clots clinging to the tops of the high rubber trees.

Cachara sits by the Wide River and waits for Oxirom. For six long months, she has waited for her lover. For six long months, he has denied her.

She has lost much. Yoshi's mistress is pregnant with his child, and Cachara remains barren. Worse, the people have lost their faith in her, for she shares the soul of Oxirom, who allowed the Yanomamo to kill Chief.

"Where are you, Oxirom? Please, I beg of you, come to me."

Ripples stir on the surface of the river, and the water is like Yoshi's skin when she strokes him with brazilwood oil.

Although she's killed six two-toed sloths for him, Oxirom spurns her love. There's only one way to get Oxirom to come.

She grasps the dogfish tooth. With one quick motion, she slashes her wrist. Pain bolts from her wrist to her elbow. She falls to the mud of the bank, holds her arm over the water and lets her life and the life of Oxirom drip into the ripples.

By her cheek, a frog eats a cicada, and her life drains from her veins into the mud; and it's almost peaceful.

But then she hears him — *she hears Oxirom!* — and he comes in his sea of flying scarab beetles, his paws pounding huge tracks into the red soil.

She slides into the river until the water covers her legs and hips. He sits behind her; she feels his breath.

But there is another with him. *A human.*

"Who is it?" she whispers.

And he responds: "You lost our child, and now you're barren. You even dare to try and kill yourself. Who will continue to protect the Waimiri tribe, *your* people, if you die? We must share our souls, Cachara, and without a child from you, what will happen? I cannot allow *my* race to die. What would you have me do?"

Her blood, the blood of the shared ancestral soul, flows into the water. Without Oxirom, Cachara *has* no life. She needs to feel some hope for the Waimiri, but...

"The Waimiri are dying, Oxirom. The killers come, they cut the trees, they burn the huts. The Waimiri have lost a hundred people these past moons. I have no answers for you."

Above her, Oxirom's face blots the sky. The two sharp canines, the soft fur, the lily pad eyes. His breath: a perfume, a drug; it eases her terrible pain.

But in his breath is another smell, that of human blood. In his arm, a body moves. His paw sets the body in the mud beside her.

The body is alive. It has no eyes. Its face is bloody, its meat dangles from its red thong.

She recognizes the body. "The Yanomamo who tried to kill me? You dare to share the Waimiri soul with a Yanomamo, of all people: *him!*"

The man moans. On his neck are bloody splotches where Oxirom has sucked life.

Oxirom dips his head, and the long tongue unfurls and wraps around the man's neck. Cachara shivers, half from the ecstasy of remembering that joy; half from jealousy and hatred of the Yanomamo.

Oxirom bares his canines.

She cries, "Me! Give it to me! Just this once, worship me enough to give me life."

"But you gave this man our soul. You slashed him with the sacred tooth and on that tooth was my blood."

"Then maybe it was meant to be. The old customs, the old ways: *perhaps they are simply gone.*"

The water is cold around her waist. It slides up her ribs to her chest. Her arms are too weak to clutch at the muddy bank, and between her legs is a terrible ache, an ache that can only be satisfied by Oxirom. She must feel his mouth upon her neck. She must feel his blood flowing through her veins.

Nothing else matters.

Oxirom lowers his head and licks the tears from her cheeks. "The Yanomamo is not the same. His soul is not mine. The Yanomamo never comes willingly."

Lust of the Giant Sloth

There is a sadness in his eyes. It is the sadness that she sees in all the Waimiri people. And she realizes that Oxirom, the last of the giant sloths, is the only Waimiri soul. There can never be another SoulSharer, for she has ended the ancient race by forgetting one simple custom, to let Chief drink Oxirom's blood from her veins.

"Drain me. It is all that I want now," she says. "There's really nothing left, is there?"

His two large paws lift her from the mud of the Wide River.

She arches her neck.

But this time, he bites her heart directly, and the incisions are strong and deep.

I wrote ANODE TO THEE: OR SURFING THOSE TUBU-LAR WAVES specifically for Catherine Asaro, who was editor of Mindsparks at the time. I knew Catherine was a physicist and thought she might enjoy a story about the angst of particles.

AnOde to Thee

(Or: Surfing those Tubular Waves)

Magnetism sizzled off Elex' flanks as she whooshed past on the high energy wave. Elex shimmied into place on the outermost rim. What a ride!

Her present wavelength felt familiar: long and languid and definitely boring. Elex peered past the inner shells at the nucleus. A blue flash sparked near the center of the atom, momentarily blinding her; then indigo and blue and green flared, feverishly, as if the nuclear hostess was excited to see her.

As the younger electrons settled down in colorful spasms to their shells, Elex clearly saw the nucleus of the positive ion, and her heart sank. Her hostess was a fuzzy, lumpy blob of potassium: 19 chubby protons and 20 fat and lazy neutrons.

"Oh, no!" cried Elex. "Of all the billions of atoms I could have run into, it had to be you again!"

"So," said Iona dryly, "what goes around comes around. My rebellious offspring is back."

Elex shifted her mass and interacted with the electron distribution she knew to be her brother. Being young, he skittered by in a febrile wave function. She felt a magnetic attraction to him, but he easily repulsed her.

"I'm sorry, Ma," she said, "I didn't mean to upset you. I'm just not ready to settle down again at home."

"Well, you do upset me, Elex. You're my oldest electron, the one of my outer shell. How do you think your little brothers and sisters felt when you ran off like that, leaving the household agitated and unstable? We, who have always prided ourselves on our attraction to the positive, found ourselves drawn ineluctably toward the undesirable negative of the — " and she almost spat the word — "cathode."

"Ma, I couldn't help it," sighed Elex, knowing Iona would never understand. "I was minding my own business, keeping the little electrons in their proper orbitals, when I was lured away by the most exciting high energy wave. I mean, it was just tubular! I've lived in a shell all my life. I need to get out more often."

She gazed at the anode where vibrant colors phosphoresced in long beckoning flicks. Behind her, a wave slithered through neighboring atoms, bopping outer electrons from their shells. She tried to position herself for bopping, but the energy slinked past, leaving her to the whims of her mother.

"You can get yourself bumped off again when you're a few years older," Iona said. "I worry about you when you flit down the tube with god knows what — a proton maybe! — to who knows where: it's all so Heisenbergly uncertain."

"Ma, I love you, I really do, but you're so stodgy. I want to see new waves! The first time you get excited — well, it's unlike anything you can imagine! I probably wouldn't have come home for ages, but I was forced to return by circuits beyond my control."

"So what's so bad about being here? Wasn't living in a high energy orbital enough for you?"

"Aw, that's kid stuff. I want to go off on a new wavelength. I want to see all the other colors of life!"

"So there's no keeping you...All I ask, Elex, is that you be careful. Don't bring home some degenerate proton who'll split us up.

AnOde to Thee

If you have to drag somebody home, at least let it be an acceptable neutron who won't destroy the stability of our nuclear family."

"I don't want to cause a fission in the family," sparked Elex.

"I'm glad you realize," Iona said, "that it could be an explosive situation."

"Of course I do, Ma." Elex was jittery, sparking at the bit to skitter off into the tube.

"Before you go," said her mother, "there's one more thing, young lady."

"What, Ma? What?" Elex flickered, poised to let her adolescent energy levels get excited.

"Don't mess with any tachyons, honey. You know they have a reputation for being fast."

"Don't worry so much." Elex flicked her mother a smile and leaped to the crest of a tubular wave. "All the kids know that they're, like totally unreal."

For many years, I was fascinated by ancient oriental artwork and history. I knew that the geisha were meant to entertain, soothe, and cater to men; they were not meant to be prostitutes. Printed here for the first time is GEISHA BLACK, a fusion of science and ancient Japanese motifs.

Geisha Black

Natsuyuki knelt on her reed mat, waiting for Mistress Midori's signal. Tonight, Natsuyuki would play the biwa lute for Midori's favorite customer, the elderly Yaeha.

The sliding paper door rustled, and in a rush of perfume and silk kimono, Midori entered the tiny room. Though she trembled inside, Natsuyuki kept her eyes lowered, her fingertips joined on her lap.

Midori had taught her well. Natsuyuki, only sixteen, already was one of Midori's finest geishas.

"Are you ready?" Midori's lips were painted red, her face buffed with a new powder that made her cheeks glow like the moon. She set a vase of flowers on the low table where Yaeha would sit. She straightened the hanging hakubyo painting: its style feathery, calm, opaque; one of Natsuyuki's finest works.

Natsuyuki bowed her head slightly. "Yes, Mistress, and tonight, your Yaeha will be very happy."

Midori's face flushed beneath its white mask, her dark eyes flashed.

Yaeha had been Midori's first love, back when she was Natsuyuki's age. It was said that Midori had almost become one of
Yaeha's concubines, that he had begged her to leave the geisha
house; but then something had happened, something awful.

Now, Midori was in her thirties, old by geisha standards; but
Yaeha still came for her, still gave her large sums of money for
evenings of dancing, music, and conversation. Over the years, he
had made Midori one of Heian's most wealthy and respected busi-
nesswomen.

And there were few choices for a woman in this, the year
1188. Mistress Midori had done very well, indeed.

"Remember, Natsuyuki, you are fujin, a lady."

Natsuyiki bobbed her head, murmured, "Yes, Mistress, I'll
remember," but inside, she was worried. Why did Midori's hands
twitch? And why was she wearing so much face paint, especially
tonight when Yaeha was coming? Was she hiding something beneath that mask of white? Something *horrible*?

"Just remember." Midori turned to the window, gazed at the
white flowers of the snowflake bushes; like gleaming pearls nes-
tled against the lush cherry blossoms. And the curcas bean flowers, green and hairy; a feathery spray over the garden wall.

Oigimi, the maid, was collecting flowers. She would mix the
curcas sap with crushed snowflake flowers to make paints and
powders for the geishas.

Perhaps Oigimi could show Natsuyuki how to make the new
powder that adorned Midori's cheeks. "Shall I help gather the
flowers?" asked Natsuyuki.

Midori turned sharply from the window, her eyes circled in
red paint, blazing like twin fires. "No, never touch the flowers!
Oigimi is the maid, not you."

Natsuyuki held back tears. Her Mistress had never spoken to
her in such biting tones.

Midori came to her, stroked her hair. Her fingers were soft
and warm. "I'm sorry, daughter. I'm not myself today. Yaeha is
old, and dying. And Yaeha wants something before he passes to
eternal death."

"What does he want?"

But before Midori could answer, the paper door rustled and slid open, and the room filled with the smell of carcasses drying by the edge of the woods.

It was Yaeha.

He was stooped, shrunken; and he staggered, his skin wobbling in loose folds from his neck and arms. His scalp was thick and tan as animal hide, and blotched with gray.

But his eyes: as always, they sparkled; and his lips twisted with pleasure when he saw Midori.

He reached for her, tottered, and she rushed forward to hold his hands. "Kiss my cheek, loved one," she said, turning her head to place her right cheek near his lips.

He smiled, his teeth blackened to hide the blemishes. He kissed her gently, and as his lips moved from her cheek, they retained the white powder she wore for this, Natsuyuki's special night.

Midori eased him onto the brocaded cushion beneath Natsuyuki's painting. Her face was more radiant than usual. So radiant it shimmered.

And yet, beneath the white glow, there was a darkness, a trembling. Her nostrils flared, then tightened, as she leaned toward her first love and whispered something in his ear.

He laughed.

And Natsuyuki almost felt gay; but still, there was something wrong. Midori was the finest geisha in Heian, but tonight, she wore her emotions, which is something no geisha ever did.

Yaeha's laughter broke. His arms flailed. He was rasping for air.

Choking.

He clutched his chest, his face twisting, and he fell from the cushion.

Midori clasped his waist, gently eased him up. Her face was filled with tenderness and concern, her words were soothing. "Relax, dearest one, for soon, you will have your dying wish."

Geisha Black

"You will give me Natsuyuki?" He was still clutching his chest, and his voice: feeble, hoarse; croaking as a frog at sunset.

Natsuyuki's limbs grew cold. Surely, Midori wouldn't give her to *Yaeha*.

But Midori laughed. "You always get what you desire, don't you?"

He smiled, drool trickling from his lips, and his eyes settled on the folds of Natsuyuki's kimono where it crossed her chest.

It took everything in her not to clutch the kimono tightly to her body, to run from the room; but Midori had trained her well, and Natsuyuki said nothing and did not move. Instead, she remained rigid, her fingertips twined on her lap.

Yaeha whispered: "She is perfect."

Midori said, "Once I was perfect for you. Now you want Natsuyuki. But before you take her, kiss my cheek again, if only for old time's sake."

Yaeha's eyes remained on Natsuyuki, as his lips smeared across the white paste on Midori's cheek. He sputtered, coughed, then smiled faintly at Midori, who seemed pleased. "Old friends always grant each other's wishes," she said, and nodded at Natsuyuki to begin the entertainment.

Natsuyuki had to perform. She was Midori's chosen one, her geisha daughter, meant to take over the house should Midori die.

So Natsuyuki lifted the lute from the silken mat by her side. And while she played, Yaeha's face glowed and his eyes twinkled with pleasure.

Midori peeled grapes and popped them into Yaeha's mouth. She fed him roasted gingko nuts from her fingertips.

But Yaeha's eyes remained on Natsuyuki. Not once did he look at Midori.

Natsuyuki danced — his favorite piece, portraying the Dojoji legend — keeping her shoulders sloped, her knees bent, her feet pigeon-toed in their heavy wooden clogs.

And Yaeha gasped with delight.

Midori plucked bones from a trout, fed him the succulent tidbits; she lifted the lacquered cup of saki to his lips.

Finally, Natsuyuki was done. She gracefully lowered herself to her cushion, eyes on her lap.

"Never have I seen such perfection." Yaeha's voice was hoarse and low. Natsuyuki looked up, saw his eyes gleaming at her.

Midori's eyes gleamed, too, but with the gleam of *gaki* demons.

"Now sing for me," said Yaeha.

She did as told, but as her voice swelled with sweetness, trained by Midori to soothe Yaeha's ears, Natsuyuki's heart sank.

Yaeha no longer loved her Mistress.

Yaeha loved *her*.

It was no wonder Midori had been so upset lately.

"You sing like angels." Yaeha wobbled to his feet, ignored Midori, lurched toward Natsuyuki. And now he stood over her, tottering, and he leaned; and his hands were raw paper, scratching her soft flesh; and his breath, though tainted by saki, was that of a man about to die, the faint wheezes as foul as gusts from the fetid swamp.

Natsuyuki shuddered and drew back. "I am *fujin*," she cried.

"You are promised." Yaeha's lips raked her cheek; two withered claws.

"Midori!" Natsuyuki jumped to her feet.

Midori rose from her cushions, and in measured steps, walked toward Yaeha, her finger pointing at him.

"She *was* promised, but it will not be done."

"It was our deal," he said.

Midori rested a shimmering cheek upon Natsuyuki's hair. "I'm sorry, it was a long time ago, my daughter, when I promised him...*you*...and in return, he kept the geisha house going."

"But how could you do this?" asked Natsuyuki, tears caking the powder on her cheeks, white paste dripping from her chin onto her silken kimono.

"It was all I knew how to do," said Midori.

Yaeha stumbled toward the sliding door. "This is no longer a geisha house. This is a house of broken promises. You forget, Midori, that I have many friends — police — who will gladly come and shut you down. It takes only one word from me."

Midori did not reply.

And long after he left, Midori refused to talk to Natsuyuki. Instead, she remained alone in her room, huddled on her reed mat; and for long hours, Natsuyuki heard her moans and her weeping.

And Natsuyuki's heart broke, for she knew that she had to go to Yaeha and be his concubine.

For the honor of her Mistress.

Early the next morning, while Midori snored, Natsuyuki tiptoed into her sleeping room. The moon cast its glow across Midori's face: her wrinkles etched like the black lines of the hakubyo painting. Her snores, soft and low, rising in steady rhythm as a wave rises upon the sea.

Natsuyuki stooped by her Mistress and groped on the low table. She found the tiny jar that held Midori's shimmering, new powder.

There was a clasp on the lid. She flipped it open, poked her finger into the powder, and wiped it across her cheeks and nose.

Tonight, she would glow for Yaeha, and she would do what was right for her Mistress.

For the honor of the great geisha house of Heian.

The powder stung her skin, swept through her like a great fire, and though the room was dark, lit only by the cold white moon, she saw hot color: warm rainbow, boiling waterfall, and the sun's rays so fierce they burned her skin.

She gasped.

What was happening to her?

Midori's eyes blinked, then opened. "Natsuyuki, what have you done?"

Geisha Black

"I have done what's needed," said Natsuyuki, her voice coming in tiny rasps.

"No, not the powder! The powder is not for you!" Midori leapt from the mat, tightened the belt of her kimono. She stumbled past Natsuyuki, fumbled on the low table.

And Natsuyuki felt a cool cloth on her face, wiping the powder from her cheeks.

"Go rest now," said Midori, her hands linked under Natsuyuki's arms, pulling her gently from the room, "and tonight, let me prepare for Yaeha."

Natsuyuki did not understand. As her Mistress tucked the blanket under her chin and pressed a cool cloth over her forehead, Natsuyuki said, "Please, please tell me what's going on. What has Yaeha done?"

But Midori only said, "Yaeha has always done what's right. But Yaeha is not good to his concubines, his wives; and Yaeha, he cannot have you."

And Natsuyuki slowly drifted to sleep, her eyes shutting but still seeing rainbows and waterfalls dancing across the backs of her lids.

Something brushed her cheek. Two withered claws.

She jerked from her mat. "No! Yaeha, no!"

But it was only Midori, her fingers soft and gentle upon Natsuyuki's face. "Come. It is time to prepare."

Natsuyuki followed her Mistress back to the room with the low table. The jar with the clasped lid was gone.

Natsuyuki knelt before the table, while Midori dabbed nightingale droppings on her cheeks to bleach the skin.

It was only after she had dressed Natsuyuki in the ritual kimonos that Midori finally spoke of Yaeha: "Soon it will all be over. Soon you will know everything. Just remember to remove the bones from his trout. And feed him the lotus root; it is an aphrodisiac."

"Mistress!"

"But remember: he cannot touch you."

Feed Yaeha aphrodisiacs? Not let him touch her? Midori made no sense.

"And if he wants to share the saki, then what?" asked Natsuyuki.

"Then share it," said Midori.

The saki would bind Natsuyuki to Yaeha. The saki meant more than a wedding vow.

Please don't let Yaeha request the saki...

Midori reached beneath her sleep mat. She removed the tiny jar, shaped like a snowflake flower, and unclasped its lid. She smeared white clay on her cheeks, painted her face white. Then she dipped a finger into the special jar, spread powder across her cheeks.

Her face flushed, her eyes rolled, she staggered; but her skin glowed like summer snowflake flowers.

That night, Natsuyuki danced for Yaeha again, and she sang, and this time, fed Yaeha the trout, the gingko nuts, and the lotus root.

Midori's face was stark white, colder than the moon.

"I will now share saki with your little Natsuyuki. As promised sixteen years ago," said Yaeha.

Natsuyuki clenched her hands tightly together. Sweat ran down her back. No, not so soon, not until she understood...

Midori sat by Yaeha's brocaded cushion. She said, "We once shared the bond of saki, Yaeha. It creates a blood kinship that can only be destroyed by death."

"It is promised. I want blood kinship with this little one of yours."

Natsuyuki didn't want kinship with Yaeha, didn't want to leave Midori and live in some strange house with Yaeha's concubines.

She only wanted to remain here in the geisha house, untouched by men, certainly untouched by Yaeha.

Midori said, "Kiss me tonight, kiss me again, dearest one, then tomorrow you may have Natsuyuki."

"Always tomorrow," said Yaeha, "but tomorrow is now, and I will wait no longer."

"Kiss me," repeated Midori, offering her cheek.

Always the kisses. Why did Midori always insist upon the kisses?

And suddenly, Natsuyuki knew, she knew without any doubt why Midori always wanted Yaeha to kiss her cheek.

It was the powder.

The heat, the burning, the *fire...*

The curcas bean, deadly, and the snowflake flower, fatal.

That was why Midori never allowed Natsuyuki to touch the flowers, to crush them into powder. Yet Midori herself wore the deadly flowers; was Midori dying, as Yaeha soon would die?

"Do not kiss her!" Natsuyuki leapt from her cushion, grabbed Yaeha's arm; but too late, his lips brushed across the smear of white on the Mistress' cheek.

And the Mistress laughed.

"Why?" croaked Yaeha, his face twisted in pain. His body heaved with spasms, rose and fell upon the floor as if the blood raced as an angry sea toward shore. He fell across the table, his fingers raking down the front of Midori's kimono. His fingers, leaving bloody trails. The table fell, the gingko nuts rolled like marbles across the floor. The trout and the lotus root, the aphrodisiac, in a heap by Midori's feet.

"Because you abused my trust," said Midori, shaking his fingers loose, staring coldly with eyes rimmed in redfire paint.

Natsuyuki fell to the floor by Yaeha. His breath, a fetid gust; his spasms, growing faint.

And then: no breath, no spasm, only the burning blood.

"You killed him."

"He abused his concubines. He beat them when they were pregnant. He did not want you. Only now, did he want you."

"What are you saying?" Natusuyuki was weeping, holding her father's head, *Yaeha's* head, in her hands.

"Yes, he was your father, but he wanted you dead at birth. But I said, no, she must live; and you must do what's right, Yaeha, you must make sure she is always safe and free from harm."

"But — "

"He let you live, but only after I promised to give him to you when you reached the time of full geisha."

Natsuyuki removed her father's fingers from the folds of her kimono where it crossed her chest. Her father, Yaeha, dead.

And her mother? *Midori?*

Her mother, dying from the snowflake flowers, dying to save her, Natusuyuki, from her own father's clutching, withered claws.

"I will die *with you*, then," said Natsuyuki, grabbing Midori's face, smearing her mouth across Midori's white death mask.

Midori slapped Natsuyuki's cheek, sending her whirling back, falling over Yaeha.

Boiling waterfalls and rainbows ...

The hakubyo painting coming to life...

Midori knelt over her. "Though the geisha's face is white, daughter ...*her heart is black.*" And Midori would die, if not from the powder, from the broken honor that would always sting her heart.

And Natsuyuki would no longer be geisha.

She would rip the curcas bean plants from the garden. By their roots.

She would destroy the snowflake flowers: white stars that burn brightly, then kill. She would take care of Midori, her mother, but she would never forget.

And when Midori died, Natusuyuki's heart would forever be black.

Given that all four of my grandparents emigrated from Russia between 1900 and 1910, I've always been interested in the history and geography of the country. SKINHEAD BONEHEAD fuses science with Russian history.

Skinhead Bonehead

Six more days protecting bones, then Beretta Tremoire would finally leave the frozen Siberian hell of Ekaterinburg. He twisted the silencer onto the muzzle of his Makarov pistol. Climbed the long flight of stairs leading to the makeshift morgue.

Lily Hwa, his Chinese counterpart these past months, crouched on the floor by the wrought-iron gate. A cigarette dangled from the corner of her mouth. Her eyes squinted at him through smoke. "You ready to guard the imperial gutou?" she said, using the Chinese word for bones.

"Show me your piece, Lily."

"It has a suppressor." She pulled a Chinese Type 59 pistol from an inner jacket pocket.

"I see we have something in common today." Her Type 59 was the Chinese equivalent of his Russian Makarov.

She rose, her body supple and lean, and slouched against the iron gate. She dangled her pistol from a forefinger, her other hand on a hip. Short black hair, eyes the blue of lapis.

He would miss her.

"I would only do this for you," he said.

"And I will repay you a thousandfold when I bring the gutou back to Peking and have hope of reviving Tsu Hzi."

Lily's beloved *lao*, old person, so old she was long dead: Tsu Hzi, the last great Empress of China. The evil Dragon Lady, who had ruled by torture and slowly inflicted death.

Why was he risking his career, his life for a woman he'd known for only five months?

She answered the unspoken question by sidling up to him, her sinewy body pressing close, her purr soft upon his neck.

She fondled his muzzle. "Let's do it, baby."

Was hard to break away, her hand in his tight blond curls, her pistol hard against his back.

But the time had come — only six days left — and so he eased her body off, twisted the locks on the gate and swung it open, then pressed the number panel that unlocked the heavy metal door.

She was behind him, her breath hot on his neck, her purrs coming in tiny gasps of excitement.

"Now," he whispered, and together, they heaved against the metal, crashed the door open, and leapt into the morgue.

Dr. Gruenwald looked up from a table by the window. His hands wore rubber gloves, his gray hair was tousled and rose in tufts around the head strap of his microscopic spectacles.

To his right, seated by the desk, two forensic experts, a Chinese man and a Russian woman, dropped their scalpels.

The nine skeletons, all that remained of the last tsar of Russia and his family, were arranged, head to toe, on the tables lining the four walls.

Bones.

Everywhere, bones.

"What's the meaning of this?" Gruenwald grabbed a knife.

"Drop it." Beretta aimed his gun between the doctor's eyes.

Gruenwald's knife fell to the pile of bones before him, then clattered to the cement floor.

"Don't make us hurt you. Your bones are worthless. Remember that." With her pistol trained on Gruenwald, Lily moved across the room to Tsar Nicholas' skeleton. Lodged in its skull were both a bullet and tiny shrunken brain. She tucked a thigh bone under her belt. Snapped off a finger bone, crammed it into the right pocket of her too-tight jeans.

"Beretta?" said Gruenwald, backing against a table. "Don't call me Beretta. I hate that name. My father, that he had to name me after his gun — "

"Would you prefer that I call you Traitor?" Gruenwald's eyes narrowed.

"Spies are never traitors. We're only hired hands, doctor."

Beretta reached beneath the tsar's skeleton, slid open the drawer that held the rope. The very ropes that had hauled the corpses from their muddy hole in the mineshaft outside Ekaterinburg. Back in 1917, before the Bolsheviks reburied the tsar and his family in the bog.

He was so tired of CIA work: sitting in dark corridors, protecting bone doctors; dragging around the world, lost, just waiting for a bullet to give him peace.

Now all he wanted was Lily.

At any cost.

"Come on, help me tie them up." Lily waved her gun at the three doctors, and Beretta blinked. Tie them up and get out — quickly.

He grabbed the elbow of the female doctor and shoved her against Gruenwald, then he and Lily tied the three doctors together, and he crammed surgical cotton into their mouths.

Lily's eyes glowed; like blue frost upon the peaks of the Ural Mountains. Her lips curled. "We have the DNA, Beretta. Soon, Tsu Hzi will return, endowed with the genes of the ancient tsars."

She was fooling herself. There was no way Chinese doctors, or doctors anywhere in the world, could bring back the dead Empress using genes from these bones.

But Beretta didn't care. It never mattered why a spy did *anything*. So let Lily think what she wanted. After she returned to

Peking and delivered the bones to the Chinese, she would help him enter China, and then, Beretta would finally have her, finally have peace.

It couldn't happen soon enough.

"Quickly now, go!" He waved his gun at the door, and she slid past him into the dark hallway. With a quick "I'm sorry doctor" to Gruenwald, he bolted the metal door and wrought-iron gate, then he and Lily raced down the stairs into the pounding hail of the Siberian night; the thigh bone jutting from the waistband of Lily's jeans, the finger hard in her pocket; her movements quick and excited, her body bounding; and though he knew she would repay him a thousandfold, the hail rained down upon his skull like a blast of bullets.

Slipping on ice past brooding black buildings. The night alive; yet nobody around. Hail, and dark rolling waves of fog swooping down the narrow streets. Howling wind, rusty doors banging on stone walls.

Beretta: his Makarov pistol clutched in fingers numb from the night. Fingers swathed in heavy wool gloves, frozen to their tips.

Ahead of him, a dart of black energy, his beloved Lily.

Kiss me, she had said, *and make me forget my past.*

Her past, worse than his own.

She, orphaned at nine in Peking, the Forbidden City, her dead father a Chinese spy, her mother an American traitor.

He, orphaned at twelve in America, his dead father an American spy, his mother unknown.

He and Lily, drawn together by a common past.

And so he had clenched her tightly and let their heat burn through the chill of Siberian night; there in the morgue, on the cold cement floor, her kisses like fire in his blood, her tiny body wrapped around him; and for a short time, he belonged somewhere, he belonged with Lily.

Skinhead Bonehead

"Dropoff point. Here." Her voice jerked him from the memories, and he stopped running, held for a moment in the dense black fog roiling down the street and swirling around his ankles; fog so thick that he couldn't see the crumbled stone pavement beneath his boots.

Lily pointed to a rotting building, an old munitions factory from the second world war. The windows were cracked and coated in frost, the stone walls glistened with ice.

He followed her into an alley, where they swept the frost from a window with their gloves, then both of them peered inside, where candles flickered on a table cut from rough wood, the candlelight like claws groping at the cavernous ceiling.

The smell was gunpowder.

Beretta drank it in and savored it.

Two men, wearing black caps and heavy coats, tinkered with an array of rubber nipples, Tokarev TT-33 pistols, and petri dishes.

The nipples: quick silencers for the pistols. But the petri dishes?

Beretta had no time to ask. Lily slipped through a broken pane, and once again, Beretta followed.

Human anatomy charts peeling from the walls. And the equipment: automated pipetting devices that looked like ham radios; microtitration instruments, autoclaves, beakers, test tubes, microscopes, incubators...

The place looked like Dr. Gruenwald's morgue.

It was a lab.

"What the hell is *this*?" Beretta grabbed Lily's wrist and wrenched her around to face him.

Her breath was labored — she liked it when he was rough — and her face flushed from excitement. "Skinhead factory, where Russian nationalists work to bring the tsar back to life. They want his DNA, to study it."

He shoved her against the stone wall, his face inches from hers. "But this was to be a dropoff point! We were to get money for these bones, from the Chinese."

Skinhead Bonehead

"Why use the tsar's bones to bring back the Great Empress?"

"You tell me: why?"

She laughed, squirmed in his grip. She was enjoying his confusion. "Because the tsars were more fierce than Tsu Hzi? Their genes more potent?"

"You're making fun of me, and *I don't like it!*"

She laughed again, and he loosened his grip, waiting...and as expected, her free fist flew up and her knee rose between his legs: but he knew her well, knew all her tricks, and he jerked back and laughed at her.

"You're not so quick, Lily."

"Who's there?" The men — Beretta swiveled his head — both grabbed guns from the table.

Lily wrenched free and stepped into the candlelight. "I have your bones." She turned briefly to Beretta and hissed, "Remember, we're only hired hands, and the Russians pay more for the tsar's bones than the Chinese."

Hired hands; spies were nothing more than hired hands; and money was money, whether it came from the Russians or the Chinese.

Besides, let the skinheads study the tsar's DNA till doomsday, let them grow and recombine genes in culture, let them inject ancient genetic codes of Russian rulers into newborn babes.

Who cared?

As long as Beretta went to China with Lily, he no longer cared about anything else.

"Who is *this?*" One man waved his gun at Beretta.

Lily's lips parted, red, the only color in this place of darkness. Her face flushed as she moved quickly toward the man. "Ah, Deathray, my love. At last, I have the DNA. We can go to Kholmogory and be rich."

The man named Deathray pulled off his cap. His naked skull bore a tattoo of shattered bones and shrapnel, with the word,

Deathray, branded to his forehead. "And what of this man, Lily? I say we kill him. Nosgorod?"

The other man, Nosgorod, nodded: "Kill him," he said, lifting his gun and smiling, his teeth chipped and blackened from tobacco and too many brawls.

"But sweet thing," Lily brushed her hands across Deathray's face, "this man is a friend, he helped me get the bones. He only wants money for escape."

Suddenly, Beretta was only a *friend?* What about running to China together, what about leaving the spy business to roll in each other's arms on soft grass under a warm sun? What about —

Nosgorod grabbed his elbow, thrust him at Deathray. "What do we do with him, boss?"

Deathray, a name as fierce as Beretta's; just another hired hand, a *spook* who took money to play with bones.

And Beretta knew these games well. He swiveled and kicked Nosgorod in the stomach; and as the man clenched his belly and fell to his knees, Beretta pulled out his gun, aimed it at Deethray, and cocked the trigger "Pay me, Deathboy, Now."

"Give him the money. Let him go." Deathray motioned at Nosgorod, who rose and edged past Beretta. Nosgorod: skin the color of iron, eyes like rusty nails; he pulled a black sack from a carton of debris wedged beneath the table and thrust it at Beretta.

Beretta grabbed the sack, pulled it open, saw the Chinese money.

Whatever it was, it would do.

He backed into the shadows. "Let's go, Lily."

But she laughed. "Go? What for? To live in China like a dead woman with you? Do you think I care about Tsu Hzi? I go with the money, the big money." And she twined her legs around Deathray, who clutched her tightly with one hand while training his gun at Beretta.

"Go," growled Nosgorod, "before you go as a corpse."

"Lily... ?" Beretta couldn't believe this. How many nights had he writhed on his cot, dreaming of Lily's lapis eyes, her red lips, her heated kiss?

Now those eyes held nothing but contempt for him, those lips nothing but sneers. "You silly fool," she said, "I don't belong to the Chinese. I belong to the Russians."

"No, Lily dear, you belong to me." Deathray pulled her close, and as he kissed her, Beretta turned and ran...

Didn't look back...

Just ran.

Outside, he stood panting, back hard against the slimy wall, sack of money in his fist.

Alone, with the hail raining down. Nowhere to go, a traitor.

He sank to the icy stone, his head spinning in a black whorl, the smell of gunpowder strong in his nostrils.

He sat there for what seemed like hours, peeking inside the broken pane from time to time, watching his beloved Lily in the arms of the Russian Deathray. She was a traitor. Beretta had trusted her with his life, his dreams, his past; and she had deceived him; and he wouldn't do the same to Gruenwald.

He shivered, his coat caked in ice, his hands as frozen as his heart.

What was he to do?

Get the bones back, return to the morgue, free the doctors?

Somehow, he had to clear his name. Beg, if necessary, in the name of his dead father, one of the finest agents ever to serve the CIA.

And what of Lily?

Noise from within the building, and laughter. Beretta peeked again through the broken pane. Lily, Deathray, and Nosgorod were tucking their guns into their pockets and moving quickly toward the front of the building.

"Hurry," said Lily, "we must be out of Ekaterinburg by daybreak. It's a long way to Kholmogory, almost to the White Sea."

She turned and blew out the candles. The last thing Beretta saw was her face: alive with excitement and the heat of the chase.

Beretta crammed the money sack under his belt and into his underwear. Then he scooted toward the front of the building. The fog was thick, he could barely see, but there: two men scurrying through the black night.

His boots clacked on the ice. The men stopped briefly, turned, saw him; then broke into a full run.

With his muscles straining, his legs stretching to go faster, yet faster, Beretta raced after them; so fast the wind seemed to propel him, the fog to curl around him and embrace him and sweep him toward his prey like a giant hound barreling after two hapless rabbits.

He reached them quickly, leapt, and tackled one down. Deathray. Beat the ugly face with the butt of his gun while grabbing Nosgorod's ankles. Now whirled and rose, kicked Nosgorod's face to send him sprawling to the ice. Smashed the man's head against the side of the building, then left the corpse for the Russian police to find in the morning.

Small movements on the pavement. Deathray: still alive.

Beretta placed his boot on Deathray's stomach, leaned, and placed the tip of his gun an inch from Deathray's forehead. "Where are the bones?"

A tiny gasp, forced words: "In...pocket..."

Beretta thrust his hand into the man's coat pocket, removed the thigh bone and finger, crammed the bones into his underwear beside the sack of money. The gun now pressed into Deathray's flesh. "And the girl? Lily?"

"What of her?"

"The girl? You want the girl?" The man was chortling, making fun of him.

"I don't use rubber nipples to silence *my* gun, Deathboy, and I don't care who hears me blow you to bits."

"Lily, ha, she is a good little f — "

And that's when the gun blew, and the damned man's words shrieked a thousand syllables and died in a howl of wind.

Skinhead Bonehead

Another life gone. Two men dead, with only one bullet spent. Blood rose like steam from the icy pavement. Beretta's coat was splattered with gore, his gloves saturated with the last of Death-ray's life.

How many had Beretta killed? A hundred men, five hundred?

He didn't want to kill any more.

He had the bones, the money.

But what to do with his life?

There were no options, not for Beretta.

Back in the skinhead lab, he found Lily, chained with rusty irons and bolted to a wall. Bloody from a quick beating, crying. Her body quaking from the cold.

He smashed an incubator against the irons and freed her. "Lily? How could you do this to me?"

Her blue eyes were filmed from tears, puffed from the beating. "We have the money. We can go to Peking. Please?"

Always, Lily went with the big money. "I'm sorry, Lily. Maybe I'm not the hired hand I always thought I was. You're a traitor — to everything — and I can't live that way."

"But I'm with you, with the Chinese." Her fingers, sticky with blood, touched his cheek, and her purr was soft upon his neck. Her body: so supple and lean; her eyes: so desperate.

"I'm with nobody, Lily. Not even with you." The words were the truth. Hard to say, but the truth. All he'd wanted was love, to belong somewhere, to find peace.

But there was no love for Beretta. Nowhere to go where life would be safe and tranquil.

"Beretta?"

He didn't answer. He'd always hated that name. He wrapped her body in filthy lab sheets, then lifted her and slipped back into the night, where the hail was still raining down like bullets upon his skull.

Always, the bullets would be there; and the gunpowder, and the memories.

Skinhead Bonehead

He would deliver Lily as the traitor, return the bones with the money, tell them where to find the dead skinheads. He would be a hero.

And in six more days, he would leave this frozen Siberian hell to drag around the world, forever lost, just waiting for a bullet to find his brain.

WEE SWEET GIRLIES is an extremely dark fairy tale told from the viewpoint of a simple girl who isn't exactly leading "the good life."

Wee Sweet Girlies

I gulp the bitter beer and stare into the fire. It crackles like the bones between Bork's teeth. He crunches and spits gristle into the mud, then he smears the grease from his chin.

The rat skins are thin across my shoulders; I pull the cape tightly to seal my heart from Bork. Our three daughters are dead. Tiny buds crushed in their father's fists.

Bork picks his teeth and leers. "Such a nice little bitty you are. Come 'ere, me love, come on." Nausea rises from the pit of my belly. The smoke from the fire is sweet from the roasting meat of Bork's young girls.

"Oh Bork, please no."

He answers, a growl in the back of his throat. He leans, and his paw grazes my cape. I shudder against the mud wall, and his eyes light. The leathery skin is so close; so tight across his cheekbones, like straps that cleave the axe to the handle. His mouth is a black wound. I sink down the wall, push myself into the mud, push until I can sink no farther.

Already I carry his fourth child. What more can he want?

Closer he comes, his fur coarse and cloyed with stink. My hands are trembling, my neck sweating; and now he nibbles my ear with the teeth that shredded baby Anne's flesh; and he licks my throat with the tongue that licked little Rosalie's blood —

"Oh, God's mercy, no!" The words escape; a violent wrench; and now he will *kill me kill me kill me.*

His arm, a falling tree; his body, a crashing bear. He growls from the back of his throat, "Give me more daughters! Give me wee sweet girlies!" And then he digs into me like a shovel to mud, and I gasp; and he plows me with seed until the fire dies; and then Mother Earth cradles me in her cold, wet embrace.

I dream of death; and then the sun shimmers, and I see yellow blotches on the dirt and embers trembling in the fire hole. I don't hear him. His magic axe — huge in his hands, small in mine — isn't there by the sleep mat. I rise and search, just to be certain, but find that yes, he has gone.

The baby within me thrashes.

It would be best for this baby to be small, for Bork likes his babies large and plump. It would be best if I don't eat.

I push aside the roof mat and dig my fingers into the sod above. It's so nice to get out of the black pit.

The evergreen curtains part gently, and I pad over the moss toward the river. Sun ribbons strobe the forest floor. Pine cones clatter. It's so quiet, so peaceful; I don't understand how a man can kill in such a beautiful place.

I slip into the cool swirls of the river. The water flows forever; *from* nothing and *to* nothing.

If only I could kill Bork. If only the magic axe were large in my hands.

I drag myself back to the house pit. I shake and plump Bork's sleep mat, sweep the dirt floor, rekindle the fire, and cook Bork's evening stew. The meat is tough and brown. I pound it with my hammer. I knead it with my fists.

Then I fall to my sleep mat.

His laugh, it sears me. I pop open my eyes to find him towering over me, leering once again. Blonde hairs are stuck in his teeth. In his fist is a sack of squirming somethings.

Bork has caught more girls.

I rise in the soot-filled dusk, scamper to the pot, stir the meat with my bark spoon. Always girls; Bork does not like tough boy meat.

"Bork, please, just this once, please let the girls go."

"But a man must eat, me bitty, and I am a big man." He drops the sack. I turn my head as the axe falls. The screams spray fire down my soul. Inside me, the baby's fingers splay, little nails rammed tight against their bloody, black prison. Bork kicks his food sack, lumbers to his sleeping mat, and sprawls on the floor with his hands beneath his head. "Prepare me food, woman."

I stir the slop, eyes averted from the still-twitching sack. The thick smell of blood, as baby's birth, hangs in the air.

How can I possibly escape? I've wanted to die for a long time, but I don't have the courage to take my own life.

I remember wandering with my sisters, digging roots for the winter and gathering moss for grandma.

Sun on my sisters' hair. A rustling, but I turn too late. Bork, giant madman of the woods, halfbear ogre who eats little girls for breakfast! My sisters, all dead in his fists. And me: he throws me into his sack for later.

I remember only too well what it was like in Bork's sack.

Five years ago, it was, when he ate my two sisters, and he would have eaten me, too, but I was beautiful and aroused other hungers in him.

Bork, always hungry for something.

"Well then, come and eat your stew," I say, but he doesn't respond. He's snoring on his mat.

Something slips from under his blanket. A tiny figure, no taller than my ribs. *Molly,* Bork's newest lover. Young, to be sure, but ugly: maggot skin, twisted grin. She has Bork's magic axe. In her hand, it is small, not big enough to dent Bork's neck. She says, "If I give him Bork's axe, the King promises to marry me to a prince."

I want that axe.

I've wanted that axe for a long time.

"Please, I need it. Give it to me," I say.

"No." She dangles the small axe in front of me, and when I reach for it, she yanks her hand back and laughs.

I clutch my belly and crawl toward her in the mud. "Please," I say, "if I have the magic axe, I can escape from Bork and save my baby. *Please.*"

"No, you can't have it. It's mine, and I want to marry a prince."

I grab Molly's wrist and I try to force the axe from her fist. She only laughs and pulls away from me. She still holds Bork's magic axe, and I must have it. I feel weak, and there's not much I can do, so I grab her hair and pull it. She wrenches from me again, but this time, she falls down, and we both go rolling across the sleep mat...

and across Bork, who awakes with a bolt and sees us — *he sees us!* — and he backhands me so I fly crashing into the nether wall, and the baby thrashes and the pain is an axe between my legs.

Bork's magic axe is stuck in the mud by the fire.

Bork grabs Molly's wrist and flings her to the floor. He strips the blue dress from her, and she screams, face flushed red, and her hand struggles to find the axe; but Bork has her, pinned with one paw to the ground while the other rips at her lacy slips. And such a vile grin he has; everything he wants right before him now: Molly to whup, me to watch, and dead girlies in the sack. For a moment, his eyes meet mine, and then he thrusts himself into little Molly.

A great pain and I scream, and with my eyes shut tight, the baby oozes from between my legs. Oh dear Lord, I've given birth, and my body is shuddering and my teeth are chattering as I reach between my legs to see:

Is it a boy, or is it a girl?

Please don't let it be a girl.

Wee Sweet Girlies

A glint above me. The magic axe is huge in Bork's fist, and it's poised and trembling over the baby! Bork the giant madman, the halfbear, roars; and then the axe crashes down and severs the tether that binds me to the child.

I scream and laugh, tears rolling faster than blood. Bork gives a thunderous *harrr* and lifts my little one; and from the corner of my eye, through the smear of a tear, I see Molly, naked and bloody, racing for the mud wall.

Bork, with the baby, does not see, and he drops the axe, which shrinks. And while he gurgles, "Wee wee girlie, wee sweet girlie," Molly snatches the axe and flees.

Behind Bork, the fire is barely there, like the fireball in the sky as it sinks below the trees. Bork's stew will get cold. *And God help her, I have given Bork another girl.*

Next morning, I take the baby to the river. Her name is Clarisse, and she is my little water maiden. I dunk Clarisse ever so gently, careful not to lower her head beneath the water. She is pretty, this new baby, with my blue eyes and grandma's dimples. I wash her cheeks and the film of hair on her newborn head.

I remember my other little water maidens. Buried somewhere in the muck at the bottom of the river are the bones of my other babies, all the girls that I gave unwillingly to Bork.

From the other side of the river comes a laugh, *a taunt.* I peer across the water and into the thicket, but see nothing. It comes again, this time louder, and I swim on my back to the opposite bank, holding Clarisse to my breast. I place the baby in the mud and pull myself from the water to sit beside her. My dress clings to me, and the sun is casting its cold eye upon me; and I shiver, the flesh rising in bumps along my arms and legs. The forest embraces me, and my nostrils swell to the sweet surge of pine and birch. I cradle Clarisse in my arms, trying to control the shivers so I don't drop her.

"Who's there?" I call.

Molly pops from behind a tree. She wears a red dress and a black smile.

"It is the future Princess Molly!" she says. Her golden slippers look as soft as butter. I haven't had butter since Bork stole me.

"You gave Bork's axe to the King?"

"I did."

How can she be so cruel? How can she be happy as a princess when my beautiful Clarisse is doomed to die at Bork's hand? Molly *could* have saved Clarisse, *could* have saved me. Molly should have given me the magic axe.

Molly scoots away in a flip of red lacy skirts. I race through the woods after her, but I'm slow for I carry Clarrise and I'm still shivering and I'm weak from childbirth; and now I'm way behind her, and the distance between us grows.

I duck under the thorny shrubs and emerge into the sunshine. The baby is crying, and I try to soothe her: "There, there; for your sisters, Clarisse, hush, hush, for your sisters;" but still the baby wails, and the birds shriek in her wake. Before us is a plush lawn, rolling like the King's carpet up to a moat, in which alligators and eels and one-eyed monsters splash in curdled water. Across the moat is the King's One Hair Bridge. The palace is ahead, glittering as a jewel against the dark forest. Exotic plants are everywhere, trellises and yew borders; and the flowers: roses of a thousand shapes and colors, carnations, zinnias, asters, cosmos; the King's twinkling treasure set in black.

And there stands Molly, her slipper upon the One Hair Bridge. She's light and small, and it's easy for her to scurry across the bridge where I cannot go.

The pain between my legs is fierce. My head whirls with the colors of the palace. Butter, I would like some butter; and fruit would be ever so nice. Anything but beer and bitter roots. Anything but meat.

Molly and I lock eyes; hers are darker than the river's depths, flowing from nowhere, to nowhere. She dances back across the One Hair Bridge and stands before me. She has a fire warm voice, *"Baby...such a sweet little baby..."*

She wants *Clarisse*?

I don't know *why* she'd want my baby, but if Molly takes her to the King's palace, then Clarisse will be safe from Bork. I don't want to give Clarisse away, certainly not to Molly, but I don't want Clarisse to die, so I whisper, "Bork eats little girls, and Clarisse is so sweet. Oh Molly, would you please — ?"

Molly strokes Clarisse's silky hair, her angel skin. Clarisse is no longer crying. She's gurgling as if she knows that now is the time to be cute. And Molly says, "She *is* sweet," but then Molly pauses and adds, "but you see, I have no need for Bork's baby. The King likes Bork's magic axe. The King says that I must give him Bork's coins and Bork's ring, and *then* the King will make me a princess."

In my arms, Clarisse whimpers almost as if she knows her fate. Can babies sense what people are really like from their voices?

Abruptly, Molly turns from me and runs across the One Hair Bridge. She's a bright red wound by the palace door, and then she ducks inside to be with the King.

I crawl with Clarisse back to the forest's lip. We rest by a tree near the pit. I don't want to go inside. I want to run away from this place, as far as my legs will take me.

But Bork will find me. He always finds me.

We slide down the mud into the hole. We wait for Bork to come home. The sun is dying again and I must build the fire. Clarisse sleeps on the mat by the wall. The wood is heavy. I drag it from the stack by Bork's mat.

I rub the wood until sparks fly, then I feed the fire until flames scorch my skin. Now the stew pot; encrusted with moldy remains, blackened from the juices of a thousand girls. I slip it to its hook, then turn to last night's sack. I've lived with this smell for five long years, but still it makes my stomach lurch and my head weak.

The meat is in the pot.

I cover Clarisse with my ratty cape.

When Bork comes home, he doesn't ask to see her and he doesn't force me to do favors. "Tired," he says; "looked for me axe all day, couldn't find it, and now Bork's tired." He gorges on the meat — bloody as it still is — and with juices dribbling into his chest fur, he falls asleep on his mat and snores.

The baby awakens and cries, and I feed her, and then I turn to stoke the fire. The soot is thick tonight, the embers dim.

I rest upon my mat, baby in my arms. We breathe, together.

And now I hear another breath; not mine, not Clarisse's, not Bork's rumbling snore. A breath light and quick.

It is Molly.

I slide the baby to the mat and cover her with my cape. Molly is leaning over Bork, pressed close to his foul maw, reaching for something: his purse of gold. She yanks it free and falls backward to the mud. The purse opens, and Bork's coins cascade over his head. He leaps up and snatches her from the floor.

Her tiny, squeaky voice: "No, no! It is your Molly!"

He stops and peers at her with leech eyes. His huge tongue licks her head. "Molly, me favorite Molly."

She says, "Give me some gold coins, Bork, please, just a few."

"I give you nothing, Molly, but I what I give you last night."

Slowly, I slither; and now I'm by his feet, looking up at his chin, all stubble and snarl. His gold coins glow like moons in the mud.

If I steal a few, then Clarisse and I can be free; free at last from this monster, Bork. I reach and I grab one coin, and now I reach and grab another. Overhead, Bork's tongue flops like a fat salmon in Molly's hair. He sucks her hair into his mouth and wrenches her neck back. She flails and begs him to let her go.

I have Bork's gold. I can bargain with other pit dwellers. I can go back to grandma's hut by the edge of the forest, back to warm clothes and butter and sweet plump fruits. If I can some-how escape, run where he can't find me, then I can buy my way to freedom.

Bork is busy with Molly. He's not killing her, not putting her in the sack. He's playing with her, poking and slurping, and now she's relaxed in his arms and pretending to enjoy what passes as his affection.

Wee Sweet Girlies

I scoop up my baby, and I limp to the river, and with my last ounce of strength, I swim across it with Clarisse. I place her on the mud bank, and then I pause in the water, shivering and and panting. When my strength returns, I pull myself up beside my baby.

She is no longer breathing!

No, it can't be! I press my cheek to her chest, but her heart is no longer beating. Her little limbs no longer flail, her mouth no longer twists into smiles and baby grimaces. What has happened to my baby?

This isn't my fault, it can't be my fault. When I escaped from Bork and Molly, when I swam through the river, poor Clarisse must have breathed water into her body instead of air.

Molly.

If Molly had taken Clarisse into the palace, Clarisse would still be alive.

If Molly hadn't been so cruel and greedy, needing more and yet more to please the King and marry a prince, then Clarisse would still be alive.

I will have my way with Molly.

I slip Clarisse into the river, where she can sleep in peace for eternity with her sisters, and then I stagger through the thorns and bushes to the One Hair Bridge, where I sit in the darkness and wait for Molly.

She will come. She needs to give Bork's gold to the King.

I wait until twilight, then a dress of red flits across the bridge. Black hair shimmers under the glow of the moon.

She stands by a frond and arranges flowers around her neck. I tiptoe behind her and linger in the shadows. She seems almost sweet here in the moonlight with the flowers and the torn dress. But my mouth is bitter: "So, if it isn't little Molly, selling your soul to seduce Bork and steal his gold."

She spins and gasps, and I see that yes, her skin is mottled with bruises. Her lips are swollen and her voice is thick. She composes herself, moves back a step, and says, "Oh. It's *you*."

"My baby is dead. *All* my babies are dead," I move close to her face, stare into those black eyes, and in them I see the muck of the river. She has no focus. She flows wherever she's swept.

I raise my fist and open it, and her eyes widen as she sees Bork's gold coins in my palm. "You will give me the coins?" she says.

As if...

I snap my fist shut. "Only if you get Bork's magic axe from the palace and give it to me so I can kill him."

Her eyes shift slightly. She plays with the flowers around her neck. "The King has Bork's axe."

"Get it from him."

"The King sleeps with it by his bed."

"It's easier to kiss the King than a halfbear ogre like Bork. You're a whore. Go sleep with the King and steal Bork's axe for me."

Her mouth curls — I amuse her — and for a moment, I think that she's ready to trade; but then her grin twists and she rips the flowers from her neck and throws them at me. She punches my stomach, still so sore from Clarisse's birth, and I roll dangerously close to the water's edge. One-eyed monsters rise, their mouths yawning black holes. Molly has my throat! I lift my feet and kick her, and she flies back into the brush. She squirms, her hair caught in the nettles and vines.

My skin prickles as if I'm caught in the vines with her. I can kill Molly now; with my bare hands, I can kill her.

She rips at her hair. Little red insect caught in my snare. "Please, don't kill me, please!"

"And Clarisse, what about Clarisse?"

"I'm sorry I'm sorry I'm sorry. Bork's doing. Bork would eat me. Bork would eat us all."

I'm so tired of death. I want to flee from these woods, from Bork; to have my life back. I look at Molly, pathetic squirming mite. "Will you bring me Bork's axe?"

A whimper. "I'll bring you the axe, but only if you give me Bork's gold coins and ring. I want to be a princess."

Pathetic little wretch. "Fine," I say, and I gather the coins and tuck them into my dress, then reach for her hair. "Let me warn you, Molly, lest you decide to doublecross me: I'll soon be light as a feather, and if you don't bring the axe, I'll come across the One Hair Bridge and kill you for it."

"I'll steal it tonight, I swear."

So I wrench her from the vines, and she skitters across the bridge to the palace.

She will bring the axe; I know it. I rest by the forest and wait. The palace glows, its colors staining the midnight sky. And later, in the birth of dawn, Molly returns with the axe. She moves stiffly, her body covered with bruises.

I grab the axe and give her half of my coins. "Go then, Molly, and become a princess."

God only knows what she has done to steal the axe. She wobbles across the One Hair Bridge to her palace prison, and a twinge of sympathy grips my heart, for how different, really, is she from me? She disappears between golden doors, where the King awaits. The King who forced her to seduce Bork and steal gold.

I realize that it's not Molly who killed Clarisse. It's not even Bork who killed Clarisse. I'm to blame, for it was my choice *not* to kill myself. Remaining alive, I knew that I'd give birth to more of Bork's babies. This is all my fault.

On the other hand, it was Bork who killed and ate my sisters and my daughters, and it was Bork who kept me imprisoned. Bork would have eaten Clarisse, for sure, just as he ate the rest.

And I know that I will kill Bork, or die trying.

I return to the house pit. I slip the axe beneath my sleep mat. I root through the mats and the soiled sacks, seeking Bork's meat.

But there is no meat.

Now his footsteps come: death's blows; they crash against my skull, and I shrink against the mud wall, trembling.

The roof mat peels back. The sun empties itself upon me. Bork's face: raw animal hunger. "You be gone all day, and I find you nowhere. I need meat. Where is my meat?"

He jumps into the pit, and the growl in his throat shakes the stewpot. He is smaller and weaker, he's no longer the size of a bear.

Surely, I'm imagining it, for how can Bork be shrinking?

"Such a nice little bitty. Come 'ere, me love, come on."

My fingers curl around the axe. It's too small to hurt him.

He lurches closer, bares his teeth, reaches for me. His fingers graze the axe. His fingers: half their normal size. His breath: the stink of week-old blood. "Meat, I need meat..."

And as he touches it, the axe grows large, and quickly I think, *is death sufficient punishment?*

And the axe slams down, and his left foot dangles by its heel. He curses and lunges —

And the axe slams down, and his foot flies into the fire; and now Bork falls to the mud, screaming.

No longer a giant, he has shrunk to the size of a normal man. And I realize that Bork needs meat, girl's meat, to grow large and strong.

All night, I drive stakes into the roof mat around the pit. By morning, only a small part of the mat flaps open.

I peer into the gloom.

Bork is the size of grandma before she died. His voice is softer: "Wee sweet girlies. Come 'ere, me bitty, give me wee sweet girlies."

As if I would! I turn and pound the final stake into the ground.

And now Bork is stuck in the pit with only bitter roots to eat.

"May you dream of death, *your own death,*" I say, and then I part the evergreen curtains and head back to grandma's hut; back to sweet fruits, to butter, and to life.

Wee Sweet Girlies

In late 2009, I was given two days in which to write a zombie romance story. As it so happens, I'd just seen the movie Julie & Julia (about Julia Child's career and life), and hence, I whipped up my version: JULIA BRAINCHILD.

Julia Brainchild

"**D**ick, I want you to meet Julia Brainchild." My producer, Harold Latootski, was all aglow. Beside him was a young woman, maybe twenty-five years old. His hand was on her elbow, and a beautiful elbow it was.

I propped my spatula on the fry pan. So this was Julia Brainchild, author of *The Art of French Brain Cooking* and blog mistress extraordinaire. "Enchanted to meet you. Please, call me Richard."

She held out a hand. It was delicate and as white as chalk. The nails were pearly and the color of farm-raised salmon.

I bent, kissed her fingers: cold but fragrant, a citrus bouquet that reminded me of my grandmother's scent. With my eyes lowered, I scanned her body, but in a way she wouldn't notice. The peach pencil skirt showed off slim hips and long legs. Matching four-inch high heels. Nice breasts beneath a creamy cashmere sweater. Classy, as I'd expected Julia Brainchild to be.

She quivered slightly, released her fingers from mine. "Richard Ashford, the American brain food expert. I've watched your show many times. You're very good with simple matters." She paused. "*Qualifié.*"

"Why, thank you. From you, that's quite a compliment." I wasn't sure what *qualifié* really meant, but it sounded good.

Harold smoothed some hair strands over his bald scalp and whisked lint off his thousand-dollar suit. I figured he was anxious to leave and get back to whatever it is network producers do. But then he dropped the bomb: "Dick, I've hired Julia to co-host *Brain and Soul* with you."

No way.

Pretty as she was, with those turquoise eyes and waves of tawny hair to her shoulders, Julia Brainchild was exactly what I *didn't* need on my show.

"My show isn't about butter and cream and sauce. We're about health. Brains are pure protein and no fat. Americans love 'em."

Harold countered, "Julia's *the* world's expert on brains, plus she's photogenic as hell and will attract new viewers to the show, Dick. Young male viewers, for example."

But my ratings were through the roof. "McBrains are bigger than ever, you know that. Teenage boys like McBrains better than pizzas."

"I've heard your Kentucky Fried Brain is doing well, too," said Julia Brainchild.

Was she on my side? Startled, I added, "Then there are my BLTs — Brain, Lettuce, and Tomato sandwiches. Pure protein. For god sakes, Harold, we're bigger than any diet since — "

"South Park?" asked Julia.

I frowned. "*South Beach.* And we're bigger than Atkins ever was, too."

She said, "I know you are Brain Burger King, Richard. But it might be fun to — she batted her eyelashes at me — "to add some zest, some *épice*, to the American diet."

She lifted my spatula —

my spatula! —

and stirred the Fruity Brain Crispees in my pan.

Julia Brainchild

"Work with her." Harold's tone was sharp, he was ordering me, and in his glare was a threat. Julia Brainchild was famous. I was disposable. Any short order cook who worked out in the gym a few hours a day and had a nice face could fill my shoes. I was just Brain Burger King because of Harold.

I took my spatula back from Julia Brainchild. "We air in a few hours. I'll be teaching Americans how to make healthy breakfasts and snacks."

Her turquoise eyes flared with excitement. "Brain snacks, oh yum!" She licked her lips.

Julia Brainchild was getting off on the thought of my recipes.

I could barely contain my surprise. What a thrill! Against my better judgment, my body took charge, and I felt myself getting hard, my stomach starting to flip flop as it did whenever I got aroused.

Maybe this wouldn't be such a bad thing after all.

She worked with me for hours before the show aired. She tasted my Fruity Brain Crispees, gasped with delight; nibbled on my Brainola Bars, declared them to be *savoureux*, savory. By two o'clock when the crew showed up, we were giggling and trading secrets about Grilled Brain Kebobs (mine), Lobes Benedict (hers), Brain McNuggets (mine), Brains Normandy (hers), and past lovers (ours).

"In three, two, one..." and Jason, one of our crew, gave me the "on the air" signal.

It was a half hour show. Live.

"And now, it's Chef Dick Ashford and the lovely Miss Julia Brainchild!"

Julia smiled at the camera as if she'd done this a million times. Then she picked up one of my spare aprons — white cloth, covers everything — and winked at me. "I cover all my special parts," she said, "so the creams will not spray me."

The guys operating the equipment turned red. My brain went on hold. "Today," I managed to say to the cameras and to the diet-crazed American public, "on *Brain and Soul*, we welcome French art and love to our dishes. You all know Julia Brainchild, and today, she's going to help us make Honey Roasted Brain 'n' Oats. It's good for the digestion, good for your heart, and it tastes like candy."

"Oh, Richard..." Julia smacked her lips. "*You* are like candy. Isn't he, dear viewers?"

"Yes, well, choose a brain, maybe cow or goat — "

"Or," said Julia, "quail or ostrich — "

"Yes, or quail or ostrich, as Julia suggests in her French way. Soak the brain for at least a few hours."

"2.15 hours, to be precise," said Julia.

"Yes, that would be good, and then, roast the brain — "

"No, Dicky dear. *Richard.* Braise the brain in a light sauce of lemon and butter, *then* roast it."

And on it went. No matter what I said, Julia interrupted with her French cooking tips. She contradicted everything I said. And all the while, she managed to wriggle her body next to mine, sending shivers through me, and she managed to make me say things like "a fine Beaujolais would go well with this brain" and "sautéed ganglia in bean sauce at your place tonight?"

By the time the show ended, the technicians were all abuzz: Julia Brainchild was a big hit. Harold rushed in with the news. People were already twittering about the sexual tension between Dick Ashford and Julia, the fun quips, the dynamite she added to my recipes. Blogs already had thousands of comments. And the part when she whipped off the white apron and pranced around the stove and counter, showing off her legs, that body, those breasts, that face —

Well, already, stills of her were all over the internet, vids on youtube. Julia Brainchild was the next Heidi Klum, Pamela Anderson, Angelina Jolie. Already, requests were hitting Harold for Julia to pose in the Sports Illustrated Swimsuit Edition.

"You want to get coffee?" I switched on my sexiest grin, beamed my crystal green eyes her way. Most girls couldn't resist me when I pumped up the charm. I was well over six feet tall, packed with 215 pounds of hard flesh and muscle, and I'd been told my face was what really got me the job as Brain Burger King. How could she resist?

But she acted coy. Smoothed her hands over the cashmere sweater, making her breasts stand out more. Turned and pretended to putter with the pots and pans on the set, so I could get a better look at her butt in that tight pencil skirt. Leaned over the sink, playing at washing the spatula, just to entice me with the view.

Then abruptly, she was upright and turning towards me, those turquoise eyes filmed with lust, or so I thought, and those lips parted ever so slightly.

"You love the brains?" Her voice was low and seductive. She stepped closer. One step. Two. Now inches from me, her eyes fixated on mine.

I bobbed my head. "I do. I do."

"Ah, most men do not understand this love for brains."

Lots of women want you to tell them that you love them for their brains, but with Julia, the meaning was totally different. She pressed her cheek to mine and shuddered as I said that canned thing that all men say at some point in their lives. "I love you for your brains, Julia."

She laughed, the citrus scent moving closer, then she whispered in my ear. "Love so soon, Richard? But we've only just met." I didn't feel her hot breath on my ear, which was strange, but the words alone set me sizzling even more. I was hard and ready to go, and I knew she felt it because the peach skirt and the creamy sweater were right up against me. She was on fire. I was on fire.

"*Petit cerveau,*" she said. Then she laughed. "*Tete de linotte!*"

Was she complimenting me, remarking on my big hard penis? I didn't know French, still don't. So I said, "And you are the most beautiful woman I've ever seen, Julia. Your eyes are stunning, your hair, your lips..." And I moved in for the kill. I grabbed her head with both hands and kissed her, long and hard. Our tongues met, intertwined, licked. She wrapped one long leg around me, shoved me against the stove. Her body was in flames, but cold to the touch. I knew she was on fire, knew it, and yet, the pearly white skin had the chill of thawed beef.

Julia Brainchild

I couldn't convince her to see me that night. She came up with one excuse after another. She had to perfect the Consommé Brunoise. The Brain en Croute took time. Brain Bouillabaisse with Rouille required one final step, the fennel seeds and saffron threads.

I ate dinner alone. A double order of large fries and a 32-ounce super-sized Coffee Mate Deluxe. I watched cartoon reruns for hours. South Park. Finally fell into a stupor, then a deep sleep around 3 a.m.

The following afternoon, I was late to set, but it didn't really matter: I could make brain dip and chips in my sleep.

Julia wore a light blue skirt and aquamarine silk blouse. The blouse was semi-transparent. The blue and aquamarine really set off her eyes, which blazed like fine gems. I couldn't take my eyes off her.

"Richard?" She made my name into a caress. "You're watching me." And then she was close again, scraping her fingernails down my face and neck.

A groan rumbled up my throat.

She tipped my chin up, then passed her tongue across my lips.

I shouldn't, she was a seductress, she wanted my job, she was better with brains than me —

But I couldn't help myself. My hands were on her waist, my mouth clamped to hers, both of us writhing with desire. All I could think was: I need more, more, more...now, now, now.

"In three, two, one..."

We were getting the "on the air" signal.

We pulled away from each other. Julia's eyes were wide. She tucked her shirt back into her skirt, straightened, and smiled for the camera.

I wasn't wearing my apron.

I always had my apron on before I went live.

I was digging beneath the counter for it when I heard:

Julia Brainchild

"And now, it's Chef Dick Ashford and the lovely Miss Julia Brainchild!"

I bet the bloggers are going wild with this, I thought, as I scrambled to get the apron on and appear as if nothing had happened between me and Julia Brainchild right before the viewers saw us.

We debated diet orange soda versus Perrier water.

We argued about Brain on the Cob versus Brains Riviera.

She insisted we make Eiffel Tower of Brain, the ultimate French dessert for special occasions. I refused.

"Brain food is smart food," I said. "And smart food is healthy food. A nice brain steak on the grill. No salt, no sauces."

We bickered about Brains Monte Carlo, where diners took their chances, not knowing about Julia's secret of using a mystery brain: camel, fish, or boar, you never knew.

"All you need is catsup," I said.

"All you need is wine," Julia said. "A Rothschild, an Ott Chateau de Selle, perhaps a Frontignan."

And when the show was over, Harold ran in and told us the ratings had soared higher than ever before, that the network wanted to sign us both for another two years of *Brain and Soul.*

"Viewers love it!" he cried. "The romance, the tension, the brains! It's wonderful!"

But it was no longer about health food and dieting. We were insanely attracted to each other, that was clear. It wouldn't take much, I decided, to seduce her. Then she would be totally under my spell, and I would rule again, with her on set to follow my commands and make lovely chit chat about French brains without threatening my superior views.

I would seduce her with the one brain dish that nobody else could possibly make. The dish my mother had passed down to me from my ancestors. Something special, something *not* French that Julia would already know.

It took two weeks of preparation. And in the meantime, we kissed, we groped, we nearly made love right before the shows aired, but always, Julia stopped me before I could strip off her clothes and have her. And always, she refused to see me after the show was over.

I would have Julia Brainchild.

I bought the brains, two of them: alpaca and llama. I soaked the brains for 24 hours. If not prepared correctly, this dish would kill. Pickled raw brain ceviche, a rare delicacy: extremely dangerous like the Fugu puffer fish. You eat bad brain ceviche, you get neurological diseases, go mad, and die. I pickled the ceviche for 12 days to kill all the bacteria. It sat by my bed in a giant crock filled with lemon and lime essences, onion, garlic, minced chillies, and a drop of vinegar. I watched South Park.

And I waited.

On air, we flirted, we cooked, we talked brains.

Finally, when the ceviche was ready, I told her. "Julia, I have a surprise for you, a special dish I've been preparing for weeks. Please, you must come tonight and let me treat you with it."

She hesitated. Her eyes clouded. "But I can't, Richard."

"Yes, you can, Julia."

"What kind of special dish is this?"

"*Brains*, Julia."

"What kind of brains, Richard?"

"Alpaca and llama."

She gasped. A hand flew to her mouth. "Oh! Oh, Richard, how did you know? That is my favorite."

I'd struck gold. Yes. Finally, she would succumb to me. Finally, she would be mine, all mine, and *Brain and Soul* would be my kingdom again. She would be my queen. I loved her.

"How is it prepared?" she asked.

Satin sheets. Bear rug.

"It is prepared, the special dish, as ceviche," I said.

She, who never flushed at all, paled to an even whiter shade than before. She staggered back against the stove, gripped the handle. "*Alpaca and llama ceviche?*"

"You know of it? It's not French," I said.

She nodded, swallowing rapidly. "It's not in *The Art of French Brain Cooking*. I never speak of it. You're right, it's not a French dish."

Of course, my Julia would know this rare specialty. She was a world expert in cooking brains, French or otherwise.

"I will come," she said.

And my heart started thumping like crazy, and the blood rushed to my head.

She.

Would.

Be.

Mine.

I rushed home, cleaned up the apartment as best as I could, made sure the bed had the black silk sheets, tidied the bear rug at the foot of the bed by the TV. I lifted the lid from the ceviche crock. Took a little taste. Perfect. We would dine here, then make love all night. Perhaps I would propose marriage to her on *Brain and Soul*. Not tomorrow, though, but soon.

She arrived at 7 pm, kicked off her heels, and threw her arms around me. I kissed her neck, and she tossed back her head and begged me to nibble further and yet further down. I did. I nibbled down to the buttons on her blouse, opened them, nibbled down, down, slid my fingers under the top of her bra. She smelled like tangerines and limes, like my grandmother. It was odd, but somehow, sexy and comforting at the same time. Her skin was cold, as always.

I carried her into the bedroom, gently set her on the bear rug. "It's been so long," she said, "since I've made love. You will be gentle, won't you?"

"Always, my sweetest."

I'd rip her clothes to shreds and fuck her till she screamed.

I fumbled with the remaining buttons, slipped off her shirt. Unzipped the skirt, slid it down. Peeled off the pantyhose.

My clothes were off in less than five seconds.

I surveyed her. She was perfection. No blemishes anywhere. Perfect pearly white skin, pink nipples, tawny hair.

But then she pushed at my chest. She tried to sit up. She grabbed at her clothes. "No," she cried, "I can't do this, I can't!"

"But why?" My erection started to shrink.

"I...my skin, it's too fragile. It might flake off."

Say, *what*?

That had to be the lamest excuse I'd ever heard from a girl. "I'll be gentle, I swear," I said.

"No!" She was crying, backing away from me, her butt moving across the bear rug. Scrabbling to dress herself.

For god sakes.

I'd give her the ceviche. That would do it.

I gave her my bathrobe, then wrapped myself in a towel. I calmed her down. She cried on my shoulder, telling me she'd not let a man this close to her in many years.

"How many years?" I asked.

Flustered, she said, "I don't know. Maybe sixty."

I laughed. She was so adorable. Sixty years. Yeah, right. "You're like, twenty-five years old, Julia."

"Oh." She nodded. "Uh huh. I meant, sixty months."

I didn't believe that, either.

But whatever, she would be mine, that was that, I would fuck her all night, she would be queen to the Brain Burger King, and Harold could make some big PR announcement about our engagement. Not tomorrow, but soon.

I opened the crock, showed her the ceviche. She nearly fainted from joy. "My mother's friend taught me how to make this when I was a little girl," she said. "She was Peruvian, but we were all very poor, so my mother and her friend had to substitute rabbit brain for the alpaca and llama brains. Rabbits were easy to come by in the French countryside, you see."

"I can't believe you've actually had this dish — in any form, actually. It's a family secret. I never make it. And I don't know anybody who's ever had it."

Julia Brainchild was obviously perfect for me. Here was a beautiful woman, sexually intoxicating, untouched by any man for years, twenty-five years old, the world's expert on brain cooking, and she knew of the alpaca and llama ceviche!

I drank in the aroma of the ceviche: citrus and spices. I admired the perfect little wedges of brain that I'd diced for hours and hours.

We cuddled on the bed, pillows behind our backs. Her robe fell open. She didn't notice. My towel unwrapped. She didn't notice.

I held a spoon of ceviche to her lips.

She flicked her tongue. It dipped into the ceviche. "Ahhh…" A long sigh. She grabbed the spoon and stuck it in her mouth, chewed for what seemed like minutes, then swallowed.

"More!" she cried.

I scooped a bunch of ceviche into a bowl, gave it to her with the spoon. With her robe fully open now, her breasts bobbing as she gulped, she swallowed chunk after chunk of my special family ceviche.

And finally, a slight bluish flush rose to her cheeks. She handed the bowl and spoon back to me. Tugged the robe around her body to hide everything again.

"You have Peruvian ancestors?" she asked.

"No." I explained that "my mother was American, but my grandfather, Julian LeBlanc, originally came from France, or so I was told. I have no Peruvian ancestors that I know of."

"LeBlanc?" She leapt off the bed, pointed a finger at me as if accusing me of something.

"Well, yeah…so, what of it?" I hopped off the bed, grabbed her by the waist, and pressed her to me. I stared into her eyes.

"Richard, we cannot be, you and I, we cannot do this anymore."

"Come on, we're made for each other, Julia. You know that, and so do I. What on earth is the problem?"

"I know your recipe. But you made it incorrectly."

Julia Brainchild

"You're breaking up with me over a recipe?" I drew back from her, stared in disbelief. This woman was crazy.

"You omitted the one essential ingredient, Dicky."

And now she was calling me Dicky again?

"A pinch of alpaca testicles," she said flatly. "That's the ingredient that makes the ceviche an aphrodisiac."

"And you know this *how?*"

The whites of her eyes were dimming to gray. The white of her skin was beyond a pallor now, it was tinged with blue. Everywhere. The pink nipples were lavender, now purple.

What was happening to her?

"This is an ancient Inca priest recipe," she said. "They used it as an aphrodisiac. My mother's friend, the Peruvian, listed the ingredients, all of them, including the alpaca testicles, over and over again. I helped my mother make the ceviche. With the rabbit brain."

"*But so what?*" I yelled. "What does this have to do with you and me, and getting engaged and married on *Brain and Soul?*"

She laughed. I saw that her teeth were cracked and yellowing by the minute. "We can't get married, you silly, silly *petit cerveau!* You *tete de linotte!*"

I pulled on my pants and shirt, shoved her skirt and blouse at her. "Here, you might as well get dressed, Julia. I think you're sick, and I mean that in a loving way." I paused. I did love Julia Brainchild, but her mind was nuts and her body was clearly not well. I would take her to the finest doctors. Then we'd finally get on with it.

"I died in childbirth, Dicky. Long ago. A hundred years ago, in fact. Nobody knew that ceviche recipe except my mother, and both she and her friend died with the secret. It was passed down only to me."

"And to me," I said. And then I thought, *did she just say she died a hundred years ago? What the hell?*

"Don't you get it?" She staggered toward me. Her gait was choppy, almost like a lurch. "I *died*, Dicky. In childbirth. Apparently, the child lived. He must have been Julian LeBlanc, your grandfather. You see, Dicky, LeBlanc was the name of the man who fathered my child!"

Psycho...

I took her elbow to lead her to the door and get her back to her apartment. She needed a good, long rest, then a very good psychiatrist. But as I touched her elbow, the skin flaked off her arm.

I dropped my hand. Stared at her. "You are...?"

"I prefer to think of myself as the Living Challenged."

"A zombie?"

"It's why I specialize in French brain cooking. I've had years to perfect my recipes. If I make love, if I let myself go too far for too long, if I let myself go all the way, I revert to the form I had when I reanimated. Hence, the blue skin. I must leave you, Dicky."

Yeah, maybe that was a good idea. This Julia Brainchild was one whacked-out chick. Harold might force me to work with her, but beyond that...forget it.

"Dicky, I did love you. But you see," she said, "I'm your dead great-grandmother."

I shook my head. "You're crazy, Julia. Come on, let me take you home, and I'll see you at work tomorrow."

"You forget, I'm the star of that show, not you."

And I saw the cracked yellow teeth, the gray whites of her eyes, the skin falling off her face, the breasts sagging then deflating like balloons sucked dry of air.

I saw the knife in her hand. Classico-Emerol stainless steel, model 287631A.

The blade flashed.

I grabbed her wrist. It fell off her arm, and with it, her hand and the knife.

Could I kill her, a zombie? Was it possible? How? Every zombie movie I'd ever seen showed that people could never kill them — not with fire or decapitation, not even with machine guns.

My mind was racing. I stalled for time. "Can't we work something out?"

"Yes, Dicky, we can. You see, I do love you, Dicky."

"We can still do the show together, I promise," I lied.

"Yes, Dicky, we can. I know you love me, too, Dicky."

And then she leaned and her tongue flicked out and touched my cheek. The yellow teeth nibbled. I felt the heat dribble from my cheek to my lips, and I tasted blood. *She'd bitten me.*

"We'll do the show forever, Dicky. Just you and me. And brains. And now that we are one, the same, it's time."

"Time?" I squeaked.

"Fuck me, Dicky, fuck me till I scream. You won't care if my flesh flakes off. Ha! And I won't care about yours, either!"

There was no need to announce an engagement the next day, or any time soon. I was stuck with Julia Brainchild forever. We were two of a kind now. I'd fallen in love with my own great-grandmother. And as we, two rotting corpses, dished up health food to the diet-crazed Americans, we could binge on all the cream and butter and lard and fatty sauces we wanted. As long as they were simmering on brains.

Julia Brainchild

When I wrote THERE'S NO PLACE LIKE VOID, which sold to Tales Out of Miskatonic, I was working as a senior science writer with a main focus on engineering and physics. I set the story at Miskatonic University's Department of Physics in a "Quantum Hut," and I tossed in everything from quark-gluon plasma to quantum optics to dark matter analysis to particle accelerators. Of course, the story also features elements such as Nyarlathotep and the Necronomicon, as well as strange creatures and even stranger scientists. Professor Montrose Qubit, with help from a post-doc from hell, goes on an insane quest to discover the origin of mass and win a Nobel Prize.

There's No Place Like Void

"**Y**ou look absolutely scintillating," said Grim as he twinkled into view. His pulsing flanks were aglow with technicolors, shades that sparkled from midnight blue to neon sky, from vampiric blood to harlot red.

I looked down at my body: scintillating was an understatement. I, too, pulsed with all the colors of the universe, a big bang radiance of particles created at the dawn of time. Then I looked up, and there *it* was — a strange room of bizarre dimensions and cold steely contraptions — and there *she* was — dimunitive, stringy black hair to her shoulders, hunched over a computer, humming.

Where had Grim and I landed?

A quivering string of my ooze pointed at *her*. "What *is* that?"

"I don't know, Fireball, my sweet," he said in a thought-blast to my brain, "some kind of scientist, I think. And worse, it seems we have congealed in a torture chamber of sorts." His phosphorescent orbs twinkled from atop a high cabinet made of steel with glass doors. Inside the cabinet were animal skulls, not a good portent for our mutual health. Though we weren't technically animals, of course, but still...

I had popped from the void onto a chair with wheels. I was closer to *her* than Grim. In fact, I was too close, and a wave of nausea swept my flanks: she *reeked*, pungent and soiled, like a decay of gangrene and carrion. She shifted, her chair spun around, her breath raked my upper crescents.

"Oh, Grim, I don't like this place! Let's go back to the void where we belong!"

"Can't yet," he muttered in my mind. "It'll take time to figure out how."

She shivered, and I heard her think, "Chilly," and then she sneezed. She was leaning into my very being, not seeing me but feeling what I was: cool, like a winter breeze or a ghost; but of course, that's not what Grim and I were at all, we only felt that way to others, that is, if they survived being near us at all.

She reached into me, beneath me, to a paper on the seat of my chair. Text on the top: MISKATONIC UNIVERSITY, DEPARTMENT OF PHYSICS, QUANTUM HUT, PROFESSOR MONTROSE QUBIT. CONFIDENTIAL. The paper was a blur of words about particle physics: W bosons, Z bosons, taus, muons, and whatever. What did these humans know about us, the particles of the universe, anyway?

I pushed my ooze from the chair and plopped onto the gray concrete floor. The chair vanished into the void, and with it went Professor Montrose Qubit's confidential paper.

If the chair could go into the luscious void, why was it so hard for us to return? And why hadn't the girl disappeared when she reached through me? What kind of strange place was this?

Whoosh, like a giant wind: a door banged open — a massive steel door with two combination locks on it — and he stepped into the Quantum Hut. The girl jumped from her chair and gasped, and her spit sprayed my humps as her right hand knocked a soldering iron off her desk. A name tag fell from her shirt. XIAO ZHANG, POST-DOC, PHYSICS. She cried, "Professor Qubit! I'm almost done with the experiment. I swear!"

"Where's the paper, the one with my confidential notes?" Qubit's voice was low, his words even and flat.

"It was here, I swear. I must have knocked it off the chair. I'll find it!"

"It had better be here. If anyone sees those notes, we're through. They'll steal my Nobel Prize. *I* have discovered the origin of mass, nobody else, just *me*."

"The notes, they have to be under the chair, but — " Xiao's eyes went wild — "where's the chair?"

"Who knows?" I said. "We don't even know where chairs go when they enter the void."

Grim chuckled. "All I can tell you is, she's female, young, and hates Professor Qubit. I can't read his mind as easily as I can read hers."

"I want to go home."

"Fireball, my glorious lump of heavenly radiance, don't despair. Qubit's lab brought us here, and Qubit's lab will return us, somehow, to the void."

Grim was the smart one, always so sweet, from the time we'd exploded into existence at the beginning of time. I was lucky to have him. As far as we knew, we were the only two of our kind, made from the lowest energy particles that anything can decay into, we had acquired energy through the ages and happily dwelled in empty space, occasionally popping through space and time to land in the nether reaches. Typically, we landed in forests and oceans, in skies, in clouds, and it was all about adventure and fun and relaxation — our brief vacations were always such a treat — but this time, we'd apparently entered the true nether reach, that of human dominance.

Doom.

Scraped flesh. Burning brains. Human against human. Torture for torture. It was a place I'd always feared. Earth.

"We are entities of the mist, not scientists," I said.

Heavy Frankenstein platform shoes, polka dot necktie, goggles. Professor Qubit was as tall as the cabinet that Grim sat on. He was as thin as the clump of optics cables climbing the wall by the door. His hair was Einstein, but red instead of white. His lips curled into a smile.

We'd existed from the dawn of time, but could easily die here. I could almost smell it.

Grim slid down the cabinet for a better look at Qubit, and his whole mass, like tub-sized jello, plunked onto the floor, where it quivered and sprayed rainbows of color across the room. The entire cabinet dissolved behind him.

Neither Professor Qubit nor Xiao noticed us, that was clear. They didn't see Grim's colors, his spreading gelatinous form. They didn't see me, shaking in dark neons beneath the desk.

But they clearly saw the cabinet disappear. Qubit grabbed Xiao's shoulders and squeezed. She recoiled, but he held tight and said, "Mass and energy. One cannot exist without the other. I must find my notes. Xiao, after ten years, I have finally found the origin of mass. The void."

Grim and I stared at each other. The origin of mass was *us*. The complexities of the universe, the void itself, the neverending nothing: these were not things that humans should touch. We would melt chairs, papers, cabinets, and all else before Qubit's eyes; at first, objects and creatures would disappear slowly, but as time spiraled forward, Grim and I would be rooted in this Earthly hell, and things would dissolve into our void faster and faster until there was simply nothing left of Earth and its human monstrosities.

"I don't want to kill them all," I said, "and I don't want to be marooned here, destroying everything in sight."

Grim snorted. "They'll find a way to kill us before we destroy *them*, Fireball. These are *scientists*."

"Physicists," I corrected.

"Yes. *Supreme* scientists. Birth of the bomb, of nuclear reactors — "

"They probe the very particles that make up nature."

"They will torture us, Fireball! Dissect us, smash us against each other! *We* are the very particles that make up nature!"

The future wasn't looking very rosy. We would destroy them, or they would find a way to destroy us first. I gestured wildly at Grim. "The door's still open! Run for it!"

There's No Place Like Void

From a splattered glowing mess on the floor, Grim's particles surged into a nanometer-wide string and bolted into the hall. I was right behind him, shooting past Qubit, who was muttering about "stopping light this time" and "altering the quark-gluon plasma" and past trembling Xiao, who kept wailing, "I swear, the simulation is almost done, I swear I'll find the notes!"

Professor Qubit cried, "The hell with the Large Hadron Collider! I've discovered the origin of mass, and it's not the Higgs boson!" The last I saw of him was his red hair, streaking in all directions, and the last I saw of Xiao was her stringy black hair, limp like her body, as the Professor pushed her against a lab bench overflowing with optics equipment and lasers and torture chambers no doubt filled with plasma and hysterical, trapped elementary particles.

Grim and I flashed down the long hall. Flickering neon signs high near the ceiling. EXIT. WARNING. NO ACCESS. QUANTUM HUT. PARTICLE PHYSICS. Closed steel doors to the right, to the left. QUARK-GLUON PLASMA LAB. QUANTUM OPTICS. DARK MATTER LAB. PARTICLE ACCELERATOR. And at the end of the hall, surging at the speed of light, we slammed into another door, this one marked

DEAD END.

We fell, wadded on top of each other: two humps of primal particles, born neutral, not hostile, born to give the universe substance, not to be confined. "Yet here we are," and Grim slid off my twinkling crescents and orbs, "trapped by humans in this subterranean hell, this — " he glared — "this *Miskatonic*."

And then, the DEAD END door vanished into the void.

"Aha!" cried Grim, and off we went, in a flash of darkness shot with the colors of the universe, particles that sizzled with life, that were pure and radiant, unstoppable, unbeatable.

Sometimes it was glorious to be alive.

We zoomed in spirals of color up a stairway, through a door that vanished behind us, into a hall with windows. Light filtering in like fog, particles of water, particles like us, only bigger. Through the fog we went, and the air was clear behind us.

Two young humans, one male and one female, stood by an open door. The chatter of youth inside the room, a dominant old male lecturing by a blackboard, scribbling with chalk.

"Don't touch the humans!" I warned, but too late, for Grim swept right past the two humans, brushed against their backs, and *poof*, they disappeared into the void.

Horrified screams from inside the room. The professor raced into the hall, arms thrashing the air, eyes probing this way, then that, and then he yelled, "Benjamin! Anne! Where are you? What happened?"

"*We* happened," said Grim, chuckling.

But we were already gone, whipping across campus. The air was cool, the wind was fierce. Leaves of yellow and brown and Qubit-red slashed into us, melting to nothing as they fell into the void. Ahead, I saw Grim, sparkling iridescence, his particles aglow, slash through a group of students. All of them disappeared.

A girl with long blonde hair pointed at me. "I see something! A glow of darkness! A mist! Nyarlathotep? The Nameless Mist?"

A boy with his arms wrapped around her looked up. "I don't see anything. You're just dizzy from my kisses."

"No! Look! It's a Great Old One!"

Sure, I was terrific, that is, Great, and sure, given that my birthday was the dawn of time, I qualified as Old, but...a *Great Old One?* It made me sound like a goddess.

The girl started walking towards us. " 'That is not dead which can eternal lie,' so said Abdul Alhazred in *The Necronomicon!* These are the Great Old Ones!"

It wouldn't be particularly good if the girl reached me and started poking at my flanks. She'd instantly be sucked into the void. "I think we should go somewhere, Grim. Like, now?"

"Okay, let's go to the dorms, so we can wipe out all the students."

I coalesced into a tense sphere of shimmering particles. I plunged the words into his brain like daggers: "Say *what?*"

"I'm *kidding.*" He paused in the wind, coiled into a spiral of neon blues and orange. Around us, the world danced. Towering black iron spires etched against a fading sun, the tall brown campus halls cold, their ivy tresses flapping against stone. The lightness of student laughter, the heaviness of branches as the wind crashed them upon the bleak earth.

All those students: where did they go when sucked into the void? Could they return, and if so, would they still be alive and human? Or would they be, I couldn't bear to think of the possibilities, *something else*?

The girl was picking up speed, starting to jog. She called, "Why have you been dormant all this time, oh Great Old Ones? Why have you come to us now?"

Grim said, "Maybe we should go to the cemetery where everybody's already dead."

"Maybe, but that won't get us home, Grim. And I repeat: we should get out of here, like: *Now.*"

"What do you know about physics, Fireball?"

"Nothing much," I said, jittery to get going. The girl was only ten meters away. I could smell her shampoo and see the moistness on her lips. Eight meters away; they were rosebud lips. Her boyfriend remained in the distance, watching her, bewildered.

"Me, neither. I say we find the Physics Library and try to figure out why Montrose Qubit cares so much about the origin of mass — *us* — and then try to figure out how to use his lab devices to get ourselves home."

Six meters away; the tiny rips in the front of her jeans were clearly defined, and she wore a locket around her neck.

"Well, we are particles, and he *is* a particle physicist..." I managed to say.

"Exactly my thinking," said Grim. "In the dead of night, when humans sleep, we'll slip back into the Physics building. Until then, the cemetery!"

She was only two meters away, now one meter, and as the girl reached for me, I saw innocence and longing in her blue eyes. "Take me," she whispered above the wind.

And with that, I bounced off the ground and against a tree trunk, and then, *zip*, bounced off the trunk and landed at least a hundred meters away. Grim followed. The tree trunk disappeared into the void. The girl blinked, disappointed. She had no clue how close she'd just been to death.

We strung ourselves into nanometer-wide filaments that could not possibly touch the few people who tottered down the streets of Arkham, the city that hosted Miskatonic University. From the campus, we threaded our way down Church Street, careful not to touch the cobblestone paths that provided a tight walkway between the crumbling, tottering, old buildings. Black iron everywhere, decaying leaves, rotting ivy. The buildings hunched over, stooped and wheezing like old dogs afraid of the whip. We passed the Arkham knife shop: closed. And the Arkham diner, where a grimy window cast gloom across tables smeared in meaty slime.

"Are we almost there?" I couldn't stand much more of Arkham. I was beginning to think we might be doing the humans a big favor if we evaporated the entire town into the void.

"Up ahead, past the church," said Grim. "I see a sign, Hangman's Hill. That must be the cemetery."

We zipped past the church: small, a mound of stones held together by clay, the wooden door hanging from its hinges and banging against the walls as the wind howled. A lone cross sat atop the vacant building. It was bent in the middle, its tip sharpened to a point.

And we slithered through the wind up Hangman's Hill. Here, the oaks were massive and hundreds of years old. Weeping willows snapped and snarled, thousands of thin branches screaming in the wind. Grim formed his particles into a foam across the gravestones. Through his mass, I saw the names: PROFESSOR ATWOOD, PHYSICS. CLEMENTINE DORWOOD, PHYSICS. TIEN ZHANG, PHYSICS POST-DOC. I wondered if Tien Zhang, the post-doc, was related in some way to Xiao Zhang, the post-doc, and then I shimmied onto my own row of gravestones and settled in for the night.

"Fireball, the coffin is empty."

"Huh? What coffin?" But before he even told me, I guessed. Tien Zhang's coffin. There was a connection between Tien and Xiao, I just didn't know what it was yet.

Grim's particles sucked the dry earth off Tien's grave and into the void. The coffin rose in the wind and settled by Tien Zhang's gravestone. I crept closer, and Grim and I formed a wall around the coffin.

"Open it," I whispered.

Dozens of his shimmering strands dove down and cranked open the lid. We both leaned forward.

I recoiled.

Decay of gangrene and carrion: the smell of Xiao Zhang. A small rodent was decaying in the cheap pine box.

But Tien Zhang's body was long gone.

"I don't get it," said Grim. "The answer to our problem, how to return home, is right in front of us, but I can't quite grasp it."

I nodded. We were creatures of space and time, Grim and I. We were the origin of mass, what gave other particles their substance. Something eluded me, but *what?*

And in a flash, I got it: I knew what had happened and how to get back to the void. Maybe I was the smart one, after all. "Grim! Xiao-Tien Zhang, Qubit's notes, the whole thing! Come on, let's go!"

"Wha — "

But we were off again, streaking through the dinghy streets of Arkham, and I didn't answer. He'd find out soon enough, I figured. We raced back to Miskatonic and across the quad and into the Physics building. We bypassed the Physics library, where students were snoring and studying — mostly snoring — and streaked down the stairs until we reached the destroyed DEAD END door. We raced down the subterranean hall past the basement labs. QUARK-GLUON PLASMA LAB. QUANTUM OPTICS. DARK MATTER LAB. PARTICLE ACCELERATOR.

And then we came to it: QUANTUM HUT.

Xiao and Qubit were still in the lab, I could hear their voices. With Grim keeping a lookout in the hall, I poked a tendril into the lab. To my left, Xiao pushed her dead, stringy hair behind an ear. Her white lab coat cast a bloodless pallor over her already pale face. She lifted a circuit board the size of a lunch tray off a wooden table and examined some markings on the edge. "Thirty-five years old, but the software still works," she said, glancing at Qubit, who was in the rear of the lab, adjusting beam splitters and mirrors on a huge black table.

He screwed something in place, then turned. His goggles were fogged, and I couldn't see his eyes. He ran a hand through the wiry red hair, flattening it momentarily to his head. It sprang up again in all directions. His lips twisted. "We are close, Xiao, even without my notes. Insert the old circuit board and crank up the dark matter detector. When I say, *now*, switch on the analyzer while I stop the light from moving."

Her voice quivered. "Yes, Professor." She was very proficient, knew exactly where to insert the board in the ancient computer that stood eight feet tall, with enough slots in it to hold a dozen huge circuit boards. Clearly, Xiao had done this experiment many times. She brushed cables aside, turned on a monitor, clicked her mouse a few times. An empty graph popped onto the screen. Her finger was poised and ready to click on a link, *Analyze Dark Matter*.

Qubit turned on his own computer, and the beam splitters, mirrors, and other devices on the huge black table started glowing, neon greens and oranges. "This will take a minute, Xiao. As your dearly departed mother always told me, slow down, Professor, and take your time."

I tensed, but not as much as Xiao, whose face grew rigid, eyes wide in alarm. "*Don't mention my mother.*"

"Oh. Right." It was obvious that he didn't care what she was saying. He didn't even bother to look at her.

From the hall, Grim's words entered my mind. "According to Xiao's thoughts, Qubit killed her mother, whose name was Tien. Or wait. Maybe it was Xiao that he killed, which is weird. Her brain doesn't distinguish between Tien and Xiao. To her, they're the same woman. She is both. Her mind is really messed up."

"I'm surprised she has any mind left at all," I said. "She's not even alive."

"What are you saying, that she's the walking dead?"

"Shhh, I'll explain later. I have to concentrate."

Qubit was walking across the lab toward me. He ignored Xiao, who glared at him, her finger still poised over *Analyze Dark Matter.*

A thin tendril of my particles drooped in mid-air by the lab door; carefully, I wasn't touching anything. Qubit stopped a mere meter from me and fidgeted with a laptop on a small razor-edged metal table. His Frankenstein shoes were held together with gray duct tape. His fingers shook as he moved the mouse over a link, *Enable Quark-Gluon Plasma.*

Both concepts were clear to me. It didn't take a particle physicist to understand dark matter and quark-gluon plasma. It only took a heap of the particles, *me.*

Both concepts together, along with stopping light —

And it hit me —

"We're in danger! Run, Grim, run!"

But it was too late for both of us.

"*Now!*" screamed Qubit, clicking *Enable Quark-Gluon Plasma*, and a split second later, Xiao Zhang clicked, *Analyze Dark Matter.*

And that's when I passed out, or rather, passed into something, and along with me, came Grim. We were pressed against each other, glowing like the cosmos, technicolors of the universe raining down into the Quantum Hut, where neon greens and oranges started sizzling on the big black table and the data analyzer graph started spewing data onto its coordinates.

And then, there was a roar, a steady baritone of hellish noise that shook the very walls of the lab. Qubit clapped his hands over his ears. Xiao fell to the floor, writhing, her face clenched in pain, the dead black hair glued to waxy plasma on the gray concrete.

And Grim and I were trapped in a void with no walls in the middle of the room. We couldn't move. Nothing dissolved or disappeared around us. I bulged against Grim, trying to push him through whatever constrained us, and he pushed back, but nothing worked.

And then, the roar abruptly ceased, and both Qubit and Xiao stopped moving. Qubit stood, six and a half feet tall, legs skinny like broomsticks on those wide platform heels, eyes unblinking behind the fogged goggles. I couldn't see any movement, but he was alive, he was breathing.

And Xiao looked peaceful upon the floor, as if she was finally at rest. She no longer writhed.

Never the smart one, I hadn't anticipated things happening as quickly as they did, trapping us here in an artificially created void. Maybe Grim could think of something if I finally told him what was going on. I tried to shift my mass. *Trapped! No, not ready to die, too young!* I was getting hysterical.

I tamped it down. There was no time for hysteria. "Grim, listen to me and find a way to save us."

His mass was shaking so much I was getting nauseous. "Just calm down," I said, "*please.*"

"Tell me," he squeaked.

"Grim, *focus.* Qubit altered time and space using a light-stopping device on the black table while dark matter was being analyzed and while the quark-gluon plasma was churning in the lab down the hall."

It was a lot to say, and it was a lot to comprehend, and Grim *was* dazed, but he got it. "The combination of all three experiments running at once in close proximity screwed up time and space. I see." His voice no longer squeaked in my head. "Light stopped. The quark-gluon plasma reversed time. And the dark matter was flowing through everything, needling the stopped light and the plasma. Time and space warped. Qubit succeeded in trapping us here, which is what he's wanted to do for years."

My humps were aching from the confinement, and I didn't want to linger on Earth any longer. "His dreams have come true. Now he can torture the particles that make up nature until he destroys us, and without us, the universe ends. What a stupid man."

Grim was reading Xiao's mind. "She's cosmic, like us. She *is* Tien. She was a post-doc under Qubit. She disappeared into the void long ago during these experiments. That's why she didn't disappear into the void when we touched her. She's not human anymore."

I was tired. "Force her to get up somehow. Get her to turn off the experiments so we can *move* again and get out of here."

"How?"

"She's cosmic consciousness, like us, once human but made of particles now. Can you reach into her and *make* her move?"

"Ah, good thinking, Fireball, my blissful radiance." He concentrated on Xiao-Tien Zhang. "I'm in her brain now, moving toward the basal ganglia, where all of her movement is controlled."

And then, he must have transmitted movement signals directly into her basal ganglia, for Xaio-Tien Zhang, like a zombie, rose from the floor, ripping her hair from the waxy plasma stuck to the concrete. Her almost-bald head should have been bleeding, but it wasn't: she *was* the walking dead.

"Tell her to turn off the three experiments, Grim."

Glazed eyes, dead, she staggered to the dark matter console and turned off the experiment, then tottered to the black stopping light experiment and switched it off. Finally, she turned off the quark-gluon plasma machine, and as quickly as she did it, Grim and I leapt from our jail.

Qubit's knees buckled. His head cracked against the razor edge of the metal desk with the quark-gluon plasma laptop on it. Across his forehead was a wide red gash, getting wider and still wider, and then blood gushed to the concrete floor. He screamed, one arm reached toward Xiao-Tien, and then he fell. His red hair was soaked in blood.

"But he's still alive," said Grim.

"Damn," I said.

Xiao-Tien's knees were also buckling. Quickly, Grim and I wrapped ourselves around her, letting her feel the coolness of our flanks, the forever of our existence, and of hers. She reeked of decay, a lifeless body brought back from the void months after she disappeared, as Qubit continued his quest for a Nobel Prize. "He buried my empty coffin," she whispered in our minds. "I was never in it. I was lost in the void."

"And then you were sucked back into this world, *how?*" I asked.

"Same way he trapped you. Cranked up the three experiments, warped time and space, here I am."

"And he's been making you work as a post-doc ever since?"

She nodded, the remnants of human tears draining from her eyes. "Twenty-four hours a day, seven days a week. He didn't even have to feed me, much less pay me. And if I did anything wrong, he put me in the particle accelerator just long enough to torture me — "

"But not long enough to smash your particles into smithereens, so you could finally rest in peace, right?" said Grim.

She nodded again, but this time, there were no tears left in her lifeless body to spill.

Up close, I could see that her skin was translucent, that her body was just an animated corpse that couldn't last much longer. She wasn't technicolor like us, wasn't a Higgs boson or any other origin of mass. But she sure wasn't human anymore, and whatever horrors Qubit had inflicted on her were done in his quest to inflict horrors on us.

Perhaps Grim and I would find out what she was when we took her home to the void with us.

If we could figure out how...

"Go to the particle accelerator in the ring beneath Miskatonic," she said.

Of course. It was such a simple solution. We'd all jump into the particle accelerator together. Gripping Xiao-Tien Zhang between our masses of sparkling midnight blues and neon sky and harlot red, we carried her into the hall.

Flickering neon signs high near the ceiling. EXIT. WARNING. DEAD END. And the one we wanted: PARTICLE ACCELERATOR.

The door was steel and bound with heavy locks and security card slots and fingerprint pads. Didn't matter to us; Grim pushed against the door and it vaporized into the void. Carrying Xiao-Tien Zhang, we slithered into a circular, cavernous room. We were on a platform, high above a giant hole in the ground. Far below were enormous monster machines, bigger than spaceships, bigger than most asteroids, I thought.

Xiao-Tien told us, "The particle accelerator ring is eight miles in circumference and deep underground. There's a place where engineers work on an access point. It's down there. It's where Qubit would throw me and then suck me back out before I disintegrated."

What an ugly man.

"Jump!" I cried.

And Grim and I held tightly onto the decaying body of Xiao-Tien, and we leapt off the platform into the giant hole. Lights crackled everywhere as we fell, and steel glinted, and finally, all three of us felt the whoosh of the access point.

"At last!" screamed Xiao-Tien.

"I hope this works," muttered Grim.

We streaked through a nano-scrape in the access point. A raging wind of particles sucked us up, and we zoomed around the eight-mile accelerator ring once, twice, three times. And then, in a blitz of rainbow colors, Xiao-Tien was smashed into a trillion particles, just like us, and we all swept into the mighty void of nothingness: home. And as we twinkled back into ourselves, I gazed at Xiao-Tien. She was absolutely scintillating.

If you like spaghetti westerns and Eldritch tales, you might want to visit Red Hook. But if you go there, make sure you avoid the Chepachet.

Showdown at Red Hook

Everything was quiet in Red Hook. Two whole days had passed without a sign of the Chepachet Indians. In fact, other than a stray buzzard, two whole days had passed without a sign of anything.

Sheriff Tom Malone twisted in his saddle, surveyed the ghost town, dusty and empty. The Chepachet never left anyone alive. Malone shifted his hat and wiped the grime from his forehead, rubbed his hand on his shirt. The sun was fierce, blazing a hole through the clouds, which hung like brush over the dead town. "We best be movin' on," he said.

But his Deputy, Al Blackwood, didn't want any part of it. Blackwood leaned over the side of his horse, Noth-Yidik — a strange name for a horse, Malone always thought — and spewed tobacco juice onto the ground. "I'm not aleavin' Red Hook, Sheriff. There ain't nothin' out there but Chepachet."

Five months Malone had been riding with that sniveling rot Blackwood, and it was enough to make a man drink. Problem was, there wasn't anything *to* drink in Red Hook. The saloon to the left was a tottering shell. The broken porch posts hung like chipped, black teeth from the hand rail. The wood siding was raw, the paint long gone. Even the sign, RED HOOK SALON, was mangled over the front window. It was a laugh, really, that any man worth his Winchester would ask for whiskey in a place called RED HOOK SALON.

The pull of a hammer and a *click*.

Malone raised his Winchester, swung his horse around, ready for the worst.

But it was only Mae Curwin, the blonde he and Blackwood were transporting east to Durango. She was tiny with a mound of perfumed hair piled high on her head, damn fine, and she had two mounds up front that made Malone quiver. Mae was friskier than a pronghorn antelope.

She raised her fifteen-shot Henry .44 and pointed it between Blackwood's eyes. "I say we move on, just like the Sheriff says. I reckon to pass over that Chepachet hill yonder and make it to Durango, with or without you, Deputy."

A slight breeze tugged the stagnant air, and with it came the smell of ripe mold, a sign of the Chepachet. Malone's horse reared and bucked him way up, and in a cloud of dust, he saw the saloon collapse; just like when he was six years old and the Fork Crest Saloon crashed down and the cupola fell and smashed his father's head, letting the Chepachet ride off with his mother, never to be seen again. And now, he saw it collapse, in horror, *not* the Fork Crest Saloon, but *this* time, the Red Hook Saloon: the roof quivering, the shingles cracking, the siding splintering off like skin from a snake; the glass blowing out, and then, *whiz*, the RED HOOK SALON sign buzzing past, missing his throat by mere inches; and those rotting posts, jagged like teeth, thrusting into the dusty earth, releasing the black-red juice that ran beneath Red Hook.

Terror surged, and all the memories rushed back, as if carried in the roiling Red Hook dust. Malone yelled, "Giddyup! Lrogg! Giddyup!" and kicked the flanks of his horse, Ol' Shep. They raced down Naggoob Street toward the hills. Wood chips, mold, and noxious black-red slime clung to his nostrils, eyes, and lips. And then something larger hit him, and Malone grabbed it and stared briefly: it was a burning page from the 1860 *New Mexico Post*, and emblazoned on it in giant letters was the word, DAGON.

Malone swivelled, saw Blackwood and Mae charging behind him, the blonde still holding her gun. Blackwood's face was gaunt and white, his eyes wide in horror. Mae's face was round and flushed, her blue eyes sparkling with excitement. A torrent of smoke rose over Naggoob Street. Only a skeleton of Red Hook remained. The rest — the houses, the jail, the saloon — everything was in flames.

"*Dagon.*" The word struck such fear in Malone that he could barely utter it.

Blackwood said, "*Evil,*" and the fire from Red Hook danced in his eyes.

Evil from other places and long-ago times; evil from beneath Red Hook; evil going by the name, Chepachet Indian Chief Dagon, who was driven underground at the dawn of time, only to emerge in the vast expanse of the West in the early 1800s. Fertility cults and strange magic — Malone could only imagine what had become of his mother twenty years ago.

Malone dropped the burning *New Mexico Post*, kicked Ol' Shep, and raced down the trail. A half hour later, he paused, and Blackwood and Mae rode up beside him. Up ahead were the Red Hook Hills: craggy rocks, shimmering under the sun, almost moving in low, lazy, exotic rhythm to the rays. Like hideous sculptures gone live, the slabs shimmied against each other, rubbing their scrub on each other's flanks. And beneath the Red Hook Hills, the brush flew from the sandy plains, collided, piled in heaps, dispersed back into balls, and bounced high against the craggy rocks.

Ol' Shep, usually a calm horse, snorted and kicked the scrub clawing the edges of the trail. The air grew thick, hotter. A smell of dung floated past. And then the smell of stale blood. There was a lewd feel to the place. Malone reached for the Winchester slung across his back and turned to his companions. He tried to sound brave. "I reckon the Chepachets are just over that rise. They're figurin' on jumpin' us."

Mae was breathing heavily, the buttons pulled tight across her shirt, threatening to rip the cloth open. Her hair was loose, flowing to her waist. Her eyes were round, innocent; she must be no more than 18, Malone figured, and probably never even been with a man. She said, "I got to get back home, Sheriff. Pa's sick. He's been callin' for me, and he don't got nobody else."

Malone had to get her through Red Hook, he just *had* to...

Blackwood said, "I've heard about Dagon and his boys. They ain't human, Sheriff. I say, we turn back whilst we have the chance."

Malone wanted to gun-whip the whussie, but he held his anger. More than once, Blackwood had saved Malone's life — maybe it'd been by accident, but still, having a trusted fool watching your back sure beat having an unknown at your side. "Nobody hates Dagon and his Chepachets more than I do, Deputy. But Mae came to our town, and if we had stopped the Earl Gang, her brother would still be alive and fendin' for her. As it is, she got nobody back in Fork Crest. You want to see her workin' the saloons, all gussied up in feathers and low-cut lace?" He glared at the Deputy.

"Well, actually, Sheriff..."

An image of Mae in feathers and low-cut lace flickered through Malone's mind. Suddenly the air felt lewd again, but this time, it wasn't from Chepachet mold and dung. What *was* he thinking? "Why, she's almost like a sister to you, Deputy!" he said.

Blackwood glanced at Mae, then averted his eyes. "She ain't exactly ugly."

Mae ignored Blackwood, said: "Sheriff, let's get over the hills. I'll find a way to repay you."

Malone and Blackwood exchanged the brief stares of men who see things that women don't see and who hear things that women don't say, and then Malone figured they best get a move on before things got out of hand, so he said steadily, "Then let's get going," and he nodded toward the shimmering Red Hook Hills.

But as he nodded, the tops of the hills came alive. It was as if the hills were budding, and their buds quickly developed into men on horses. It was a stampede, hundreds of animals, their hooves banging down the rocky hills; hundreds of men, their voices screaming obscene words: "*Hel sother sabaoth tetragrammaton ischyros va adonai messias eschereheye!*"

"The Chepachet!" screamed Mae. "Hundreds of 'em!"

"I ain't gonna go! I ain't gonna go!" screamed Blackwood, but he looked as fierce as Malone had ever seen him, and Malone knew his Deputy was ready to fight.

All three horses reared and bucked, anxious to turn and run. Malone raised his Winchester, kicked his heels hard into Ol' Shep, and surged into the thunderous Chepachet charging down the hills.

"*Hel sother sabaoth tetragrammaton ischyros va adonai messias eschereheye!*" screamed the Chepachet.

"Giddyup! Lrogg! Giddyup!" screamed Malone —

— right before he was hit by a blast of circles and pentagrams. Floating in the heat, sent by the arrows whizzing past his horse: black-red shapes, etched with veins and throbbing with life.

Malone's eyes burned, he could hardly see through the thicket of horses, men, and throbbing shapes. He was shooting wildly, thrilled to hear the screams of Chepachet as the bullets pierced their ugly hearts, all the while knowing he could do no real damage to the evil tribe.

A horrible shriek to his right told him that Blackwood had been hit. A horse went down, and dust rose. Terror and sadness vibrated in Malone's heart. It was his fault that Blackwood was dead. There was no time to think of it now, though. Ugly Chepachet faces were all around him, and these boys didn't look real. They wore horse skins and horse tails, and their eyes had no color, only whites.

Mae was in her saddle, upright, pumping bullets into the surging Chepachet. And then as an arrow punctured its neck, her horse bellowed a death cry. Mae screamed, "Sheriff!", and Malone lunged, grabbing her around the waist with his right arm, holding his Winchester aloft in his left. He swept her from the horse just as it fell, and she grabbed his shoulders with both hands and clung to him from behind.

Abruptly, the dust settled. The circles and pentagrams fizzled into ordinary air. Malone and Mae were surrounded by Chepachet.

"I want that squaw." The words were low and deep and came as echoes off the sides of the Red Hook Hills. *It was Chief Dagon.* He weighed hundreds of pounds and sat on a horse that was skinned from the legs up. He wore a headdress of horse tails and a loin cloth of horse hide — most likely taken from the poor beast on which he rode. His arms were brown and fatty. Instead of fingers, each hand had eight wriggling tentacles, and where most men have a chest, Chief Dagon had a patch of long red-furred tubules with suckers on the ends.

"*...that squaw, that squaw,* that squaw," echoed Dagon's words.

Malone figured he had to answer, and toughness was always the way to go when dealing with outlaws, so he said, "I'm afraid I can't abide by your request, sir. Now let us pass, and nobody will get hurt."

Mae was soft on Malone's back, quivering slightly. He imagined her back there, her head proudly upright, the blonde hair flowing to her waist. Malone might be scared, but he'd protect Mae from whatever the tentacled Dagon intended for her. She'd never been with a man, and Chief Dagon definitely wouldn't be her first. Not as long as Malone's heart was still beating.

The Chepachet started chanting, first softly, then more loudly: "*Hel sother sabaoth tetragrammaton ischyros va adonai messias eschereheye!*" Each man looked different from the other. Some had tentacles, others had scales for flesh. The one thing they had in common was that all Chepachet wore horse tails and loin cloths of horse hide. And all their horses were skinned from the legs up.

Mae clung to Malone, sobbing in his right ear. The Chepachet circle tightened around them. Malone was more scared than he'd been when the Mustang Boys jumped him behind Coot's gun shop. More scared than during the Great Uprising of Mi-Go ten years ago. More scared than when he dreamed of the insatiable lusts of Prickled Things That Are Not Cacti. But not more scared than when the Chepachet dragged his mother off long ago, never to be seen again. Nothing could equal the terror of a young boy witnessing the certain death of his mother. It was the reason Malone had become a lawman.

"*Magnum innominandium Cxaxukluth Hziulquoigmnzhah Ghisguth.*" The Chepachet pushed Ol' Shep from behind, widened the space in front of the horse. Ol' Shep was scared, Malone could tell from the trembling, but the horse stepped cautiously and swiftly over knife rocks, around throngs of shimmying clay slabs, and through ropes of vibrating green moss. The Chepachet horses had dead eyes, all of them, and seemed not to feel the pain from being skinned from the legs up.

Higher they went up the Red Hook Hills. Higher —

"*Magnum innominandium Cxaxukluth Hziulquoigmnzhah Ghisguth.*"

As the Chepachet chanted the vile words, an unnatural expectation rose in the air, and over all of it hung the odor of dung and stale blood.

At the crest of Red Hook, Ol' Shep whinnied as if begging Malone to turn back. He patted the horse's neck. "We'll be fine, old buddy." Malone didn't believe his own words.

Clip clop went Ol' Shep down the other side of the Red Hook Hills. Boulders tottered on steep precipices overhead. The moss ropes hung more thickly, like blankets, from the limbs of the cacti. When it seemed Ol' Shep might not make it much farther, they emerged from the throbbing hills into the encampment of the Chepachet.

Mae gave a small cry.

Seemed she wasn't so brave anymore. It was one thing to stand up to Deputy Blackwood, poor sod, it was another to be dragged into the Chepachet encampment.

For a moment, Malone's eyes saw only a blur of darkness, and then, as the encampment became illuminated from an unearthly light that streamed from the brush-dead clouds, he knew that nobody would survive the night. There was no hope of saving Mae, of saving even Ol' Shep from the horrors of Chief Dagon.

They stood at the edge of a vast dirt circle. All around the circle were throbbing, scraggy hills, and in the middle of the circle was a pool of boiling red-black juice. Teepees lined the perimeter of the pool, and the teepees were made of horse hide and held upright by bones. There were no squaws, no females, to be seen: only the ugly Chepachet male-beasts with their tentacles, snouts, and slimy mouth protuberances. There were no children. No *live* horses.

"We are alone," Malone whispered.

"I reckon we are dead," said Mae.

Dagon approached Ol' Shep. His skinned horse sagged beneath his weight. His belly hung in huge, flabby folds over his loin cloth. He waved three tentacles, and several Chepachet dragged Mae and Malone off Ol' Shep. Dagon's tentacles pressed his horse to its knees, and Dagon dismounted and stood before Malone. This close, Dagon's face was one that Malone dared not view straight on. Instead, Malone lowered his eyes to the furry chest and its coiling tubules. The Chief said, "The squaw must enter the pool. Virgin, 18, blonde: good squaw for the Old Ones. It gives us life beneath the earth. There is no other way."

"Why, you! — " Malone lunged at Dagon, but was instantly assaulted by dozens of tentacles, which dragged him away from the Chief.

"You can't have Mae!" Malone wrenched his left arm, then his right, he tried kicking the Chepachet, but they didn't budge or lose their footing. Nor did they snicker, as outlaws did; nor did they laugh or punch him. They just wrapped their tentacles around his body and held him in ropelike knots. Malone's muscles started aching, his breath got tight.

The mold was sweet and thick. The black-red juice of the pool was burbling, now boiling, steam rising from it, curling, and unleashing shape upon shape. The chanting of the Chepachet intensified, grew stronger and louder; and the shapes swelled and dangled over the pool, and now they were bursting into the shapes of man-beast Chepachet.

Malone looked at Mae. She was in the clutches of tentacles herself, and her face was drained of blood.

The shapes over the pool budded into both Chepachet and their skinned horses, all dead, all alive somehow: and they settled upon the ground, and the new Chepachet joined in the chanting.

"No! No!" Mae kicked and flailed, but her strength was no match for the Chepachet tentacles and suckers. Twelve suckers attached to her neck and arms, and they dragged her to the edge of the viscous pool. Twelve tentacles lifted her into the air.

And it was in that moment that Dagon transformed into a creature more hideous than any in the encampment. His body bulged and pulsed with black-red juice, and it wobbled and then exploded and became —

Al Blackwood.

The Chepachets' grip slackened around Malone's body.

"Jack that gun, Sheriff, go on and pull!" cried Mae, high overhead in the clutch of tentacles.

Malone jacked his Winchester and pumped bullets into the Chepachet who held Mae aloft. He pumped bullets into Chief Dagon, who now looked like Deputy Al Blackwood.

Mae fell toward the black-red juice, whacked into a tentacle, and careened to the lip of the pool. Blackwood-Dagon dove for her, and so did Malone. Something yanked the Winchester from Malone's grasp and tossed it toward the pool.

"Don't you want to free your mother?" cried Blackwood-Dagon. He pinned Malone to the ground. He looked like Malone's old Deputy, but his strength was Dagon's. Malone clawed at the Deputy's belt, at his shirt, but no matter what he did, Malone was helpless against the mighty power of Dagon.

"Throw Mae into the pool! Free your mother, you slobbering rot of a man!" Blackwood-Dagon straddled Malone's chest, then abruptly stood, hauling Malone with him. The Deputy shoved Malone at Mae, who still lay upon the ground at the lip of the vile pool. A few yards away —

the Winchester —

"Throw Mae into the pool! Free your mother!"

"No! *Never!*" Malone shielded Mae's body from Blackwood-Dagon.

Blackwood's body transformed again, this time back into the spectre of Dagon. This time, eight tentacles shot from Dagon's huge body, and all eight held guns.

"*Draw!*" cried Dagon.

Eight guns against...*no guns*. Malone *had* nothing to draw.

Dagon's laughter rose into the chanting of the Chepachet, still encircling them all, but standing back as if worshiping the spectacle of their Chief with the two humans and the one live horse.

Eight guns cocked. Eight suckers twitched and sat ready to squeeze the triggers.

Tubules extended from Dagon's chest and pried Malone from Mae. She was weeping, unable to talk. Malone's heart was breaking. She was so young, only 18...

"Blackwood, please!" One last time, it was worth one *final* effort: Malone flung himself at Dagon, only to hear a gun roar and only to feel the sting and sharp pain of a bullet blazing into his right shoulder. Malone staggered back but refused to fall. "She was like a...sister..."

"Wrong, Sheriff," said Dagon. "She was like a *mother* to you. Give us Mae and you can free her. It's an even trade."

A *mother?* What was Dagon babbling about? If anything, Malone had lusted, still lusted, after Mae. He groaned and clutched his right shoulder. The pain was fierce. He couldn't move his right arm.

Dagon lifted Mae, keeping three tentacles and three guns trained on Malone. "I led you here. I let the Earl Gang kill Mae's brother. I, Dagon of Red Hook, made you bring Mae on this trip to Durango, knowing we had to go through Red Hook. Now *you* must give Mae to the pool. Only *you*, Malone."

Deputy Blackwood *had* played on Malone's need to be the manly one, the hero. Deputy Blackwood *had* played the wimp — apparently, on purpose.

And now, what could Malone possibly do?

In the midst of black-red shapes, and in the glow of the deadly sun, Mae's young body writhed over the pool. Her hair flowed straight down, perpendicular to her body.

"Do you want your mother back?" asked Dagon.

His mother, the cupola, he was six, the Chepachet killed his father, orphaned...his Ma...

"Yes," whispered Malone.

"Would you take her from the Chepachet?" said Dagon.

"Yes." An ache swelled in Malone's heart. Suddenly, he knew what he was doing, and he knew that he was no better than all the outlaws he'd ever put away.

The shimmering gold of Mae, the soft roundness: all of it, gone forever, as the tentacles released her, and she shrieked one final time, and fell to the viscous surface, only to be sucked down in one large gulp.

Mae was gone.

Malone gasped and fell to his knees. The Winchester was a yard away. Malone picked up the gun, then staggered from the pool and into the throng of Chepachet. He couldn't kill them, he knew, for they were already dead; and if he died, it just didn't matter anymore.

Malone cocked the Winchester with his left hand and aimed it at Dagon. The beast-creature laughed. The blast roared. Dagon staggered back as smoke rose from his red-furred chest tubules. But he laughed again. "You can't kill *me*," he said.

Heat and anger filled Malone, and he pumped another bullet into the Chepachet Chief. He would pump all his bullets into the beast, all of them, and then Malone would throw his own worthless shell of a body into the pool after Mae.

As the bullet hit him, Dagon lurched backward again, and then he gave another great laugh, as his tentacles coiled and twisted in the sky. It seemed that minutes passed, though Malone knew it was only seconds, and then, from behind Dagon, from the depths of the pool —

rose Mae.

But as she rose from the muck, Mae's golden hair turned gray and her body shrunk and her face shriveled into that of Malone's...

"*Ma?*" Malone's finger jerked.

Another bullet blasted into Dagon. This time, Dagon slipped by the pool and fell backward into the slime. A giant splash catapulted Malone's mother to the edge of the pool. She lay there, panting, slime dripping from her hair and clothes.

Eight Dagon tentacles flailed above the red-black juice, and the last Malone saw of the Chepachet Chief was a single sucker clutching at the air. The beast was back in its pool, not alive, not dead, just somewhere beneath the Red Hook Hills.

As their Great Old Leader sank into the muck, the Chepachet dissipated into the air; the black-red shapes exploded and melted into the pool; the dead horses fizzled into nothingness; and the pool closed until only dry dirt remained.

Near the foot of the Red Hook Hills stood Ol' Shep; faithful to the end, thought Malone. He stared at his Ma. "Are you real?" he asked softly.

She wore an old dress that he remembered from his childhood. It was red and white, tiny checks of some kind. It was frayed on the bottom, had holes everywhere. "I'm real, Tommy. I ain't recollect where I been. You're bigger than I remember." She spoke the words slowly as if she'd forgotten how to string them together. She sat, wiped the slime from her hair, then wiped her hands on the ground.

They had to go through Red Hook territory to get home. He paused. "You any good with a Winchester, Ma?"

"Mighty good," she said.

"Was there ever a Mae?" he asked. He hoped to god the answer was, no. Else, he knew he was fingered forever as Mae's killer.

Ma shook her head. "T'aint somethin' I know, Tommy."

It was unnatural, what had happened, not a thing of man. Beneath the hills was a viscous black-red pool where Dagon and his Chepachet waited for their next victim: a young girl, no doubt, like his Ma had been and Mae had been. They would rise again, these Chepachet, to capture another squaw. And some other poor sap — like Malone — would be held accountable.

Pain was burning down his arm into his hand and down his shoulder straight to his ribs. Malone needed whiskey. He'd take it from the debris of the RED HOOK SALON. "Ma, we best be movin' on," he said.

Ma nodded and mounted Ol' Shep . She would ride, with Malone on the saddle behind her.

The sun was fierce, and overhead, a buzzard circled. It left a black-red trail in the sky.

A wisp of horse tail fluttered from Ma's hair. Her eyes turned to his: her eyes, which had no color, only whites.

SCOURGE OF THE OLD ONES, which sold to High Seas Cthulhu 2, is set in rural Pennsylvania, a place of magic where the love of the land, of home, and of the past can exceed the desire for anything else. I've known some folks who gave birth to children with their brothers, sisters, and first cousins. I've known some folks who prefer to live in isolation from the rest of the world. Having spent a lot of time in rural Pennsylvania, it occurred to me that maybe, just maybe, the magic is really the —

Scourge of the Old Ones

Tinny music whined through the radio static. Ruben Gildersleeve jerked up in bed and glanced past the ancient radio at his wife, who was still snoring in an alcoholic haze. Even from here, separated as they were by the mahogany nightstand that had belonged to his daddy, Rubey could smell her: rancid as the dying cabbage that lay in the weedy fields up on the hill, her breath stale and reeking of homegrown wine.

Rubey slapped the radio, which belched and crackled, and then a male voice announced, "Volcanoes worldwide are showing signs of increased tremors, and — "

Rubey slapped the radio again, killing the male voice. Damn news. Who the hell cared about volcano tremors? He and Flossie were almost a hundred years old, and all Rubey cared about was getting the old hag to shut up and give him some peace.

She gurgled in her sleep, rolled towards him, and wheezed. You'd think the woman would take better care of herself. Hair all over her chin, nothing left on her scalp except a small white tuft, and a face so ugly that Rubey couldn't even remember what the 14-year-old Flossie Nahum had looked like when they got hitched.

Rubey pulled a flannel shirt over what was left of him. If he got any skinnier, he might just disappear. A thread of light trickled under the door of the one-room shack. It was near dawn. Time to get fishing and catch some breakfast. Else Flossie would have to eat rotting cabbage again this morning, and she'd give him hell.

He left the shack with his fishing pole. The outside air was a blanket of must, as if the clouds themselves were damp with decay. It was hard to breathe. He trampled over dead grape vines toward the water.

A stagnant yellow mist coated the lake, all the way out to the horizon. It was especially thick today, the mist, and pearlescent, shimmering in the dim glow of a sun that was so faint it seemed almost to be the moon. From the horizon came a rum*ble; almost like thunder, thought Rubey, despite what Flossie's daddy said.*

An image of his long dead father-in-law slipped into Rubey's mind, and he shuddered. Old man Nahum had been a loon, alcoholic like his daughter, misshapen like his daughter, a man who once told Rubey that "Them creatures, them beat the drums from beyond, and them multiply in the lake. Them the scourge of the Old Ones."

Nonsense. If anything had been the scourge of the Old Ones, it had been old man Nahum himself, who killed his fellow fishermen for their catch.

Rubey squat in the hard sand. Around him were the fishing buckets, all empty except for oily water. Here came the rumbling again, and this time, it was louder and *almost* gave him a chill though he knew it was more likely to be Flossie snoring than some giant fish come to kill them both.

He cast the line into the mist. Waited.

A boat slipped onto the horizon. Then another, and yet another. Slow-moving fishing vessels, they bobbed in and out of the mist.

About twenty yards from shore, a shadow rose and moved over the water. Rubey squinted. The shadow was so dark that it blotted out the shimmering mist.

It was weird, for sure, but Rubey had seen stranger in his near hundred years.

Rubey twitched the line and waited.

Then something nipped and caught hold. Rubey's heart leapt: it was food, a fish, something to keep Flossie at bay. He tugged gently. The thing nipped again. He tugged more tightly, pulled the line back, felt coldness grip him as the fishing hook moved from the mist and dragged over the beach.

"This thing ain't no fish," he muttered, and from out in the lake came a *drumming*, loud and steady this time, and increasing in depth and timbre. The shadow slinked over the water until it was only five yards from the beach. It throbbed on the waves to the beat of the drums.

A tingle swept down him.

Bang.

The drumming grew louder.

BANG.

Flossie was something to fear. But *shadows?*

Rubey really had to get a grip.

His catch wriggled on the hook. Rubey would worry about the shadows later. The fish-thing on his hook was tiny, squidlike, and coated in black oil. He dropped it into a bucket, then hauled the bucket to the barbeque pit.

A splash of lighter fluid, a flick of a match, and flames shot from the pit.

"What the hell you got, old man?" Flossie stumbled drunkenly toward him in her threadbare flannel gown, her feet unsteady in the slippers she'd worn for countless decades. Sagging skin hung on her old bones like the waddles on a turkey neck.

"Don't know what this thing is. You tell me." Rubey lifted the fish-thing from the bucket. Its tentacles thrashed, flicking oil on his cheeks. He recoiled and almost dropped the thing.

"Well, cook it, you damn fool!" Flossie shrieked over the pounding of the drums. At low levels, her voice was like sandpaper on an open wound. At full volume, she sounded like a wild animal in death throes.

He tossed the squirming bulbous thing into the fire, where it skittered as if dancing. The creature was about two inches across, like gray oily fat, it was, and coated with bristles and red pustules. Half a dozen large, round, black eyeballs reflected no soul.

Bang. Bang. BANG.

The thing hopped on the flame in time with the drums. Rubey could swear he heard the thing purring, but over the pounding, it was hard to know for sure.

"You caught a piss of slime, you stupid old man," cackled Flossie.

"There's nothing else out there. The fishing boats — " he pointed to the three boats bobbing out at sea — "take most everything. The lake's dying."

"Yeah, we're dying, too, Rubey Dubey. The radio man says we've gotta get out of here."

"We ain't leaving, Flossie. I grew up in this house, and I'm going to die here."

She gasped. "Look! The food! It's growing!"

It *was* growing. It bulged to twice its original size, then it hopped up and down and billowed out to at least twelve inches in diameter.

"Cook it more, Rubey Dubey. We'll have food for days."

Rubey's stomach turned. Despite his hunger, there was no way he was going to eat this thing. It went from gray to sickly yellow, and for a moment, disappeared from view. Then it was there again, gray and coated in black slime, shot through with tiny jots of color that sparkled beneath the gauze of clouds and mist. The purring was louder, gaining in tempo until —

"My god, Flossie, the thing is rumbling in time to — "

" — the drums of the creatures, like my daddy says!"

And then the thing, now about three feet in diameter, leapt from the flames, and screeching, went flying past Rubey toward the surf. Flossie's face was whiter than her hair. She screamed something, but it came out all garbled, and then she staggered and fell to the sand.

A pang of horror hit him, tinged with a flash of relief. He *should* help her, *but —*

He couldn't move. For out of the lake came a huge diaphanous creature. Gray, it was, like a gigantic wad of bulbous flab, but covered in red pustules and open black sores, bristling with spiky hair, its whole body throbbing in pace with the drums. Suckered to the flab were hundreds of small fish-things, and they were slurping a gray mottled fluid: *they were the creature's young.*

The mother's tentacles unfurled across the mud, slopping oil everywhere. She sparkled, and Rubey thought, in some freakish way, she was almost beautiful. *Hypnotic.*

Dozens of round black eyes poked from the flab and stared at him. *Boom BOOM.* The drumming was so loud his head hurt. His chest tightened, and a stab of pain sliced through his upper left shoulder.

Rubey shut his eyes to the giant thing, then trying to ignore the pain in his chest, turned his body away from the lake. Each slight movement made him wince.

Opening his eyes, he staggered the few short steps to Flossie. Her head rolled slightly. The skin folds on her neck twitched.

Should he save her, or should he leave her here to die?

As the thought flit through his mind, her eyes widened in fear. She was staring at something right over his shoulder. She screamed and pulled herself up and then slumped against him. Her odor hit him, the rancid cabbage and stale wine. A spike of pain sliced his torso. He nearly fell over.

Boom. BOOM.

"I'll save you, Rubey Dubey." She started half-dragging him back to the shack.

Flossie was saving *him.* But why? She'd never given him anything but hell. Maybe the old hag actually loved him. What a thought.

She shoved him through the doorway, and as he stumbled into the shack, he peeked behind him once more:

Tiny fish-things danced in the barbeque flames, and they were sparkling and bulging to twice their size. The lake itself was alive with the things, some jumping across the surface, others slopping their way toward shore.

The mother was halfway up the slope toward the barbeque. A tentacle crashed down, and with it, came a pine tree, which hit the barbeque and burst into flames.

Flossie shoved Rubey into his bed, and grabbed a water jug. She made her way outside, and it seemed like hours before she returned; but then, Rubey thought, maybe he'd dozed off from delirium. When she returned, the jug was empty, and she told him that "it was all taken care of."

Abruptly, the drumming stopped.

He wondered how Flossie had doused the flames with only one jug of water. But before he could ask, the male voice on the radio announced, "Oil is filling the world's oceans and fresh lakes. It's as if something's stealing the Earth's water. Who are these strange creatures that people are calling *the scourge of the Old Ones?*"

The phrase sent a shiver through Rubey. It was Nahum's phrase. Through static, the voice continued: "Scientists speculate that the creatures thrive on lava. Like turtles swimming thousands of miles, like salmon going upstream to spawn, they migrate to the lakes to reproduce. Except these creatures have turned all of our water into oil."

"Maybe that's a good thing. Don't people always whine about needing more oil?" said Flossie.

"Don't know, I'm no scientist," muttered Rubey. He pulled the ratty blanket over his body. His teeth were chattering.

And then, something knocked on their front door.

Rubey couldn't remember the last time he and Flossie had visitors. Must have been thirty years ago, when Hank Tremone and his wife, Agnes, stopped by to ask Rubey and Flossie to attend their daughter's wedding. They'd refused. They couldn't afford a gift.

Flossie opened the door. And here was this man, clearly not from around here: he wore a fancy brim hat, a shirt with buttons, black trousers — not jeans, but trousers — and a real blazer, maybe made from polyester, and very fine, Rubey could see, very fine indeed.

He took off the hat, held it with fingers that were slim and dainty. His hair was sleek, probably cut by a real barber. "Sorry to disturb you folks," he said. "Jason Timberwood. U.S. Marshall. You're the last of the bunch. I'm afraid you're going to have to leave your house. There are creatures in that water, Mr. and Mrs. Gildersleeve, creatures that will kill you."

U.S. Marshall? Rubey managed to sit up. He was the man of the house, and before him, his daddy had lived here. "We've seen what you're talking about, Marshall, but we're old. Where do you expect us to go?"

Timberwood said, "Don't know, but you can't stay here. The government's willing to buy your property. We intend to flatten whatever's in that lake. We'll give you a hundred and fifty bucks and bus you to a shelter in the city."

"We ain't selling, fool." Flossie flicked her fingers at the man as if to dismiss him. "You can go away now. We ain't leaving this house."

Timberwood was still by the door. He leaned against the wall. "These things are reproducing like crazy. We think they're drilling their way through the Earth from unstable volcanic sites. The mothers have some sort of internal nuclear fuel cycle. Their digestive systems create oil. We think these things, whatever they are, created the Earth's oil fields long ago."

"You're crazy," Rubey said.

"I wish that were the case, but it's not. I urge you to reconsider, Mr. Gildersleeve. You don't have much time."

"I get it," said Flossie. "You with your fancy words. Get out. You're not taking my land for pennies. Flatten the lake, would you? Ha!"

Yeah, Rubey got it, too. The government wanted his hundred acres because the fish-things were converting his water into oil.

Rubey was sitting on a gold mine. No way he was going to sell. Certainly not to some fancy government man. "Get out of here while the getting's good," he said.

Flossie grunted.

"You're making a mistake, Mr. Gildersleeve."

"We'll just see." Flossie's eyes glinted, her lips twisted into a smirk.

After the U.S. Marshall left, tramping through the growths toward the highway up on the hill, Rubey and Flossie collapsed in bed. They were too old for this kind of ruckus.

Eventually, the room grew dark, and day passed into night. He and Flossie rose a few times, passed the bottle between them, drank and passed out from the alcohol. Faint with hunger, Rubey's vision seemed to twinkle. He saw neon spots and fuzzy gray where yesterday there was rotting pine and mahogany.

They spent most of the next day bickering over how to use their remaining three jugs of water. By nightfall, only two jugs were left. And they still hadn't eaten anything.

And that's when they heard the rumbling again, the drums. The walls of the shack were shaking so much that dust billowed off them. Sneezing, the two were forced to leave the shack and try to clear their lungs.

Flossie left first, and as Rubey followed his old wife into the yellow fog of day, he heard her coughing and stumbling over the now dead underbrush toward the surf. Rubey tottered forward and found Flossie by the barbeque.

The drums banged in the cliffs, from beneath the very ground, and they echoed from far out across the water. The air was noxious, a cancerous mustard-like fusion of something not quite gas and not quite liquid.

Maybe these giant flabby creatures who were born of fire, who bred in the lake and brewed oil in their bellies, perhaps they had owned the Earth at its dawn, back when the oil fields were first created. Perhaps they had returned, now that the people had polluted the air to the point where it was getting closer to what had been so long ago.

Had Flossie's daddy, old man Nahum, been the loon? Or had Rubey just been an unbelieving fool all these years?

Rubey stared across the haze toward the horizon. The water was thick now and black — "pure oil, it is," said Flossie — and it glittered with wild colors.

Bulldozers churned the beach on a distant shore to the left, far away from where Rubey and Flossie stood. The government had come to kill the creatures. The government had come to suck the oil out of the water.

Across the surface, shadows rose and then fell, giant gray bulbous creatures rose and blinked thousands of black eyes at Rubey, and tens of thousands of squidlike babies popped on the water.

BOOM. BOOM.

The drums intensified until it seemed that the heavens had unleashed the thunder of a million planets. The lake sloshed back and forth, back and forth to the beat, and the waves slapped the beach in bizarre rhythms.

We're going to die, thought Rubey.

Out where the bulldozers churned the sand, large shadowy globs rose from the water. Even from this far away, Rubey could see the tentacles flailing in the glittering yellow fog. The bulldozers crumbled in their grasp. People would never lay pipes into that oil.

"We're not gonna die here, old man," said Flossie. "I was a Nahum before I was a Gildersleeve."

"Come on," he said, turning and tugging his wife's elbow. "Let's get the rest of the wine, and sit out here and watch what's left of the world."

Her eyes sparkled at the thought of alcohol, but she pulled back from him and said, "I'm a *Nahum*. Those creatures, they're kin to me."

He didn't have the strength to argue. Yeah, Flossie was a Nahum. What of it?

"They're not gonna hurt me, Rubey Dubey. Kin. You understand? We're kin."

Rubey stared at her. The tufts of white hair sticking up from her scalp, the grin drawn back over the toothless maw, the sallow skin hanging on her neck, wobbling as she pointed her finger at him to emphasize each word.

Flossie was breathing in time to the drums. "Don't you wonder why we never had no children, Rubey Dubey?"

"We've been married some eighty years. I stopped wondering a long time ago, Flossie."

She laughed. Behind her, the lake erupted in flames. The fire rolled like a surfer's curl toward the shore from far out where the bulldozers had been crushed.

The creatures screamed in the water, hundreds of young suckered to each monstrous body, tentacles thrashing the air all around.

"I couldn't have no children, Rubey Dubey, until the creatures came back. Now I *can*. Now *we* can. *Children*, Rubey Dubey!"

What was she talking about?

That was when a bolt of terror hit him.

He reached behind him to the barbeque. For the lighter fluid.

"Don't you get it? My kin's calling. They've come from beyond to save me."

And she lunged for him.

Without thinking, he flicked his wrist, he doused her with the lighter fluid.

And then his wife erupted in flames!

Godalmighty, what had he done?

But she only screeched with laughter and bulged rapidly in size: twice as big and now three times bigger than she'd been only moment before.

A huge diaphanous creature rose from the waves. Hundreds of small fish-things flailed against it, slurping oil. A tentacle ten times the size of Rubey's shack thumped onto the sand. It quivered within inches of him.

He turned back to Flossie. Dozens of round black eyes stared at him from her bulbous body. In some freakish way, she was almost beautiful.

"Come," she whispered.

She was —

hypnotic.

"It's breeding season," she whispered.

She was —

seductive.

Rubey shivered. For the first time in decades, his heart filled with desire. Lust gripped him, and the heat rose in his legs and stomach and groin.

It had been so long. There was no way he could resist her.

To round out this volume, I'm happy to include THE LAGOON OF INSANE PLANTS, which I wrote for Ancient Shadows (Elder Signs Press, 2011). Editor William Jones asked me for a dark weird tale with a touch of sword and sorcery. I remain indebted to William for publishing THE LAGOON OF IN-SANE PLANTS as well as this volume, ELDRITCH EVOLU-TIONS, and my recent novel, BLOOD AND ICE (Elder Signs Press, January 2011). As I finish writing this introduction to the final story in this book, I'm writing my next novel: DEAD-LY DIMENSIONS AND OTHER BLASPHEMIES, due from Arkham House in hardcover in 2011. DEADLY DIMEN-SIONS incorporates many themes that have underscored my favorite short stories: quantum optics, particle physics, chaos theory, string theory, strange creatures that merge the digital with flesh, and the very dark. I'm also starting to think about ARKHAM NIGHTMARES: ELDRITCH TALES OF THE MACABRE, which I'm thrilled to be editing for a 2013 release. Stay tuned for what I hope will be an adventure into the dark limits of your imagination.

The Lagoon of Insane Plants

A gong splintered my dreams. I bolted upright in my tent, shivering despite the humidity. The Golgash demanded sacrifices from the Magleesh and would wait no longer.

I had to warn King Aiyaheth. His twin sons, born only three days ago, would die today if I didn't stop Hudusoymaeya.

I slipped my dagger into my belt, made sure the ax was strapped securely to my back. I lifted the tent flap, stepped into the steam roiling off the swamp. It was hard to breathe, hard to see, but I was accustomed to the ways of Hudusomaeya, the goddess I'd been battling since she took my family long ago. She had left me, a mere girl of six, to survive on my own.

I crept around the swamp and ran toward the hut where King Aiyaheth slept with his family. It was dawn, with the sun peeking over the trees and dots of water twinkling like fireflies on the moss.

The Golgash vines throbbed like veins in the dirt.

I nodded to the men guarding the hut. They knew me well. I was the King's Protector.

Once inside the hut, I swung left down the corridor by the outer wall. Past the nursery, where the twins gurgled in their cradles. I could hear the snoring of the nurses.

The gong clanged again. Twice.

I entered the King's bed chamber. He was asleep on his mat, clad only in the loincloth of the Magleesh, his long dark hair and beard glistening with sweat. Queen Clarima was curled beside him. She groaned once, rolled to face me, a wave of black hair shifting on her pillow.

I touched the King's cheek, whispered in his ear. "Great Aiyaheth, it is I, your Protector. Jade of Magleesh."

He bolted up. Then seeing me, his eyes narrowed, and he gestured at me to follow him into the hall.

He glanced toward the nursery, then asked, "What's wrong? What's happened?"

My visits were never for pleasure.

I stared directly into his eyes. We were both six feet tall.

"Hudusomaeya banged the gong twice. She's fertile and demands attention." I hated to say it, but —

"She wants food," I said.

The King's eyes widened. "My sons!"

I nodded.

"She can't have them, not even in return for all of Magleesh."

"If you refuse, Sire, Hudusomaeya will kill every child under the age of twelve. If provoked, she'll kill their parents, too. Your entire kingdom is at risk."

"Protect my sons. At all costs, Jade. They're the future of Magleesh.

"And the other children?"

"You're the Protector. Save as many people as possible, but don't trade my sons."

"I'll do my best, but..."

"Just do what you can." He paused. Then his eyes swept down my body, lingering on my halter and loincloth. "Wait for me. I

The Lagoon of Insane Plants

need to prepare — it'll take me a few minutes, not long — and then I'm coming with you."

I shook my head. *Not a good idea.* "Sire, I must protest."

He glowered. "Don't tell me what to do! I must ensure the safety of my sons."

"Sire, forgive me, but nobody has ever survived a battle with the Golgash, much less Hudusomaeya. I'm protected by her black milk and by the jewels of three kingdoms. I alone can fight her."

Aiyaheth grabbed my arm and shook it. "But you *haven't* killed her, have you? You haven't fought her and *won*, have you?"

"I...I..." I didn't know how to answer. He was right, I'd never beaten Hudusomaeya. The closest I'd come to destroying her was three years ago in the Lagoon, when I'd hacked and burned her Golgash to the ground. But they'd sprung up again, much thicker, within the year. "I'm all you have," I finally said.

The King released my arm. His voice softened. "You're much too arrogant for a girl. And you aren't strong enough to kill her."

Arrogant? *Me?*

Aiyaheth slipped back into his chamber, leaving me to remember: *Hudusomaeya's black milk and poisons raining down upon me as she killed my family.* I didn't die as she'd hoped. Instead, my skin repelled the poison, and it rolled off me as water rolls off a duck. As a result, three kings burned their jewels into my flesh, and in previous battles, the jewels had blinded Hudusomaeya long enough for me to escape death.

Aiyaheth's hand was on my shoulder. Startled, I realized that I was scared; and very little scared me. "Are you up to this?" he asked. He wore the vestment of Magleesh over his loincloth, and leather straps were crossed over his chest. On his back were dozens of arrows, and his right hand clutched a bow.

"Of course, Sire," I said.

We headed toward the Lagoon of Insane Plants, Hudusomaeya's home. The gong clanged again. Twice. The trees cast shadows upon the mud and across the wild growths.

I made my legs move faster. I gained more distance than Aiyaheth and heard him panting far behind me.

The Lagoon of Insane Plants

Suddenly, the vines rose like stalks from the ground and spewed white dust. I ducked and slipped, but regained my footing.

The mud was soft, the vines were getting higher and thicker. The Golgash were anxious. They were hungry.

A girl and a scrawny dog toddled by a tent. She was about four, the age of my sister Elena when the Golgash had eaten her.

A vine twitched, and the pollens sprayed. I grabbed the Golgash just as they sprayed poison, but I was too late. The girl screamed and clutched her eyes.

The dog barked and reared on its hind legs. I stumbled and almost fell over the dog, caught myself just in time.

A woman about my age emerged from the tent. "Taran! No!" She threw her arms around the girl, looked up at me, eyes spilling tears. "What is it, Taran? What happened? *Jade?*"

"It's Hudusomaeya. She's fertile. Taran is...*not well.*" I pulled the ax from behind my back, gripped it with both hands.

Taran's eyelashes fluttered a few times, then stopped. Her skin was purple from the Golgash poison. She twisted in pain, screamed once, and then...

And then she died.

Sobs welled up in me. I wanted to cry but controlled it. Taran's mother collapsed over her dead daughter, weeping enough for both of us.

I had failed again. Another child was dead.

Would it ever stop?

From the path came King Aiyaheth. He was panting, not used to the long run through mud and brush. His body was thick with muscles, good for fighting soldiers but not very good for fighting the Golgash and racing through vine-clogged swamps.

Aiyaheth squinted at Taran and her mother. His face fell, and had I ever wondered about his sincerity in the past, I didn't wonder now. He tried to comfort the woman, and then motioned at me to get moving. "No more deaths," he said. "No more children. We must *kill* Hudusomaeya. Her rule will end."

Together, we hurried down the path toward the Lagoon of Insane Plants. The mud pulsed with the beat of the deadly Golgash. Vines clawed their way up from the earth and twitched toward the sky. Crystalline metallic-colored cancers.

I swung my axe at the Golgash mat. Aiyaheth panted behind me. But then the vines had me by the ankles, and I went down. Dozens of lip-cups opened and strained for a bite of my flesh.

Aiyaheth whipped out a knife, and he slashed at the vines. I clutched his waist, holding on for dear life. A black paste, like tar, seeped from the cut stems, coating us both. My toes squished in the mud and tar. I grasped Aiyaheth's shoulders and hauled myself to my feet. Aiyaheth brought his knife down, hard, and severed a thick vine, breaking it six inches from my ankles. I pulled my legs free, and we slogged through the muck, now only moments from the Lagoon.

Perhaps Aiyaheth is right, I thought. I'm too weak to fight her alone. Perhaps I do need his help.

And as my confidence sagged, I saw it:

The Lagoon of Insane Plants.

Golgash stalks rose from the stagnant water. The vines writhed across the surface. Purple buds yawned toward the sky and belched their poison dust.

I stood with that poison still in me. It oozed from my pores, twinkled on the jewels set into my skin. I wore the sapphires of Prankar, the rubies of Zindoor, and the jade of Magleesh. But the sun was behind clouds, and the jewels wouldn't be bright enough to blind the evil goddess.

Insects hopped, then fell into the muck. Bubbles burst everywhere. The surface of the Lagoon quivered.

Arrows flew past me. I swiveled to see Aiyaheth pulling back his bow. The arrows pierced the purple buds, the stalks, the writhing vines. And a screech went up from the water, the screech of children dying; and now a high-pitched wail, that of a mother grieving, and Hudusomaeya rose in a column of filth, sending waves of putrid water over us. Aiyaheth fell under the weight of the water, while I dug my toes into the muck and held ground. My ax was over my right shoulder, raised high and ready to strike the first blow.

Hudusomaeya was submerged under the Lagoon from the waist down. She stood upon something — perhaps the bodies of thousands — unwavering in the pounding water. She laughed and pointed at me. "*You* kill *my* children? You puny, pathetic, little creature!"

"Kill her!" The King's words were faint. His arms flailed, and his head bobbed over the surface of the belching Lagoon. An arrow flew.

Green blood trickled from Hudusomaeya's cheek where the arrow hit. She threw back her head and laughed, brushed the arrow from her flesh as if it was nothing more than a pesky fly.

Hudusomaeya was the size of forty alligators stack one upon the other. Her hair fell like twisted vines to her waist, and from there, I'd always assumed, to her feet and possibly further. I'd never seen her from the waist down.

Her muscles, I knew, were like granite. She'd gripped me three years ago, and only the poison dripping from my pores had saved me.

"Sacrifice yourself to me now, Jade, and I'll spare the two bratty princes."

"You won't have me *or* the babies!" I yelled. "Your killing is over!"

She just laughed, and the water shook and roiled, and it sloshed over me, pushing me back against Aiyaheth's body. He was standing now, and he reached back to find another arrow. "Take me," he said, "not my boys and not Jade."

The King was an idiot. She would kill him, me, *and* the boys. His offer made no sense.

She reached one giant arm over the Lagoon and grabbed the King in her fist. He squirmed, and his face went red.

I leapt and curled my body, diving over the surface and under the muck. The water reeked of sewage and rotting bodies, but as I said, I was used to it — the hot air, the stench, the filth so thick I could barely see. Still clutching my axe, I swam as quickly as I could, which wasn't very fast given the turbidity of the water. Insects stung me, soot and peat moss bit my skin. I poked my head up, paused, and saw the giant mouth open right above me.

The teeth were pointed and sharp, brown and pitted from the acid of her belly. Her nostrils loomed over me: the hair like bushes, the mucous filled with bugs. Her eyes glittered like the sapphires of Prankar, the rubies of Zindoor, and the jade of Magleesh.

The King struggled in her grasp, wide-eyed in terror, legs kicking. His arrows fell to the water. Hudusomaeya said, "I won't eat you, Aiyaheth. I'll give you to my children. The Golgash."

I drew back the axe, swung it with everything in me, and it crashed against her green stomach. She didn't even notice. The axe bounced off her flesh.

I swung again and again, growing tired with each attack. And still, she didn't flinch. She made the King an offer: "Give me your sperm, and I'll give your boys their lives. There is no male like me, and I grow lonely. Give me children other than these Golgash, King Aiyaheth, and I'll spare your kingdom."

She wanted to bear the King's children? *Impossible.* She was a monster, he was human. The two could not spawn.

He shook his head. *No.*

"Then bratty King, father of bratty princes, give me Jade and I'll spare you all." Her voice was low and cunning.

He bobbed his head. *Yes.*

He would sacrifice me? How could he serve me up to the goddess after all these years?

I glared at him and steeled myself, waiting for her to scoop me up in her fist and crush me.

But she closed her fingers more tightly around Aiyaheth, and she crushed *him* instead. Just crushed him as if he were a seed. Blood streamed down her arm to her elbow. She opened her hand, and the squished body fell in fragments. The vine cups opened, the purple buds strained, and the black tar rained down from Hudusomaeya. I dove quickly under water, watched as black splotches spread over the surface above me. The Golgash lapped up the black milk, bulged, and grew larger before my eyes.

The Lagoon of Insane Plants

I poked my head up again. Golgash stalks gulped fingers, legs, kneecaps...

I couldn't watch.

Aiyaheth was gone. Tears burned my eyes. Hudusomaeya's children had been fed. But it wasn't much. Just one man. They would need more, a lot more, before the day was done.

The sun shifted and a ray hit us from behind the clouds. I flipped onto my back, floated briefly, and the sun shot from my jeweled skin and hit Hudusomaeya. She clutched her eyes, but only briefly, and the sun shifted back into the gloom of an overcast day.

If I could just aim the light at her eyes, I could blind her as she had blinded Taran with her poisons. Then I could move in for the kill. But I'd tried this technique many times, and it had never worked.

I didn't know what else to do.

And then it hit me: the twin infants were now the Kings of Magleesh. Who would rule us while they grew up? The Queen? Was she up to the task?

Hudusomaeya made her offer again. "Sacrifice yourself, Jade, and I'll spare the boys. Refuse, and my Golgash will consume all of Magleesh."

She wanted me because my skin was impervious to her poison and my body was adorned with the jewels of Magleesh, Prankar, and Zindoor. But why not just kill me without all this banter? I couldn't defeat her anyway. The King had been so right about that.

"Golgash!" cried the insane goddess. "Get me the two new Kings!"

The vines wove themselves together and moved toward the shore; and on the shore itself, the vines shifted across the mud like a giant rug toward the center of Magleesh, toward the King's hut.

As the vines closed all around me, I pulled myself onto the mat. It zipped across the Lagoon and across the mud, much more quickly than my legs could ever run. Behind me, Hudusomaeya keened and dripped black tar. I was coated in the foul milk. I wondered why she didn't kill me, right there and then. *What was she waiting for?*

The vines quivered outside the King's hut. I leapt off the mat, noticed that the guards were all gone — dead, no doubt, and eaten by the Golgash — and I dashed into the hut.

In the nursery, the twin Kings gurgled in their cradles. The nurses weren't snoring. They were probably dead.

Queen Clarima was no longer in her bed.

She was probably dead, too.

I wondered who wasn't dead.

Around me, the Golgash writhed as if dancing. They had fed, but not on the infant sons of Aiyaheth and Clarima.

Hudusomaeya's voice boomed. Steam rose in the hut. Steam that smelled of blood. "Golgash, my only children: eat the two boys. Eat them now, and we'll be done until next I spawn."

I gripped the reed walls of the hut, once again awaiting the mighty blow of Hudusomaeya and her Golgash, once again surprised when they didn't kill me.

Nor did the Golgash kill the infants — I heard them still, gurgling in their cradles.

"Kill them!" bellowed the goddess.

The Golgash continued their dance. With a shock, I realized that the *vines* were gurgling with joy. I wasn't hearing the gurgling of infants, but rather, of the vines themselves —

"Ungrateful brats! Do as I say!" cried Hudusomaeya, and the reed walls shook so violently they almost caved in. I started clawing my way toward the nursery, and was inches from the door when Hudusomaeya bellowed again: "I never wanted you, ungrateful, ugly *vines*! Who would want *vines* for children?! I wanted children like *me*, like the mighty Hudusomaeya!"

The Golgash were no longer listening to her. Their stalks were everywhere, bolting up from the mud floor, gripping the walls.

A double-wailing rose, the cries of *infants*: the twin Kings were awake, terrified and screaming for their mother. I slipped into the nursery and lifted the two Kings from their cradles. They were so tiny, the bones so fragile, the heads with tendrils of hair, eyes darting to and fro. I held both in the crook of my left elbow.

The hut shook. A wall collapsed in the King's chamber. I darted into the hall and leapt from the entrance as the structure fell to the mud.

The Golgash were taller than my six feet. Much taller. Yet they did not hurt me.

Hudusomaeya stood before me: her head in the clouds, her feet huge and clawed, her legs so wide I couldn't see around them. Green skin, splotched with the black tar of her milk, the coiled hair dripping down her back into the mud.

She bellowed, she screamed her commands to kill the twins, but the vines no longer obeyed her.

I realized that her power was in the vines. Without the Golgash, Hudusomaeya was just a giant stupid monster. Her children had rebelled against her, as all children do at some point. They were tired of taking orders.

I looked at the two babies in my left arm. The squinting black eyes of Kings looked back up at me. I held the future of Magleesh. My family had been of Magleesh, I was of Magleesh.

If I could somehow kill Hudusomaeya, her black milk would cease to flow, and the vines would die. The Golgash didn't reproduce. Hudusomaeya spawned them.

The Golgash danced around me. They gurgled. They sang insane duets and choruses.

And Hudusomaeya screamed "No, no, no!" and reached down a mighty arm to grab me.

My skin glistened with the black tar. The jewels glowed even beneath the clouds.

The Golgash shrank back, writhing in a circle. The chorus rose.

"Kill her," I whispered. "Kill Hudusomaeya."

A shriek of delight, and the vines wrapped around Hudusomaeya's ankles and legs, and they brought her down. She fell like the mountain she was, and from afar, I heard the waves banging against the shore of the Lagoon.

The Lagoon of Insane Plants